Beyond the Shadow

of

Canderlay Manor

by

Dee Julian

Copyright © 2013

Cover illustration by Tibbs Design

For information on the cover art, please contact Valerie Tibbs at www.tibbsdesign.com

Dedication

This book is dedicated to the people in my life who supported, encouraged, and guided me through good days and not so good. And for the ones who constantly pushed me to the finish line, I owe you a wealth of gratitude. Thank you, Elaine, Kim, Chris, Amber, Stephen, Horn, Missy, Lisa F, Brenda N, and of course the man who ignited my path to romance - my husband, Paul. You are all very much loved and dearly appreciated.

A hearty thanks to Loy Leffingwell of the Germantown Fire Department. His expertise and willingness to help saved me a great deal of tedious and time-consuming research. And I would also like to thank his lovely fiancée, Shannon, for allowing me to disrupt their plans from time to time.

And most of all...thank you, God, for blessing me with a small amount of creativity and for giving me a genuine appreciation for romance. I hope I did not disappoint You.

The countryside of Kent
Near the eastern coast of England
June, 1811

Chapter One

Despite his Scottish grandfather's tales of ghostly apparitions, Morgan Spence had never met one. Nor did he believe in them. Growing up in a centuries old castle appropriately named Dragon's Breath had taught Morgan to disregard the occasional odd or unexplainable sound, especially after the sun sank below the horizon. But in all his nine and twenty years he had never once encountered something he could not easily rationalize.

Until now.

Thief?

Unlikely. Canderlay Manor possessed nothing of real value.

Curious trespasser?

Perhaps but then...local curiosity would've waned several decades ago.

Ghostly visitor?

Out of the three possibilities, the latter seemed the more reasonable explanation. How else could he account for the brief flickering of candlelight in the second floor window of an English manor that had been deserted, except for an occasional renter, for three decades?

A decisive chill slithered across his skin, replacing the warmth of a mild summer day. Thunder rumbled low as storm clouds billowed in the distance, threatening to extinguish the last gasp of sunlight before its time.

Morgan banished any ghostly thoughts from his mind and dismounted. "What say you, Ares?" He stroked the horse's neck. "Granted this place needs a few repairs, but I believe we will be content here."

If I can convince Lydia's father that I am a worthy suitor.

With hair the color of fine silk and soft hazel eyes, Lydia Adderly was more than pleasing to any man's eye. As were the seductive curves of her enticing body. But her most endearing feature, without a doubt, would be her generous dowry. It would be more than enough to foot the bill for Canderlay Manor's restoration.

Brief remorse pricked his conscience.

He wasn't penniless.

Not at the moment.

And any decision regarding his future bride should not rely exclusively upon a generous dowry.

Morgan stared at the manor's dark windows, but the mysterious light he'd witnessed earlier failed to appear a second time. The stately three story manor stood as silent as death now, completely void of any sign of life. Tomorrow, its resurrection would begin.

At age twelve, he'd gotten his first glimpse of this once grandiose estate, and for the next seventeen years, it had stubbornly occupied his thoughts. The architectural design was unmatched. Jacobean, his father had said. And rare. Constructed in 1599, this was a home well-suited for a nobleman.

A marquis.

A pity he could claim neither title.

He led his horse through the break in the low brick wall and into the inner courtyard. An elegant facade made of white stone projected outward from the manor, shielding the massive front door from severe weather. The top section of the facade ended just below a third floor window. He'd visited Canderlay only once and during that impromptu visit, he'd committed to memory each empty room and its position inside the manor.

The wind picked up, swirling dust and debris about Morgan's feet, prompting the thought that he might wish to seek shelter. He glanced at the front door. What did he expect? That it would suddenly open wide and an ancestral spirit would bid him enter?

Had he truly seen the soft glow of candlelight earlier or did exhaustion interfere with his vision? After all, he hadn't slept much the last two days. Mostly due to the numerous bottles of brandy he and Bartholomew had consumed.

Lightning branched out in random formation.

Ares snorted, one hoof nervously pawing the ground.

"Easy, old friend. We'll be off soon." Morgan withdrew an apple from his saddlebag and offered it. Having successfully distracted his restless companion, he glanced again at his dismal surroundings. "What the devil have I done, Ares?"

Bartholomew, trusted friend, brother-in-law, and recently titled Duke of Chase, argued that a gentleman should never allow mere sentiment to influence business decisions. According to Bart, purchasing this estate was not and likely never would be a wise investment. At the time Morgan had been suffering from acute nostalgia and staunchly defended his actions.

A trait he likely inherited from his headstrong mother.

No, Canderlay might never be touted as a worthy investment, but it didn't matter. It was something Morgan had desired. As the first born son, he would've become the rightful owner at some point. Instead, George III's blind hatred and inexcusable greed had forced Morgan to purchase his own birthright. A realization that would've left a bitter swirl inside any respectable man's gut.

He left his horse and walked around to the side of the manor to gain a better view of the outer buildings. The laundry house looked intact but needed a fresh coat of paint and several shutters. One of the doors to the carriage house had been propped open, but he couldn't see inside. Outside, the roof appeared solid enough but probably needed repairs. The stables had suffered the most decay, for its roof had collapsed at the far end.

Have I bound my dwindling finances to a colossal mistake?

Too late to cry foul, for this afternoon he'd hired two dozen skilled laborers from Maidstone, and repairs would begin come morning.

Once again Morgan considered the light he'd witnessed. If spirits did indeed roam the empty corridors of Canderlay Manor, as some of the locals had suggested, he doubted they would require candles.

The sky lit up in a dazzling display followed by a loud crack of thunder. Darkness descended almost at once, and an eerie sadness surrounded the old manor house.

A sense of loneliness pervaded Morgan's soul. A feeling he did not expect. Returning to his horse, he grabbed the reins. Ares pranced, eager to be off. Morgan swung into the saddle and could scarcely hold him back. He carefully guided his mount back through the break in the wall and took extra care on the parched and uneven road that was nothing more than a jagged pathway. This too had been grossly neglected over the years.

Neglected.

Abandoned.

Discarded.

Had anything connected to this estate been cared for over the years?

Renewed determination rose inside him. No matter what the cost or how long it took, he would return Canderlay Manor to its previous glory...to a time before his father's lands and title had been unjustly taken away. He needed only one thing to make this plan a complete success.

Lydia Adderly. And if her father objected, he'd find another lady of comparable wealth. One whose father harbored no misgivings about pledging his daughter's well-being to a man with no title.

A fine mist blew across Morgan's face. He kept the pace slow until he reached the end of the narrow road. As an afterthought, he turned his horse for another glimpse at the place where his father had been born and raised to manhood.

And there it was again. Unmistakable candlelight. Only this time it peeked through a window on the main floor before disappearing.

"What the bloody hell?"

7

The sensible, English side of Morgan's character warned that he was close to being caught in the middle of an unpredictable storm and urged him to flee now and return in the light of day. With several armed men. But the reckless, Scottish side had become dangerously curious. And no storm, English or otherwise, would keep him from defending what rightfully belonged to him.

"Come, Ares," he coaxed. "Let's face this dragon together."

* * *

Lightning burst through the tattered and worn drapery adorning the long windows of Canderlay Manor's once expansive library, exposing the barren walls and near empty bookshelves. A series of consecutive rumblings followed as the storm drew closer.

Standing in her bare feet and wearing the last stitch of clothing she could truly claim as her own, a thin night dress, Isabelle Lindley raised the candle high and frowned at the only two books she had avoided these last few months. One boasted an expertise at breeding championship horses while the other offered advice on producing and maintaining all manner of flowering plants. Normally these subjects wouldn't interest her in the least, but beggars could not afford to be discriminating.

And a beggar I have now become.

Belle chose the book on flowering plants, blew the dust from the cover, and promptly sneezed. The sound resonated around the room void of all furnishings except for a faded gold and blue striped sofa and a small table with unsteady legs. It was a shame Canderlay Manor stood deserted once again. With the passing of time, it had seen too little care.

So different now than when Uncle Magnus had rented it.

Sadness jabbed her insides. Canderlay had become a pitiful reminder of its former greatness. Destined to share the same gloomy existence as Belle.

Tears burned her eyes. No, she wouldn't cry. Wouldn't dwell on the past.

With book in hand and candle in the other, Belle headed across the room toward the secret passageway beside the stone fireplace, but an unexpected creaking stopped her midway. She whirled around, her heart pounding so hard she thought she'd faint.

Had a strong wind somehow jarred the main door open?

Relief washed over Belle, but it was short lived. The front door likely weighed at least seven stone, and it would take quite a strong wind to—

Footsteps, slow and methodical, landed on the marbled foyer.

Thud...thud...thud...thud.

A frightening sound. And then...

Nothing.

Had Samuels returned?

Not by way of the front door. Unless he'd come into possession of a key.

Had one of the locals picked the lock?

Unlikely. No one dared cross the threshold of Canderlay Manor. Most considered the place haunted. And yet...

Someone had.

The man with the scarred face? The same man who'd burned her cottage to the foundation and chased her into the forest? Had he somehow found her?

A fierce clap of thunder snapped Belle to her senses. She extinguished the candle's low flame, cold fear impeding her every breath. Rooted to the spot, she tried not to panic, but her hands shook so violently she nearly dropped the candle. No longer trusting her numb fingers, she placed the book on the sofa then set the candle and holder gently on the floor.

Footsteps again.

Heading down the corridor this time.

Belle picked up the hem of her nightdress and scurried across the room. As she reached the secret passageway, she realized she needed the light from the candle in order to operate the temperamental latch.

Blessed Father, help me!

Light flickered in the corridor outside the library, and elongated shadows danced upon the bare walls. The light gradually became stronger until it stood on the verge of invading the room.

Belle dashed toward the nearest corner, tripping over a loose brick in front of the fireplace. Acute pain pricked her big toe. She bit her lip to keep the tears in check before slipping behind a portion of the drapery.

Within seconds the shadows vanished, and light poured into the room, stealing through haphazard holes in the once fashionable drapery. She pressed her shoulders against the window as the intruder walked about, his boots heavy upon the wooden floor. Every other step, he paused. Regaining an ounce of bravado, she leaned forward and peeked through a tattered, moth-eaten hole.

Someone strolled into her line of vision. Tall. Dark hair. Dressed in gentleman's clothes. He carried a lantern in one hand. This wasn't the scarred villain of her nightmares, thank God. If he had come to Canderlay in search of her, he didn't appear in any hurry to begin the task.

Who was he? And what was he doing standing inside the empty library of a deserted manor house?

After studying the room for longer than necessary, he finally headed to the fireplace, tripping over the same loose brick she'd tripped over earlier. Reseating the brick with the heel of his boot, he stood in front of the finely carved mantel and slowly ran his hand along the wood as if stroking a loyal hunting dog.

Or cherished woman.

Good heavens! And me a vicar's daughter!

Embarrassing heat crept into her cheeks. Such wicked thoughts should've never entered her mind. Yet they had, and she couldn't pretend otherwise.

Regaining her composure, Belle cautiously peeked through the damaged portion of the drapery again. The man had turned his back with his face tilted up and held the lantern above his head as though he thought to inspect the room's high ceiling. Whoever he was, they shared a common interest.

A deep fondness for Canderlay Manor.

The wind pelted rain against the window behind her, hitting the glass with force. She turned her head, careful to keep the rest of her body motionless. A flash cut through the darkness outside, so bright it momentarily blinded her. She squeezed her eyes shut, bracing for the resounding clap. When it finally came, she nearly cried out.

Footsteps neared the drapery.

Heaven help her! *Had* she cried out?

She drew a nervous breath and held it.

All of a sudden the tattered drapes slid into the corner where Belle stood, folding in upon one another like an accordion and safeguarding her hiding place but at the same time disturbing years of accumulated dust. Throat burning and eyes watering, she clamped her hands over her nose and mouth.

Dear lord, please do not let me sneeze!

* * *

Morgan turned away from the raging storm outside, thankful he'd shut Ares inside the carriage house.

His gaze shifted about the library. Faded blue wallpaper with white sheep grazing in a field of yellow daffodils covered the area beside the two long windows. This would have to go. Along with the shabby sofa and odd table the last tenant had obviously abandoned.

The wall to the right of the room's wide doors was adorned with empty bookshelves as was the far end. To the left stood a large fireplace flanked by exquisite oak paneling on each side. Above the doors was another hint of Jacobean artwork. The high ceiling probably displayed the same.

His attention returned to the empty bookshelves.

Books were not a necessity at the moment.

Oh, how his dear mother would disagree.

Without warning her last parting words came to mind.

Morgan, you cannot plan every detail of your life nor can you expect every detail of your life to go as planned.

It was as though she could see directly into his soul and didn't care for what she found. Her logic might be sound, but it didn't apply to Morgan. He knew exactly what he wanted.

Knew exactly how to get it.

Acquire Canderlay Manor. Marry a wealthy nobleman's daughter. Add to his dwindling fortune. In that order.

He had accomplished the first goal.

As for the second, he should've stayed in London another two weeks to finish out the Season. At this very moment he could be dancing with the beautiful Lydia upon his arm. Or strolling into a moonlit garden to steal a kiss. Instead, impatience had gotten the better of Morgan, and now he was stumbling around Canderlay Manor searching for imaginary spirits.

As he turned to leave, he noticed a book lying in the middle of the old sofa. Almost as if someone had recently sat down to read but had been interrupted. On the floor beside the sofa lay a brass candle holder with a nearly spent candle.

Could this be the light he'd seen earlier? Not once but twice?

Uneasiness clawed its way up the back of his neck. Gripping the handle of the dragon dagger sheaved at his belt, he set the lantern down and briefly glanced about the library.

Bloody hell! Am I a man or a frightened lass?

He loosened his grip on the dagger. As with the sofa and table, the candle and holder had likely been left behind years before. But then...why did the faint smell of beeswax linger in the room? He knelt and touched the tip of the candle's wick.

No, this was not imaginary spirits.

This...

He stood.

Was a trespasser.

Suddenly a fierce wind broke against the manor, howling with a vengeance as it whipped around one corner. A haunting sound. A cry of loneliness and desolation. Then, just as quickly, the wind died, leaving silence in its wake.

Somewhere beyond the stillness, a door creaked

softly.

Rather careless, my uninvited friend.

Morgan picked up the lantern, along with the candle and holder, and crept from the room.

* * *

Why is he stealing my candle?

Whatever the reason, Belle intended to take it back whenever the opportunity presented itself. She waited until the light from the lantern gracefully faded from the library before cautiously emerging from her hiding place. With her injured toe still throbbing, she carefully crossed the room. Pausing at the door, she peeked down the corridor. Dim light glowed from the foyer.

Instinct cautioned her to return to the safety of the dusty drapery, but she ignored the warning. Swallowing intense fear, she crept along the dark corridor. Reaching the foyer, she spied the candle. It had been joined to the brass holder and was now lit. Both had been placed on the floor near the bottom of the stairs, illuminating the lower portion.

But where had the gentleman disappeared to?

Her gaze rose to the second floor and beyond...into a black void with no shape or definition.

Is he watching me?

Lightning intruded through the tall windows, exposing the foyer and forcing the oppressive darkness obscuring the upper floors to retreat briefly. She crouched in the shadow of the staircase before a clap of earsplitting thunder followed, shaking the manor to its foundation.

Somewhere upstairs a door slammed shut followed by something heavy falling to the floor.

What is he doing?

What does it matter? Take the candle and make your way to safety.

No. He'll realize he's not alone in the house.

And when he fails to discover anyone, he'll think he's encountered a ghost.

She smiled.

And he'll leave.

Before she could talk herself out of it, Belle sped around to the base of the stairs. Her bare feet on the marbled tile sounded like fish flopping about upon the deck of a boat. Was she truly making this much noise or did fear exaggerate the sound her feet made?

Upstairs, another creak.

If she didn't act now...

Summoning all the courage she could muster, she snatched the candle, splashing hot wax onto her hand and burning her skin. Biting her lip, she carefully switched her grip. In the process, the brass holder came loose and fell to the floor with a loud clatter before rolling onto its side.

Terrified she'd be discovered any second, Belle left the holder where it landed and made a mad dash back to the library.

* * *

Slivers of bold light illuminated the master bedroom as thunder boomed and strong winds continued to punish the manor. Rain fell in a downpour now, so loud it drowned out every other sound.

Ignoring the profound ache in his shin, Morgan swiftly closed the window. He turned and righted the chair before placing it next to the fireplace. If the wind hadn't suddenly slammed the bedroom door shut, startling him, he might've remembered the chair had been positioned in front of the window and avoided tumbling over it. Instead of searching for an intruder as he'd planned, he'd been thinking of how this room would eventually look with new furnishings.

A faint rustling sounded behind him. He turned, his gaze focused on the corner of the room nearest the fireplace. It was almost as though someone had slid their hands down the oak paneling in quick fashion, but that someone would've had to vanish into thin air within seconds.

A mouse?

Most likely. The thought crossed Morgan's mind to investigate, but he decided to postpone that particular venture until he could actually see what he wished to explore.

Wandering about unfamiliar surroundings could be hazardous, as he'd just proven.

His father had never mentioned secret passages or anything of that nature, but that didn't mean they didn't exist. Dragon's Breath concealed numerous passageways behind its massive fireplaces. Dangerous passageways that spiraled downward in a maze of sharp twists and turns where one misstep could send you to a horrible death.

Morgan's attention swung back to the fireplace. Was someone hiding behind there this very second, watching his every move?

He released a pent up breath. This was Canderlay Manor. Not Dragon's Breath. If either of his younger brothers ever discovered how skittish he'd become, their teasing would never cease.

Thunder erupted again, violently shaking the windows and rattling the glass. The fierce storm seemed to be hovering over the manor, refusing to move on. He'd better check on Ares. The Arabian was likely stomping around the carriage house with nostrils flaring and eyes as round as coins.

He picked up the lantern and hobbled out of the room. Midway down the stairs he came to an abrupt halt as thick blackness once again consumed the foyer below. A sharp draft must've extinguished the candle he placed on the floor. As he reached the bottom of the stairs, light from the lantern exposed a portion of the marbled tile. The brass holder lay on its side, but it no longer held the candle. In fact, the candle was missing.

"What the devil?"

A sudden break in the downpour outside coincided with an unexpected thump upstairs.

Morgan whirled around, but his vision failed to penetrate the murkiness hovering like an ebony blanket over the floor above.

This will end.

Tonight.

He hung the lantern on a hook that had once supported a wall sconce and turned down the wick until complete darkness closed ranks around him. Making his way back up the stairs to the second floor, he kept his back to the wall, bleeding into the rest of the shadows. Passing the entrance to the portrait gallery, he moved into the corridor. And that's when he heard the floor creak directly above him.

Eager for the confrontation, Morgan exited the corridor and holding onto the balustrade for guidance, he crept up the stairs to the third level.

A few more steps, friend, and you're mine.

A distorted shape slowly emerged from the black hole of the corridor, strangely stooped and moving awkwardly.

Morgan squinted, logic battling sheer panic. Fear was not an emotion he was accustomed to, but at this precise moment he got acquainted with it. As he stared, trying to determine what the devil he was looking at, lightning entered the large window near the third floor landing, exposing bleak surroundings along with the small, cloaked figure standing a few feet in front of him. Before he could process what he was staring at, the light disintegrated, leaving him with a chilling image burned into his brain.

The ghostly image of...

What?

He swallowed hard.

A banshee with no face?

Terror slithered up Morgan's spine, and the hair on the back of his neck stood on end. "Listen, friend," he said, forcing his voice to remain calm. "I've no idea who you are or what you're doing in my house, but you're trespassing, and I'd like you to leave." He swallowed to relieve the sudden dryness in his throat. "Immediately."

Strained silence. Severely pronounced.

Had this thing, whatever it was, vanished?

"And if you have a key," he added boldly, "you may leave it in the door on your way out."

He held his breath.

Waiting.

Listening.

Light from the storm funneled in and flickered around the walls, creating a host of formidable shadows. One of which was all too real.

No, it hadn't vanished. Or heeded his warning.

Suddenly its right hand stretched forward, and one long finger pointed in his direction, as though accusing him of some crime.

He backed away. "Holy mother of...good God!" His heart thudded hard as though it wished to escape the confines of his chest. "What the..." He forced air into his starved lungs. "Hell and damnation!"

Shocked beyond coherent speech, the instinct for survival seized Morgan's feet, taking precedence over every emotion, real or imagined, and he quickly backed away from the disturbing figure.

And right over the third floor balustrade.

Chapter Two

Good God!! I've killed him!

Belle stood frozen to the spot, petrified with fear. Finally warm blood returned to her hands and feet, replacing the icy numbness. She rushed to the balustrade, peering into the hushed void below. "My lord, are you hurt?"

No response.

He's just fallen to the second floor landing. I doubt he's unharmed.

"I'm terribly sorry, sir...whoever you are. I didn't mean to..."

Frighten you? Oh, yes. You meant to do just that.

True, but hopefully she hadn't killed him.

"Heavenly Father, he cannot be dead." Belle carefully made her way down the stairs to the second level, but she could see nothing. "Merciful Lord." She turned around and felt her way down the corridor, muttering beneath her breath, "Sweet and gentle Father, I beg you, please do not punish this man for my misdeeds." She continued through the antechamber and into the master bedroom. "Oh, please."

Stopping at the fireplace, she slid her hands along the wall then tapped the oak panel in the center. Left unlatched, it popped open immediately. "Please, please." Inside the secret room, she grabbed the candle she'd left burning and raced back to the second floor landing, all the while whispering beneath her breath, "Please, please don't let him be dead or horribly maimed."

Setting the candle on the floor, she knelt beside the stranger. He lay on his side with his right arm pinned beneath him, and his left leg thrust forward in an awkward position. Carefully she straightened his leg then rolled him over.

His breathing came and went in a steady rhythm.

Relieved, she placed her hand over his heart.

A strong beat.

"Thank you, heavenly Father. Thank you, thank you."

Guilt quickly replaced relief, and tears welled in Belle's eyes. She touched his forehead. A handsome face, marred only by the swelling of a dark bruise over one temple. She had never in her entire life caused anyone harm. Never. Until now. If this man died, or became a simpleton, the fault would be hers.

"I meant you no harm," she whispered. "Truly." Hot tears overflowed and slid down her cheeks. "I simply thought to frighten you into leaving but you..." Angrily, she wiped the tears, her hands shaking uncontrollably. "You didn't react the way I expect3ed."

He remained silent, unmoving.

"You could've broken your neck."

But his neck and everything that held it in place appeared undamaged.

Thank God for watching over foolish men!

Not knowing what else to do, she unbuttoned the top two buttons of his shirt. It might've successfully revived this gentleman had his unconscious state been due to tight fitting stays.

"You're not very clever, are you?" she admonished. "No one with any sense whatsoever enters an empty manor house after dusk or during a wicked storm." Thinking better of this rash judgment and disingenuous accusation, she added, "Unless, like me, you had no other choice."

Was it fair to blame this gentleman for reacting normally?

She caressed his brow. His skin felt cool to the touch, but the swelling from his bruise continued to spread outward.

"Did you even consider the consequences? How could you be so careless?"

"Miss Isabelle?"

Her head snapped around.

A white-haired old man holding a straw picnic basket in one hand and a glowing lantern in the other stood at the foot of the stairs. She didn't immediately recognize him until he added, "Who are you speaking to?"

She blinked through the tears and rose to her feet. "Oh, thank heavens it's you, Mister Samuels! I didn't expect you until tomorrow evening. How did you know I needed help?"

"I feared the storm might've alarmed you, miss. I had no idea you needed me. What's the trouble?"

"Come up and see. Hurry please."

The old caretaker climbed the stairs but not quickly. He never did anything in haste. Not the way he walked, the way he spoke, or even the way he went about his normal duties. As he neared, his gaze fell upon the injured stranger. "I see you found yourself in the company of a gentleman."

"Yes, but he failed to provide a name before his accident."

In customary slow fashion, Samuels managed the rest of the stairs to the second floor landing. "What happened to him?"

"Toppled over the balustrade," she replied before resuming her position beside the stranger. "Backward."

"From the third floor?"

She nodded.

His brow wrinkled. "On purpose?"

"Well...no." Tears filled Belle's eyes again. "Not exactly."

Thunder grumbled low and continued for several seconds. The storm had finally decided to move on.

"Is he dead?" Samuels asked.

She shook her head.

"He can thank the blessed saints the second floor landing is a bit wider than the third, otherwise he would've fallen all the way to the foyer." He placed the basket at her feet and the lantern beside it. "Here now, miss. Stop that. You know it pains me to see you cry."

"I'm sorry. It's just..." She wiped her eyes with the hem of her nightdress. "If this man dies, I'm to blame."

"You?" His good eye, the brown one, widened as he stared at her. "No. I'll not believe that."

She choked back the tears. "It's true. I caused his

accident."

His hand rested on her shoulder. "Did this blackguard assault you?"

"No." Again she wiped her eyes. "I don't believe he was sent by the same person who wishes to harm me. I suspected he was merely waiting out the storm, and I thought to frighten him off, but Mister Samuels...look at him." Shivering, she released a sob that racked her entire body. "He's hurt and likely needs a doctor. What are we going to do?"

"Calm down, Miss Isabelle. Take a deep breath." He knelt beside her, one knee objecting to the strain with a loud creak. "I doubt your papa told you but when I was a lad, I spent two years assisting a country doctor." He examined the man carefully before declaring, "No broken bones. No visible wounds except for the bruise there. Breathing does not appear distressed." He turned to Belle. "No need to fret, miss. If this dandy's good fortune persists, he should live to a ripe old age."

She exhaled from sheer relief.

"How did he get inside the manor?" Samuels asked. "Through the broken window around back?"

"No, he walked in by way of the front door."

"He likely has a key then." He searched the man's pockets and found what he was looking for. "Another renter." He shook his head before replacing the key where he'd found it. "Why anyone would be willing to lease this old girl is beyond me."

"Being abandoned for many years does not make this house undesirable. It was beautiful once and could be again with a caring master."

"If you say so, miss, but I doubt any reasonable lord would lay down good coin for the likes of Canderlay Manor. Not in its current condition."

"Actually..." She gathered her thoughts. "I believe this man did."

"What's that? You spoke to him?'

"Well, no, but he is the new owner. I'm sure of it. I'm sorry I didn't recall it sooner, but the shock of seeing him take such a wicked tumble—"

"Owner, did you say?"

"Yes, but allow me to start at the beginning. No, that might take too long. I'll begin in the middle, after my visitor made his entrance." She drew a breath. "You see, Mister Samuels, I'd entered the passageway through the library and climbed the narrow stairway to the second floor to spy on him, but as I exited the secret room..." Recalling the tender knot on her shin, she glared at the helpless man lying on the floor. "Was it truly necessary to move that chair over by the fireplace? I could've broken an arm or leg."

"Miss Isabelle?"

"Forgive me, Mister Samuels. Where was I? Oh, yes. I exited the secret room and then made my way up to the third floor. You wouldn't believe—"

"In complete darkness?"

"What? Well, yes. I couldn't very well carry a lighted candle, now could I?"

"No, I suppose not, but how did you see anything at all?"

"I've recently had plenty of practice maneuvering in the dark."

"I imagine so. Well, miss, you must be more prudent in the future. Why you decided to go up to the servant quarters while this gent was roaming around downstairs is beyond me. You should've kept to that room."

"I wanted to retrieve the cloak I'd found. I'd left it on the third floor this morning when I—"

"Miss Isabelle, did you not stop to think you might create a noise that this dandy would be obligated to investigate?"

"It was a chance I was forced to take. And besides—"

"You could've returned for the cloak come morning. Why risk discovery?"

"Because I thought the cloak might be useful in my silly amateurish attempt at frightening away a grown man." She sighed. "Please, Mister Samuels. I'm having a little trouble understanding what occurred myself and if you keep interrupting, I'll likely become more confused."

"Apologies, miss. Proceed."

"Thank you." Gathering her thoughts, Belle drew a

quick breath. "After retrieving the cloak, I crept back down the third floor corridor. It's impossible to see anything up there and as I emerged, I almost collided with this gentleman. If not for a brilliant burst of lightning, I likely would have. Had I not been so shocked, I might've screamed."

"You cannot afford to be so rash, miss."

"Well heavens, I didn't expect him to be lurking about the third floor. When I saw no light from his lantern on the stairs below or from the foyer, I assumed he had gone back down and into the library. In error, I decided it would be safe to make my way down to the second floor and into the secret passageway in order to continue spying on him."

With difficulty, he stood. "Did he see your face?"

"No. It's more likely he thought I was a ghost. I quickly realized I couldn't fool him for long, but he blocked my escape down the stairs. If I turned and ran back down the corridor, he'd catch me in no time or I'd be trapped in the servant quarters. I wasn't sure what to do and as we stood staring through the blackness at one another, this irritating gentleman suddenly proclaimed himself the new owner of Canderlay Manor and ordered me to leave. Not to be outdone, I raised a finger and pointed, silently ordering him to do the same." She winced. "But that didn't go as I'd planned either."

"I expect not."

Thunder, a last dying gasp, rumbled through the manor.

"He must've suffered quite the shock," Samuels declared behind his usual stone-faced expression.

The composed countenance he always wore. The face of a loyal servant. It never changed no matter the situation.

"Had I seen what I believed to be an apparition," he added, "I might've run straight into a wall and knocked myself senseless."

"Better a wall than over a balustrade."

One corner of the caretaker's mouth twitched, but he successfully avoided a smile. Had he ever smiled? Ever laughed?

"Pardon me, miss, but..." He pointed to her bare feet.

"Did you misplace your slippers again?"

She grimaced. "No, I purposely refused to wear them."

One white bushy brow rose. "You realize, of course, that you could catch your death walking about this drafty old manor?"

"They pinch my toes, and since I've only one pair of stockings..." She sighed. "Never mind the discomfort of my feet, Mister Samuels. At the moment, we've a more pressing problem."

He eyed the stranger. "New master of the manor, is he? Well, I'd best get his lordship downstairs. I'm certain his tender backside has never suffered this much abuse."

"We can place him on the sofa in the library."

"Very good. You take hold of his feet, miss, and I'll grab his shoulders."

Belle did as instructed, but the man's weight placed her back under considerable strain. "I cannot speak for the burden you're carrying, but I can hardly budge this end."

"Yes, he is rather burdensome." He rested the stranger's shoulders on the floor then straightened. "We'd better leave him."

"Leave him? You mean...here on the landing?"

"Well..." He rubbed the gray stubble on his chin. "I suppose I could roll him down the stairs."

"Heavens, no. You might injure him further. Oh, wait...I've an idea."

Belle snatched the lantern and hurried down the stairs. In the library, she yanked down a portion of the worn drapery. Gathering the musty cloth in her arms, she exited the room and raced back up the stairs, sneezing several times along the way. As she approached, the caretaker uncorked a near empty bottle. "Mister Samuels, surely there is a more appropriate time to partake in a glass of brandy?"

He glanced up. "It's been fifteen years since I tasted strong drink. Not since the day your papa, God rest his soul, hired me as caretaker to the church. I recently discovered this bottle in the kitchen pantry and meant to toss it but..." He poured what was left of the liquid down the front of the gentleman's shirt. "Now it's served a better purpose."

"What do you mean?"

"Gent claims he owns the place. If you wish to avoid unnecessary confrontation—"

"Rather late for that," she mumbled.

"Yes, well..." He cleared his throat. "Is it your intention to remain here at Canderlay Manor so that I may continue to look after you until the time comes to claim your inheritance?"

"Unless you have a better idea, yes."

"In the meantime, we must convince his lordship that he got soused earlier this evening and fell to the second floor on his own."

"Oh...the smell of brandy on his clothes. Yes, I see. An excellent idea, but what if he remembers me? I mean...remembers seeing a cloaked figure?"

"More than likely he will come to the conclusion that the brandy caused his eyes to see something that wasn't there. You may trust my experience in this matter, miss." Samuels re-corked the empty bottle and placed it beside the stranger. "What do you plan to do with that musty old drapery?"

"I thought perhaps we could roll our unexpected guest onto it and thereby safely carry him down the stairs to the sofa."

The caretaker shook his head. "Even if we managed to lift this gent, the rotted cloth will likely tear straight through, and he'll roll down the stairs without our help. Unless of course..." He paused briefly. "That was your intention."

Belle frowned. "No, Mister Samuels. Indeed, that was not my intention. Even though this gentleman caused more than his share of trouble this evening, and likely throughout his life, I am not a heartless woman." She covered the stranger with the drapery and stood. "And I would never roll an unconscious person down the stairs, with or without genuine cause."

"Very well then." He picked up the basket and handed it to her. "There's food in there along with some extra candles, and I purchased a needle and some thread for you."

"Splendid. I discovered another hole in my..." Her voice stalled as intense heat inched up her neck and into her face. The sorry condition of her drawers was no one's business but her own. "That is...the gray frock I found in an attic trunk will need to be taken in a few inches."

"I fear you're wasting away, miss."

"Not at all. It's just...well lately I've not had much of an appetite."

"Your anxiety can be blamed on an uncertain future."

"Tremendously uncertain. If I fail to claim what Uncle Magnus left me by my twentieth birthday, which is a mere two months away, it will go into a charity fund. I've nothing against charities, you see, but with the fire and my supposed death, I lost the stipend Father left me. I need that small inheritance in order to survive."

"I'll travel with you to Dublin, miss. Make sure you arrive at the solicitor's office safely."

"Thank you, Mister Samuels, but that's not necessary. You've already done more than I could've hoped. If not for you, I would've never survived."

"Your clever mind would've come up with something, miss. Oh, I stopped by the church this morning and spoke with the cleaning woman. No news as to when the new vicar will arrive but..." He reached inside a pocket of his coat. "Mrs. Kemp discovered this strapped beneath the chair in your father's office."

"Is that one of his journals?"

"It appears to be." He handed it over. "Likely the last one before..."

Before his heart failed.

Grief closed Belle's throat. "Yes, I imagine so."

"You will eat what I brought, will you not, miss?"

She nodded.

"See that you do. I'll return in the morning. If our guest has suffered no ill effects from his fall, I'll introduce myself and inquire as to a position in his household."

"A clever idea. I doubt the locals will be interested."

"My thoughts precisely."

"Oh, but...what if he's still unconscious when you return?"

"Then I'll drive posthaste to Maidstone and leave him with a doctor. That is...if we can manage to get him downstairs without breaking his neck."

Belle's attention shifted to the stranger. "The bruise on his temple worries me."

"I've seen worse. He'll likely experience a slight headache and overall stiffness, but I doubt he loses the capacity to reason."

"I should hope not. Perhaps we could take off his boots. Or bring him a pillow. He might even be thirsty. If we sit him up—"

"No, miss."

"But...could we not—"

"Miss Isabelle, you've done all you can for his lordship this evening. Now take that basket and go on up. I prefer to see you safely locked inside that room before I leave."

"Very well, Mister Samuels. Good night."

"Good night, miss."

She picked up the candle. "I'm certain our intrusive friend did not travel here afoot. Should we not see to the care of his horse?"

The caretaker frowned. "I saw no horse in the courtyard, miss. Nor fancy carriage."

"He may have brought the animal inside the stables or carriage house to wait out the storm."

"I'll check. If there's a horse, I'll see to it."

"You are a wonderfully kind man, Jasper Samuels."

"It isn't difficult to be kind to someone such as yourself, miss."

With a smile, Belle turned and climbed the stairs. Alone in the hidden room, she set the candle on a round table before placing the basket on the small uncomfortable cot she slept on. Inside she found several candles, a fresh supply of rose-scented soaps, a chunk of cheese, baked bread, roast beef, butter, cinnamon apples, grapes, and a slightly warm pot of tea.

And as promised, the needle and spool of thread.

Clutching her father's journal, she sat on the edge of the cot.

My life used to be so simple.

So ordered.

Not anymore.

Was it possible Uncle Magnus had sired an

illegitimate child, and that child now wished to share in Belle's meager inheritance? But surely his solicitor would've mentioned it in the letter he'd sent.

Unless...Magnus had requested otherwise.

No, her uncle was a decent man. He loved children. If he'd sired such a child, he would've never hidden it. He would've gladly taken responsibility and seen to the child's welfare.

Belle sighed. She'd lost everything she owned due to a raging fire set by a madman, and she could provide no answer as to why her quiet life had been purposely and maliciously placed in turmoil. Behind the darkness of Canderlay Manor, she'd found protection as well as familiarity. She'd felt safe.

Until the gentleman lying helpless and unconscious on the second floor landing unknowingly intruded, forcing her to accept a bitter certainty.

She wasn't safe. Would never be safe as long as she remained in England.

It's not his fault. Why shouldn't he inspect what belongs to him?

Belle stood. She should return. Take a pillow and try to make the injured man more comfortable.

Don't be a fool. If he wakes, he'll ask who you are and what you're doing inside his house.

A valid point.

She eased onto the cot.

No, I simply cannot leave him lying on the cold floor.

It would be terribly uncivilized.

Think of your own safety.

How could she when her dear father had always preached compassion for others? Especially for those less fortunate.

Belle stood.

But...what can I do?

Indecision reigned, and she sat down again.

It would be impossible to move the unconscious man. She couldn't even lift his feet for more than a few seconds. She might be able to help him if he came to his senses. Which, considering the ugly bruise on his temple, seemed unlikely as more time passed.

Belle toyed with the journal and tried to ignore thoughts of the injured man, as well as his obvious discomfort, but leaving him on the landing didn't seem proper. If he awoke before morning, he might not recall where he was. Surrounded by darkness he might even become disoriented and...

Her heart plummeted, and she jumped to her feet.

Dear God, he might take a tumble down the stairs!

Chapter Three

Between the murky realm of sleep and consciousness, something delicate tickled the tip of Morgan's nose. Irritated by whatever had intruded upon his restless slumber, he brushed it away, but the strange tickling sensation soon returned, forcing him to crack open an eye.

The familiar face of Bartholomew, Duke of Chase, came into focus.

"Good morning, princess," Bart said with a grin, twirling a white feather in one hand. "Did you sleep well?"

Morgan groaned. "Not particularly, duchess." He covered his head with a pillow and rolled over, but the stiffness and dull ache in one shoulder wouldn't allow him to go back to sleep. And besides, the duke had begun poking him in the back. "Bart, you and I have been friends ever since our time at Cambridge, but at this very moment I find I do not care at all for you. Away, you devil. Allow me to wallow in my own misery."

"When you departed London two days ago, you indicated you were riding straight to Chase Manor."

"And your point is?"

"Does this Godforsaken place look anything like Chase Manor?"

"I wouldn't know," Morgan replied. "Oddly enough, my vision seems a bit impaired."

"No bloody doubt!"

"Speak softly, old friend. In fact, I'd rather we not speak at all until much later. Say around midday?"

"That won't do as your sister has made plans for my free time."

"I warned you not to marry her, did I not? But you wouldn't listen."

"I've never followed anyone's advice. Particularly yours. Here, let's get you on your feet."

"Leave me, Bart, I beg you. I've a terrible headache, and seeing your noble yet arrogant face before I've had a decent breakfast will put me in a foul mood."

"Are you a damsel or a man? Take your punishment and be done with it."

"Believe me, I have. This mattress is as thin as a board. It should be taken outside and flogged."

"You're on the floor, Morgan. Not lounging on a mattress."

"The devil, you say." He peeked out from under the pillow. "Good God, no wonder my body feels as though it aged a century overnight. I must've rolled off the bed."

"Take another look, my friend. There is no bed."

With difficulty, Morgan sat up, but his surroundings, everything he glanced at, seemed to bob up and down like a cork on the ocean. "My eyes...are they're bouncing around like musket balls on a marble floor?"

Bartholomew laughed. "Your eyes are closed."

"Never mind then. My head throbs intensely. I fear any second now it might separate from my neck and drop right off my shoulders." Without warning, a sick churning began inside his gut as the contents of whatever food he'd consumed the night before threatened to come back up the way it'd gone down. He placed his head in his hands, fighting waves of debilitating nausea.

"I'm curious," Bartholomew said in a much too cheerful tone. "Please enlighten me, Morgan, as to what on earth would make you choose to spend the night here?"

"What do you mean?"

A slight hesitation. "On the second floor landing of Canderlay Manor."

Morgan slowly raised his head. Little by little his surroundings came into focus in the gray light of early morning. Stark and bleak. Nothing to boast about except the beautiful grand staircase. A masterpiece actually. At least from his vantage point. And he was indeed sitting where Bartholomew claimed. On the second floor landing covered in...

"What the devil...is this tattered drapery?"

"Apparently. Did you start a brawl last evening with a fellow twice your size? You know, Morgan, I've always enjoyed your odd brand of humor, but not every Englishman is as agreeable as me."

"My humor is fine, thank you. Not at all dry, like yours."

"And yet your beautiful sister married me in spite of this glaring fault."

"Strange, is it not? By the way, where is Margaret?"

"At Chase, hoping I can convince you to return." Bartholomew sniffed the air and frowned. "Why does your shirt reek of brandy?"

"I assumed that sour smell originated from you."

"Hardly." The duke picked up an empty bottle lying next to Morgan. "A poor choice from inferior stock."

"Your knowledge of brandy is astounding, but you'll be pleased to know I did not purchase that bottle."

"Is that so?"

"I swear it's the truth."

"Oh, I believe you," the duke declared, but his tone lacked sincerity. He set the bottle aside. "Engaged in a bit of fisticuffs, did we?"

Morgan glanced at his hands, but they showed no signs of recent injury. "No, Mother, I did not get into a brawl. Any other misconduct you'd care to accuse me of?"

"My suspicions arose not from your nefarious reputation but came about due to the nasty bruise to your temple."

Morgan raised his hand to the throbbing area on the right side of his face and promptly winced. "What the bloody hell happened?"

"Precisely my point."

Morgan pushed aside the dusty material he'd obviously wallowed under all night and got to his knees. Shaky and lightheaded, he announced, "There's not a muscle in my body that doesn't ache. Kindly help me to my feet."

The duke chuckled before offering his hand.

Morgan stood. Holding onto the balustrade for support, he made his way down the stairs. Along the way, he noticed the light of a low-burning lantern hanging from a hook on the wall. His lantern. He vaguely recalled turning down the wick but little else. After several stops to ease the nausea, he finally reached the foyer. "I know how this must look, Bart, but I swear on Grandfather Ethan's grave..." He turned to face his friend. "I did not get soused last evening, I did not get into a brawl, and I've no knowledge as to how or why I received this bruise."

"And the empty brandy bottle?"

"A mystery as well, along with the ghastly condition of my shirt."

"You are far from dimwitted, Morgan. Put those two clues together, and I'm quite certain you'll come to the same conclusion I did."

Morgan sucked in a deep breath, attempting to clear his thoughts, but the pain inside his head diverted all efforts to concentrate.

"What exactly did you do last evening?"

"You mean after leaving London?" Morgan's mind eased backward to the day before. "I stopped in Maidstone and hired about two dozen skilled laborers. They should arrive around seven this morning."

"That was half an hour ago."

"Oh...well, perhaps they were delayed."

"Yes, I imagine so. Where did you travel after Maidstone?"

"Here. To inspect the house and grounds." Morgan massaged the stiffness from his neck. "It was close to dusk when I arrived, and a storm was brewing. I realize I should've waited until the light of day, but you well know how impatient I am."

"Indeed."

"I was about to head off in the direction of Chase Manor when I spotted a light in a window downstairs. Actually, that was the second time I noticed this light. I'd originally seen it earlier through a second floor window. When I came inside to investigate, I discovered a nearly spent candle sitting on the floor in the library, and it had obviously been recently used."

"An intruder?"

"That's precisely what I suspected but upon further investigation..."

The remaining portion of last evening's events crowded into Morgan's mind in quick succession. Shock mingled with disbelief, and his reasoning bordered upon complete denial. Unwilling to trust this memory, he raised his gaze to the semi-darkness still hovering about the third floor.

"You were saying?" Bartholomew prompted.

"I discovered a..."

Had it been real? Or a clever intruder?

"You discovered what...exactly?"

Morgan shrugged. "I've no idea, Bart. Whatever it was, I pray to the Good Father I never see it again."

The duke sighed. "Are you certain you were not stewed? Perhaps you suffered from an overindulgence of inferior brandy."

"I drank no spirits last evening, but I may have encountered one. And I have never been so pickled as to see something that couldn't possibly be there. Yet it *was* there, right in front of me."

"Well what the bloody devil was it?"

"A ghost. Apparition. Spirit. Banshee. Take your pick. It was dark, and I couldn't make out any details except between flashes of light from the storm, but what I did see..." Part of the pain in Morgan's head shifted to a tender spot behind his eyes, and he lowered his tone. "As I said before, I'm not sure what it was, but it reached out to me, and I was so stunned I backed right over the third floor balustrade. And that's where my memory of last evening abruptly ends."

In a casual manner, Bartholomew glanced up the stairs. "A spirit chased you over the balustrade?"

"Chased? Yes, I suppose that's an accurate assumption."

"And after doing you this terrible injustice, it made amends by leaving you with a soft pillow and tattered drapery for your comfort?"

Morgan frowned. "I understand your reluctance to accept my version of events, strange as they are, but I swear I have no idea how the pillow and drapery came into my possession. I certainly didn't bring them with me. Unless you choose to believe I packed them behind my saddle."

"Isn't it obvious? Either someone provided for you, or you came across them while staggering about the manor."

"Staggering? Ridiculous. While I agree with the first part of your theory, the latter part makes no sense at all. If I can recall seeing that...that thing upstairs and slipping over the balustrade, why would I not recall searching for a pillow? And why would I curl up on the second floor landing when Ares and I could've simply..." With a start, he stared at the front entrance. "Ares."

"Pardon?"

Stumbling toward the door, Morgan rushed outside. The air felt brisk and refreshing as it entered his lungs but with each movement, he suffered pinpricks of pain in his muscles. A few aches reached deep into his very bones. Somehow he'd turned into an old man overnight.

Making his way around the manor, he halted before the two doors of the carriage house. Open doors. Not closed. And no Ares. Had he not bolted those doors the night before?

"Morgan?"

He spun around, his head spinning as well. "Bart, if that bloody creature stole my horse—"

"Stole? What use would an apparition have for a horse? No, never mind. I've no wish to discuss possible answers to a question that has no obvious validity. Not to worry. Your horse is quite safe."

"You've seen him?"

"As I rode up." The duke nodded in the direction of the stables. "He's found himself a nice spot of pasture behind that pile of rubble."

Morgan hurried around to the back of the stables. Sure enough, Ares stood grazing in the tall grass. He whistled softly, and the Arabian's head jerked up. Another whistle and Ares trotted up to a damaged area in the fence.

"Good morning, old friend." He scratched behind the horse's ears. "I apologize for not seeing to your comfort last evening, but it seems you weathered the storm better than me. I didn't expect to spend the night here or I would've..." He stopped abruptly and stared in complete amazement.

35

"Bart, did you remove his saddle?"

"Certainly not. Why the devil would I?"

"Well someone did."

"Morgan, are you trying to convince me that someone other than yourself saw to the comfort of that temperamental beast last evening?"

"There's no other explanation." He glanced around. "Look there. Ares' saddle is resting upon the fence near the entrance to the stables, and I didn't set it there."

"Perhaps he grew tired of waiting for his master and snatched the saddle off his own back," Bartholomew quipped. "You did say he was rather clever, did you not?"

"Clever, yes. A magician, no. And how did he break out of the carriage house? I distinctly remember bolting those doors."

The duke rested his hand on Morgan's shoulder. "You've given me cause for concern, my friend. I believe the wound to your temple is playing tricks upon your memory, and I urge you to visit a physician at once."

Before Morgan could respond, he spied a horse and cart approaching the rough road leading down to Canderlay Manor. One man sat upon the driver's bench. "This cannot be good."

The duke turned and shielded his eyes against the glare of the morning sun. "Did you not say you'd hired two dozen laborers?"

"I did."

"Where are the others?"

"Apparently they reconsidered."

"For what possible reason?"

"Haven't you been listening, Bart? Canderlay Manor is haunted."

"Morgan, you should know better than to encourage such uneducated postulations."

"I haven't but unlike you, I cannot avoid something that is difficult to explain. Especially when I saw it with my own eye. I mean...eyes. Now, if you will excuse me, your Grace, I must go and greet my first visitor."

Morgan entered the courtyard as the horse drawn cart came to a stop a few yards away from the main door. The driver, a thin older man with a full head of white hair, set the brake before gingerly climbing down.

"Good morning, my lord."

"Good morning," Morgan replied. "What's happened to the others?"

The man's deep-set eyes, one blue and the other brown, dimmed with confusion. "Others, sir?"

"The laborers I hired from Maidstone yesterday. Where are they?"

"I wouldn't know, sir. I was told a new master had taken over Canderlay Manor, and as my own father, God rest his soul, was once the caretaker here, I rode over hoping you might offer the position to me." He reached into his breast coat pocket. "Here are my papers, sir. I have many years of experience, and I'm an honest and capable worker."

"I'm sure you are, Mister...?"

"Samuels. Jasper Samuels."

"How do you do, Mister Samuels. I'm Morgan Spence."

Something flickered in the old man's eyes but immediately disappeared.

"No need to address me as lord," Morgan added. "I've no worthy title. Unlike my brother-in-law and good friend the Duke of Chase here."

"A pleasure, your Grace."

Bartholomew nodded once.

"Did you say your father was once the caretaker here?"

"For the last marquis to hold the title. Yes, sir. My father retired soon after King George claimed this place. So you see, sir, I know this estate well, for I lived here until I turned four and ten." Samuels glanced at the manor house. "She's far from it now, but at one time this old girl was quite the beauty."

"And she will be again," Morgan declared.

"I seem to recall there was a Jasper Samuels working in the employ of the local vicar," Bartholomew noted.

"That would be me, your Grace."

"I met the late Reverend Lindley on occasion. A godly man, and you'll be pleased to know he spoke highly of you,

Samuels. It's a shame about his daughter. My wife was extremely saddened over the matter."

"As was I, your Grace." He turned to Morgan. "I served as church caretaker to the vicar for fifteen years until his untimely death last winter. He left me a fair stipend in his will, but I'm not a man to suffer idle hands. I'll accept any position you offer, sir. As you'll note in my papers, I've worked in the stables, assisted a doctor, been a head groomsman for a viscount, a footman and then butler to an earl, and manservant to a duke."

"Manservant is low on the priority list," Bartholomew insisted. "In fact, if a man cannot dress himself, what good is he?"

"On this, Bart, we can agree." Morgan glanced over the caretaker's papers. "You've held quite a few prominent positions, Samuels. Should this concern me?"

"I merely thought to expand my knowledge along with my experience, sir."

"And so you did. Very well then. You're hired."

"Thank you, Mister Spence. I'm most grateful for the opportunity to serve you. Pardon me for being so bold, sir, but did you suffer some sort of accident?"

"Oh, you mean the bruise? Yes, I..."

An amused grin lifted one corner of the duke's mouth, but he said nothing.

Morgan realized his strange experience might sound far-fetched but more important, he didn't wish to frighten off his only servant. "It's nothing," he said. "I merely tripped on the stairs."

"I see. May I suggest pressing a damp cloth to the wound, sir, to take away the swelling? And you might wish to clean and dress it afterward. I have ointment and would be happy to see to the wound, if you like."

"On the job at once. I like that, Samuels. No, I'll take care of my own needs, thank you, after I change clothes and clean up."

"Very well, sir."

"Oh, Samuels," Bartholomew said in the curt tone that accompanied his noteworthy title. "I feel I must warn you. Your new employer believes a ghost resides in his manor house."

The old man's white, bushy brows rose as he studied the duke. After a few moments, his gaze drifted back to Morgan, his stoic face betraying none of his thoughts on the subject. Nor any amusement whatsoever.

"Pay no attention to my brother-in-law, Samuels. His Grace is highly excitable and easily frightened."

Bartholomew huffed. "Unlike Mister Spence, I am not a man who caters to delusions. Now if I were a child or an emotional female—"

"Just because you did not witness a certain incident, does not mean it did not occur."

"I won't argue the fact that you crossed paths with something peculiar, Morgan, but I doubt it was an apparition. More than likely, it was an intruder."

"As much as it grieves me to admit this, Bart, you're probably right. And if I ever discover the identity of this trickster, I'll have him stripped and flogged."

Samuels' face reddened, and he cleared his throat in an unusually loud manner. "Mister Spence, may I inquire as to my position, sir?"

"Yes, of course. What position do you desire?"

"Why...whatever position is of the utmost need."

Morgan smiled. "Bart, I like this man."

"Yes, he seems a capable enough fellow, but I suspect there's a great deal of drudgery in his future. Now see here, Samuels, if this gentleman fails to pay you your full worth, bring your grievance to me at once, and I'll make certain he's reprimanded. Now then, Morgan. What do you plan to do regarding the repairs to the house and outer buildings? Obviously few workers are willing to approach this property."

"I can complete some of the work myself."

"You've experience as a skilled laborer?"

"No, but I'm certain I can accomplish a few simple tasks."

"And what of the more difficult ones?"

"Begging your pardon, gentlemen, but I believe I can be of service in this area as well," Samuels declared. "Mister Spence, the locals in Maidstone will be of no use to you. They know this place well, and their misguided superstitions will keep them away. If it's laborers you seek to hire, you'll have to travel to London or Cambridge. I'd be pleased to take on that particular task for I know where to look for these men and can negotiate a fair price. If you will permit me, sir."

Pleasantly surprised, Morgan nodded. "Certainly, Samuels. I leave you in charge then. Hire whomever you please. Domestic help as well. Inspect the house, outer buildings, and grounds to get an idea of the supplies the workers will need. I intend to see that every portion of this estate is repaired and in suitable condition in record time. Oh, and make sure the larders are well stocked by the time I move in next month."

"Understood, sir."

"In the meantime, you'll need funds. I'm staying temporarily at Chase Manor and will await your visit this afternoon to discuss the budget as well as your salary. Let me know if you have any questions or concerns at that time."

"Very good, sir."

"Oh, Samuels, where are your lodgings?"

"In Maidstone, sir. I've a room at the boarding house."

"I'd prefer you stay here. Bring whatever belongings you possess, personal items and furniture, and take up residence as soon as possible."

"You're requiring the man to stay?" Bartholomew glanced around, his frown deepening noticeably. "*Here*?"

"What's the matter, Bart? Afraid he'll validate my claim of a resident ghost?"

"Ridiculous. I was merely expressing concern over the man's comfort. He has no cook. No housekeeper or any other servants whatsoever."

"Not to worry, your Grace. Mister Spence, I neglected to mention it nor is it included in my papers, sir, but I was once employed as a cook."

Morgan stared at the man. "Cook?"

"Oh yes, sir. A position I rather enjoyed."

"May I ask how long and with what family?"

"Four years for the *Prince of Scotland. A* merchant ship from Glasgow."

"Yes, I know of it. Were you a decent cook?"

The old man's posture straightened considerably. "I believe so, sir, as I received few complaints."

Morgan turned to the duke. "Does this meet with your approval?"

"If you do not wear the man down until he can no longer walk, yes."

"His duties will be light. They will not include taking care of an entire household or staff. His main concern will be me. And unlike you, Bart, I am not a demanding gentleman." Morgan turned to the servant. "I've changed my mind, Samuels. I'll not wait until next month to take up residence. In fact, I'll return early next week. Would you be uncomfortable staying here alone until that time?"

"Not at all, sir."

"Splendid."

"What will the man eat?" Bartholomew inquired.

"Excellent question, and one I hadn't thought of. I suppose I could purchase a cow, several goats, and a dozen or so chickens."

"Where will you house them? The barn and stables are in shambles."

"Pardon me, your Grace, but there's a local farmer who lives no more than an hour away. With your permission, Mister Spence, I'll work out a price with him to deliver eggs, potatoes, butter and milk, and anything else we require. I suspect he will occasionally have wild game and fish."

"Thank you, Samuels. That will do nicely, will it not, Bart?"

The duke dipped his head in acknowledgement.

"No need to sleep in the third floor servant quarters," Morgan said to the old man. "I've seen the butler's private room downstairs, and it's rather spacious. If it pleases you, it's yours. If you need something purchased for your personal use, let me know, and I'll see to it."

"Thank you, sir. Am I to be your butler then?"

"Let's begin with supervising the laborers you bring in. After this estate is restored to its previous glory, we'll reexamine your status. Will that suffice?"

"It will indeed, sir."

"Oh, you might need this." Morgan reached inside his

pocket and retrieved a key. "It fits the front door. I've other keys and will hand them over when we meet this afternoon."

"I see. Very good, sir. If you'll excuse me, I'll begin my inspection."

"Of course. And Samuels..." Morgan offered a sincere smile. "Welcome home."

"Thank you, sir."

Once Jasper Samuels disappeared inside the manor, Morgan turned to the duke. "You mentioned the vicar's daughter earlier. What happened to her?"

"Tragedy, I'm afraid. She perished in a fire several months ago. A blaze so fierce it consumed the entire cottage and everything inside."

"How do you know she didn't escape?"

"Because she failed to turn up alive," Bartholomew replied.

Morgan could find no fault with this conclusion, and his gaze casually drifted up to the second floor windows.

* * *

Panic jolted Belle from her daydreams, and she darted back from the window. Why had she foolishly dared to stand so close? Had the gentleman seen her? He'd stared up at the window as though something had caught his eye. Hopefully, it wasn't her face. Whoever he was, it appeared he suffered little from last evening's accident. And...he'd given Samuels the key to the front door.

She waited until both men rode away before entering the secret room. Closing the door and securing the latch, she rushed down the narrow steps. Near the bottom floor, a familiar tapping sounded on the oak paneling.

"One moment, Mister Samuels."

"No rush, Miss Isabelle. Our guests have departed."

"Yes, I saw them." With a bright smile, Belle unlatched the panel, pushed it open, and stepped into the library. "Good morning."

"Morning, miss." The old caretaker held up a key. "Not sure of my title, but I've acquired new lodgings. Morgan Spence, he's your gentleman visitor and the current owner, asked me to move in immediately."

"Oh, thank God." She hugged the old man briefly. "You've no idea how relieved I am that I shall have someone other than my imagination to talk to."

"It won't be for a few days, miss. I'm off to Chase Manor this afternoon to discuss the household budget and then on to London."

"London? Whatever for?"

"Laborers. Mister Spence aims to see this estate restored in record time. His exact words."

"Oh, but this is wonderful news. I pray the workers are not frightened off. You referred to the owner as *mister*. Has he no title then?"

The old man shook his head. "Comes from nobility though. Even if I hadn't recognized the surname, I would've eventually remembered the face. Except for the blue eyes, he's the very likeness of the last Marquis of Canderlay."

"So that's why he looked at everything with such fondness. It once belonged to his father. He's come to take back what George III stole."

"Stole is the correct word, miss. If Morgan Spence's character is half as noble as his father's, he's a decent enough gent."

"You knew the Marquis of Canderlay? Well, of course you did. Your father worked as caretaker here."

"I admired young Lord Canderlay and his loyalty to his dear mother. A dark haired beauty with green eyes. She had a gentle spirit and a kind soul. Like you, Miss Isabelle."

She recalled the portrait she'd discovered in the dusty attic, wrapped securely in a faded linen sheet and leaning against one corner. Samuels was right. Lord Canderlay's mother had been quite the beauty.

"As I said, miss, I'll be away for several days, but I'll make sure to leave you plenty of food and water. Oh, and I should warn you. Mister Spence will be taking up residence early next week."

Belle frowned. She hadn't considered losing more of her freedom.

He added, "I'll be pressed for time upon my return, busy readying the manor house."

"Then allow me to help. Given a broom and dust cloth, I can—"

"No, Miss Isabelle. I'll not ask it of you."

"But Mister Samuels, you didn't ask. I volunteered. And besides, I am not a delicate lady of the nobility."

"You are to me, miss," he declared and offered a loyal servant's bow.

The gesture warmed Belle's heart. "My dear Mister Samuels, I feel you have misjudged me."

"Unlikely, miss, and I'll not watch you chaff your tender hands performing tasks made for common folk like me."

"Nonsense. Father always said work was good for the mind and soul. Please, Mister Samuels. Allow me to help."

He hesitated.

"Do you not wish to make a good impression on your new employer?"

"Certainly, Miss Isabelle, but how would I explain a manor house that had been tidied while I was away for several days?"

"Oh...considering you've no domestic help, I suppose that might seem a bit strange."

"I imagine so."

"Be there a soul in 'is godforsaken place?" shouted a male voice from the foyer. "Anyone breathin', that is?"

"Sounds like one of the locals," Belle whispered.

Samuels placed a finger to his lips then called out in the head servant's formal tone, "In the library at the end of the corridor." Rushing Belle toward the passageway, he whispered, "Hurry, miss."

She stepped inside, closed the panel, and secured the latch.

It wasn't long before footsteps sounded on the library's wooden floor and when they ended, a muffled voice asked, "You Samuels?"

Hesitation and then, "Yes. What can I do for you?"

"Name's Amos Barlow. Spoke with Morgan Spence on the road back there. Claims he owns this estate."

"Yes, Mister Spence is the new owner."

"Inquired if he needed a carpenter. Said I should

speak with Samuels his overseer. That be you?"

"It is, but unfortunately I've already hired the carpenters. This morning, in fact. I regret I neglected to inform my employer, and I apologize for any inconvenience this has likely caused you."

Belle sucked in a breath. She'd never known Jasper Samuels to speak anything other than the truth, but he'd clearly lied just now. Why?

"I've experience patchin' stone and brickwork. Don't care for climbin' onto a roof, but I'm familiar with tar and pitch." The man's tone became aggressive. "I'm in need of a job, old man. And Morgan Spence promised there'd be plenty of coin to go around."

After a noticeable pause, Samuels responded. "Very well, Barlow. If Mister Spence has approved your hiring, so be it. Return Monday morning."

The stranger walked away, and the sound of his footsteps gradually faded.

Belle waited a few minutes before she opened the panel.

Samuels stood with his back to her, his gaze fixated on the corridor beyond the library.

"Who was that man?" she whispered.

"Judging from your previous description, miss..." The caretaker turned, worry shadowing his expression. "I assume that was the scar-faced scoundrel who attempted to murder you."

Chapter Four

Rain trickled down the window of the sleek landau as it drew to a halt near the outer edge of the infamous Seven Dials District.

Philip Taft, Earl of Glenhawk, drew the curtains and waited patiently inside the darkness of the carriage. Beneath a decorative pillow, he'd hidden a flintlock pistol.

Had Isabelle Lindley been clever, she would've denied her father's journals ever existed. Did she not understand? Not comprehend what was at stake?

He'd been so clever, sending that letter claiming to be a renowned London publisher offering to purchase those journals under the pretense of publishing them in memory of a dedicated man of the cloth. Mindless chit. She had wanted nothing to do with his generous proposal. The journals were private, she'd written in response. Private words and private thoughts of her beloved father, and therefore she didn't feel comfortable allowing others to read them.

Were the vicar's written words as damning as the man claimed?

It no longer mattered. Whatever thoughts he'd committed to paper had been destroyed by fire. Still...

The girl knew. How could she not?

Why hasn't she contacted me to issue a demand? Is she waiting for an engraved invitation?

The carriage door opened, and for a brief moment the heavy darkness gave way to the faint light of civilization. Hawk lowered his head, shielding the upper portion of his face under the wide brim of his topper, as the man he'd summoned slid into the cushioned seat across from him.

After the door closed, Hawk asked, "Have you news?"

"Not a blessed word, milord," Amos Barlow replied,

his rain-soaked coat reeking of some offensive smell it had recently come into contact with.

"Nothing in three months? Where the devil is she?"

"Forest is plenty dangerous at night. Could've fallen into a bog. That'd take care of your problem, would it not, milord?"

"What does a ruffian with no conscience know of my problem? You were hired to follow orders. Not offer illiterate opinions."

"I got ears, milord. I hear the concern in your voice, and each hour the Lindley chit continues to breathe throws you into deeper despair. What'd you do? Poke your manhood between her ivory thighs? Get her with child, and she threatened to run straight to your lady wife?"

"Rutting with a vicar's young daughter?" Anger nearly consumed Hawk. "Have you no morals? No decency?"

Barlow sported a wicked grin, stretching the scarred skin on the left side of his face until it looked as though he wore a grotesque mask.

"I am a gentleman of the nobility," Hawk declared. "I would never sacrifice my honor by committing such depravity."

"And what of murder, milord? Wouldn't such a crime tarnish that sainted honor?"

"Watch your tongue."

"Or perhaps you've talked yourself into thinkin' there's no sin in hirin' someone like me to carry out the deed."

"How dare you." Hawk tried to rein in his anger, but it was dangerously close to the breaking point. "Do you have any idea who I am or what I could do to vermin like you?"

"No, milord, and I don't care to know you. Whatever occurred between you and the late reverend's daughter doesn't concern me. My interest lies solely in how much coin you're willin' to part with in order to safeguard your secrets."

"Then we understand one another perfectly, but a word of caution, Mister Barlow." Hawk's left hand slid beneath the pillow, searching for the pistol's grip. "Our association is the product of an evil decision I was forced to make, and one I cannot turn my back on until it is finished.

Once our business is concluded, you'd do well to forget we ever spoke."

"That won't be difficult as you've given me no name to accuse. No face to identify. And if I were to ever go against my nature and loosen my tongue, how would I point the finger at you without placing a noose about my own neck?"

Hawk leaned against the cushions, concealing his face in deeper shadow. He didn't trust this man, but he'd made a bloody bargain with the devil and couldn't back out. Surely God would not judge him so harshly for protecting what belonged to him.

Foolish girl! If she'd only taken the money.

"Isabelle Lindley must be found," Hawk declared. "Do we understand one another, Barlow?"

"We do, milord."

"If she made it out of the forest alive, then someone must've hidden her."

"Seems likely. She knows my face. Knows I set the fire. Can't figure why she didn't run straight to the constable."

"The authorities in Kent are not interested in whatever mishap befalls a vicar's daughter. The overworked constable would likely put the matter to bed by drawing the inevitable conclusion that Miss Lindley must've started the fire by accident and simply became too mortified to admit it."

"That may be but if she decides to talk—"

"It's been three months. Have the local authorities tracked you down? Questioned you regarding your whereabouts that night?"

"That don't mean the chit won't accuse me at some point."

"If she does, I'll take care of the matter."

"And just how, milord, would you be doin' that?"

Hawk smiled. "You'll simply disappear."

"With a modest amount of coin, I pray?"

"Yes, you'll be properly paid."

Properly, indeed.

"Did you speak to the cook?" Hawk inquired.

"Didn't have to. She's stayin' with her sister. Moanin'

and cryin' to anyone who'll listen 'bout how cruel life's been with Miss Isabelle gone. That worthless old hag don't know the meanin' of cruelty."

"What about Miss Lindley's friends?"

"Most believe she perished in the fire. Don't blame 'em." Barlow's laugh sounded unusually cold and depraved, as though sheer madness possessed his soul. "Was a wicked blaze that night."

"Thankfully you upheld that part of our bargain."

"Weren't my fault she crawled out the bedroom window."

"If you had snapped her neck while she slept—"

"Wasn't asleep. The wench spied me comin' up the stairs and barricaded her door." Barlow licked his lips. "Always did like auburn curls and sweet young innocents. A pity I couldn't spend a few hours with the girl."

"Enough," Hawk growled, keeping his voice low. "I've no wish to hear your decadent thoughts."

"One man's sin is another man's pleasure, guv'na. I weren't born into nobility. Society don't impose their strict rules upon me and my kind."

"Then keep your vulgar urges and back alley misdeeds to yourself." Sweat beaded Hawk's brow, and he wiped it unceremoniously. Madness was hereditary, was it not? He dismissed the answer even before it formed in his mind. "What of the other servants employed by the vicar?"

"The housekeeper returned to Glasgow."

"And the caretaker?"

"Jasper Samuels. Found the old man last week in Maidstone and followed his dray to the rundown estate of Canderlay. Figured I was on to somethin' till I learned he'd been hired as overseer by the new owner."

"Someone purchased Canderlay Manor? What gentleman would saddle himself with such a monstrosity?"

"Morgan Spence," Barlow replied and went on to tell what he knew of the man, including the fact that he was educated at Cambridge.

Curiosity piqued Hawk's interest. "Has this Spence fellow no title?"

"The workers address him as mister, not milord.

Boasts about his sister though. Seems she did well for herself. Married the Duke of Chase."

"Yes, she did well indeed. I suspect Morgan Spence is likely counting on the duke's generosity to restore his estate."

"Could be, but I hear his coin came from his own coffers. An inheritance."

"How do you know so much about the gentleman?"

"I spent the last two weeks workin' as a day laborer for him and overheard a conversation he had with Samuels."

"A day laborer? Really, Barlow, do I not pay you enough to keep your saucy trollops happily upon their backs?"

"Good enough, milord, but Jasper Samuels was the only servant of the late vicar's I hadn't questioned. Got little out of him though. A cold fish, he is. Not one for conversation and when he does speak, he looks down that long servant's nose of his."

Hawk sighed. "Find her, Barlow."

"She'll be found, milord. One way or another. Now if you don't mind, there's a keg of ale in the Cock's Round with my name on it."

After the man departed, Hawk tapped his cane on the roof, and the vehicle jerked into motion. Perhaps Reverend Lindley had possessed a modest amount of decency after all and hadn't disclosed the name Glenhawk in his bloody journals.

No, it's foolish to trust this line of thinking.

Reverend Lindley had been present as Mary drew her last breath. He'd heard her confession. Even before their first confrontation that afternoon eleven years earlier, Hawk had glimpsed the truth in the vicar's eyes.

And had instantly despised the man.

A foreboding chill inched down Hawk's spine, spreading numbness throughout his body. As long as Isabelle Lindley lived, the threat to expose his identity would remain. Had he suspected for one moment that Mary, a simpleminded prostitute and the woman who had given him life, would one day break the vow of silence she'd made with his father, he would've snuffed out her miserable existence long ago.

* * *

The fog of sleep drifted inside Belle's mind before gradually dispersing. Noises intruded upon her consciousness, echoing again and again inside her head. She groaned and rolled onto her stomach, crushing a pillow tightly about her ears, but the dull pounding continued, driving her to the brink of insanity. No matter how hard she tried, she could no longer separate the pounding in her head from the pounding outside. The workers seemed to be everywhere all at once. Inside the manor. Trudging up or down the stairs. Outside the manor. On the roof. All around her. Every hammer connected with a nail or board in a disjointed compilation of similar sound. Every day, all day long, for five days now. The noise did not cease unless interrupted by foul weather or until the workers left.

She flipped onto her back, the pillow still covering her ears, and stared up at the ceiling. What day was it? Saturday. A few more hours and she could enjoy a blissful and peaceful day without the presence of Morgan Spence.

He would be away most of the day tomorrow, as he was each Sunday.

She sighed. How she missed her dear father and his insightful sermons. Even though she dutifully said her prayers each night, she often felt detached from God. It was a strange and discomforting feeling, and one she truly did not wish to grow accustomed to.

Belle glanced at the leather-bound journal but couldn't bear to read his last thoughts.

A slight breeze stirred, fluttering the candle's flame. Her attention drifted to the stone steps leading down to the main floor. Had she carelessly left the panel to the library unlatched?

Her pulse quickened. It took a few moments of silence, and no footsteps coming up the steps, to calm her fears. She had felt that odd breeze before, when she and Uncle Magnus had first explored the secret passageway.

"Drafts are common inside manor houses as old as this one," he had explained. "Perhaps a door opened.

Perhaps one closed. Nothing to fear, Belle."

Nothing to fear, Uncle.

Her thoughts turned to the present. Stuck inside this room from dawn to well past dusk, she'd lost what little freedom she'd previously gained. Mostly for fear of running into Amos Barlow. She was completely dependent now upon the kindness of Jasper Samuels. The old caretaker may as well be her jailer because this...her gaze shifted about the confined surroundings...*this* was her prison.

Lately she rarely saw a reprieve. Even at night. For at the oddest times, the new owner would appear as if by magic. He casually roamed the upstairs and spent a great deal of his free time inside the master bedroom where he'd set up a bed.

To his credit, Morgan Spence did not issue orders while others worked. He set about emptying the upstairs bedrooms by his own hand and wouldn't allow Samuels to help. The fact that Samuels had encountered difficulties hiring domestic help didn't seem to discourage his employer in the least. He seemed to take pleasure in general labor. Even with the dusting and cleaning duties normally performed by maids.

She had often watched his comings and goings through the small peephole in the antechamber. In fact...studied him.

Such an intriguing man.

Belle shifted onto her side, carrying the pillow with her. Despite all the trouble he'd caused, she liked Morgan Spence. Liked his pleasant humor as well as his handsome smile. Both came natural and quite often but especially when he spoke to Samuels or the Duke of Chase.

She exhaled a deep sigh, and the candle's low flame sputtered again.

If only I could leave this room for more than a few minutes at a time.

She *would* leave. And soon. Oddly, the very thought saddened her.

Belle closed her eyes and must've dozed off for when she awoke, the pillow had fallen to the floor and the endless noise from the hammering had ceased.

Completely.

Oh, the joy of silence!

She sat up and, holding her breath, listened intently. Nothing.

Had she slept through lunch? Was it now evening? Stuck inside her prison without the benefit of a clock, she had no way of monitoring the time.

Had night fallen?

Curiosity bypassed caution and with a sudden overwhelming urge for freedom, Belle reached for the dark cloak and headed down the passageway to the library.

* * *

Morgan stared at the pair of frilly white pantalettes spread upon an old table inside the washhouse. By devil, the master mason had spoken the truth. Indeed it was a female's undergarments. But what were they doing here? Had the workers hired a prostitute for a bit of sport? Not likely, for they would've never slipped the wench past the watchful eyes...one brown, one blue...of the ever-present Jasper Samuels.

No. Samuels would've never allowed such depravity.

To whom did these belong?

He thought back to a week earlier. Had he truly seen a woman standing behind one of the second floor windows?

His bedroom window?

It could've been nothing more sinister than a shadow. A trick of the eye. Knowing the extent of Bartholomew's opinion regarding the existence of ghostly apparitions and spirits, he'd kept the incident to himself.

Reluctantly Morgan picked up the garment and caught the faint hint of roses. Had he not detected that fragrant scent before? Whoever owned this once frilly garment must've been hard pressed for coin, for she'd patched it in several places using different colored thread.

He marched out of the washhouse, undergarment in hand, stepping aside for the last cart hauling away a small mountain of refuse. On his way to the rear entrance, he thanked the Good Father that Samuels had encountered trouble hiring staff to serve inside the manor. At the time, it had irritated him. Now...there would be no smirks, no sly glances. No giggling maids. As for the laborers, he'd sent them home for the afternoon.

Inside the kitchen the smell of food surrounded Morgan, and his stomach rumbled with anticipation. Samuels had proved to be an exceptional cook, but at the moment he was nowhere in sight.

Morgan marched straight to the dining room. No Jasper Samuels. As he reached the foyer, he thought he caught sight of coattails heading into the corridor leading down to the study, drawing room, and library. Curious, he decided to follow but was stopped short by a portrait resting against the wall near the main entrance.

The lady in the portrait possessed exceptional beauty. She wore a flattering gown of rich amber. Hair the color of blackest coal had been coifed, displaying a slender neck. Emeralds adorned her ears and throat. Green eyes, the same as his father's, stared back at him with a gentleness that covered her entire face.

He bowed low. "A pleasure to meet you, Grandmother Celeste."

Did her spirit still roam Canderlay Manor?

Take hold of your sanity, Morgan. This is a portrait. Not a ghost.

Where had it been discovered? Were there others?

"Samuels?"

Silence met his request.

He entered the corridor. "Samuels?"

Again, no response.

Morgan halted at the entrance to the formal drawing room and glanced inside. No Samuels. He turned, crossed the corridor, and inspected the study.

Empty as well.

"Where the devil is he?" Morgan raised his voice. "Samuels, are you in the library?"

No reply.

He headed down the corridor. "Samuels, am I to chase you about the manor the entire afternoon?"

Rounding the entrance to the library, he ground to a halt. Unfiltered sunlight burst in through the unadorned windows and into a tidy but empty room. Had he not seen the old servant head down this corridor a few seconds earlier?

Well, no. Actually he hadn't.

He'd merely glimpsed coattails.

Had Samuels returned to the foyer and walked past Morgan as he stood admiring his grandmother's portrait?

It was possible, but he likely would've offered a comment.

Morgan returned to the foyer. "Mister Samuels, show yourself this instant, as I have need of your services."

"You called, sir?"

Morgan glanced up to the second floor landing. "How the devil did you get up there?"

"By way of the stairs, sir."

"That's not what I bloody meant."

"Pardon?"

"How did you...did I not see...were you not just in the..."

The old man raised a brow. A common occurrence.

Morgan couldn't seem to put two sentences together that made any sense so he decided to drop the matter and change the subject. "You brought the portrait downstairs, I assume?"

"The one of your grandmother? Yes, sir." Samuels began a slow descent. "It saddened me to leave her ladyship in the attic with all that dust."

"Are there other portraits?"

"None, sir."

"A pity. Perhaps I'll hang Grandmother Celeste above the mantle in the drawing room."

"If I might make a suggestion, Mister Spence...I believe it once hung in the library, where her ladyship spent most of her free time."

"Oh? Well then...after I've had the portrait cleaned, I shall return it to its rightful place of honor." Morgan studied the old man. "How did you know she was my grandmother?"

"I recognized your surname that first day, sir, but it was your face what made me think we'd met before. It once belonged to another. Your father." The caretaker's hand slid along the balustrade as he descended one step at a time. "Except for the eyes, you're the very image of him."

"So my mother says."

"Does he live, sir?"

"Yes, and rather well. Wed a highlander's daughter. I have three younger brothers and a sister...formally known as the Duchess of Chase."

"I see. Your father is blessed then. Perhaps one day he will pay us a visit."

"Perhaps. That reminds me, Samuels. Are you aware of any hidden passageways inside this manor?"

Reaching the foyer, the servant halted. "Passageways?" He thought for a moment before clearing his throat. "Not that I can speak of, sir."

"And you've encountered no problems here? No...ghosts?"

"Ghosts, sir?"

"What I mean is...do you not feel at times as though someone is watching you?"

"Occasionally, but I try not to dwell upon it. Any uneasiness is rare and likely stems from being surrounded by far too much emptiness."

"A reasonable assumption. Never mind then. Forget I mentioned it."

"I've prepared a meat and potato stew with fresh baked bread for lunch, sir. And for dessert, there's cinnamon apples warming in a pot.

"You've been busy this morning."

"I enjoy keeping busy. Makes an old man feel useful."

"You certainly are that. Useful, I mean. Since I've yet to obtain domestic help, you've become cook, housekeeper, and scullery maid. Not to mention overseer, caretaker, and stable boy. Oh, that reminds me. Is Ares giving you any trouble?"

"Not at all, sir. He recognizes my voice now, and I bring him treats. He's quite fond of apples."

"Yes, he is. Am I paying you enough, Samuels?"

"I daresay you've been most generous, Mister Spence. I do not mind the extra work with Ares. Keeps my hands busy. Now then, if you'll go into the dining room, I'll bring your lunch out from the kitchen."

"Splendid. Oh, one more thing." Morgan held up the undergarment. "I found this in the washhouse spread upon a table. Do you know any reason why it would be there?"

Color flooded the servant's normally chalk white face, but his voice showed no trace of discomfort. "One might assume it was placed there to dry, sir."

"Any idea to whom it belongs?"

"I would imagine to a lady."

"*Lady?*" Frustration crept up the back of Morgan's neck. Was the old man being purposely obtuse or had his mind slowed to match his steps? "By the pitiful condition, I highly doubt this belongs to a gently bred woman." He held the undergarment out until Samuels took it. "See to it that this indecent thing is tossed into the fire."

* * *

Mortified with embarrassment and afraid her rising emotions would snap like a dry twig, Belle hurried from the library and back up the steps to the secret room. "Mister Spence *highly doubts*, does he?"

Her face burned with humiliation as she paced back and forth.

"Not gently bred, am I?"

The more she thought about his words and the arrogant tone of his voice, the more her temper flared.

"What does a pompous, crude and insensitive dandy know?" She removed the cloak and threw it angrily against the wall. "What does he know of poverty? Of waking each day, wondering if you'll be granted one more night or if you'll be murdered in your sleep?" Tears temporarily closed her throat. "What does this poor excuse for a gentleman know of nightmares? Of disappointment and loss? He's likely been pampered his entire life."

And to think I was just beginning to admire this insufferable man.

But in his defense, Morgan Spence had no idea of her dire situation. Was unaware the owner of the shabby undergarment was standing in the library, listening to his conversation with Samuels.

Defeated and suddenly drained, she sat on the edge of the cot. Her life, like the pitiful state of her pantalettes, was indeed appalling. Both might well be beyond repair. She would eventually purchase new undergarments, but building a new life would require much more effort.

Why had she been threatened? Chased? She was a vicar's daughter. No one of importance.

Her thoughts traveled back to the night of the fire. The night she'd barely escaped from the scarred man, Amos Barlow.

The housekeeper and cook had been given the night off, and she'd been alone in the cottage, reading in bed when she heard a noise downstairs. When she opened the door to investigate, he'd been standing at the top of the stairs, his shadow menacing as he rushed toward her. She had quickly closed and bolted the door before climbing out the window. Escaping to the darkness of the forest, she'd easily lost her way, so frightened she couldn't think. Shadows sprang up all around her, evil and ominous. She hadn't known which way to turn or what to do, except to pray. And she had kept praying all night...kept running. Once he'd almost caught up to her, but she'd hidden inside a hollow log.

"His lordship will be none too pleased," he'd muttered to himself as he passed her hiding place.

Who was his lordship and why does he wish to harm me?

By dawn the next morning, exhausted and parched with thirst, she'd stumbled onto the main road leading to Maidstone...and straight into the path of a horse and cart. Fortunately Jasper Samuels had been the driver. She learned from him that her cottage had been burned to the ground the night before.

I should've asked him to take me directly to the constable.

But she hadn't. Mostly because of her father's strong distrust of the authorities in Kent.

A tap sounded upon the oak paneling. "Miss Isabelle?"

Her cheeks warmed.

Lord, but she couldn't face Samuels now.

"I've placed your..." He cleared his throat. "Your belongings are on the chair, miss. I'll bring a washbasin of hot water to the library later on and set it beside the fireplace so you can wash up."

Belle swallowed her pride and rose. Halfheartedly she walked over, unhooked the latch, and opened the panel. But Samuels had already disappeared, likely far more embarrassed than she. Snatching the offending pantalettes off the chair, she closed the panel and secured the latch.

I am not a vengeful person but...

Morgan Spence had become a nuisance.

And he'll be more so after Canderlay Manor is restored.

"I wonder...how does one go about getting rid of a nuisance?"

Impossible. This one owns the manor.

Belle sighed.

Apparently sharing his home with a 'spirit' no longer bothered him.

Guilt prompted a grimace, and she tossed her threadbare pantalettes onto the foot of the cot. Perhaps the man's commonsense had been lost in the fall from the third floor. Nevertheless, he treated Samuels well, and she suspected the loyal and faithful servant had already grown fond of his new employer.

Her opinion of Mister Spence seemed to change daily. No. Hourly. She couldn't deny she shamefully enjoyed spying on him. Perhaps because he reminded her of Uncle Magnus. Tall and handsome. A confident, beguiling smile. Honorable. All fine qualities but...

He stole my drawers, for heaven's sake!

And had the audacity to mock her impoverished circumstances in front of Samuels. Should she allow such crude behavior without retaliation?

Unfair. The gentleman has no clue as to who you are and therefore he cannot possibly understand the severity of your circumstances.

True, but rational thoughts no longer prevailed.

War had been declared.

Morgan Spence just didn't know it yet.

Chapter Five

After dinner and polite conversation, Morgan followed his sister and the duke into Chase Manor's private parlor. Reaching inside an inner pocket of his coat, he withdrew the book he'd found and handed it to Margaret.

"What's this?" she inquired.

"Instructions on how to produce all manner of flowering plants. I found it in Canderlay's library and immediately thought of you."

"Thank you, Morgan. How very thoughtful." She briefly flipped through the pages. "Oh...it has instructions on how to build a solarium. Bartholomew, this is exactly what I've been telling you about. Come and see."

"We'll discuss the matter later, my love." He strode to the liquor cabinet and filled two glasses with brandy. Before he turned to offer one to Morgan, Margaret had pulled her husband aside to whisper in his ear. With a slight smile, the duke nodded once in response to whatever question she'd asked. Afterward, Margaret's voice grew even more hushed. In fact, she became almost giddy with excitement.

Giddy...like on the rare occasion when she drank too much champagne.

"Am I to decipher this particular conversation?" Morgan inquired. "Or would the duke and duchess prefer me to leave the room?"

Margaret's gaze shifted from her husband, and her expression turned demure. "Why, whatever do you mean, dearest brother?"

"I mean, darling sister..." He chose an overstuffed chair next to the sofa and sat down. "There is a disturbing glimmer of mischief in your eye this evening, and it concerns me."

"Oh? Which eye?"

He frowned. "Mags, what are you up to?"

Her expression became defensive. "I haven't the faintest idea what you're talking about."

"And if you did, which I wager you do, why on earth would I assume you would admit it?"

Flashing a playful smile, Margaret set the book aside. "Ah, it's a wager you wish to make, is it?"

"You'd better flee, Morgan. While you're still in possession of the shirt upon your back."

"What? Run away like a cowardly rat? Never. While I admit to a certain fondness for the gentler sex, I've never been blinded by a lady's charm or beauty. At least not to the extent that I'd wager a diamond mine and then promptly lose that wager. Let's see now...what was the name of that foolish Englishman?"

Bartholomew's expression soured. "You know perfectly well I allowed Margaret the victory in that particular circumstance."

"Allowed?" she echoed. "Husband, you did no such thing."

"Admit it, Bart. You married a clever cheat."

"I am not a cheat, Morgan."

"Apologies, Margaret. Are you not still the owner of said diamond mine?"

"Yes, but I never cheated, and—"

"No excuses," Morgan touted. "The charges have been brought forth and upheld." He turned his humor upon his brother-in-law. "What devilish scheme has she drawn you into this time?"

The duke handed him a glass of brandy. "I've no idea what you mean."

"No, of course not. But perhaps I should speak to my nephew. As you both are well aware, the child listens at keyholes."

"Jonathan is away," Margaret announced before sitting on the sofa. "He's enjoying a bit of a holiday with Bartholomew's mother."

"Is he now? How convenient."

Her eyes misted.

The desire to tease his beloved sister suddenly vanished. Margaret adored children, but shortly after the difficult birth of her son, doctors informed her she would never again conceive. The news had been devastating.

Life was often cruel.

But Margaret Katherine Spence Drake, the Duchess of Chase, was a strong woman. After the initial shock and sadness, she had made it a point to make peace with the Good Father.

"After Father's death," Bartholomew said, "my mother decided to shed her mourning clothes and spend her remaining years on permanent holiday."

"I daresay that devil Napoleon has put a snag in milady's recent plans."

"Indeed. Now Mother spends half the year in London, attending balls or visiting with friends, and the remainder with relatives. She begged Margaret to allow our son to travel with her to Dover for an extended stay with a distant cousin."

"Jonathan's nose is constantly stuck inside one book or another. This will be a nice change for the lad. When do they return?"

"The end of October," Margaret replied.

"Samuels and I should have Canderlay Manor in fair condition by that time. I'll ask Jonathan over for a visit. I rather think he'd enjoy exploring his favorite uncle's manor house." He finished his brandy. "That is, if he can avoid running into the resident ghost."

Margaret's expression perked up. "Ghost?"

Morgan eyed the duke. "You didn't tell her?"

"No."

"Well why the devil not?"

"Because she would've insisted on investigating the matter on her own."

"I see. How did you explain the bruise to my temple?"

"An accident involving Ares."

"And she believed you?"

"Obviously."

"Bartholomew," Margaret chided. "Kindly explain yourself. You well know I despise secrets."

"You're one to talk, Mags."

"Oh, hush, Morgan. This does not concern you."

"Actually—"

"Bartholomew, I demand an accounting from you. What have I not been told regarding my brother's accident? The truth, if you please."

Amused, Morgan's attention centered upon the duke.

Surrounded by his wife's indignation, and with no verbal assistance from his childhood friend, Bartholomew relented with a sigh. "Very well, my love, you shall have it. But I warn you. It will not be pleasant." Another sigh, deeper this time. "You see, Margaret...your brother, whose sanity I have long questioned, encountered an intruder roaming about Canderlay Manor one night and mistakenly thought—"

"An intruder? Heavens! Who was the man? Was he violent? Morgan, you must've been terribly alarmed."

"To the point of swooning," the duke remarked with a snide chuckle.

"I did not swoon, Bart. You gravely offend me."

"My mistake, old friend."

Margaret, clearly annoyed by their teasing barbs, alternated her glare between them. "Will one of you please explain?"

"I was about to, madam, when you interrupted," her husband replied. "You see, Morgan believes his accident can be blamed on the ghostly apparition of a deceased ancestor."

"I never claimed it was an ancestor."

"In his haste to get away from the apparition, he backed over the third floor balustrade and ended up on the landing one floor below. That's where I found him the next morning."

Her eyes widened. "By the Good Father, Morgan, please tell me you were not soused?"

"No, but I fervently wish I had been."

"What caused you to believe you'd encountered a ghost?"

"Perhaps, Margaret, because whatever this was shouldn't have been in the manor at all. Perhaps because it hid behind a dark cape and spoke not a word. Or perhaps because it walked strangely, as though on a deformed leg."

"How odd."

"You've no idea."

"Am I to understand you didn't see it clearly?"

"How could I? A fierce storm had overtaken the manor, and I'd turned down the lantern's wick."

"Whatever for?"

"Because..." Morgan sucked in a breath, waiting for a small amount of patience he suspected would never come. "I assumed complete darkness would better aid me in capturing an elusive and clever intruder."

"Oh, but...how does one go about capturing a ghost?"

"I hadn't considered it a ghost at that point. I believed it to be a man."

"And you believe different now?"

"Don't answer that, Morgan. Margaret, not another word. I forbid any further discussion of this nonsense."

Sharp annoyance flashed in her eyes.

"Or am I to assume, sweet wife, that you believe in spirits as well?"

"If you had spent half a lifetime at Dragon's Breath, you wouldn't dare ask such a question. Would he, Morgan?"

"Indeed, little sister."

Frustrated, the duke turned his back.

Margaret smiled at Morgan. "So..." Her eyes sparkled like fine jewels. "Has it appeared again?"

"Who?"

She glared at him.

"Oh, you mean the..." He shook his head. "I never came upon it again, but the next day..." No, he wouldn't admit to his sister that he'd witnessed someone standing at his bedroom window. "Well, like Bart, I've come to believe my impression as well as my vision was at fault that night."

"The man has an ounce of commonsense after all," Bartholomew declared before turning a stern gaze upon his wife. "As I said before, Margaret. What your brother encountered was an intruder, not an apparition or ghostly ancestor. Do not allow your head to be filled with such ridiculous notions."

Her eyes narrowed dangerously at the stinging rebuff. "Please forgive my addlebrained and strictly female logic, your Grace."

His tone softened. "My words were not meant to offend, my love. I merely thought to instruct you."

"Of course, dearest," she said in a restrained yet formal tone, aware no doubt that the servants were somewhere within earshot. "I daresay I must require instruction often. However did I get on without your wise tutelage?"

"Now, children, let's be civil to one another," Morgan implored, jumping in before Bartholomew's pride perished in the frigid shadow of his wife's cold demeanor. "Margaret, you and Father spoke often about his life at Canderlay Manor. Did he ever mention secret passageways?"

"Not that I recall. Why do you ask?"

"Curiosity, I suppose." The clock in the foyer chimed eight times, prompting Morgan to withdraw his pocket watch. The hands beneath the dial pointed precisely to eight o'clock. "Would you look at that?" He glanced up. "Grandfather Ethan's watch has decided to keep proper time again."

"If you require the services of a master clockmaker," the duke offered, "there's a reputable man in London who set up shop on Front Street."

"Can he repair my memory as well?" Morgan asked. "Stop me from misplacing a key? Keep my candle lit when I leave the room?"

"Morgan..." Margaret's expression showed deep concern. "Perhaps you're still suffering the effects of that nasty fall. Shall I send for the doctor?"

"I'm perfectly fine. Well, not perfect but..." He sighed. "The past few days I seem to have been plagued by forgetfulness. And the smell of roses. It pops up at the oddest times."

"Perhaps you're overly fatigued," Margaret remarked.

"Perhaps," Morgan agreed. "The watch is usually most reliable, but lately it's run either an hour slow or an hour fast. Next time I'm in London, I'll visit the clockmaker." He replaced the delicately crafted heirloom inside his watch pocket and stood. "Margaret, thank you for a lovely dinner. Enjoy the book."

She arose. "You're not going?"

"I'm afraid so. It'll be ten o'clock before Ares and I reach Canderlay, and I wouldn't wish to worry Samuels."

"I doubt he'll think anything's amiss. Stay the night," she pleaded. "We'll take the carriage to Canderlay come morning."

"*We?*" he echoed.

"Did I speak a foreign language, dear? You've extended an invitation to my husband on numerous occasions. Am I to be forever excluded?"

"Of course not, Mags, it's just that...well, there's little for you to see at Canderlay. No drapes, rugs, or furniture. I can offer you tea and refreshments, but there's no sofa to sit upon."

"You discovered a dining table and chairs in the attic, did you not?"

"Yes, but they're poorly matched...nothing to boast about and certainly not what you're used to."

She walked over and offered a warm smile. "I'll not look down my nose."

"I'm not concerned about your delicate nose, but why not postpone your visit until I've purchased a few pieces of quality furnishings? Or at the very least, a decent sofa."

"Oh, but Morgan—"

"Bart, please explain to my sister how uncomfortable she will likely be."

"Little good it would do. She's as stubborn as her mother."

"That stubbornness has served me well, husband. Especially in the presence of arrogant gentlemen."

"If you're referring to me, dear wife, arrogance has never been my calling card."

"It's every gentleman's calling card at some point. Now then, Morgan, about your travel plans—"

He held up his hand to cut her off. "Very well, Margaret. I give in. Like a spoiled child you've gotten your way again. I'll stay here tonight, and tomorrow you shall receive the full and rather uninspiring tour of Canderlay Manor." He kissed her brow then leaned close and whispered, "And if you see something you can't quite explain, you cannot claim I didn't warn you."

＊ ＊ ＊

Midmorning the next day, Belle stood hidden behind the closed door of the master suite's antechamber, listening to the comical scene playing out in the corridor.

"Frederick Jenkins," Samuels declared in a gruff manner. "If the master owned a bottle of port, I'd swear you've been swigging it."

"I'm not soused," the worker insisted. "But I'll repeat myself in case you didn't understand. Never again, sir...never will I set one foot, nor any part of my person, inside that room. Not if the entire house caught fire and through there lay my only path of escape."

Belle clamped her hand over her mouth to keep from laughing aloud.

"And what explanation, pray tell, should I offer my employer as to why you did not finish papering the wall in his antechamber?"

"The truth, sir."

"By the truth you mean..?"

"I heard someone sneeze and that someone was a woman. A *woman*," Jenkins stressed again. "There be no women here, but I heard that dainty sneeze as clear as a church bell. As though she was standing right behind me. When I turned...bless the saints, I was alone. I got a chill down my spine this very moment just thinkin' about it."

"And so you've concluded it must've been a female ghost peering over your shoulder?"

"I heard the rumors same as the others. This house is plagued with angry spirits. And one in particular wants ole George's head. The last Marquis of Canderlay, that's who. You know the story, Samuels."

"Yes, indeed, but there are errors in your reasoning."

"What errors?"

"The last Lord Canderlay was not female nor is he deceased. But if he were a ghost, I'm certain he would be pleased to learn his eldest son had purchased his lordship's former estate."

"Son? You mean...Morgan Spence is..."

"I do."

"By devil then, it's his lordship's sweet mother who haunts this place."

"Rubbish. There are no spirits tormenting this house."

"Couldn't be nothin' else."

"No? Your imagination perhaps?" The caretaker did not wait for a reply. "For shame, Jenkins. You've allowed foolish rumor to frighten you off a perfectly good job. If you leave now, this incident will likely follow you and sully your good reputation. And I can assure you...you'll not be paid for a room half-finished."

"Keep your coin, Samuels. It weren't merely the sound of a sneeze that alarmed me. My shears are missing. I cannot work without my cutters."

"Nothing strange about that. You likely misplaced them."

"No, sir. I left 'em on the floor in that...that..."

"Antechamber?"

"Yes, sir. I went downstairs to relieve myself and was gone no more than five minutes. When I returned, they were nowhere to be found. And that's not all. I smelled roses."

"Roses? I see." A slight pause. "Wait downstairs, if you please."

Footsteps headed down the corridor. After a prolonged silence, the door opened, and Samuels entered the room. He closed the door and without muttering a word, turned and stared at Belle. His bushy brows rose as though he didn't quite know what to do with her.

She offered a timid smile.

By his disapproving expression, he obviously did not share her amusement. Holding steadfast to silence, he held out his hand expectantly.

Feeling like a child who'd just been caught stealing a tasty treat, she turned and marched across the antechamber, through the bedroom, and popped open the paneling. After retrieving the shears, she returned a few seconds later and handed them over. The thought crossed her mind to explain her actions, that she'd only wished to keep Jenkins from covering the peephole, but she feared Samuels' sour disposition had not lightened, and thus she doubted he'd listen to an explanation.

Valid or otherwise.

As the door closed behind him, Belle trudged back into the bedroom. Had she lost her only friend? She walked over to the window. Most of the outside work had shifted from the exterior of the manor to the stables and carriage house, and she could stand close to the window now without fear of being seen.

As the early morning sun rose above the distant trees, she longed to spend a few hours walking about the grounds. She settled for raising the window instead. Unhampered by the burden of heavy curtains, a gentle breeze floated into the room and caressed her skin. She closed her eyes, basking in the warmth.

Was it so long ago that Uncle Magnus had stood at this very window and waved goodbye as she and her father had driven off?

Ten years come October.

Ten long years and two months since he and his entire crew had been lost during a violent storm at sea.

Magnus had been called away unexpectedly, as he often was, but he had never failed to leave a note for her to find. Until that last time.

As a child of eleven, she'd prayed to God for his survival, hoping he had washed ashore on some tropical island and was simply waiting to be rescued. Her father did everything he could to discourage this line of thinking. Still...she'd held out hope. And she'd prayed. Until the post delivered a letter from Barrington and Huff declaring her beloved uncle deceased. The letter stated he'd left a great deal of his fortune to various charities, setting aside the prearranged portion for Belle when she turned twenty.

Point five percent of ML Shipping.

She had no idea how much that amounted to.

Although Reverend Lindley loved his younger brother, he cared little for Magnus' wealth or extravagant lifestyle. He feared the promise of riches would corrupt Belle, but her uncle had argued that wealth would ensure Belle married well. His argument fell upon deaf ears. Finally Magnus had reluctantly given in and accepted the vicar's proposal of half of one percent.

The day she'd finally accepted the truth, that her uncle would never return, was the coldest day she could ever remember, with a wintery mix of snow and sleet covering the frozen ground. She would never again speak with Magnus. Never again hear his voice.

There was no body to bury. No grave to visit.

Only memories of a kind and generous man remained. A man whose eyes crinkled at the corners when he laughed.

The door to the antechamber creaked.

Expecting Samuels and a well-deserved reprimand, Belle turned and waited patiently for her just punishment.

Footsteps thudded upon the wooden floor before pausing.

Heavy footsteps.

This wasn't Jasper Samuels!

Instant panic numbed her reasoning, and she fought to clear her head.

Had the master of the manor returned?

She glanced across the room. Thank God she'd closed the secret panel but with the bedroom door standing open, she couldn't make it to safety without being spotted.

As footsteps neared the bedroom, Belle quickly ducked beside the bed then rolled beneath it, making sure to drag the hem of her frock with her.

A man casually strolled into the room and walked over to the window, his brown boots dirty and scuffed at the heels.

No, not Morgan Spence.

He kept his black boots spotless.

"You weren't useless after all, Jenkins."

With the sound of Amos Barlow's crude voice came the crushing sensation from her nightmares. The sensation of being hunted...of being trapped. But this was no dream. It was terrifyingly real.

"Them's roses sure enough. Smelled 'em once before. On a fair auburn-haired wench." His laugh sounded like a cruel sneer. "Now if I was a young woman with a need to disappear..." He turned from the window, the toes of his boots pointed toward the bed. Scuffed, like the heels. "This old house might be the proper place to hide, seeing as the church caretaker is newly employed by the owner."

Barely breathing, Belle held her hand over her mouth and prayed she wouldn't be discovered.

"Does Morgan Spence know who's been visitin' his room? Or maybe the handsome gent invited sweet and innocent little miss into his bed."

A long pause.

"You payin' for his silence? He protectin' you?

She thought to cover her ears to the insults but dared not move.

"You've made an enemy, girl, but I'd wager you already know that."

With whom? Tell me!

"Don't know what you did or why he wants you dead. Can't say that it bothers me. I'll not strangle the life out of you right away though. You and me will get to know one another first."

Bile rose in Belle's throat, and she almost gagged.

"And if you think to ask for help from someone like Morgan Spence or that Samuels fellow..." He walked forward and stopped beside the bed. "Then you'll force me to take care of those two as well."

Chapter Six

Footsteps approached from the antechamber, and Belle carefully turned her head to face the door. The blunt tips of Samuels' polished boots walked into the bedroom.

"What are you doing in here, Barlow?"

"I'm no thief, Samuels, if that's your meanin'."

"Regardless of my opinion, you've no business being in the master suite."

"Thought I'd see for myself if Jenkins spoke the truth."

"If you're referring to what he believed he heard, then you've clearly wasted your time and therefore Mister Spence's coin. Jenkins heard nothing. As it turns out, his commonsense was overcome by superstition."

"Said he smelled roses. I smell 'em as well."

Samuels turned and marched straight to the night table. "This is Mister Spence's bath soaps. Would you care to inspect them? I believe you'll find they're rose-scented."

"I worked alongside Morgan Spence for the last three days cleanin' out the attic. Sweated with the man. He never once smelled like roses. That's a woman's delicate scent."

"Not that it's any of your business, but I suspect my employer's sister sent him these soaps only recently."

"I follow your reasonin', old man, but that don't mean it's the truth."

"It bothers me not at all what you chose to believe or disbelieve." Samuels walked to the door. "My only concern is your presence in the master suite without an invitation, so I'll ask you to leave. Now, if you please."

As the strained seconds ticked by without Amos Barlow's cooperation, Belle grew concerned for the caretaker's safety. If Barlow dared lay so much as one finger upon Jasper Samuels...

"All right, Mister High and Mighty Overseer. I meant no harm." Barlow edged around the bed and headed across the room. At the door, he paused. "Just thought I'd catch a glimpse of what spooked Jenkins."

"And now you know. The man was overcome by his imagination."

"Yes, indeed." Barlow's laugh, low and menacing, mocked his civil tone. "Now...I...know."

Belle waited until the two men exited the bedroom and the door closed behind them before emerging from her hiding place.

Dear God! He knows!

She paced back and forth beside the bed, the heaviness of complete despair burrowing inside her chest.

He recognized my scent! Knows I've been hiding here!

Belle had no idea how long she paced about the room in an agitated state of panic, but the sound of the door creaking open again brought her back to the present. Heart pounding, she whirled around, ready to do battle this time.

At the sight of Samuels, she nearly collapsed to the floor. "He knows I'm here," she whispered. "I should've been more careful. You're constantly warning me of the dangers, but I didn't listen because I foolishly and stubbornly believed in my own cleverness. And now..." Shaking, she sat on the edge of the bed. "You and Morgan Spence are in danger as well."

"Do not concern yourself with me. And it matters not what Barlow suspects. As long as you stay hidden inside that secret room, he'll never find you."

"Mister Samuels...I cannot stay hidden forever. What if he burns the manor to the ground as he did my cottage?"

"Calm yourself, Miss Isabelle. Mister Spence would never allow that."

She glanced at the bedroom door.

"We're free to speak. I've locked the outer door to the antechamber."

Belle sighed. "I fear we've underestimated Amos Barlow and his obsessive determination to end my life. How will I travel to Dublin when this wicked man is constantly watching and waiting for me? And what about you, Mister Samuels? What if he tries to harm you?"

"I wouldn't worry about that." He sighed heavily. "What were you thinking, miss, playing tricks upon poor Jenkins?"

"I didn't mean to sneeze. It's dusty in that small room."

"I'm referring to the fact that you stole his shears, did you not?"

"Well, yes, but he was about to cover the antechamber's peephole."

"As well he should. It isn't proper for a lady to spy upon a gentleman in all manner of undress."

Intense warmth permeated her cheeks. "I never spy upon Mister Spence unless he is dressed. How can you even think such a thing? I use that particular peephole to make sure he's departed his suite before I exit my prison."

"Do you not understand, Miss Isabelle? You can no longer walk about the manor freely. It's simply too dangerous."

"I agree but...I've grown weary of hiding and so very tired of being isolated that I cannot stomach the sight of my dungeon a moment longer. If not for emptying my chamber pot in the darkest hours of night, I'd get no reprieve at all."

"You've a month before you depart for Dublin. I beg you, miss. Please endure the discomfort a short while longer."

Pain swelled in her throat. "Very well, Mister Samuels. I shall resume playing the role of the good vicar's daughter and do what I'm told." Her bottom lip quivered as tears filled her eyes. "As I've always done."

"I'm greatly relieved, Miss Isabelle. Soon you'll be free again. Free to do whatever you like. Go wherever you please."

"Will I?"

"Why would you not?"

"Have you forgotten Amos Barlow? Will he follow me? Will his puppet master ever cease this maddening pursuit? Assuming my inheritance has nothing to do with the man's murderous intentions..." Belle sighed. "When will this horrid nightmare end? Dear lord, the constant fear has dulled my spirit." She stood, and a quiet determination settled over her. "Mister Samuels, do you own a pistol?"

"Yes. Why do you ask?"

"Because I wish to change the rules of Mister Barlow's game."

He frowned. "This is not what we discussed."

"I realize that, and I'm sorry to disappoint you. Again. Now please...go retrieve the pistol and then ask Mister Barlow to—"

"Retrieve the pistol? For what purpose?"

"Is it not clear? I cannot believe I didn't think of it before. But of course, I was too preoccupied with portraying the helpless vicar's daughter. So deep into the pitiful role that I couldn't see the ruthless predator could easily become the helpless prey."

"Miss Isabelle—"

"No need for alarm, Mister Samuels. I'm not insane. Yet." She clasped his hands. "I've a plan. We'll tie Amos Barlow to a chair and force him to tell us who hired him to torment me."

"If by we you mean you and I...it's a worthy idea, miss, but not a prudent one. We, as in you and I, are not burly men nor are we the bullying sort."

"True, but your pistol might convince Barlow otherwise. And by holding him hostage with the threat of ending his miserable life, he could be inspired to reveal the name of the person who wishes me dead."

"I doubt we could force that vile man to reveal anything he doesn't wish to. Barlow is shrewd. He would, I suspect, see right through our pretense and refuse to divulge anything of importance. And then...what would we do with the man? We couldn't allow him to leave. If Mister Spence stumbled upon our hostage, how would we explain our actions?"

"I hadn't thought of that." With a sigh of pure dejection, she walked over to the fireplace. "Once again we must suffer Morgan Spence's interference." Before entering her dreary prison she turned. "Mister Samuels, how did my rose-scented soaps get inside a drawer of his night table?"

"After speaking with Jenkins, I placed several pieces in my pocket and was on my way up to hide them in this room so that if anyone else believed they smelled roses, including Mister Spence, there would be a perfectly logical explanation. I had no idea Barlow had come up to investigate while I was gone."

"Rather clever of you." Belle smiled at the old man. "I'm sorry. From now on I promise to be more cooperative." She opened the panel wide. "And I'll do my best to be more disciplined."

"Then you..." He cleared his throat. "You're no longer considering holding my pistol to Barlow's head?"

"Since I have very little knowledge of weaponry, I suppose that horrible man is safe. For now."

The sound of a conveyance traveling down the road leading to the manor distracted Belle's attention. Curious, she wandered toward the window.

With a scowl that would've made her father proud, Samuels blocked her path and turned her again in the direction of the secret room.

"I merely wished to learn the identity of our visitor," she defended over her shoulder.

"It's likely the farmer's son delivering eggs and milk," he declared before heading to the window.

Belle remained silent until she could no longer stand the suspense. "Well?"

"I was mistaken." After another lengthy pause, Samuels turned from the window. "There appears to be a rather large caravan headed for the manor."

* * *

Mindless of the Chase carriage trailing close behind, Morgan reined in Ares. "What the devil?"

Along the winding road leading down to his estate, he counted at least thirty carts, drays, or covered wagons lined up in succession all waiting to reach the front entrance of Canderlay Manor.

"Margaret, love, did I not say we should've started out an hour earlier?"

"Yes, dear husband, you did, and I accept the blame entirely, but now is not the time to scold. How can I direct the deliverymen as to what goes where if I cannot force my way to the beginning of this procession?"

As their discussion slowly invaded Morgan's awareness, he turned in the saddle and discovered the duke and duchess had exited their carriage. "Margaret, what have you done?"

"Not now, Morgan." She hitched up her skirts and marched over to him. "I am in dire need of transportation, and since yours is the only horse not attached to some sort of conveyance, I'm respectfully commandeering him."

"Ares is not a ship, Mags, and if you haven't noticed...I'm not sitting in a fancy sidesaddle nor are you dressed for riding astride."

"I'm fully aware of the way I'm dressed." One hand on her hip and the other holding her skirts, she tossed him a look of pure defiance. A look that warned she would permit no argument.

He recognized the unwavering stance and her determined expression. Both belonged to their mother. With a sigh, he dismounted and handed his sister the reins. "Try not to embarrass your husband."

"His Grace will recover, no doubt." She stroked the Arabian's nose and leaned close. "Hello, Ares, my love. Have you missed me?"

Morgan lifted his sister into the saddle in a dignified side position. After she rode off, he turned to question his friend.

Bartholomew, however, was busy giving instructions to his driver. "Take the carriage home, Oxley. Return to Canderlay by three o'clock this afternoon."

"Very well, your Grace."

"Morgan, do you intend to stand there like a simpleton? Help me get these horses backed up far enough to allow this contraption room to turn around."

Within minutes, the Chase carriage headed back the way it came, and Morgan and the duke set out on foot for the manor. As they passed each conveyance, he noted the painted words on the side.

Porterhouse...Suppliers of Fine Persian Rugs.
Caruthers and Son. Premium Glassmakers of London since 1757.
Mrs. Simmons Fabric Shop.
Wickham Bookstore.
Hammerstein Quality China.
Montpelier Cabinet Makers.
Sanderson Linens.
J. Talbot...the finest kitchens in all England.
Beckman Brothers Furniture Makers.

And several more. These were not ordinary merchants but superior ones.

Beckman Brothers had ten covered wagons waiting in line. One third of the long procession. As he walked, it eventually dawned on Morgan why his sister had been so insistent last evening about visiting Canderlay. "That little minx." He eyed his friend. "How much?"

"What?"

"Do not play the part of ignorant buffoon, Bart. It does you and your title a severe injustice." Suddenly distracted by a huge six-wheeled wagon promoting *Hillcrest Porcelain Sinks and Bathtubs*, Morgan raised his eyes to heaven. "Oh, Good Father, thank you!"

"What are you babbling about?"

"Never mind." Reluctantly his attention returned to the duke. "How much did this cost you? And I prefer the truth, if you please."

"Not one shilling."

"That's difficult to believe for I highly suspect this project was paid for with coin from your coffers."

"You're mistaken. Margaret spent her own monies."

Morgan halted.

The duke did not.

"Margaret sold the diamond mine?"

"That worthless piece of property? I doubt she could give it away."

"What about her inheritance?" Morgan hurried to catch up. "Is that what my sister did? Used those monies to pay for all this?"

"Yes."

"From Grandfather Ethan or Great Uncle Charles?"

"Both."

Again Morgan halted. "Both?"

Bartholomew stopped and faced him. "Yes."

"But that's...good God, well over twenty thousand pounds."

"Twenty thousand three hundred four to be exact."

"Why would she do this? That money was to be Jonathan's."

"You think I cannot afford to see to the welfare of my own son?"

"I implied nothing of the sort, Bart. I'm simply trying to understand the reason your wife, my sister, lied to me."

"She didn't lie. I was present when you and she discussed the particulars of her inheritance several years ago. Margaret clearly stated at that time that the monies would be held in trust for someone she loved dearly. She was referring to you."

"She couldn't have known at that time that I intended to purchase Canderlay Manor."

"Morgan, your sister is far from daft. In fact she's quite perceptive. This estate is all you've ever talked about with genuine enthusiasm. Do you think she planned this and then put it all together in a matter of a few short weeks? No. She set this in motion over two years ago. Broke into the manor house, on her own and without my approval, to jot down the dimensions of every room and what each would need to become respectable."

"*Margaret* broke that window around back?"

"What? Well, no. Her driver did the deed. My point is...she placed the order for the furnishings, drapes, and rugs two years ago. Even the china pattern. She put a great deal of thought into this and—"

"Except for the fact that she failed to get my permission or my opinion on the matter."

"Precisely the reason I advised her against such a venture. Right or wrong, she planned all this because she adores you."

Morgan glanced down the road where his sister and Samuels were busy rerouting several of the carts to the back of the manor. "I'll repay the monies. I swear, Bart...I'll repay every shilling if it takes fifty years."

"You've sworn that promise to the wrong person. Speak to Margaret of your intentions."

"You can bloody well count on it."

"My only request...keep in mind your sister's tender heart and sensitive feelings."

"I'd like to put a strap to her tender feelings. Is that sensitive enough?"

They proceeded on and nearing the front of the line Morgan noticed a cart with the name *Conrad Graf* painted on the side. "A fortepiano?" He eyed the duke. "Has your generous wife forgotten I've a deaf ear when it comes to music?"

"Hardly, but at some point you'll be required to entertain."

"Believe me, if I played the fortepiano, it would not be entertaining."

"I suspect that particular gift is intended for the future Mrs. Spence."

"How clever. Indeed, I hadn't thought of that. Say, Bart, you don't suppose Margaret purchased one of those for me, do you?"

"A wife?" The duke laughed. "I daresay if she thought for one moment she could get away with it, it would've already been arranged."

"Well then," Morgan remarked with a bit of sarcasm, the shock of what his sister had done beginning to wear off. "That's one addition I can look forward to selecting on my own."

* * *

Canderlay Manor was returning from the dead!

Belle could hear it. And even though the transformation had kept her imprisoned inside the secret room for the better part of the day, she couldn't be more pleased. But poor Samuels! Fearing her curious nature and overwhelming excitement, as well as her recent penchant for getting into trouble, he had taken the time to provide updates. Or perhaps he merely thought to check on her. To make sure she hadn't crept outside the secret room. His concern was well-grounded for she couldn't wait to explore each room adorned now with new furnishings.

Particularly the library.

Muffled voices soon caught her attention. Deep voices. Male. She could hear them walking about in the antechamber. Probably the deliverymen bringing up more furnishings. The commotion continued for a long while before the voices and footsteps faded into the background.

Without warning a quiet stillness settled over the manor, and she could detect no sound at all. It made her feel more alone...more isolated than ever.

Struggling to overcome a surge of melancholy, Belle briefly considered slipping outside. Fortunately her better judgment, along with the thought of seeing Samuels' vinegary expression, quickly snuffed that idea. Instead she picked up the candle and maneuvered around the stone steps to the far side of what she now referred to as her private dungeon. Located beyond this wall was the antechamber.

She extinguished the candle and set it aside before easing a wooden peg the size of a knitting needle from its place on the wall.

A tight beam of light burst into her dark prison.

Holding her breath, Belle rose on tiptoe and placed one eye near the opening. Something blocked her view. She wasn't sure what until it moved away, and she finally realized she'd been staring at the naked backside of a man.

Shocked and thoroughly appalled, she jumped back and nearly tumbled down the stone steps behind her. Fighting to keep her balance, her cheeks burning with intense heat, she moved away from the steps and placed her back against the wall. With one hand over her pounding heart, she sucked in a deep breath and tried in vain to erase the image from her mind.

Heavenly Father, please forgive this sinful and shameful act. It was not my intention to...to...

Heavens! Had she truly seen..?

Heat flooded her face again. In fact, her entire body.

A strange heat.

Disturbing.

Swallowing hard and deathly afraid the man had turned around to face the wall, *her* wall, Belle raised on tiptoe and squinted one eye before leaning toward the small opening.

Dark hair glistening from dampness, Morgan Spence lounged inside a deep and luxurious bathtub, the soapy water reaching midway up his muscular chest. He'd closed his eyes, and a smile of pure enjoyment curved his lips.

She backed away, tingling with excitement.

Bless the saints! Could it be?

She wet her lips and once again stared through the narrow opening.

Sweet and kind Father!

A delicate shiver traveled up her spine. Then right back down again until it reached her toes.

At last! An answer to my prayers!

Too many nights she had longed for it. No, dreamed of it. And now...now it was within reach. Waiting for her. Beckoning like a siren's call.

A bathtub!

And Belle couldn't wait to use it.

* * *

After the workers and deliverymen departed, Morgan and his guests ate a late lunch before settling into the newly furnished drawing room where Samuels had built a cozy fire in the hearth. "I'd offer you a brandy, Bart, but I'm afraid I haven't gotten around to stocking the wine cellar."

"A pity. I expect this matter to be corrected before my next visit."

"Properly noted, your Grace."

Margaret sat down on the fashionable coral-colored sofa. "I vow, Morgan, if you employed more than one servant, I'd be tempted to make use of your bathtub."

"If it's a bath you desire—"

"I certainly do, but I'm far too exhausted to disrobe without the attendance of my dear Hilary."

"Yes, of course. My apologies." He drew a quick

breath. "Listen, Margaret, I'd like to discuss the terms of this loan."

"What loan, dearest?"

"Mags, I'm most grateful to you for filling my home with expensive furnishings, and I'm sure my future wife will be pleased as well. However—"

"I didn't do this to please Lydia Adderly."

"Did I mention her name?"

"You didn't have to. I well know your intentions. Bartholomew told me."

Morgan cut his gaze to the duke, but his friend avoided eye contact, so he turned his attention back to his sister. "Margaret, while I appreciate your kindness and generosity, I cannot accept charity. I intend to repay you."

"Well of course you'll repay me, Morgan. I never expected otherwise."

"You didn't?" Was she saying merely what he wished to hear or was she sincere? "Yes, well...I'm glad it's settled then."

"Margaret, my love, I commend you. You've outdone yourself."

"Indeed she has. Fluttering about like a butterfly from flower to flower. Giving orders and instructing the workers as to what furniture goes where."

The duke smiled. "Then changing her mind and rearranging the entire room for no practical reason or purpose."

Her gaze narrowed. "Am I to be mocked by worthless scoundrels?"

"Worthless?" Morgan echoed.

"Scoundrels?" the duke quipped. "Why would we mock you, sweet wife? There's little doubt of your exhaustion. I can see it in your lovely face."

"Yes, Mags, I daresay you've suffered far greater than we gentlemen."

"Suffered? You and Bartholomew? In case you do not recall, brother, you and my beloved husband did little. No, that's not entirely true. You both managed to get in the way quite often."

Morgan feigned surprise. "Bart, was that not our job?"

"Indeed. I distinctly recall my wife giving instructions to 'walk about the manor and look important.' Were those not your exact words, Margaret?"

"That's not what I meant."

"No? Then you cannot fault Morgan or me for the miscommunication."

Clearing his throat to garner attention, Jasper Samuels stood just inside the drawing room door. "Pardon the interruption, Mister Spence, but the Chase carriage has arrived."

"Thank you, Samuels."

"Oh, Mister Samuels?" Margaret called.

"Yes, your Grace?"

With an endearing smile, she stood. "I realize you went to a great deal of trouble for my husband and me, preparing a splendid lunch with no help whatsoever. I simply wished to thank you again."

"You're most welcome, my lady."

After the door closed behind the old man, Bartholomew turned to his wife. "Margaret, I believe Samuels will make a respectable gentleman out of your brother."

"I *am* a respectable gent."

"Of course you are." Margaret sighed. "Poor Mister Samuels. He's rather fatigued, is he not? I haven't seen the man smile once the entire day."

"That's because he's forgotten how."

"Ridiculous, brother. How does one forget how to smile?"

"I'm not sure but if Samuels' lips turn upward, I suspect they would crack from the unusual position."

"If I were the only servant charged with the upkeep of this manor," the duke declared, "I'd display a constant frown as well."

"Trust me, Bart. Samuels enjoys his unique position."

Margaret walked over to him. "Morgan, I'm sorry if I gave you quite the shock this morning, and I pray I've not offended you."

He took her hand. "You mustn't worry so often about me. And I apologize for not properly thanking you for such

84

undeserved generosity."

Her smile turned pensive. "If there's anything you don't care for...anything at all—"

"Margaret..." He held her at arm's length. "You have exquisite taste. Rest assured there is nothing I dislike. Everything you selected suits this house perfectly. Particularly the bathtub."

"Splendid. Oh, I've just had a thought. What do you think of inviting Mother and Father to Canderlay for Christmas?"

"Do you suppose they'd enjoy it?"

"I'm certain of it. Shall I write them?"

"If you wish."

"Now that that's settled..." Bartholomew rested his hand at his wife's back. "Shall we go, my love?"

"Yes, of course. Now, Morgan..." She slid one hand inside the crook of his elbow and the other inside her husband's. "You should consider hosting a party." All three walked out of the drawing room together. "Why not throw a ball in honor of Canderlay Manor's reemergence into society? We'll schedule it around the harvest festivals. That will give us plenty of time. Perhaps you'll be successful in procuring domestic help by then."

"And in persuading Miss Adderly to become your bride," the duke said.

"Bite your tongue, husband, and feed it to the vultures. I'll have no such talk. You know how impressionable Morgan is. Give him an idea, and he runs with it when he should be going about on tiptoe."

"Mags, why are you against my acquiring a wife?"

"I'm not opposed to the idea, dear brother. Just Lydia Adderly."

"And if I disagree?"

She sighed. "Then I shall pray that the Good Father bestows a generous amount of mercy upon you for the remainder of your time upon this earth."

Standing near the door, Samuels bowed respectfully as they passed. Outside the driver waited dutifully beside the Chase carriage, his hand holding onto the open door.

"Mister Samuels is quite wonderful as well as efficient

but, Morgan..." Margaret halted outside the façade. "He is one man. He simply cannot maintain this household without the proper help."

"I agree, but I doubt he would."

"The workers you hired did a splendid job repairing the manor house," Bartholomew remarked. "How long before they finish the stables?"

"A few days, I suspect."

"Have you considered restoring the cottages for tenant farmers?"

"I've given it some thought but not much planning." Morgan walked around in front of his sister and gripped both her hands. "Margaret, you are an amazing woman. Has your snobbish husband ever told you that?"

"Often and with shameless abandon."

"As well he should. I meant what I said, Mags. I will repay you."

Her expression turned serious. "Why not start by marrying a lady who pleases your heart instead of your dwindling purse."

"Was that the thought behind this rather expensive venture? To save your brother from an unpleasant union?"

"Can you think of a more worthy cause?"

"I'm flattered, my lady. I rather thought the monies should've gone to Jonathan, but your prickly husband has already reprimanded me for daring to suggest that he cannot take care of the lad."

"And rightfully so."

"Mags, you are too much like our dear mother. In fact, if I close my eyes, your voice sounds remarkably like hers."

"And what, pray tell, is wrong with our mother?"

"Nothing. Nothing at all. You know I adore the woman, but you have to admit she's a bit headstrong and severely outspoken."

"Devil take it," the duke quipped. "You've stuck your foot in it this time, Morgan, and I'll not help you extract it."

"What? Am I not allowed to express an opinion?"

With a firm crossing of her arms and a fiery glare, Margaret began a verbal assault, claiming that the fine qualities she inherited from their mother made up the better part of her character. And how dare he imply a woman could not use her clever brain if the Good Father chose to give her one.

As she ranted on, Morgan's gaze casually drifted upward to one of the windows of the second floor where something had disturbed the newly hung curtains. It was only a slight movement, like the flutter of a gentle breeze, and would've been dismissed altogether had the window been open. But it was obviously closed, and these were the curtains adorning *his* bedroom window.

"Morgan, have you heard one word I've said?"

He glanced down at his sister. "I apologize, Margaret. I was momentarily distracted. Listen, love, I'm going to make a request of you and Bartholomew. One you may find strange, but nevertheless I'm going to ask you to do it without question."

"Without question?" The duke laughed. "Morgan, either you've forgotten your sister's inquisitive nature or you've gone completely mad."

"Bartholomew, you rogue. I shall deal with you later. Morgan, what is it? I can see something troubles you."

He ducked inside the façade.

Margaret followed.

Morgan stopped her before she reached him. "I'd like you to stand there, where you are, and do not move," he said low. "Make sure you are in clear view of my bedroom window but don't look up." He backed away. "Oh, and pretend you're still speaking with me."

"I was right, Margaret." Bartholomew walked up behind her. "Your brother is quite mad."

"Morgan—"

"I've no time to explain, Mags," he whispered. "Humor me. Please."

She and the duke merely stared at him in complete confusion.

Until a sudden, mischievous spark lit Margaret's eyes. "Oh, Morgan, I neglected to tell you my plans for the Harvest Ball. You will attend, will you not? Well, of course you will. I simply cannot believe the time has passed so quickly. Bartholomew was saying just last week that we should visit

Dragon's Breath, but I told my dear husband that it's far too soon to abandon my brother."

As she prattled on, going from one subject to another with fine-tuned ease, Morgan slipped inside the manor and hurried up the stairs to the second floor. He unlocked the door to the antechamber and finding the room empty, snuck inside and crept to the door of his bedroom.

Pausing, he exhaled a slow breath before turning the latch and pushing the door open. It swung wide, crashing against the inner wall.

Near one of the windows stood a slender young woman, thick auburn curls trailing down her back. The moment she whirled around to face him, a mixture of dread and overwhelming fear instantly appeared in her large brown eyes.

"Who are you?" he demanded.

She blinked, her gaze shifting apprehensively toward the fireplace.

His attention strayed there as well. To a long oak panel that looked out of place. It quickly dawned on him that this was probably the means she used to come and go as she pleased. "It was you...that first night." He pinned her with a harsh glare. "That horrible misshapen creature."

She swallowed hard, her fear so intense it practically radiated off her body.

"You caused my accident." He inched closer. "My near fatal trip over the balustrade."

She darted toward the panel.

Morgan quickly cut her off. "If your desire was to carry out a mischievous prank upon some unsuspecting gentleman, you certainly succeeded. But why me? Was I the only person available for your amusement?" He suddenly noticed her shabby attire. A simple frock with worn sleeves. Toes peeked out from under the tattered hem. No shoes. No stockings. Compassion stirred inside his heart, and his attention returned to her face. "Why are you living at Canderlay Manor?"

She backed away, keeping her eyes trained on his every move.

He followed, steadily closing the distance. "Though

you played the part well...you're obviously no ghost. So I ask you again." He edged around the foot of the bed. "Who are you?"

Instead of replying, she scurried across the bed to the other side.

Before she reached the door, Morgan caught her around the waist.

"Let go of me," she hissed, struggling to break free.

"Ah, the lovely spirit speaks." He drew her against his chest. "And she smells sweetly. Like roses. Another mystery solved." He turned her to face him before trapping her against the wall. "Let's be civil, shall we? My name is Morgan Spence." He offered his most beguiling smile. "And you are?"

She opened her mouth. Then promptly closed it.

"Stubborn, are we? Well now, I've a cure for stubbornness." He grabbed her hand. "Come along, Mistress Spirit. It's time to meet the rest of the clan."

In protest, she kicked the back of his knee.

Wincing from the pain and barely avoiding a muffled curse, Morgan turned. "Not only are you a stubborn lass, but you've a violent streak as well." Releasing her hand, he picked her up, hauled her over his shoulder, and strode from the room. "You realize, of course, that I'll be forced to summon the local constable?"

"What an excellent idea," she snapped, fighting to loosen his hold. "I'd cherish the expression on your arrogant face when I explain to him how you accosted me."

He whacked her on the rear, expecting her to calm down or at least stop struggling. She did neither. In fact, his action had the opposite effect, prompting her to beat her fists against his back.

"Stop that at once!"

"Certainly, my lord. Provided you keep your hands off my rear."

"Fair enough. And there's no reason to address me as lord. I've no title."

"Obviously."

"What does that mean?"

"It means you are an uncivilized, ill-mannered brute with a brain the size of a...ouch!"

"Was that the sound of your head smacking against the edge of the door?"

"You did that deliberately."

"No, you did that on your own. Now stop flailing about like a fish out of water before you inflict serious damage to your person."

"Gladly. If you set me down."

"Now why would I do that?"

"Are you a child? Must even the simplest matters be explained?"

"Are the barbs from your tongue strictly for me?" Morgan shot back. "Or are others cursed with them?"

"If you set me down, I'll consider speaking to you with respect."

"Not likely. Besides, it's far too late to offer a truce."

"Truce? Are you daft? Well, of course you are. Otherwise you would've never brought up the subject. And where are you taking me?"

"Downstairs. Kindly restrain yourself until we reach the foyer. As to the explanations, allow me to clarify something, strange spirit. *You* are an intruder. *I*, on the other hand, am the owner of this estate and have a valid reason to be here. Who do you believe the courts will side with? You, the intruder? Or me, the legal owner?"

Her struggling ceased. "Are you always so smug?"

"When proven indisputably correct, yes."

At the foot of the stairs, Morgan paused briefly to adjust her weight on his shoulder. Heading across the foyer, he met Margaret coming in the door with the duke not far behind. The shocked expression on both their faces was rather amusing if not downright comical.

Bartholomew found his voice first. "What goes on here, Morgan? Who is this woman and why are you carrying her in such an undignified manner?"

"I'm carrying her because I cannot trust she'll follow peacefully behind. As to her identity...Margaret, Bartholomew, may I present..." Morgan set his burden down none too gently, and she plopped onto her backside in the middle of the foyer. "The ghost of Canderlay Manor."

Chapter Seven

Ashamed of her ragged attire, Belle drew her bare feet beneath the frock.

"This is no ghost," Lady Chase insisted, her blue eyes round with disbelief. "Miss Lindley? Is it you?"

"Yes, my lady."

"Bless the Good Father!" Her Grace extended a hand and pulled Belle to her feet. "But...where have you been these last three months? Oh, never mind, dear girl." She hugged Belle briefly before pushing her at arm's length. "Forgive my lack of a proper greeting, but you've caused quite the shock."

"Yes, I realize that, and I'm terribly sorry."

"Margaret, are you implying that you recognize this woman?"

"Well of course, Morgan. She's Isabelle Lindley. Miss Lindley, this is my brother, Morgan Spence. And you remember my husband, do you not?"

"Yes, of course." Belle curtsied. "Good evening, your Grace."

The duke nodded. "Miss Lindley."

"I'm surprised you survived that horrible fire," his wife continued. "Where are your shoes, my dear? You must be quite chilled. Oh, listen to me prattle on. How thoughtless when you are likely in need of a doctor."

"No, my lady. I'm well, thank you."

"I'm relieved then. We feared the worst. That you'd perished."

"We were left with no other possibility," his Grace concluded. "And you've been here at Canderlay all this time?"

"Lindley?" Morgan Spence echoed. "Yes, of course. The vicar's daughter." Sudden comprehension soured his expression. "It makes perfect sense now."

"What makes sense?" his sister inquired.

"Everything. I've been duped. Tricked and deceived. Ah, Samuels, there you are. Join us, if you please, as I'm quite certain you are very much involved in this intrigue."

Belle followed the old caretaker's approach to the center of the foyer, his steps slower than she remembered. He didn't glance her way, likely disappointed she hadn't heeded his warning to stay hidden.

A ton of guilt settled upon her shoulders. "It's not his fault."

"What's that, Miss Lindley?" A half sneer spread across Mister Spence's lips. "Have you decided to favor me with an apology? Some sort of explanation?"

"I cannot blame you for any mistrust, as I'm certain I deserve it, but you must understand that Mister Samuels is innocent of any wrongdoing. Out of genuine desperation, I..." She bit her lip. "I forced him to help me."

"No, Miss Isabelle. You did no such thing."

"Hold on, Samuels. Let's allow this trickster enough rope to hang herself."

"Morgan," Lady Chase chastised. "How utterly rude. Is it your intention to conduct an interrogation?"

"It certainly is."

"Then must you do so in the middle of the foyer? Can you not see Miss Lindley has gone through a horrifying ordeal?"

"Margaret, this is clearly none of your concern."

"I disagree, brother. I suggest we continue this discussion in a more civilized manner and in the proper setting."

"The workers left earlier this afternoon, Mags, and as you know, I've no servants except Samuels. There are no strangers listening at keyholes."

"What my wife is suggesting, Morgan, is that she and Miss Lindley would likely be more comfortable in the drawing room."

"Bart, I believe I've already made Miss Lindley more than a little comfortable."

Belle's composure snapped. "Comfortable? Then I

daresay you've never been imprisoned inside a small room with no windows, breathing the same stale air day and night for months, with hardly a glimpse into what goes on outside that room except for an occasional glance through a tiny peephole. Each hour crawls by in the same excruciatingly slow manner as the one before it, with nothing but the flame of a candle to break a lonely and dark existence. I can assure you, Mister Spence, there was hardly any comfort in that hidden room except for the knowledge that for the moment I was safe."

"You poor child," Lady Chase remarked.

"Save your sympathies, Margaret. This young woman is..." His eyes narrowed on Belle. "Hidden room?"

She nodded. "Behind the fireplace in the master suite."

"Another mystery solved," he muttered. "Miss Lindley, you snuck in through the broken window around back, did you not?"

"Yes, but I broke no window."

"Did I accuse you of that particular misdeed? I'm amazed you have the audacity to..." He stopped short, and his gaze hardened. "Peephole? Good God! You likely spied on my every move."

"Your comings and goings did not interest me in the least," Belle retorted. "And the only reason I peeked was to make certain you were not present when I exited my prison."

"And exit you did, on numerous occasions, so do not play the role of prisoner here. And why on earth were you hiding?" Again his stare cut right through her. "Tell the truth. What do you know about the fire that destroyed your cottage?"

The heat of injustice warmed Belle's cheeks, almost consuming her.

"Morgan," Lady Chase said. "What are you implying?"

"I believe I spoke rather plainly, did I not?"

"Indeed, but you've no cause to browbeat Miss Lindley. I won't have it." Her Grace wrapped one arm around Belle's waist. "Come, dear girl. We'll go into the drawing room and sit beside the fire. Oh, Mister Samuels, would you bring us a pot of tea?"

"Right away, my lady."

"Hold on, Samuels. I give the orders at Canderlay. Not the Duchess of Chase. And as I'm hosting no social event, I'm under no obligation to furnish refreshments. Which leaves you free to accompany us to the drawing room."

"Very well, sir."

"Pay no attention to my brother, Miss Lindley," her ladyship instructed as she led Belle down the corridor. "Morgan is decent enough, but he can be an uncivilized brute at times."

"My character is not in question, Mags. Coming, Bart?"

"I wouldn't miss it."

"Mister Spence, shall I inform his Grace's driver of the delay?"

"And give you the opportunity to escape? No, Samuels, I'll explain the situation myself."

Inside the drawing room, Belle hardly noticed the new furnishings as she marched straight to the fireplace. If this room hid a secret panel, it would be difficult not to make a mad dash to safety.

But there was no safe place to run.

Not here.

Not now.

"Miss Lindley?"

Belle turned.

Lady Chase smiled. "Would you care to sit beside me on the sofa?"

"I appreciate your kindness, my lady, but I believe I'll take my punishment standing and with my back to the wall."

"An understandable strategy. Forgive me, my dear, but...it looks as though your frock has seen better days. Have you nothing else?"

"No. Everything I owned, except for the nightdress I wore that night, was lost in the fire. I discovered this frock in a trunk in the attic. It was in poor condition and smelled of must, but it's provided a change. I suppose your brother will consider this theft and ask me to pay for this offense as well."

"Oh, I wouldn't worry about Morgan. His anger will be short-lived. You'll see. As to your attire, I believe I can help."

"Thank you, Lady Chase." Belle turned. "Mister Samuels, I'm terribly sorry to have gotten you into trouble with your employer."

"Do not overly concern yourself with me, Miss Isabelle. I'll find other employment."

"Not until you're dismissed from your current one." Morgan Spence strode through the door, accompanied by the duke. Stopping in front of her, he offered a disingenuous smile. "Now then, Miss Lindley..." With a glare that could wither a delicate rose, he added, "Let's begin with what happened the night your cottage burned."

Belle drew a breath then recounted the details of the circumstances she'd been forced into for the last three months. She had no wish to further involve Samuels, but he'd played a key role in her rescue, and she found no credible method to extract his participation. Without lying, that is. And so she told the truth.

All of it.

During the process, she realized she no longer swallowed around a tight knot lodged in her throat. No longer carried the full burden of dread inside her heart and upon her shoulders. Sharing her troubles had liberated her. She was still afraid for her life, and with good reason, but that fear no longer dominated her thoughts.

She finished with, "I've been hiding as well as sleeping in the secret room I mentioned earlier."

There was a moment of silence before the duke exclaimed, "Good God!"

"Calm yourself, Bartholomew," his wife advised. "My dear Miss Lindley, you are a brave young woman. I shudder to think of the horrors you must've suffered. And that horrible Barlow fellow...coming here on the pretext of—"

"Samuels," Mister Spence interrupted. "Did you see Barlow this morning?"

"No, sir."

"Nor did I. Did you inquire about the man's absence?"

"Frankly, sir, I was rather grateful for the reprieve."

"Understandable so, but you should've come to me, Samuels. I would've tossed that man out on his..." Morgan Spence did not finish the thought. "Miss Lindley," he said, his tone more civil. "Had I known what Barlow had done, you can be certain I would've taken immediate action. But I'm confused. Why not go to the local authorities? Surely you must've considered they'd question Barlow, and in turn you might discover the identity of the man who'd hired him."

"My father did not trust the authorities in Kent. His opinion, right or wrong, swayed mine."

Mister Spence eyed Samuels. "And you agreed with this? Agreed to help her? Bring her food and water?"

The caretaker nodded once. "Miss Isabelle had no one else, sir."

"You should've trusted me." He turned to Belle. "Both of you."

"We didn't know you," she countered. "We *don't* know you at all." She swallowed her pride. "Please do not dismiss Mister Samuels. He didn't lie. He never lies. He merely—"

"Spoke around the truth? Yes, I've already deduced that much." With a weary sigh, he ran his hands through his dark hair. "I've no intention of releasing Samuels. He's too valuable a servant." He aimed a tolerant smile toward the man. "Too valuable a friend."

Jasper Samuels' expression remained stoic. "Thank you, sir."

"But from now on, I expect complete honesty. Is that clear?"

"Quite, sir."

"Miss Lindley," the duke said. "Have you no idea who the mysterious man is, the one Barlow referred to as his lordship?"

"No idea at all, your Grace."

"What gentleman has reason or motive to do away with you?" An amused smirk cracked Morgan Spence's lips. "Besides me, that is."

"Are you a gentleman, Mister Spence?" Belle inquired in a clipped tone. "I thought perhaps you'd been determined a cad. Or brute, I believe was the term."

Lady Chase giggled then tried to cover the offense by pretending to yawn.

"You find the situation amusing, Margaret?"

"Of course not, Morgan, but you must admit...Miss

Lindley is rather refreshing."

"Oh? You find dishonesty refreshing?"

Guilt kept Belle from issuing a cutting denial. She *had* been less than honest, but she was being truthful now. Nevertheless, this crude man's accusation severely wounded whatever remained of her pride.

"You exaggerate, brother."

"Is that so, Mags? Well then, you haven't spent the last month with this trickster. Do not be deceived. This woman's words seem as lovely and as innocent as her face, but they're just as misleading."

Why that pompous, overbearing...

Belle's mind halted, replaying his last words.

He thinks my face is lovely?

The inadvertent praise caused a delicate tingle to travel over her skin, much like the embrace of a cold draft on a humid day.

"Miss Lindley?"

Heart racing, she responded, "Yes, Mister Spence?"

"You failed to answer my question. Who in the nobility wishes you dead?"

"I've no idea," she replied, her heart returning to the usual dull thud.

"Ridiculous. Think back. You must've had contact with this mysterious nobleman. Had you recently been in a confrontation with anyone?"

"Yes," she retorted. "You."

"If your plan is to provoke me," he said with an arrogant glare, "I daresay you'll eventually succeed."

"And what, sir, will you do then?" Belle crossed her arms. "Lock me in a hidden room?"

He stared...as though he could not quite understand her.

Samuels cleared his throat. "Pardon me, Miss Isabelle, but I'm reminded of the gent who wished to purchase your father's journals. He was most adamant in his attempts to persuade you to part with them."

"Oh, yes. I'd forgotten about those letters."

"Who was this man?" Mister Spence asked. "What was his name?"

Belle thought back. "I don't recall."

"How convenient."

"Hardly," she countered. "I believe he claimed to be employed by a London publisher."

"Which one?"

"I...I'm not sure. I wasn't interested in his offer so I discarded the letters."

Morgan Spence turned to Samuels. "Did you notice a name on any of the letters?"

"Harry...no, I believe it was Henry. Henry Darling." The old man's brow wrinkled. "Or was it Downing?"

"Very good, Samuels. You may return to your duties."

"Yes, sir."

After the door closed, the duke remarked, "There's a Henry Downsworth who's employed by Shutterby's Publishing. A cocky gentleman, short and thin...about sixty years in age."

"Since I merely corresponded with the gentleman, your Grace, I've no idea of his age or his appearance, but why would he lie? He wrote that his employer had become aware of my father's death and wished to purchase the journals as a memorial to Father's devotion and service to God."

"But you turned him down?" Mister Spence asked.

"I most certainly did. I replied to each letter. I wrote that my father was a man who respected others' privacy. Under no circumstances would he ever have allowed his thoughts regarding his parishioners to be published."

He raised a brow. "Reverend Lindley kept track of his parishioners' sins?"

"Heavens, no!"

"Behave, Morgan," Lady Chase admonished. "Miss Lindley, how did the London publisher learn of your father's journals?"

"I've no idea, and it didn't occur to me to inquire. I should've. I see that now. I cannot believe Father would've told anyone." Belle's ire returned to Morgan Spence. "And he did *not* keep a written record of anyone's sins and certainly not his parishioners."

He merely stared at her, as though he disagreed.

"Whatever the vicar did or did not do..." the duke

edged closer to the long windows before turning, "I fail to see why his daughter's life is in danger now."

"Seems rather obvious to me," Morgan Spence declared. "There are secrets written in those journals. Secrets she read."

Lady Chase rose. "Miss Lindley, why did your father feel the need to keep a journal?"

"Several years ago he began to lose the ability to recall people and events. He was often forgetful and the only way he could conquer this demon was to put his thoughts to pen and paper for future reference. Later on, when his hands shook so badly he couldn't read what he'd written, he asked for my help."

"Do you not see, Miss Lindley?" Mister Spence asked. "Whether you're willing to admit it not, your father committed to paper the sins of those under his spiritual care, and you became a witness. That fact alone might've given someone cause for alarm."

"Enough to incite murder," the duke remarked.

Belle shook her head. "How would anyone know I had helped Father? And he spoke of no one's sins. Not really. There was nothing severely incriminating in those journals. Nothing more than minor offenses."

"How many journals?" Mister Spence inquired.

"I'm not sure. Probably twenty or more."

"You read them?"

"No, of course not, but— "

"Then how can you be sure of their content?"

"I cannot, I suppose. Still...Father never used proper names when referring to his parishioners. He used Lady J or Lord S or Mister P. He would certainly never repeat any of their offenses. Especially to me."

"I daresay someone believes otherwise," the duke insisted.

"What became of the journals?" inquired Mister Spence.

"They were lost in the fire. Except for the one Mister Samuels recently brought to me."

"I wonder..." the duchess mused aloud. "Miss Lindley, was your father ever called to witness a person's dying confession?"

"Occasionally, but he never recorded anything spoken in confidence or in the nature of a confession."

"Are you certain of this?"

"I believe so, my lady."

"A pity we cannot question the gentleman who sent those letters," the duke stated.

"But there is someone we can question," Morgan Spence insisted. "Amos Barlow. I'll have the constable waiting in the morning to arrest him for arson and attempted murder."

"Thank you, Mister Spence." Belle expelled a breath of sheer relief. "If you've no objection, I've a few questions to ask before he's taken away."

"I'm afraid I must object, Miss Lindley. You're not to go anywhere near the man, nor should you speak to him."

"But...he tried to murder me."

"Yes, I'm well aware of that."

"Splendid, but I wish to know who hired him and why."

"Were you not listening when I said I'd have that answer for you come morning?" He set his hand gently upon her shoulder and offered a rogue smile. "But I must ask for your cooperation as well as your trust."

Her heart fluttered.

Dear Lord! I'm being charmed by a smooth as velvet voice and an incredibly handsome face. Add another besotted female to this man's collection.

Belle raised her chin in defiance to that last repulsive thought. "Very well," she said. "I'll do as you ask, but you should know that if you fail to extract the answers I seek, I'll question Barlow on my own. With pistol in hand."

With an amused grin, he stepped back. "Fair enough."

"I'd like to hear his story as well," the duke declared.

"Certainly, Bart. I'll expect you around eight."

Lady Chase approached Belle. "Miss Lindley, have you family?"

"My mother's older brother, but he and his wife sailed for America nine years ago. Father and I never heard from them again."

"I see. Well, you must come to Chase Manor then."

"Thank you, my lady, but until I discover who wishes me harm, I'd rather not involve anyone else. Particularly you or your husband."

"My dear girl...you cannot remain at Canderlay. You've no chaperone."

"She has Samuels," her brother insisted. "And Canderlay is not only safe, it's logical."

"But, Morgan, it wouldn't be wise. You must think of this young woman's reputation."

"I believe it's a bit late for that, Mags."

"I beg your pardon?" Belle snapped, heat rising up her neck.

"I meant no offense, Miss Lindley, I assure you. Margaret...you employ a large number of servants, and servants have a habit of gossiping about their employers, along with anyone else associated with said employers. I doubt they'd hesitate to discuss the reappearance of their beloved vicar's supposedly deceased daughter. This is precisely how rumor and misinformation spread."

"He's correct, my love. As Miss Lindley has been at Canderlay all this time, it's a bit like closing the stable doors after the horses have escaped. It might be unwise to relocate her at this point and would only encourage gossip."

"I understand, Bartholomew, but I simply wished to extract Miss Lindley from a potentially disgraceful situation, thereby protecting her reputation from further damage."

"Margaret, there's been no damage or disgrace. Rest assured...there's absolutely *nothing*, and never will be *anything*, disgraceful going on between Miss Lindley and myself."

Belle's eyes narrowed. "And I couldn't agree more fervently."

Morgan Spence's amused gaze settled upon her briefly.

"Have you no other relatives, my dear?" Lady Chase inquired.

"None. My mother died when I was a child, and her parents before I was born, as did my father's. He died, as you know, last winter. His younger brother, Magnus, was lost at sea ten years come October."

The duke's somber expression changed drastically. "Miss Lindley, are you telling us that your uncle is...was...Magnus Lindley?"

"Yes."

"The Irish shipping magnate who perished at sea? The man who owned ML Shipping, *he* was your uncle?"

"That's correct, your Grace."

Morgan Spence whistled low.

Lady Chase glanced from brother to husband. "I fail to see how a deceased relative pertains to Miss Lindley's immediate situation."

"It doesn't, I suppose," her husband remarked. "Though I had no idea Reverend Lindley was of Irish descent."

"My father and uncle were half-brothers, your Grace. Magnus' mother was Irish."

Morgan Spence paced about the room. "I find it odd and a bit reckless that this prosperous uncle failed to provide for his brother and niece."

Annoyance pricked Belle's ire. "Forgive me, Mister Spence, but you never met my father and therefore could not possibly understand his aversion to wealth. As to Uncle Magnus...he did provide for me. I'm to collect one half percent of the value of his shipping business when I turn twenty and one, which occurs four weeks from today. So you see, I am not to become a pauper, if I can reach Dublin and still draw breath."

"Half a percent? Why such a meager share? Were you not cherished?"

Swine!

Morgan Spence might have the manners of a crude boar, but he certainly didn't look the part. She drew a quick breath. Nor did he smell like one. In fact, his scent was rather pleasing...clean with a trace of cinnamon.

No. Mint.

Do not lose your temper. Whatever the cost to your pride can be offset by future bathtub privileges.

"Yes, of course I was cherished," she said and paused to purposely sweeten her tone. "But you see, my father would not accept monies from Uncle Magnus, and he refused to allow a higher percentage for me."

"Seems rather selfish, does it not?"

"Not at all. Really, Mister Spence, you've no cause to..."

Focus your thoughts on the bathtub! Not his insensitive barbs!

"Forgive me. I spoke out of turn," Belle said. "Had you met my father, you'd understand. He used to say that if a man's heart..."

No, do not sacrifice your integrity! Putting this cad in his place is much more important than bathtub privileges.

Belle smiled. "He said that if a man's heart yearns for nothing more than luxury and wealth..." She aimed an innocent glance at her adversary. "Then that man's life is meaningless."

One corner of his mouth turned up in a half smirk. "Spoken like a true vicar's daughter. Please, Miss Lindley, continue this valuable teaching."

"Morgan, have you no shame?"

"When my character is being broadsided, no. And you, Mags...shouldn't you or your noble spouse be mildly offended by this woman's holier than thou attitude?"

"You're twisting my father's words. He meant no offense to anyone as kind and as generous as the Duke and Duchess of Chase. Only the nobles who remain greedy. Those who refuse to soften their hearts and loosen their purse strings."

The expression in his eyes became guarded. "Since I possess no noble title, does that make me exempt from the vicar's criticism? From God's eternal damnation?"

"All must eventually give an account to God. No one is exempt."

A glimmer of respect flashed in his eyes. "Indeed, you are correct."

Forced sincerity or mild sarcasm?

"My father knew firsthand what he spoke of. He gave up his birthright for the hand of a farmer's daughter. A quiet girl who owned nothing but a sweet soul and gentle nature. My mother." Belle swallowed the ache in her throat. "Father discovered long ago that it took more than fancy clothes or fine carriages to make a man noble. Honor wasn't the centerpiece of the large estate he once lived on. In fact, it was often pushed aside or forgotten."

Lady Chase lowered her gaze. She recognized the story. It was written in her expression. Her husband knew it as well.

"Miss Lindley?"

Belle shifted her attention. "Yes, Mister Spence?"

"You look a bit flushed. Are you ill?"

"No. I...I'm fine."

Without warning his harsh gaze softened, and the sarcasm and mistrust vanished. As he continued to stare, his eyes filled with sympathy, as though he now saw the gaping hole in her heart caused by her beloved father's untimely death. As though he finally understood the loneliness she faced.

As though he cared.

In a moment of weakness, tears brimmed in her eyes and spilled over.

He reached up, and barely a whisper of his fingertips brushed her cheek as he wiped away her tears.

And once again...

Heaven help me if my heart ever dares to yearn for this man.

The haughty way he treated Belle made her fume. Still...his undeniable and overpowering presence glowed like sunshine over a bleak and barren land. When he looked at her with compassion, as he did now, her heart warmed, and his gaze left her weak-kneed. Confusion reigned inside her soul. She wasn't accustomed to this much emotional turmoil.

"Honor comes not from a man's noble bloodline," the duke muttered low, breaking the trance-like spell. "It is found in a man's actions, and actions speak of a man's true worth." He favored Belle with a smile. "Yes, Miss Lindley, I've listened to the vicar's sermons with interest."

"Father spoke highly of you and your wife, your Grace."

"With Margaret, it would've been difficult to find anything critical."

"Not if the good reverend had bothered to ask the lady's four brothers," Morgan Spence quipped.

Lady Chase laughed. "Yes, I daresay he would've gotten quite an earful from my family." She drew Belle's hands into her own. "What I remember about Reverend Lindley was that he was a selfless man of God who preached that one is not born into peace and contentment. Those gifts cannot be inherited, neither borrowed or purchased, but must be earned. I will never forget those words."

Belle smiled. "He would be pleased, my lady."

"You were indeed blessed with a wise and devoted father, my dear, and by the tone of your voice when you speak of your uncle, I suspect he was a fine gentleman as well."

"Magnus was indeed generous beyond measure, but others saw him as a man who never missed an opportunity to add to his vast fortune. In this my uncle succeeded, but I fear it gave him little comfort in the end."

"At the risk of sounding callous," Mister Spence remarked, "I suggest we steer clear of all reminiscing until we eliminate the problem at hand and tie up any loose threads. I've given this some thought, and I believe it will be in our best interest to explain to the constable that my uninvited guest has been unwell these past few months and that she's been staying with friends in an attempt to mend."

"But...that would be a lie."

"A rather sanctimonious response, don't you think, Miss Lindley? This explanation would merely be a slight deviation from the truth, as you and I are clearly far from the status of friendship."

"We certainly are, but what if the constable wishes to know the names of these friends?"

"Why the devil would he? But if it comes to forcing a lie, allow me to commit the misdeed to save your conscience as well as your saintly soul."

Belle frowned at the intended insult. "And what of your soul, sir?"

He offered no rebuttal. "Bart, I'm sending Samuels to the constable's office come morning. Margaret, as the man will no doubt wish to question Miss Lindley, she'll require a suitable change of clothing."

"I've considered her immediate needs, Morgan, and you can be certain I'll attend to it."

"Then we'd best be on our way, my love," his Grace advised.

"Yes, of course."

Once the duke and duchess said their farewells and the door closed behind them, Morgan Spence turned to Belle. "Am I to assume that the journal Samuels discovered is here at Canderlay?"

"Yes. In the secret room."

"You mean...your prison cell?" he teased.

She nodded.

"You've not read it?"

"No."

"Where was this journal discovered?"

"At the church. Mister Samuels said the cleaning woman found it in my father's office, strapped to the bottom of his chair."

"As though he wished to keep it hidden from prying eyes?"

"I...yes, I suppose."

He paced toward the long windows before turning suddenly. "Would you object if I examined the journal? Before you give your answer, let me remind you that you were responsible for my near fatal tumble over the balustrade."

"I truly meant you no harm. Very well, I'll hand over the journal for your perusal. With one stipulation."

"Let me guess. My silence regarding whatever secrets I come across?"

She frowned. "Two stipulations then."

The light of curiosity reflected in his eyes. "I'm listening."

"I'll hand over the journal in exchange for..." Belle swallowed the last shred of pride she'd held onto, hoping she wasn't about to make a bargain with the devil over such a trivial matter. "For frequent bathtub privileges."

Chapter Eight

"Well?" Hawk stared at his driver. "Is Barlow here in Maidstone?"

"Yes, milord. I was told he's been arrested."

"When?"

Three nights ago."

"On what charge?"

"Murder."

Was it true? Had Amos Barlow finally caught up with Isabelle Lindley?

"Pray tell..." Hawk could hardly contain his excitement. "Who is our *friend* accused of murdering?"

"A bloody Scotsman, milord."

Not the news he desired.

A lanky commoner stumbled out of the noisy King's Men Tavern then turned his back to relieve himself.

Standing beside the carriage door, the driver briefly glanced around. "See that man, milord? His name is Jenkins. He worked at Canderlay Manor last month. Said he visited this tavern last Friday to celebrate a new job he'd taken. He never cared for Canderlay. Afraid of the spirits, you see. Well now, about an hour after he arrived, in staggers Barlow, half soused. Not five minutes goes by before he gets into a brawl with the Scotsman. Gutted the man for starin' at his scarred face."

"We've no choice then but to part ways with Mister Barlow."

"Welcome news to me, milord. Pardon the crude vulgarity, but Amos Barlow was every bit as annoying as piss on a polished boot. He's been rather difficult to deal with. Always asking questions."

"Questions?" Hawk's gut soured. "About what?"

"Mostly about you, sir."

"Why did you not inform me?"

"There was no cause, as I told him not a blessed thing. You instructed me to keep strict silence in regards to your identity, milord, and I did."

"I'm relieved you followed orders."

The soused man, Jenkins, stumbled toward the carriage. "Evenin', good sirs," he said with a noticeable slur. "Would either of you have the time?"

Hawk shied away from the open door.

"Near midnight, I imagine," the driver replied.

Jenkins tipped his cap. Shoving his hands inside his trouser pockets, he turned and continued down the street, whistling a tune.

"Did they take Barlow to the local prison?"

"Yes, milord. Jenkins says he hears Barlow will be transferred to Newgate soon to await trial."

Newgate.

"When?" Hawk inquired.

"Tomorrow."

"A fitting end."

As for the vicar's elusive daughter...

"There's more, milord."

"What is it?"

"Jenkins claims that before Barlow was carted off he said to the tavern owner that if his brother came lookin' for him...I suppose he wanted folks to think that fellow was me...the proprietor should say, 'Barlow says he found her but won't tell where until he's freed.'"

Brother.

One word. A word that should've generated familiarity or at least a feeling of endearment and camaraderie. Instead of comfort, it hurled a dagger of fear straight into Hawk's heart.

Had Barlow known the truth all along?

That Hawk was his half-brother?

Impossible. Unless...

Bloody stupid hag! Filthy prostitute!

Thank God Mary Barlow was now dead, for in life she'd obviously been unable to keep her mouth shut. Not only had she confessed her sins to the local vicar, but she'd likely recounted the details of her sordid life to her youngest son as well. A scarred misfit who possessed no morals whatsoever.

What would Barlow do with this information?

A dismal future flashed before Hawk's eyes. He could lose everything he'd grown accustomed to. His title and wealth. His wife.

Everything!

Bloody hell, he'd slit his own throat before suffering humiliation at the hands of his dimwitted brother.

A burst of anger flooded his soul like a devastating tidal wave. Barlow might've learned the truth, but so far he'd kept his fool mouth shut. Did he think to blackmail Hawk from a prison cell? No one would believe the rantings of a madman and without the vicar's journal, Barlow could never prove he and Hawk were brothers. Even if he were foolish enough to confess to the authorities that Hawk had hired him to murder Isabelle Lindley, there was no proof.

None.

His driver knew nothing. He had merely arranged the meetings.

Hawk leaned forward. "Did Barlow tell you about our business?"

"No, milord, and I didn't ask."

Relief soothed Hawk, and he realized he'd been given a golden opportunity to create a façade that his peers, should it become necessary, might actually believe. "Because you are a loyal servant, Tibbs, I shall tell you my dealings with him. You see, there's a stain upon my youth. An indiscretion with a woman who was not of noble birth." He paused briefly before continuing the lie. "I sired a daughter with this woman and foolishly hired that crude ruffian to find her."

"You're a decent man, milord. I doubt others in your position would be so kind as to take responsibility for a bastard child."

"Yes, well..." He almost smiled. "I do what my conscience bids."

Had Barlow truly found the vicar's daughter? Or were his words of bravado a feeble attempt at salvaging his worthless life?

***

Disrobing in record time, Belle stepped inside the magnificent bathtub and sank down, the heat from the water soothing her skin. Until this very second, she hadn't realized how much she'd missed such a simple act as bathing. And she didn't intend to suffer such hardship ever again.

Scrubbing every inch of her body with the sweet smelling rose-scented soap, she sank deeper into the tub and briefly closed her eyes. Washing her thick curls and then brushing out the tangles would take time and plenty of effort. Fortunately sleep did not beckon to her.

Not this evening.

Even though Morgan Spence had graciously given up his master suite and enormous new bed for her comfort, she wasn't in any particular hurry to place her head upon his soft, satiny pillows. Not when the master of the manor had breathed new life into the silent corridors and empty rooms of Canderlay.

Not when there was so much to explore.

Oh, how Uncle Magnus would've approved.

No, he would've outright applauded.

Lounging in sheer luxury for half an hour, the water became cold, and so did Belle. She arose and stepped out of the tub, picked up a towel, and quickly dried off before heading across the room to the roaring fire. A white nightshirt hung across the back of a nearby overstuffed chair.

Did it carry his scent?

She held it beneath her nose.

Lye soap, starch and...

She sniffed again.

Liniment?

Not the clean scent she'd expected.

Belle slipped the nightshirt over her head then turned and studied her reflection in the long floor mirror. The material practically swallowed her. Although the length was decent enough, coming to just above her ankles, there were slits running up both sides.

Long slits that exposed her calves and rose up to her knees.

She fastened the garment's three square buttons. On an average man, they would've rested high on his chest. On her the buttons drifted well below her bosom. No matter the ill fit, she would be grateful and thank Mister Spence come morning.

With towel in one hand and a brush in the other, she walked into the bedroom and sat down on the edge of the bed. As she began the daunting task of brushing the tangles from her hair, her thoughts returned to Morgan Spence. Though often ill-mannered and quick to judge, he clearly could be a fine gentleman when he put his mind to the task.

As he had this evening.

Not wishing to burden the elderly caretaker, Mister Spence had heated the water for her bath in a huge kettle situated outside the door to the laundry house. He'd carried that water across the yard, through the kitchen and down the corridor to the foyer, up the stairs and into the antechamber himself.

Seventeen buckets in all!

Belle had offered to help and received a curt refusal.

After filling the tub, he brought her clean towels and stoked the fire in the hearth. With a stiff frown, he'd inquired as to the location of the peephole. When she pointed it out, he'd promptly marched across the room and covered it by moving the floor length mirror a little to the left. Satisfied with his cleverness, the wallpaper unexpectedly triggered a second glance, dividing his attention between the wall where Jenkins had hung the new paper and the adjoining wall where the old paper had been left undisturbed. Though both sported matching colors of brown and gold, the individual patterns of tall wheat grain in the new paper blew in a distinctly opposite direction than the grain in the old paper.

Mister Spence had clearly wished to ask the obvious question, but for some reason he did not. After turning and politely inquiring if she needed anything else, and receiving a 'no, but thank you', he'd taken her father's journal and departed the room.

He was an enigma, this man. Strange and confusing.

One minute he fairly seethed with hostility and arrogance, the sort of person she disliked immensely. Then all of a sudden his character would change, and he'd be kind and generous, giving up his personal suite to someone he hadn't known for even one day.

Belle set the brush aside. With a sigh, she ran her hand along the smooth material of the bedcovers...a comforting pattern of forest greens and deep golds. She wasn't sure she could sleep here.

Wasn't sure she'd feel safe.

Not even with the door locked and bolted.

It had nothing to do with Morgan Spence, but rather her mind kept returning to the fact that Amos Barlow knew her whereabouts. Knew she'd been standing in this very room.

A light tapping sounded against the outer door to the antechamber.

Thinking it might be the old caretaker coming to check on her, she rushed into the room and said through the door, "I'm afraid I'm not exactly dressed for a polite visit, Mister Samuels."

"It's not Samuels, Miss Lindley."

Morgan Spence!

What could he possibly want at this hour?

"And as much as I hate to admit it," he added, "I've been far from polite to you. I realize the hour is late, and you are a modest young woman, but what I have to say cannot wait until morning."

At a momentary loss for words, she glanced down. No shoes. No stockings. The borrowed nightshirt hid most of her female traits admirably, but the slits were indecent, and the ill-fit would definitely prompt amusement.

She grimaced.

Not to mention acute embarrassment.

"Miss Lindley, I understand your reluctance. I appreciate the fact that you might not be dressed in what some would consider respectable attire, but I believe I've discovered the answer to something that's eluded you for the last three months."

She cracked the door open an inch. "An answer?"

112

He smiled. "To the question of who wishes you dead."

***

Morgan studied the young woman shrouded in soft candlelight who sat demurely upon the sofa, awaiting an explanation. Long auburn curls with a splash of gold, still damp from her bath, clung to her shoulders possessively.

Auburn and gold.

The vivid colors of a fiery midsummer sunset.

With chin lifted in quiet expectation, her flawless face a portrait of innocence, she tugged a worn blanket about her body and held his gaze.

Isabelle Lindley was indeed beautiful in every sense of the word, but her expressive deep brown eyes were her best asset by far.

His gaze lowered.

At least the assets he could clearly form an opinion of.

Under his intense scrutiny, she squirmed then tried valiantly to cover her actions. "Mister Spence, I trust you found a clue in my father's journal?"

"As to your unknown tormentor...yes, I believe so. The vicar writes of a nobleman and refers to the man as Lord H. Does that name bring anyone to mind?"

"Not particularly. Why would he wish to harm me?"

"Patience, Miss Lindley. I'll get to that in a moment. I find it strange you never read your father's journals."

"I suppose I was never curious."

"Seems he was well acquainted with Lord H." He held up the book. "Will you allow me to read a few pages?"

"Very well."

Morgan sat in a chair across from her. "Some of this story you might recognize. If so, please feel free to speak up." He opened the journal and turned several pages. "The entry dates are in chronological order, but they span more than a decade."

"A decade? That's odd. Father wrote yearly journals."

"I gather this one was special."

"Apparently."

"This first entry is dated February 3rd, 1800."

I ministered to a woman today. A woman known only by her wicked profession in which she walked the streets of London. A gravely ill soul with the mind of a child. God has warned her, she said as she wept, that she's not long for this world. And He has instructed her to give an account of the sins she committed as well as the sins that were committed against her. Atrocities against innocence. Evil deeds hidden behind locked doors and a noble crest. Lies that never once saw the light of truth. Her name is Mary B.

Morgan glanced up.

Miss Lindley shook her head.

He continued reading.

As I spoke with Mary, I soon learned the details of her sad and pitiful life. And dear Father, it was indeed shameful what was done to this woman. Thirty and five years ago she'd been a scullery maid employed in a wealthy and prominent household. A simple but beautiful child of fifteen who caught the eye of a corrupt nobleman with a lustful heart. When the gently bred lady of the house discovered Mary was with child, she promptly gave her the boot and with Mary's own family disowning her, she took to the streets of London. At the end, when her beauty had faded and she could no longer survive in such a disgraceful manner, she returned to Kent. Weeping, she fell at my feet and asked me to witness her confession.

"That poor woman."

Morgan flipped a page. "The next entry is dated ten days later."

Mary B drew her last breath today with my hand upon her fevered brow. She wasn't angry with God and didn't curse Him as I feared she would, as so many others in her position have. No, this brave woman had the grace to leave this earth at peace with her creator. God, in His tender mercy, redeemed her tormented soul, turning fifty years of cruelty and hardship into nothing more than a distasteful memory.

He glanced up.

Tears glistened in Miss Lindley's eyes.

"The next entry is dated three months later."

114

My knowledge of Lord H's birth gnaws at his soul. Since he fraudulently inherited monies and a title through illegitimate means, he lives in constant fear of discovery...terrified of the day his mother's deathbed confession fractures the noble mask he so meticulously crafted.

"His mother was Mary?"

Morgan nodded. "As an infant he was taken from her and sent to live in his father's house. According to the vicar, only a few people knew the truth."

"And you believe this is the nobleman who wishes me harm?"

"It makes perfect sense. Lord H learns of the vicar's death and fears you will discover this journal and read it. He hires Barlow to burn your cottage, thereby destroying any evidence of his illegitimacy. And if you had perished in that fire..."

"It would've ensured that I never betray his secret."

"Precisely."

She sighed. "Illegitimacy is far too common in England."

"As is murder." He turned another page and read:

With much internal debate, I've decided to commit Mary's tragic life, as much as I dare, to the pages of this journal. Not in fear that I will ever forget...bless the saints, if only I could...but to protect my only child. My daughter Isabelle.

"I understand now. Lord H has a great deal to lose."

"He has everything to lose. All he owns would be stripped from him in the blink of an eye, and your father made certain his lordship understood that. There are numerous other entries in this journal, each pertaining to Lord H. His marriage to a marquis' daughter, the birth of his children, and even his daily routine with the servants."

"You're suggesting my father spied on him?"

"No, it was implied in the journal. After Lord H's threat to harm you, the vicar took note of everything his lordship did. Knew of his appointment in the House. If he heard that his lordship stepped one inch off the noble path, obtained a mistress or beat one of his servants, Reverend

Lindley states that he penned a letter to him."

"But...why? Did Father not realize this constant interference would be dangerous? Good heavens, it's like poking a stick at a venomous snake."

"The vicar was clever. More so than you give him credit. He no doubt wished to remind Lord H that he would be held accountable for all he said and did. And if that didn't place the fear of God into his lordship's heart, then the existence of this journal would."

"That sounds rather devious and not at all like my father."

"Perhaps, but you forget he was trying to protect his only daughter."

"How do you suppose this horrible man discovered my father kept a journal?"

"He was purposely made aware of it," Morgan replied. He turned another page then read:

And so I keep this journal hidden as security for Isabelle's safety and as a warning to the man who now claims the title he does not deserve. God help him if he ever dares to harm my daughter, for I won't hesitate to go straight to the King of England. Somehow I found the courage to tell him this, and I daresay he was livid. A small consolation. My heart is still heavy, and my guilt grows daily for I feel an obligation to Mary B, yet I dare not reveal her confession. I can only fervently hope and pray that God, and Mary, can someday forgive me.

"He had no right." Isabelle stood, and the blanket she'd draped around her body slid to the floor in a forgotten heap at her feet. "My father had no right to dishonor Mary with his silence. To keep what was done to her a secret in exchange for my well-being. Mister Spence, you must promise to hand his journal over to the Prince Regent."

He stood as well. "I understand your concern, but—"

"Concern? Dear Lord, I'm outraged."

"I believe you, Miss Lindley, but as of this moment we've no idea who Lord H is, and until we do...until he's rotting in a darker cell than the one you've just spent three months in...justice will have to wait."

"Should we delay until he murders me?"

"No, of course not. You're forgetting Amos Barlow and the fact that I intend to question him come morning." Morgan softened his tone before adding, "I wonder...could we possibly dispose of the stiff formalities and simply go forward with Morgan and Isabelle?"

She blinked. Then sighed. "No."

"No?"

She pushed up the sleeves of her nightshirt. "I prefer Belle."

He chuckled.

She frowned. "You find the name amusing, sir? Or has my ill-fitting attire given you cause to smirk?"

"I wasn't smirking, but I have to admit...that nightshirt is most distressing. Obviously it belongs on an old man with wrinkles and white hair."

"Then it...it doesn't belong to you?"

"Me? Good God, no. I sleep without such primitive restraints."

Color tinged her cheeks, and her lashes lowered.

Morgan realized it would be inappropriate to offer further comment on this particular subject. "As to the cause of my amusement, I was reminded that before my parents wed, my father gave my mother a gift. A spirited white Arabian mare. She was quite the beauty, and her name complimented her perfection." His gaze slid over the vicar's daughter. "Her name was Belle."

The color in her cheeks deepened.

"However," he added with a touch of genuine remorse, "I've suddenly become aware that using Belle when speaking or referring to you might be looked upon as an endearment and could possibly be misunderstood." He hesitated. "By others, I mean."

Her gaze avoided his. "Yes, of course."

"Tell me, Isabelle...would you strongly object to my using that name?"

"No. My father preferred it as does Mister Samuels, but Uncle Magnus..." After a slight pause, she skillfully avoided whatever memory had caused her brief pain and changed the subject. "I've admired your horse from afar, Mister Spence. Ares, I believe you call him?"

Though she would allow him to use her given name, she did not intend to use his. No matter. He wouldn't press the issue.

"After the Greek god," Morgan replied in response to her question.

"He's magnificent. Does he belong to Belle's lineage?"

"As a matter of fact, he does."

"Mister Samuels worked for your father, the previous Lord Canderlay, but you were born in Scotland, were you not?"

"On an island off the western coast. Dragon's Breath."

"How lovely, and yet your voice shows no hint of a Scottish dialect."

"My mother was born in America and lived there for many years."

"Oh...I see."

"Her father was Scottish," Morgan added. "Her mother English. My father's mother was French and his father English. So you see, when it comes to speech, Scotland was outflanked by foreigners."

"I've seen the portrait of Lady Canderlay. She was quite beautiful, and I'm told most kind. It's a pity you never met her."

"Indeed. I'm having her portrait cleaned. It will eventually be returned to the library to hang over the mantle where Samuels claims it belongs."

"Has Lady Chase seen it?"

"Not yet. I'm saving that as a surprise. Forgive me, Isabelle, but our conversation seems to have strayed."

"Yes, but there's not much more to say, is there?"

"Perhaps not. You realize, do you not, our plan has changed somewhat?"

"What plan?"

"I can have Barlow arrested for burning your cottage, and I can hand your father's journal over to the Duke of Chase, but I cannot accuse Lord H, whoever he is, of hiring Barlow to murder you. Nor can you."

Her eyes narrowed. "I most certainly can."

"But you won't, because you and I possess no titles. Anyone bearing false witness against a lord is subject to suffering a horrible death."

"Yes, but we wouldn't be lying. We'd be speaking the truth."

"A truth we'd be required to prove."

"Wouldn't my father's journal do that?"

"Perhaps, but we cannot be certain of it, can we?"

"No, I suppose not." She sighed. "I realize nobles are exempt from most prosecution, but this is clearly different. Lord H's peers may not care if the life of a lowly vicar's daughter is threatened, but surely they will take offense with a man who gained his title and lands by covering his own illegitimacy."

"I'm certain of it, but you've missed the point." He ran one hand through his hair. "Listen to me, Isabelle. Listen carefully. If charges of attempted murder or illegitimacy are to be brought against Lord H, it must be done through a trial by his peers in the House of Lords, not by a man with no title. Not by the vicar's clever daughter and not by an inferior constable whose sole ambition might be to gain local acclaim. Plainly speaking, the Duke of Chase is in a better position, a more prominent position than either of us, to handle this matter. Do you understand?"

"Of course I understand. Do you consider me a child?"

Morgan's gaze cut to the slit in her frumpy nightshirt. From her nicely formed calves down to her slender ankles.

No, not a child. A desirable woman.

An attack of conscience forced his attention back to her face.

She frowned. "Mister Spence, I can well appreciate your reluctance in this matter, but we must not lose sight of our moral duty. We must find this detestable Lord H. Find him and force the crimes of his family from behind locked doors. See that he's held accountable and right the endless wrongs committed against Mary B."

"For the life of me, Isabelle, I cannot disagree," Morgan admitted. "And while I admire your strict sense of duty and moral honor, I fear it will no doubt cause me a great deal of trouble." He turned and strode across the room. At the door he paused and with a backward glance added, "And I suspect that your rather obvious pristine reputation is precisely the reason your life is in danger now."

Chapter Nine

Hawk tethered his horse's reins to a low branch before walking several yards through dense underbrush. Crossing a shallow ditch, he waited beside the dusty road, his gray overcoat blending in with the shadows of early morning light.

He knew exactly what to look for.

Knew exactly when it would be passing through this lonely stretch of road.

He held no reservations.

No misgivings.

Hawk drew a long breath and closed his eyes. As the forest behind him came alive with the sound of birds chirping praise to their maker, a long ago pain cut through his heart.

Felicia.

The woman he once called Mother. A cold woman who never missed an opportunity to show Hawk how much she despised him. As a child, he hadn't understood her hatred. When he became a man, he told himself he no longer cared. On the day she died, he'd felt no remorse.

Merely relief.

From the moment his father told him about a woman named Mary, Hawk had been obsessed with hiding the shameful details of his birth. Obsessed with preserving his family lineage. He had hoped to keep the truth from breaking his sanity but no matter how hard he tried, or how much he wished it, he could not erase who he was.

The bastard child of a lowly servant girl.

A slight breeze caressed Hawk's face, reminding him of where he stood. He scanned the deserted road in both directions then withdrew his pocket watch.

Quarter to six. Not much longer.

He had never intended to force the vicar's hand by threatening his young daughter. It had been a mistake. A bold bluff that did not go as planned. But Hawk had been younger then. And foolish. The vicar far too cunning.

Now...

He had no choice but to silence Isabelle Lindley. There was simply no other solution. If he allowed the girl to live, his shame would one day be exposed. He had no doubt about that. And that fear kept his mind sharp. Kept him from sacrificing his soul to insanity.

The sound of an approaching conveyance broke the chains of self-inflicted pity, shattering them like thin glass from a beveled mirror.

Hawk forced his attention down the road.

Before long two sturdy horses rounded the tight curve, drawing a slow moving prison cart behind them. Two men sat upon the bench seat. Driver and guard. The latter carried a long rifle.

Patience. You cannot afford a mistake.

Clutching his side, Hawk lowered his head and staggered onto the road.

***

Belle woke with a start. Complete darkness enveloped her surroundings, causing a moment of confusion and panic.

Where am I?

As her mind reconstructed the events of last evening, a surge of relief calmed her racing heart.

In the secret room. The candle must've burned out during the night.

An odd disturbance caught her attention. Gradually the sound grew louder, as though someone pounded upon a distant door.

She drew back the covers and slipped from bed. As she felt her way to the wall panel, the pounding ceased and a muffled voice began calling her name with urgency.

"Miss Lindley, where are you?"

"Here," Belle replied. "Inside the room behind the

122

fireplace." She popped open the panel and peeked through the crack.

From across the room, Morgan Spence stared at her with an expression that would've soured fresh milk. "What the devil are you doing in there?"

"Forgive me for not coming out to politely greet you, but I just this moment awoke, and I'm not yet dressed."

He stomped over to her. "You have a most disturbing habit of not answering my questions."

Belle briefly considered sticking out her tongue but dared not. "What I'm doing in this room is none of your concern."

"It most certainly is." He appeared to take a second to calm his demeanor. "Did I not surrender this entire suite for your comfort and privacy?"

"Yes, you did, and I'm very grateful, but—"

"Along with my bed?"

"What? Oh, yes. The bed. It was most inviting but—"

"Did you by chance sit upon the mattress?"

"Actually I—"

"It's stuffed with the softest goose down. I can tell you with the utmost sincerity that my mind as well as my body regretted not having the pleasure of sleeping on that mattress last evening. Obviously you prefer this dark prison cell...your words, Miss Lindley, not mine...to the luxury of the master suite. Is that not odd?"

"Well, yes, I can see why you'd think—"

"I find your actions extremely confusing," he remarked, posturing about like a noble bull about to charge. "Indeed, most perplexing."

Belle feared if he continued in this state of blustering, he might collapse from lack of oxygen. "If you'll wait in the antechamber, Mister Spence, until I'm dressed, I'd be happy to offer a satisfactory explanation. That is..." She didn't try to hide a smile. "If you will permit me to speak."

His glare lasted several long seconds. Finally he presented a quick bow before turning on his heel and returning to the antechamber.

At the sound of the door closing, Belle stepped into the bedroom. Sunshine and warmth filtered in through lace curtains. She hurried over to the chair in the far corner where she'd placed her dress the night before. "I'm curious," she said as she lifted the borrowed nightshirt over her head. "How did you get inside this room? I distinctly remember locking the door last evening."

"Apparently you've forgotten who I am," he quipped. "Allow me to remind you. I am the master of Canderlay Manor which means I possess the keys to all the rooms. Including the one to my private suite."

"Which, obviously, you used." She stepped into the worn and tattered gray dress, despising the way it looked and felt. "Without my permission, I might add."

"I had no idea I needed your permission and if you had responded when I called to you, I would not have been forced to trespass upon your privacy."

"I wonder, Mister Spence..." Belle stuck her arms through the sleeves and pulled the dress over her bodice and shoulders. "Am I the first female who didn't respond or come running to your side when you called?"

"Hardly." A slight pause before the sarcasm disappeared from the tone of his voice. "I was worried about you, Isabelle."

Worried?

Her fingers trembled as she laced the ties about her bosom.

About me?

It had been far too long since she'd actually heard those words. Tears of self-pity formed, but she brushed them away. "You needn't have worried, Mister Spence."

"Obviously," came the snide retort. Then once again his tone became more civil. "I've brought up your breakfast."

Thoughtful, generous, and handsome.

A deadly combination.

Belle sighed. Whatever the future held, she doubted she could ever forget Morgan Spence. And she must guard her heart to keep this insufferable man from stealing it.

Sadness quickly consumed her. She would soon leave Canderlay, and the very thought of never returning pressed a heaviness into her soul.

Or is it the master of the manor you cannot bear to

leave?

Ridiculous! How could I feel affection for a man I do not know?

Belle combed her fingers through her hair and smoothed the wrinkles from her frock before opening the door and entering the antechamber. "You prepared breakfast?"

With a quirky grin, he shook his head. "I'm afraid I'm rather lost when it comes to the kitchen. Oh, I might recognize a spoon or fork, and possibly a knife, but anything else would be merely speculation on my part."

"You're teasing, are you not?"

"Somewhat." He indicated the tray sitting upon the table in front of the stylish beige sofa. "Samuels prepared the food this morning before he left for Maidstone."

"When do you suppose he will return?"

"A few hours."

"Did you speak to Barlow this morning?"

"No, he didn't accompany the other workers. Do not worry, Isabelle. I intend to see that he's sent to prison for the crimes he committed against you. Now come and sit down. You'll want to eat before the food grows cold."

Belle headed for the sofa. The breakfast tray contained a plate of eggs and bacon, a saucer of soft butter, containers of cream and sugar, and a thick slice of bread. To the side he'd placed a napkin, eating utensils, and a cup matching the china teapot pattern of pink and white floral.

"Three trunks arrived this morning from Margaret."

"For me?"

"Well I highly doubt they were meant for me. I've set them in the corner over by the door."

"How wonderful." Belle quickly forgot all about the food and headed for the trunks, intending to dive in with both hands.

Morgan Spence stepped in front of her. "Breakfast first."

Obediently she sat down on the sofa and picked up the napkin. "I shall have to think of some way to thank Lady Chase for her extraordinary kindness. Is she returning later this morning?"

"I was told she'd be along shortly. And you can thank my sister by getting rid of that horrendous frock you're wearing. It should've been thrown into the fire two decades past." Amusement flashed across his face. A second later his mischievous grin unexpectedly faded. "It's suddenly come to my attention that I must offer you a sincere apology."

"An apology? For what offense?"

"For the incident with the..." He tugged at the stiff collar of his white shirt. "For asking Samuels to burn your..." A half-hearted smile crept into one corner of his mouth. "I'm assuming they were yours, were they not?"

And then the *incident* finally dawned upon Belle.

My pantalettes!

Intense heat rose up her neck and into her face. So hot it could've torched the entire second floor.

What have I done, Heavenly Father? What sin have I committed that I should suffer such humiliation?

Drowning in a rush of sheer embarrassment, she plucked an ounce of dignity from within. "Yes, they were mine."

He had the audacity to grin like a buffoon. "I'm terribly sorry to hear it," he teased. "I had no idea those...things...were still in use. I mean...they didn't appear to be—"

"Are you finished?" Belle snapped. "If so, I should like to inquire as to why my attire concerns you in the least. In fact," she added defensively, "I care not one farthing what you think. This conversation is most inappropriate."

To his credit, Morgan Spence tried to cover his amusement, but at this point his intentions seemed more placating than honorable. "I'd be happy to make restitution, if you like."

Heavenly Father, please save me from this man's merciless ridicule!

Before I do something You would highly disapprove of.

"No need for restitution," she replied sweetly, dodging the urge to hide behind modesty. "I've already received vindication."

His eyes narrowed with suspicion. "Have I been the

victim of a vengeful prank or do you refer to the night we first met?"

Belle set her napkin aside and rose, wishing for just this brief moment that she stood as tall as he and could look him directly in the eye. "Do you recall an *incident* with your pocket watch?" With a sugary smile she added, "Constantly losing or gaining an hour must've been rather annoying."

He stared. "That was your doing?"

"Precisely."

He offered a dismissive shrug. "I see nothing vindictive in a harmless prank. You'll have to do better than that."

"What about the key to your room? Did you ever stop to think that you didn't lose it or misplace it? Did you ever once wonder why the candle you'd just lit seemed to go out whenever you left your bedroom? And did you not release a stream of foul curses when you couldn't find one of your boots?"

"Yes, but I had no idea an intrusive young woman had her ear to the door, spying on me."

"I wasn't spying," she defended. "I was downstairs in the library."

He relented with a sigh. "Very well, Isabelle, we are now on even ground, but I warn you. No more tricks." He moved closer, determination simmering in his eyes. "Or I will be forced to turn you over my knee."

"I rather think you'd enjoy that."

Amusement curved his lips. "And you'd be correct."

A burning sensation began low in Belle's stomach before spreading and reaching lower still. An unsettling urge she had never felt before. She shivered, unsure what had come over her.

After a lengthy pause, he added, "Eat. It would be a shame to perish before receiving your inheritance."

Unnerved and at a loss for words, she sat down again. Lifting the teapot, her hands shook as she poured a cup of tea. She covered her nervousness by blurting out, "I shall definitely put whatever her Grace sent to good use."

"I should hope so. Did you sleep in there?"

She glanced up.

He now stood at the door separating the bedroom and antechamber.

"If you're referring to the secret room, the answer is yes."

"Why?" He faced her. "Did you fear you couldn't trust me?"

"No, not at all. Oh, you might bully me or threaten to put me over your knee, but you've never once given me real cause to distrust your honor."

Briefly his gaze raked over her before returning to her face. "Then why the self-imposed imprisonment?"

"I came to the conclusion that trusting Amos Barlow would not only be foolish, but could become quite fatal." She spooned honey and cream into the cup of tea. "He knows I'm here. I was afraid he would come back. Afraid he'd slip inside the manor and..."

"I should've realized. Forgive me."

Belle sipped the tea. The hot liquid soothed her parched throat. Out of the corner of her eye, she noticed her benefactor had quietly entered his bedroom. Perhaps he needed a clean shirt or stockings. Perhaps he'd forgotten his pocket watch. Deciding it was none of her business, she picked up a fork and attacked the plate of eggs and bacon. Finishing breakfast, she noted Mister Spence still had not returned to the antechamber, and she could no longer pretend disinterest.

What is he doing?

Curious, she stood and walked to the bedroom door. The panel to the secret room stood open. As she neared the fireplace, she could hear him moving about the small room. She glanced inside, but the deep shadows hid him. "What are you searching for?"

"You're blocking the light."

She stepped back. "What are you doing?"

"Exploring," he replied. "Tell me, Isabelle, are there more hidden rooms here at Canderlay?"

"I'm not sure. Perhaps you should ask your father."

"I doubt he could provide an answer as he never mentioned this one."

"I see. Well...Uncle Magnus and I never discovered

any other rooms. If you'll wait until I light a candle, I'll give you a tour of the passageway that leads down to the library and demonstrate how to open the panel."

He reappeared at the small opening. "I accept your offer."

The sound of carriage wheels outside cornered Belle's attention.

"On the other hand, perhaps we should postpone this tour until later." He stepped through the panel and strode over to the window. "It's Margaret and the duke." He turned. "I'll leave you to your rummaging. No doubt Mags will be up shortly to supervise."

She smiled. "I'd like that."

"Have you finished breakfast?" he asked as he walked from the bedroom to the antechamber.

Belle followed him. "Yes. It was delicious. Thank you."

"Thank Samuels." On his way to the door, Mister Spence picked up the breakfast tray then turned, a fond expression softening his gaze. "I believe that man is the finest servant I've ever had the pleasure of employing."

***

"Incredible." The Duke of Chase shook his head as he read Reverend Lindley's journal. "There are several noblemen in Kent who could claim the title of Lord H, but we've no idea the man's age."

"He may not reside in Kent." Morgan took the journal and turned to the beginning. "This first entry is dated February 3, 1800. A week later, Reverend Lindley makes a reference to the fact that Mary B died at the age of fifty. If my calculations are correct, she would've been born in 1750 or possibly 1749. At age fifteen she got with child, so that would put Lord H born in the year 1765 or 66."

"Setting his age around forty and five. Nicely done. That narrows the possibilities, but there's no way to know for certain who this man is. A pity the vicar did not reveal more. What do you intend to do with his journal?"

"Keep it safe until we've positively identified Lord H."

"And afterward?"

"Hand it over to you."

"I see. I'm to present it to the Prince Regent, is that your plan?"

Morgan released a tight breath. "My plan, in fact the only plan that came to mind, was to hand the vicar's journal over to someone whose name and title are above reproach. If that someone is you, Bart, then I offer my congratulations but be warned. Whatever you do with this journal will forever weigh upon your conscience."

"So noted."

"Once Barlow is thrown into prison, I suspect he'll betray the man who hired him quickly enough."

"Of all the blasted misfortune. Barlow was finally to receive what he richly deserved, and what does he do? He fails to show up for the hanging."

"He smelled the roses," Morgan muttered.

"What?"

"Isabelle's soaps."

The duke's brow rose. "Isabelle, is it? You'd best not let Margaret hear that. She'd faint dead away with the sheer impropriety of it."

"Well then...perhaps your sainted wife shouldn't be so childish."

"It's not a matter of maturity, Morgan. Surely you realize this."

"Yes, Bart, I do. Now...can we please return to the subject at hand?"

"Am I preventing you?"

Morgan collected his thoughts. "Miss Lindley despised being cooped up in that small, dark room. I believe she snatched every moment of freedom. After seeing firsthand what she's been forced to endure these last several months, I cannot say I blame her."

"No one could."

"At the risk of exposure, and indeed her own life, she frequently escaped to my suite, searching for a breath of fresh air or to watch the sun rise over the meadow." Morgan favored his friend with a brief glare. "Without my presence."

Bartholomew smiled. "Of course."

"Her rose scent often lingered inside my bedroom. I

discovered only this morning that Barlow had stole inside my room last week."

"In your private suite? What was he doing?"

"Searching for Isabelle...that is, Miss Lindley."

The duke sighed. "He knows she's here."

"And that's precisely why he must be arrested. Today."

At the break in conversation, the sound of a conveyance approaching the manor drew Morgan's attention, and he headed to the drawing room window. "It's Samuels."

"Does the constable accompany him?"

"No."

"Perhaps he'll arrive later."

Morgan hurried from the room. As he reached the foyer, by chance he glanced up to the second floor landing. And the hands of time ground to a halt. He forgot what he'd been doing, forgot whatever he'd been thinking, for next to his sister stood a radiant vision of loveliness dressed in a gown of shimmering deep gold. With auburn hair neatly coifed, Isabelle Lindley held her head high before lowering her gaze and briefly offering him the most dazzling smile.

His breath hitched then escaped his lungs in one long swoosh. At an utter loss for words, he vaguely realized he was staring, but he couldn't take his eyes off this woman. Until something thumped him in the back of the head. With a great deal of annoyance, he redirected his attention.

The duke stood by his side, sheer amusement stamped upon his noble face. "Put your eyes back where they belong, my friend," he whispered. "Unless you wish to tip your hand."

"Tip my hand? What the devil are you talking about?"

"A fool disregards instruction pertaining to something he's never before experienced while a wise man listens intently. Which are you?"

"Bart, did you rattle the brandy bottles this morning?"

"Gentlemen," Margaret announced, regaining their attention. "May I present to you...Miss Isabelle Lindley. Niece to that well-known and wealthy Irishman, Magnus Lindley."

A combination of anger and fire fused up Morgan's

spine, creating a knot of tension at the base of his neck. "So that's your logic, is it, Mags? Your solution to the question of this young woman's future?" He had no idea why a sudden foul mood had cast a shadow over his commonsense. "You intend to foist her upon the first nobleman who fancies her."

Isabelle's eyes widened with shock.

"Foist?" Margaret repeated in a sharp tone. "Morgan, precisely what are you accusing me of?"

"Is it not obvious, madam?" He eyed Isabelle, whose injured expression instantly hardened. "Why is she dressed like a debutante?"

"If you have to ask, dear brother, you clearly have no idea what goes on inside a young woman's head."

The duke's hearty laugh caught everyone off-guard.

"You find the situation entertaining?" Morgan snapped.

"Immensely," Bartholomew replied.

The distinct sound of a door closing behind them cut through the banter.

Morgan turned.

Jasper Samuels stood just inside the foyer, his hat in his hands.

"Where's the constable?" he asked the servant.

"Preoccupied with an urgent matter, sir."

"What's more urgent than putting Barlow in prison where he belongs?"

"Searching for the person who ended his life."

Morgan approached him. "What are you saying?"

"You heard correctly, sir. Amos Barlow is quite dead."

Chapter Ten

At the unexpected news of Barlow's death, Belle grabbed the balustrade for support, a mixture of horror and immense relief simultaneously washing over her.

Morgan Spence faced her, and their eyes locked briefly before he once again shifted his attention back to Samuels. "What happened?"

"Murdered, sir. Early this morning."

"A fair and just punishment," surmised the duke.

"Bartholomew," Lady Chase scolded, her clipped tone a polite yet stern reminder to guard his tongue. She placed an arm around Belle's waist. "Perhaps it would be wise if you gentlemen continued this conversation without the presence of Miss Lindley or me."

"I beg your pardon, my lady, but I'd rather stay." Recovering from the shock, Belle descended the rest of the stairs, joining the men in the foyer, her interest attached to the caretaker. "Unless Mister Samuels thinks Mister Barlow's death does not concern me."

"Well, look at you, Miss Isabelle," he declared, but his pleasant tone seemed at odds with the concern in his expression.

"You cannot fool me, Mister Samuels. You are hedging. I should like to hear proof that Barlow's death is unrelated to my present situation."

"I'm not sure he can prove anything," Morgan Spence stated. "Not with any certainty."

"Precisely why I wish to hear the details."

The old man cleared his throat. "Miss Isabelle, you've nothing to do with Barlow's misfortune."

"The man's numerous misdeeds likely laid the foundation for his demise," the duke remarked.

"Constable Foley drew the same conclusion, your Grace," the caretaker stated. "He believes Barlow was the victim of a robbery. A highwayman on the prowl for wealthy nobles."

"You spoke to the constable?" Mister Spence inquired.

"I did, sir. He said to tell you to expect his visit this evening."

"Did you explain why I asked to see him?"

"No, sir. I thought I'd leave that up to you."

"Very good. Thank you, Samuels."

"Yes, sir. I shall be in the kitchen if anyone has need of me."

Tears welled in Belle's eyes, and she couldn't prevent them from escaping. "That's the end of it then. With Barlow's death, we've lost the opportunity to discover the identity of Lord H." A knot of self-pity temporarily closed her throat. "Perhaps I will discover the man's name just before he offs me himself."

"You'll be safe at Canderlay," Mister Spence vowed. "You have my word."

"And mine, Miss Lindley," Chase declared.

"I shall be your champion as well," his wife insisted. "As I've decided to remain at Canderlay until this dreadful situation is resolved."

Emotion swelled inside Belle's heart. "That's kind of you, my lady, and I truly appreciate each of you for making me aware I've friends I can turn to."

"Well of course you have," Lady Chase stated.

"Certainly," her husband agreed.

"And I value your friendship more than words can express, but perhaps..." Belle glanced at Mister Spence. "Perhaps it might be unfair to press my kind benefactor for more."

He shrugged. "To this point, Miss Lindley, you've asked for very little."

"That may be true, but I fear I will quickly become a burden."

"No more of a burden than before," he teased.

"Morgan Sebastian Spence," his sister admonished. "Must you constantly play the troublemaking scoundrel?"

She pinched his arm before turning a warm smile upon Belle. "At Dragon's Breath, there was an old woman with a special gift for seeing the future. She taught me a great deal. The most important was to never lose faith. Keep a light heart, a true heart, and the Good Father will make certain you weather each and every storm."

"Words my father would've appreciated."

"Then I daresay Reverend Lindley would've gotten along famously with Old Edwina." Lady Chase clasped Belle's hands. "You are not alone, dear girl. If you forget everything else, you must remember that."

"I will, my lady."

"Margaret," her brother said with a frown. "If you stay, you'll have to do so without the use of servants."

"Or adequate brandy," the duke quipped.

"You will survive, Bartholomew," the duchess insisted. "And as always, Morgan, you exaggerate. My Hillary does not believe in ghosts or spirits. Besides, this manor house no longer lies abandoned and therefore has lost the power to play upon the locals' imaginations. Why, I wager I could staff this house and grounds within three days."

"I've no doubt, Mags."

Her ladyship raised a brow. "Then I've your permission?"

"No."

"What? Why on earth not?"

"We've discussed this matter before. Did I not give you a valid enough reason then?"

"Yes, and I repeat...you are overtaxing Mister Samuels."

"I understand why you'd draw such a conclusion, but that's clearly not the situation."

"In your opinion, but I should think, Morgan, you'd be overjoyed at the opportunity to acquire additional servants."

"Under normal circumstances, but let me explain once again. Allowing strangers to roam about Canderlay would only complicate matters more than they already are."

"My Hilary is not a stranger."

"My love," the duke interjected. "I believe your brother is reminding you that servants often engage in a healthy dose of gossip with their meals. Even your sainted Hilary. And any speculation or reference to Miss Lindley's presence at Canderlay, however insignificant, might very well endanger her life."

Her ladyship sighed. "A logical assumption, I suppose, but I believe you gentlemen have missed an important consideration. If Mister Barlow suspected Miss Lindley is here, would he not have informed his employer?"

Dread crept into Belle's heart. She hadn't even considered this.

"Therefore," Lady Chase concluded, "staffing Canderlay with an adequate number of servants would not only be prudent, it would likely discourage would-be murderers."

"Mags, you failed to take into account that servants' loyalties can be easily bought. Especially recent hires. I would feel more comfortable knowing with a certainty that I can trust the people I'm surrounded by." He glanced briefly at Belle. "Margaret, if you insist on staying, I'll not object. Unless, of course, your husband does."

The duke shook his head.

"Splendid." Mister Spence turned his smile upon Belle. "Does this please you, Miss Lindley? Put your mind at ease?"

"Yes. Tremendously."

The earlier dread that had threatened to consume Belle's thoughts began to evaporate like mist escaping a warm sun. She longed for the companionship of another female, and she truly admired Lady Chase, but something unexpected now lifted her spirits.

The subtle yet appreciative glance Morgan Spence tossed her way.

He obviously approved of her fancy gown and polished looks.

Why, then, had he been so angry a few seconds later?

***

How dare she!
Morgan waited until Isabelle and Margaret had

climbed the stairs to the second floor and disappeared down the corridor before he turned his anger upon the duke. "How bloody thoughtless of your wife to expose that innocent young woman to such debauchery."

"Debauchery? Morgan, have you lost your ability to reason?"

"Isabelle is different from most young ladies her age. She's not a prize to be dangled at will."

"I do believe you're acting like a jealous lover."

"Ridiculous, Bart. I'm on to Mags. I know exactly what she's up to."

"Oh? And what would that be?"

"She's set her mind on finding a wealthy husband for the vicar's daughter."

"And what, pray tell, is so immoral with this?"

Morgan opened his mouth to offer a rebuttal, but he could think of no valid argument. Thankfully he didn't have to for a familiar shadow standing in the corridor beyond the foyer snagged his interest. "Since you're not one to eavesdrop, Samuels, I must conclude you've a pressing matter to discuss."

The servant inched forward. With a brief glance up the stairs, he nodded once. "On my way to Maidstone this morning, I happened upon a gruesome discovery." He lowered his voice even more. "A prison cart with two men lying on the ground beside it and one prisoner in back. All three dead."

"Did you inform the constable?"

"No need, sir. He and his men had arrived before me. I didn't think the ladies should hear this sort of news, and I had no wish to alarm Miss Isabelle."

"I agree, but why would she be alarmed?"

"The prisoner was Amos Barlow, sir, but his death wasn't the result of a simple robbery as I led you to believe."

"You'd better begin this tale again, Samuels. From the beginning."

The old man nodded. "I recently learned that after he left Canderlay last Friday, Barlow was arrested for murder."

"Bloody hell," Bartholomew declared before recognizing he should lower his tone as well. "Has there been a sudden demand for that vagabond's services?"

"That's the reason he didn't return to work yesterday and today," Morgan remarked. "He'd been arrested."

"Yes, sir."

"Whom did he murder?"

"A foreigner," Samuels replied. "Got into a brawl at a local tavern called the King's Men. I overheard the constable discussing how he'd been held at the tavern for several hours until the prison cart arrived. This morning he was being driven to Newgate to await trial when someone stopped the cart on a deserted stretch of road, shooting both the driver and armed guard."

Morgan shook his head. "No experienced highwayman would rob a prison cart and expect to acquire enough coin for his trouble."

"Precisely, sir. Oh, the money those men had been allotted for the trip to London was indeed stolen and their firearms taken as well. Even their inexpensive pocket watches, but robbery was not the thief's true purpose."

"Unless the highwayman was of the incompetent variety," Bartholomew offered. "Otherwise one might assume Barlow was shot to eliminate a potential witness."

"He wasn't shot, your Grace. Barlow was purposely released from that cart before someone slit his throat."

"I see your cause for concern, Samuels," the duke said. "If the motive was robbery, it would've made more sense to leave Barlow locked inside the cart. Why release him if the intent was to simply eliminate a potential witness?"

Morgan paced toward the main door then turned abruptly. "Whoever committed these murders wanted something more than Barlow's death. He likely wanted information."

"You suspect Lord H obtained the whereabouts of Miss Lindley then murdered the only man who could betray him?" Bartholomew inquired.

"That's exactly what I think."

Instinctively Morgan glanced up the stairs. The threat to Isabelle's life was now far greater than before, and he wasn't sure what to do about it. Samuels must be worried as well for he'd purposely lied to her. Isabelle's situation was without a doubt connected to Barlow's death.

"We must protect her, sir. She has no one else to look out for her."

"Yes, Samuels. I'm fully aware of that."

"I can supply armed men from Chase," the duke offered. "Men who can patrol the grounds after dark."

"An excellent idea, Bart, but allow me several hours first."

"Why? Morgan, where are you off to?"

"To visit the King's Men Tavern," he replied over his shoulder.

***

Hawk glanced at his hands...at his fingers streaked with the dried blood. The blood of his worthless half-brother.

He had never before killed anyone. It had crossed his mind once or twice but until this morning, he had avoided it.

Hawk reined in his horse next to a slow-moving stream. Dismounting, he removed his overcoat before wading in. The coolness of the shallow water refreshed him, and he knelt in the middle of the brook to wash his face and hands.

So much blood.

He hadn't considered that.

Released from the prison cart, Amos Barlow's expression had been one of genuine relief.

"Knew you'd come," he'd said with an ugly smirk.

But then he had stupidly supplied the very guarantee that kept him safe.

Where to find Isabelle Lindley.

Barlow probably expected he would soon be on his way out of England and therefore had little to fear. Having no idea what Hawk was capable of, he had turned his back. As Barlow began taunting the dead men, boasting that he planned to steal their boots as well as their coin, Hawk had drawn his blade and slipped behind his brother.

It took little effort to slit the man's throat.

He'd felt no emotion as he waited for Barlow to draw his last breath.

Waited for the disbelief in his eyes to become a blank stare.

I've become what I feared most.

More evil than my father.

Hawk stood. Retrieving the overcoat, he removed all the items Barlow had attempted to steal. Two firearms, pocket watches, and a small knife. He tossed these into the middle of the stream but kept the pouch of coins. He tried to remove the blood from his overcoat, but the stains refused to disappear as easily as they had from his hands. At length he gave up and stuffed the overcoat beneath dense underbrush.

Tying the bag of money to his saddle and mounting his horse, Hawk turned the animal north. Though slightly different now, he recognized this particular area of Kent. In younger years, he'd often explored these woods during visits to Westwood. Uncle Miles had been kind to Hawk. But then...the old gent likely never knew the truth.

Why did I not slit Reverend Lindley's throat when I had the chance?

It would've removed a decade of fear.

But Hawk understood clearly why he'd allowed the vicar to live.

The threat of those bloody journals!

Within a half hour, he came upon a familiar establishment. Leaving his horse at the edge of the forest, Hawk walked up to the old white-washed church. It hadn't changed much in ten years. Perhaps a bit more weathered.

Drawing a deep breath, he pushed open the door and slipped inside.

Draped in semi-darkness, he half expected Reverend Lindley's ghost to jump out from one of the pews to accuse him of every sin he'd ever committed. Instead, a glaring silence hummed in his ear.

Hawk proceeded down the center aisle until he reached the highly polished pulpit where the strong smell of beeswax permeated the air. He tossed the money bag onto the wooden platform and turned. Before he'd completed two steps, he noted the sound of a conveyance drawing to a halt outside. He hurried around the pulpit and ducked inside the vicar's office, leaving the door slightly ajar. A few minutes

140

later, voices broke the silence inside the church.

"You mustn't give a man too much liberty, Jenny, or 'e'll quickly turn it against you."

"Nothin' I can do about it, Mrs. Kemp. I got five children to feed."

"With anot'er on the way. Lord, girl, you're a saint. If my 'enry ever tried to plow another wench's field, I'd cut off 'is man'ood and feed it to the pigs. Course..." A soft snort. "E's never been w'at you'd call overly endowed, so I daresay I'd nary miss it."

Course laughter echoed around the room.

"I could do worse than Freddie, I suppose. 'E may suffer a roamin' eye, but 'e works 'ard, and most evenin's 'e's home afore my feet grow cold."

"I'll say a prayer for you, Jenny girl."

"From your lips to God's ears."

Hawk peeked through the crack in the door. Nothing but shadows.

"New vicar wants cleanliness above all. Says 'e won't tolerate untidiness. I says, 'tis clean and tidy, sir.' 'E says, 'Too much dust. 'E can smell it. I says to myself...'is nose is long enough 'e can smell a cooked goose in the next county."

"Go on. Surely you didn't."

"Oh, but I did, dearie."

A low grunt followed by a long pause.

"I've fond memories 'ere, Mrs. Kemp, truly I 'ave, but now...seems far too sad for my likes."

"W'at do you mean?"

"I'm referrin' to w'at befell the vicar and 'is daughter. All that misfortune. I've often wondered if it were a sign of God's disapproval."

"Close your lips, Jenny. Reverend Lindley was a good man, and 'e enjoyed givin' to folks in need. W'at 'appened to 'im 'appens to all of us."

"Yes, but 'e suffered more."

"More 'an me and 'enry? No, dearie. The vicar may've suffered 'is portion of troubles, but 'e was by no means cursed."

Hawk almost smiled. He'd cursed the man often.

"Now Jasper Samuels...'e's a man livin' under a curse,

'is young wife and infant daug'ter taken by the fever all those years ago. Nearly drank 'imself to an early grave afore the vicar took 'im in."

"Poor devil. 'E found Reverend Lindley, did 'e not?"

"Yes. In 'is office, slumped over in 'is chair."

"And later on, the vicar's daug'ter lost in a 'orrible fire."

"Truly dreadful, it was. Broke my 'eart." A heavy sigh. "Nary a bone of Miss Isabelle's was ever found."

Because the chit's alive, you foolish old cow!

Alive. For the moment.

Hawk eyed the open window across the room.

"New vicar's a bit jittery. Say's 'e'd like the furniture replaced. 'E's a waste of man'ood, if you ask me. I'd wager 'e fears Reverend Lindley's spirit still resides 'ere." A long pause. "I can feel it even now."

"The good reverend's spirit? Bloody 'ell, you're givin' me the willies."

Hawk decided it was time to make his escape and crept to the window.

"Tell me, Mrs. Kemp. Is it true?"

"W'at, dearie?"

"You discovered one of Reverend Lindley's journals?"

Hawk hesitated, his hand braced against the window sill.

"I did indeed."

"Did you read it?"

A long moment passed as Hawk held his breath.

"'Ow could I?" came the response. "I never learned to read."

"A pity. I might've discovered if my Freddie's been pokin' the comely Widow Ames or the blacksmith's big-bosomed wife."

"Poor Jenny. Reverend Lindley may've understood the sinful nature of men, your man in particular, but I doubt he ever wrote of it."

"Well...w'at did he write of?"

"I'm sure I've no idea, and it's none of my concern."

"W'at'd you do with it?"

"The journal?"

Hawk swallowed, his throat suddenly parched.

"I gave it to Samuels."

"W'at'd he want with it?"

"I didn't ask."

"Does he read?"

"Don't know. Don't care."

Oh, but I do, madam.

"Bless the saints, Mrs. Kemp!"

"W'at is it? You spotted a mouse?"

A sharp intake of breath. "It's a bag of coins."

"An offerin' to lift a 'eavy burden."

If only it were that easy.

"Leave it be, Jenny. We'd best finish our work afore noon."

While the women went about their chores, Hawk crawled out the window and slid to the ground, heading into the forest. Reaching his horse, he took a second to gather his thoughts.

Samuels had likely taken possession of the one journal Hawk feared the most. The one book he'd fervently prayed had been destroyed in the fire.

Damn his bloody misfortune!

And damn the vicar as well!

What now?

How do I get my hands on that journal without risking my identity?

Hawk ran a hand over his eyes, his head pounding and his pulse racing. He hadn't slept solidly in three months. Now that he knew precisely where Isabelle Lindley was hiding, he'd bide his time. Chose his moment carefully.

Was the journal still in her possession?

More than likely.

What about Samuels?

It wasn't as though Hawk's soul teetered between a heavenly realm and fiery hell, waiting for one good or bad deed to tip the scales. No, if he truly had a soul, it was far past the point of redemption and could not be salvaged.

Not after this morning.

Drawing a deep breath, Hawk closed his eyes.

The old man must die as well.

Chapter Eleven

"Well, your Grace?" Belle held her breath. "What do you think of this one?"

"I simply adore it more than ever," Lady Chase replied. "I cannot tell you, Isabelle, all the compliments I received when I wore this gown to a Harvest Ball two seasons past, but now that I see it on you..." She shook her head and sighed. "I daresay the deep forest green is much richer. Perhaps because of your lovely auburn hair. Let's see now...turn about."

"Turn?"

"As if you were dancing in the arms of a handsome gentleman."

Belle secured the hem of her gown and twirled about the antechamber. Halfway through the third spin, she tripped, lost her footing and almost tumbled backward over the sofa.

"Careful, dear girl," the duchess warned with a chuckle. "We cannot have you all bruised and battered before your first ball."

"I'm the daughter of a vicar, my lady, and someone is trying their best to murder me. Although I appreciate your generosity in providing this fancy gown, you must realize I've little use for such finery as I doubt my future will include attending balls or parties."

"You're not allowed to become a perpetual skeptic, my dear. You're far too young. Remember, a lady must be prepared for every occasion. One never knows for certain what the Good Father has in mind."

"Unless one was raised in the presence of a gifted seer. Tell me more about Edwina, your Grace."

"Oh, she was simply amazing. She would often send

for me or my brothers, claiming she'd had a dream or some sort of vision. Do you know..." She grabbed Belle's hand, and they sat upon the sofa. "When I was ten and three, Edwina described to perfection the man I would marry."

"She saw the duke in a vision?"

"Incredible, is it not? She said and I quote, 'He's got black eyes, Mags, but dinna ye fear, child. He's a good and honorable mon, and yer heart will flutter from the moment he speaks.' She was right, Isabelle. And my heart flutters still."

Belle sighed. "Every woman should be as fortunate."

"I may not be as clever as Edwina, and I may not possess her gift of seeing the future, but I believe that one day you will find a true and worthy love." She offered a reassuring smile. "Perhaps even sooner than you think."

"I'm not as confident as you, Lady Chase. I'm afraid I have nothing of value to offer."

"But that's simply not true."

"Sadly it is. I've no funds to provide a dowry."

"Isabelle, you possess so much more than wealth. A gentleman would have to be blind not to see your exceptional qualities."

"Exceptional?"

"Well, yes. You've a kind and tender heart. You're clever, loyal, and honest. Not to mention your delicate beauty. Why, in that gown...I daresay if you were at a ball this very instant, your face and slender figure would garner attention from every male who draws breath."

"The gown is truly worthy of high praise, your Grace, but..." Belle slid her hand across the satiny material. "It belongs to a duchess. Not a vicar's daughter...a woman who will never achieve anything higher than the state of impoverishment. As for my invaluable traits..." She stood. "I've learned that clever females are often avoided while loyalty takes years to recognize and appreciate. And although I try my very best to be truthful, such honesty generally annoys most gentlemen."

"Yes, but those swine are not for you, dear girl." Lady Chase stood as well. "My mother taught me three valuable lessons. How to ride a horse without a saddle and how to fire a weapon with deadly precision."

"And the third?"

"To guard my heart. I've found that most gentlemen can be compared to seashells lying partially exposed in the sand. At first glance, they pique your interest but when you dig a bit deeper, you realize they are not worthy of your interest. Sift through the sand and seashells, Isabelle. Find your precious pearl."

"As I said before, my lady, I doubt I'll have the opportunity."

"But of course you will. You're going to be a guest at my Harvest Ball. You must promise to be discerning though. A respectable lady mustn't be impulsive when dealing with potential suitors. She must be selective, elusive, and stand apart from the others. What she says and what she does should be well thought out. My mother put it this way. A lady should survey the dance floor before stepping onto it."

Is it hopeless to dream?

No, but it might be pointless. And eventually become unbearable.

"Very well," Belle declared half-heartedly. "If the opportunity arises to entertain suitors, I promise to be discerning."

Flashing a smile of approval, her ladyship headed across the room. On the way to the adjoining bedroom, she noticed the slightly mismatched wallpaper and paused. "How odd yet...it fits Morgan's character." With a dismissive shake of her head, she picked up a bundle of gowns from the chair. "Come, Isabelle. We must hang these in the wardrobe or they'll become horribly wrinkled."

Belle followed obediently and by chance caught sight of her own reflection in the floor length mirror.

What would it be like to twirl around a dance floor?

Hopefully she wouldn't stumble over her own two feet. Would her handsome partner whisper words of endearment? Speak of his profound love? Would her heart race as he gazed into her eyes?

She sighed.

Did love truly hold the power to change the beat of a woman's heart?

Belle's pulse rarely stayed the same while in the presence of Morgan Spence, but that could be explained. He was a constant source of irritation.

She hurried into the bedroom then over to the tall oak bureau where Lady Chase was busy putting away undergarments and stockings. "My lady, I heard you speak of your brothers earlier. You've four?"

"Yes. Two older and two younger."

"I'm curious...did Edwina describe their future wives?"

Her ladyship paused, her slender fingers entwined in the lacings of a sheer bodice. "Yes, she did. Let's see now. Alexander, who was born after me, was to marry an English widow with two daughters, which he did last year, I'm pleased to say. My brother Jules, born before me, will be married to Dragon's Breath Castle until he reaches the age of forty, at which time he will meet and marry a woman of mysterious origin."

"Mysterious origin? What do think Edwina meant?"

"We haven't figured that out yet, and Jules has another twelve years before he crosses paths with that particular lady. As for Cameron, the youngest brother, he'll wed a high-strung lowlander's daughter and be blissfully thrown into chaos. A condition he seems drawn to, and I suspect secretly craves."

Belle giggled.

"Oh, you wouldn't laugh, Isabelle, if you knew Cam as I do."

"Mischievous, is he?"

"Not exactly. That description is almost honorable and is never used when describing Cameron." Her Grace sighed. "Think of the loudest, most annoying child you've ever had the displeasure of being in the same room with. Now give that child a tantrum."

"He couldn't be that dreadful."

"I suspect the word melodramatic is engraved upon Cam's calling card."

Belle drew a nervous breath. "What about your oldest brother?"

"Morgan?"

"Yes. What sort of wife did Edwina predict for him?"

"Oh..."

Belle's heart thumped painfully as she waited for a reply.

Lady Chase closed a bureau drawer before opening another. "It's really rather strange that you should mention Morgan's future."

And most improper.

Belle blushed. "I...I'm sorry, my lady. I shouldn't have been so forward."

The duchess stared at her for several seconds. "Goodness, Isabelle. I didn't mean that the way it sounded. I simply meant that Morgan never trusted in Edwina's predictions. He's always plotted his own course and knew exactly what he wanted. Oh, she tried to tell him on several occasions, tried to warn him about certain things, but Morgan is stubborn. He refused to listen."

"Tried to warn him? About what?"

"I'm not sure, and Morgan would never say, but I overheard Edwina tell Mother once that her oldest son must allow his heart to choose his direction. If not, he'd regret it for the remainder of his life."

"Was she speaking of a wife or of Canderlay?"

"I suppose it could've been either. No one understood with complete certainly everything Edwina predicted. She could be purposely vague at times."

"I see." Disappointment beat a path to Belle's soul, but she quickly pushed aside any frustrations. "What of your father, my lady? Did he approve of the purchase of his former residence as well as the plan to restore it?"

"I actually believe he was quite proud of Morgan." Lady Chase paused and with a faint smile added, "I had no idea you knew of my father's connection to this estate."

"Mister Samuels told me," Belle confessed. "His father was once the caretaker here."

"Oh, yes. Bartholomew mentioned it."

After they'd stored the rest of the clothing and unmentionables inside the bureau and adjacent chest, Belle sat down on the bed. "Lady Chase, what's Dragon's Breath like?"

"Like nothing you could ever imagine, Isabelle." She wandered to the window and casually pushed aside the sheer drapes. "Impressive. Formidable. Daunting. Imposing." She turned, traces of a smile still visible. "And unbearably cold in the winter. From the first moment my mother glimpsed that black castle, she swears she fell in love with it. Even though Father is English, he grew fond of it as well."

"It sounds fascinating."

"Yes, I imagine it is in some fashion."

"But...you've come to care less for it?"

"Oh, it's not that I've little or no sentiment for the place, it's just...well, as a child, it was a bit too isolated. Perhaps one day you'll visit and judge for yourself."

"I would enjoy that," Belle said, but she doubted she'd ever be so fortunate.

Her ladyship strolled to the center of the room and paused at the foot of the bed. "The Macgregor Clan is fiercely loyal, and their dislike of strangers is well documented, but I have never known a people with more generous hearts."

"To be surrounded by the love of one's clan..." The pain of too many years of loneliness and despair stole into Belle's thoughts. She quickly swallowed around the lump forming inside her throat. "I expect it would be most comforting."

The duchess did not respond as her attention had become fixated on the wall next to the fireplace.

Belle could almost read the woman's thoughts. "Would you care to see the secret room, your Grace?"

She turned. "If it would not impose upon your privacy."

Belle arose from the bed. "Not at all."

"Morgan told me you continue to sleep there."

"Yes. It provides a feeling of security."

"I understand."

Belle walked to the fireplace and popped open the panel. Stepping inside the semi-darkness of the secret room, she headed straight to the oil lamp Samuels had recently given her and turned up the wick.

Lady Chase followed. After surveying the dank and dismal surroundings, her gaze settled upon the small end table and uncomfortable cot set against one wall before going on to an old trunk occupying space in one corner. At length her attention returned to Belle, her eyes moist with emotion. "This is incredibly suffocating, my dear. How have you managed to tolerate such misery?"

"With a great deal of prayer, my lady."

"I would imagine so." She pointed to the stone steps disappearing downward into darkness. "Where do these lead?"

"A panel in the library," Belle replied. "Would you care to descend?"

"No, I believe I've seen quite enough." Retreating to the bedroom, Lady Chase marched to the door then suddenly halted. "It just occurred to me, Isabelle. Did Morgan inform you that he and Bartholomew determined the age of Lord H to be forty and five?"

"No, he did not, but how did they accomplish this?"

"Through clues in your father's journal."

"Oh, I see. How very clever."

"You know, for some reason I'd considered Lord H ancient." Lady Chase's expression suddenly changed, and her eyes grew wide with excitement. "Dear me, Isabelle. I believe I might've stumbled across a way to figure out who this ghastly nobleman is."

Belle's hopes soared but before she could inquire as to what her ladyship meant, a knock sounded outside the antechamber door, and the duchess rushed away to answer it.

Outside in the corridor stood Samuels. "Forgive me for disturbing you, your Grace," he said in his normal monotone voice. "I've prepared a light lunch, and his Grace requests you and Miss Isabelle's presence in the dining room."

"I had no idea of the hour. Thank you, Mister Samuels. You may tell my husband we'll be down shortly."

The caretaker bowed as low as his age would permit before turning on his heel and retreating back down the corridor.

Lady Chase closed the door then turned, her eyes alight with mischief. "Do you trust me, Isabelle?"

"Of course, my lady. Why do you ask?"

"Why? Because, dear girl, you have an inclination to speak the truth. An honorable trait and one I admire, but I'd rather Morgan and my husband remain unaware of our plans until it is much too late to oppose them."

Belle frowned. "I'm not sure I understand. What plans?"

The duchess laughed. "It matters not. Be dressed and ready to travel by nine o'clock tomorrow morning. I'll explain everything when we're safely inside the carriage."

***

Half an hour past noon, Morgan arrived in Maidstone. Leaving an unusually docile Ares in the capable hands of a stable lad, he crossed the street to the two-story, red brick establishment called the King's Men. Inside, the place looked and smelled like any other English tavern. Dim, smoke-tinged main room with a long bar at the far end. Two small windows, one on each side of the front door. Oil lamps positioned throughout. Several patrons sitting at square wooden tables, their tin cups never far from their lips.

A barmaid strutted up, her dark eyes measuring the cut of his clothes with a well-honed expertise. "You lookin' for a spot of ale, milord?" She cocked her head to the side, and a strand of long black hair slid over one bare shoulder. "Or a bit of sport?"

Morgan scrutinized her the same way she'd studied him. Though not beautiful in the traditional sense, her face fairly glowed with the shine of youth.

"Sorry, love," he replied. "I do not engage in, nor approve of, the popular sport of bedding young girls."

Her smile withered. "I'm ten and seven years, milord. 'Ardly a child." She leaned close. "But an expert at pleasin' 'andsome gents such as yourself."

His gaze drifted to the peaks of her small breasts, straining against a tight-fitting bodice.

Inviting.

Seductive.

"Yes, I'm certain you're rather gifted, miss..?"

"Regina, milord, but most folk call me Regi."

Morgan thought to inform her he wasn't a nobleman but decided against it. "While I appreciate your generous offer, Regi, I'm afraid I must decline."

"A pity," she remarked, her tone suddenly indifferent. "Will your lordship be requirin' a pint of ale? 'Ow about a plate of beef stew?"

"Ale will do, thank you. I'll take it over at that table in the corner. Tell me..." Morgan withdrew two shilling from his pocket. "Who is the proprietor of this fine establishment?"

She eyed him suspiciously. "Mister Browder."

"Is he in residence?"

After a slight hesitation, she nodded.

Morgan reached for her hand and then placed the coins squarely into her palm. "Do you suppose you could fetch him for me?"

Her smile returned. "I'll see to, milord."

The way her rounded hips sashayed as she walked away would've normally provoked a painful stirring from his manhood. He had played this provocative game before and thoroughly enjoyed it, but Regina seemed far too young to be peddling her feminine wares at the King's Men.

He walked over to the table in the corner. As he sat down, he thought of Mary B. A girl of fifteen who had tried to make an honest living. Had she freely given herself to the master of the manor? Or had Lord H's father simply taken what he desired without any thought to the consequences? Reverend Lindley had sympathized with Mary, and he clearly feared Lord H. Considering what his lordship had tried to do to Isabelle, the vicar's fears were justified.

Several minutes passed before the barmaid emerged from one of the back rooms followed by a short man around middle age. She halted, speaking a few words to him before pointing in Morgan's direction.

As the man approached, Morgan appraised him. Thin brown hair balding at the forehead. Short turned-up nose and plump cheeks. Round wire spectacles that made his eyes appear overly large, like those of an owl.

"Gilbert Browder, milord." Mild concern shadowed the man's expression, and his tone betrayed a certain reluctance. "You wished to speak with me?"

"How do you do, Mister Browder, I'm..." Morgan hesitated, suddenly aware he might need to ensure the proprietor's cooperation. "I'm Bartholomew, Duke of Chase."

Browder's eyes widened before his mouth dropped open. "Your Grace, I...well," he stuttered. "I'm delighted you've chosen to honor this establishment with a visit. Pray tell, what can I do for you?"

"Sit down, will you?"

"Oh, yes. Certainly." Browder's head snapped around. "Regi, hurry up with his Grace's ale!"

"Keep your trousers on, luv," she retorted from the bar. Swinging around with two pints of ale in her hands, she carried them to Morgan's table. "Give me a w'istle if you grow thirsty, your Grace."

"I will," Morgan replied, wondering if this little charade would eventually cost him more than he was prepared to pay. After all, was it not a crime to impersonate a nobleman? Fortunately Bart would never lower his high standards by entering such an establishment. As the barmaid returned to her duties, Morgan shifted his attention again to the proprietor. "Mister Browder..."

Careful. Suspicion can restrain a man's tongue.

"I'd like to speak with you regarding my wife's brother. You see, he recently purchased Canderlay Manor and—"

"Canderlay? I've been told the old estate acquired a new master."

"Yes. His name is Morgan Spence."

"Wife's brother, is he? Well, he must be a fine fellow."

Morgan grinned. "I believe so." He drank a hearty portion of ale before setting it down. "A pity Mister Spence could acquire no workers from Maidstone. Can you believe he had to send his overseer to London?"

"I heard. A bloody shame, your Grace. Everyone knows Maidstone workers are far and above those idlers in London."

"Agreed. As for domestic help..." Morgan made a disparaging gesture with his hands. "Unfortunately he's found no servants to work the manor."

"Maidstone women don't care none for Canderlay," Browder stated in a flat tone. "Simpleminded females, the lot of 'em, afraid spirits roam that place. Some of the men believe it as well. Not me." He emptied his pint in four gulps then expelled a loud burp. "I'm a bit more educated."

Morgan almost laughed. "I can see that," he quipped. "Trust me, Browder, there are no ghosts or spirits at Canderlay. I've visited there on several occasions. In fact, my wife and I are staying in one of the guest rooms at present."

"Do tell, your Grace."

"It's true."

"I'll pass that along. Might help your lady's brother with future inquiries regarding domestic help."

"Precisely why I came to you," Morgan declared, hoping he'd erased all amusement from his tone. "Yes, Mister Browder, you are quite the clever fellow. I knew you'd be able to help."

The proprietor beamed, his smile large and wide. "Happy to be of service, your Grace."

"There is another matter though."

"Oh?"

"Well, I'm not one to gossip, you see, but..." Morgan hesitated slightly as he toyed with the pint of ale. "I've come across a concern worthy of mentioning, and I'd like to get your opinion."

"Of course, your Grace. Whatever I can do."

Morgan leaned his arms on the table and said low, "Mister Spence hired a man of questionable character recently. A man I suspect might be a thief."

"Do tell."

"His name is Amos Barlow."

Browder nodded. "I know of him. Can't say if he's a thief or not, but I wouldn't waste good coin on the fellow."

"Precisely my thoughts, but how do I persuade my brother-in-law to listen to such sage advice?"

"I wouldn't worry none about that, your Grace. Barlow's been arrested for murder. He's likely on his way to Newgate as we speak."

"Murder?" Morgan pretended shock. "Whom did he off?"

"A Scotsman. I was minding my own business behind the bar over there when the bloke was knifed. I ordered Barlow locked inside my wine cellar until the prison cart arrived."

"How did he defend his actions?"

"With curses and foul language, your Grace. The man's not normal, if you ask me. Always ranting about this or that. Giving folks the evil eye."

"The devil, you say. Does he have any friends or family?"

"Friends?" Browder shook his head. "As for family, Barlow was born on the wrong side of the blanket. Never knew his papa, but his mum came from a family of tenant farmers on the outskirts of town. Mary gained employment in a fine house, she did."

Mary?

Mary B...Mary Barlow.

Morgan's interest doubled. "What house?"

"How's that, your Grace?"

"Do you recall the family who offered Mary employment?"

"That would've been years before I was born. All I know is one day she found herself surrounded by unfortunate circumstances and moved to the streets of London. At least that's the story she told."

"When did she return to Maidstone?"

"Must've been eight years ago or longer."

"Mary B," Morgan muttered.

"Aye, that's what we called her."

Lord H and Amos Barlow were brothers!

"Tell me, Browder. Did Mary produce other children?"

"She never said."

Disappointment gutted Morgan's insides. Had he been wrong? Was this not the same Mary B? Was this not Lord H's mother? Absolute certainty would be difficult if not impossible as there must be other Mary B's.

"She was a simple woman," Browder added. "Didn't associate with others unless she needed coin. Although, now that I think on it..." He paused to adjust his spectacles. "She must've given life to another bastard."

Morgan leaned forward. "Why do you say that?"

"From Barlow's own lips. As he was tossed into the back of the prison cart, he told me if his brother came lookin' for him to give him a message. First I heard of a brother."

"What was the message?"

"He said, 'tell my brother I found her.' Then muttered something about not saying where until he was freed."

"Did Barlow's brother come looking for him?"

"Not at the King's Men."

"Did he mention his brother's name?"

"Not that I recall, your Grace, nor did I care to ask. As for the woman Barlow spoke of, I've no idea who he meant."

Morgan knew. And that knowledge only deepened his growing fear for Isabelle's safety.

Chapter Twelve

"What are you implying?" Constable Foley puffed on a cigar then leaned forward, one large hand splayed upon his desk. "That Reverend Lindley's daughter did not perish in that fire?"

"That's exactly what I'm saying," Morgan replied.

"And this was the matter you wished to speak with me about?"

"It was...and is. Since I had business in Maidstone this afternoon, I thought I'd save you the trouble of traveling to Canderlay."

"Business?"

Morgan did not respond, aware that the constable wished to probe further.

"Where's she been?" Thin trails of smoke rose from the tip of Foley's cigar. "Hiding, perhaps?"

"Not from the authorities, if that's your insinuation. She's under the protection of my sister. As I said before, Miss Lindley feared for her life."

"Frightened, was she? By whom?"

"Amos Barlow."

"Barlow? What's he got to do with this?"

Morgan described in detail what had happened to Isabelle the night her cottage burned but omitted the fact that she'd hidden at Canderlay for the past several months. And since Barlow was now deceased, he figured the man sitting on the opposite side of the desk might eventually divulge that information.

Foley leaned against the back of his chair, a leer upon his thick lips. "You said you hired Barlow to work at Canderlay?"

"Yes, but I assure you that was before I learned of his

157

brutal attempt to put an end to Miss Lindley's life."

"Where's the girl now?"

"Did I not mention she's under the protection of my sister?"

Foley's gray eyes narrowed. "Your sister...she have a name, sir?"

"Margaret," Morgan replied. He didn't care for this man. Arrogance and self-importance dripped off his person like fat off a roasted boar's backside. "You may've heard of her husband. Bartholomew, Duke of Chase?"

The cigar slipped from Foley's lips and onto his desk. Embarrassed, he snatched it up, raking the ashes onto the floor. "Apologies, Mister Spence. I meant no offense with these questions. An obligation to get to the bottom of matters, you see. Of course I know the duke. Well, not personally, you understand."

But not the King's Men, thank the Good Father!

What the devil was I thinking, impersonating a duke?

"His Grace is a most generous man," Foley gushed, sweat beading his worried brow. "Most generous indeed. Paid the expense to repair several of our churches three winters ago, and your sister donated clothing and food to the poor. A saintly woman."

"Yes, Margaret is quite the..."

Busybody. Troublemaker. Interfering meddler.

"Quite the saint," Morgan declared, still perturbed by the dubious future his sister planned for Isabelle. "Getting back to Miss Lindley—"

"No need to concern yourself for the vicar's daughter, Mister Spence. No need at all." Foley leaned across his cluttered desk, grinning as though he were about to spin a gaudy and vulgar tale. "Amos Barlow was murdered this morn."

Morgan waited a full five seconds. "By whom?"

"Highwaymen. We've plenty of cutthroats in these parts. And that's just what they did. Cut Barlow's throat and left him beside the road."

No mention that he was headed to Newgate?

Or of the two guards who forfeited their lives?

Why is this man being purposely vague?

Perhaps it was the nature of his position.

"Am I to assume the matter of Miss Lindley is closed?" Morgan inquired.

Foley stood. "It is for me, sir."

Morgan rose as well. On his way to the door, it occurred to him that it might be prudent to place a genuine concern into this pompous man's head. "Constable..." He turned, his hand resting on the door latch. "Would you say Amos Barlow was a man of means? A man who might be mistaken for a wealthy nobleman?"

Foley grunted with amusement. "Not likely."

"Why then do you suppose he gained the attention of an experienced highwayman?"

"I couldn't say, but his was a life filled with trouble. Drawn to misfortune at an early age. In my opinion, sir, he received exactly the fate he deserved."

"A harsh judgment, is it not?"

"Why do you suppose he broke into Miss Lindley's cottage? It wasn't to beg for a cup of tea, I can promise you that."

Morgan agreed but still...was it not the purpose of this man's position to solve crimes? To seek justice for those who've been wronged? Unless the victim possessed a noble name, it likely wasn't much of a priority.

Foley sat on the edge of his desk. "He tell you how he got disfigured?"

Morgan shook his head. "As it was none of my business, I didn't ask."

"Fell amongst hot coals when he was a child. Mary carried him to the doctor's residence, but there was nothing to be done."

"Mary? His mother?"

"That's correct."

"She was born here in Maidstone, was she not?"

"I wouldn't know, sir. Worthless Mary, I called her."

"Were there other children born to her?"

Foley hesitated, mistrust entering his expression. "Why the concern for an old prostitute?"

"You mentioned misfortune, reminding me of Mary's

troubles when she was but a young girl. She worked for a noble household, did she not?"

"The only employment Mary set her mind to was that of a prostitute. I doubt she ever held a position for any length of time except for the one lying on her back."

Morgan knew better. Disappointment surfaced for the second time that day, but he refused to give in to frustration.

"The vicar's daughter was fortunate," Foley remarked. "Perhaps the next time she'll come to the proper authorities."

Morgan's gaze narrowed. "The next time?"

"Was I not clear and to the point, sir?" The constable puffed out his chest like a rooster about to crow. "We cannot have common folk pestering the Duke and Duchess of Chase with every frivolous matter that comes along."

"Frivolous?"

"If Miss Lindley feels threatened, she should come to me." His lips stretched into a cocky grin. "For a modest amount of coin, I'll see to her protection."

Is that your game then? Slip the constable a few coins and all is well?

A growing anger simmered behind Morgan's calm facade. "Well, as you say, Constable, my sister is surely a saint and enjoys playing the part." He made no attempt to hide the sarcasm in his voice. "Although I doubt Miss Lindley has ever been a problem to anyone throughout her young life, I'll certainly remind her of your sterling reputation as guardian over the common folk. Good day, sir."

* * *

Belle sat across the table from Lady Chase, the duke positioned at her left. Over a lunch of roasted quail, boiled turnips, fresh bread, and baked apples, his Grace shared his plans for the afternoon.

"I shall ride over to inspect the tenant cottages and afterward, I intend to travel on to Chase. I've several men who can serve as guards outside this manor."

"A splendid idea, Bartholomew," his wife remarked. "I wonder, dearest, if you'd do something for me while at Chase."

"Of course, my love. Whatever you wish."

"I've written a list of the items I'll need. Would you see that Hillary receives it?"

"What list?"

"For the clothing and other necessities she's to pack in our trunks."

"Trunks?"

"Bartholomew, stop repeating my words. You sound like a trained parrot."

He frowned.

"Surely you realize, husband, that you and I cannot function normally without the proper attire? Oh, and I've written instructions for the laundry women, asking them to find someone to provide service for Canderlay." Lady Chase offered the old caretaker a timid smile. "You are competent at every task, Mister Samuels, but Miss Lindley and I cannot ask you to wash clothing we consider most private."

Relief appeared briefly in the servant's expression.

As he finished his lunch, the duke asked his wife to retrieve the list she'd penned for her maid as well as the request to the laundry women. He then reminded her that she and Belle should remain inside the manor at all times while he was away.

Following them to the foyer, Belle waited until Lady Chase climbed the stairs before she turned to the duke. "Guards, your Grace?"

"I've no wish to frighten you, Miss Lindley, but we mustn't underestimate a man who clearly has strong motive and no conscience. It has been my experience to side with caution. In your particular situation, I feel it's wise to be ever-vigilant."

"You may depart without worry, sir," Samuels stated on his way to the foyer. "I've a pistol and will carry it upon my person at all times."

"Very good. I leave the safety of my wife and Miss Lindley in your capable hands. If given just cause to shoot, I beg you...do not miss."

"You can be certain of it, your Grace."

As the duke began a casual conversation with Samuels regarding the future hiring of tenant farmers, Belle wondered why no one had offered an explanation regarding Morgan Spence's absence. She had expected at some point during the meal that the duchess would inquire, but strangely she did not.

Fending off an attack of unwavering curiosity mixed with unbridled speculation, Belle had wished to ask Samuels but held her tongue admirably. It wasn't her place to inquire as to the master of the manor's whereabouts. In fact, her questions might be considered vastly improper.

After his conversation with the duke ended, Samuels resumed his duties in the kitchen, and Lady Chase returned to the foyer. She handed her husband two notations. He then excused himself with a perfunctory bow and a promise to return by early evening.

"Well, Isabelle..." The duchess remarked. "It would seem you and I must suffer the rest of the afternoon in confinement. But of course, you've weathered imprisonment before. I, however, am certain to resent it."

"I have indeed, your Grace, but the present internment is more lenient and includes an entire manor house. Why not explore the newly furnished rooms?"

"I believe I've already admired each and every one."

"I see. I'll leave you to your privacy then." Returning to the dining room, she began the task of clearing the dishes from the table.

"Privacy is a rarity for me, Isabelle. At Chase Manor, there is always someone or some matter that needs my immediate attention." Her Grace gathered up a bowel and stacked it onto an empty plate. "Explore Canderlay to your heart's content, my dear, while I assist Mister Samuels in the kitchen."

"Oh, no, my lady. Although your offer would be quite sincere, I fear he's much too proud to accept."

"He'll simply have to accommodate my intrusion. I'll not be as uncaring as my brother, placing the duties of this manor upon that kind old gentleman's shoulders until one day he no longer enjoys life. It's quite cruel."

"Actually..." Belle hesitated as she gathered the eating utensils and cups. "Your brother has been most kind. He and Mister Samuels converse not as employer and servant but almost as friends."

A brief silence ensued.

"You care for Morgan, do you not?"

Heat crept up Belle's neck and into her face, hindering any thought of a quick response. Unwilling to face the duchess, she lowered her gaze. Yes, she did care. How could she not? "I do not dislike him, my lady, but if you're suggesting that I might...I might have designs upon him—"

"Goodness, Isabelle. I implied no such thing. I was merely offering a casual observation."

Casual observation?

Good heavens! Did that mean her thoughts could be read so easily?

"Do not look so forlorn, my dear," Lady Chase remarked. "I wouldn't dare accuse you of inappropriate feelings. However, I know Morgan. He's quite the handsome charmer. It would be far too easy for an innocent young woman to become disillusioned or hurt, and I couldn't bear it if such a tragedy fell upon you."

The heat in Belle's cheeks became unbearable. "You've no cause to worry about my feelings, your Grace. I know my place."

"My dear Miss Lindley." The duchess walked around the table. "Do you honestly believe I could be so haughty as to place my own importance above others? Me?" Her eyes widened for effect. "Daughter to an English spy. Granddaughter of a nefarious Scotsman who was often accused of smuggling. And to this day, my mother refuses to step one foot upon English soil."

"I had no idea, my lady, and I sincerely apologize to you and your notorious relatives."

"Thank you, Isabelle, but I believe the apology should come from me. I'm afraid I've given you the wrong impression." She grabbed Belle's hands. "Your place is where you make it, dear girl. Whether it be nobleman's wife or farmer's. I would applaud, indeed welcome, someone like you into my disturbing yet lovable clan." With a sigh, she shook her head. "Especially when I think of the lady Morgan might wed."

Belle's heart sank. "Has he someone in mind?"

"Unfortunately, yes. Lydia Adderly. She's the daughter of a wealthy earl, and I've never met a more vain creature. She boasts endlessly of her beauty and conquests. If my brother's heart is set upon marrying this woman to support the upkeep of Canderlay, I'm afraid his life will become intolerable."

Cold realization seeped like poison into Belle's soul.

Of course. Marry a wealthy bride. It's expected.

"And I do not fall into that category," she muttered to herself.

"I wish you did," Lady Chase whispered with sincerity. "With all my heart, I wish it."

Embarrassed she'd said the words aloud, Belle focused on clearing the dishes. She could pretend indifference, but her heart knew the truth.

Canderlay would one day belong to this conceited woman...Lydia Adderly.

And Morgan...he would be hers as well.

The very thought sickened her to the point of nausea, and she thanked God she would not be required to witness such a tragedy.

"Well now," the duchess remarked after a prolonged silence. "Let's find Mister Samuels and annoy him with our presence, shall we?"

Battling a tempest of emotions, Belle managed to nod.

* * *

Morgan arrived at Canderlay late in the afternoon near the end of a brief summer storm.

Samuels met him at the door. "We expected you hours ago, sir."

"My apologies. My return suffered an unavoidable delay as I decided on the spur of the moment to pay Constable Foley a visit."

"I see. You missed a splendid downpour."

"No, I did not. Unfortunately it passed me several miles back as Ares and I waited beneath an oak." Morgan handed over his hat. "I gave him a brisk rubdown before I came inside."

"I'll see to his food and water, sir."

"Thank you, Samuels. Seems my horse is more fond of your hand than mine. I hope he's not too much of a burden."

"No, not at all. I've become an expert over the years at managing temperamental horses. Households as well."

"A pity you cannot expand that expertise to the ladies."

"Pardon?"

Morgan laughed. "Never mind."

"Here, sir. You'll catch your death in those wet clothes. Allow me to take your coat while you run upstairs and change. I've kept lunch warming in the oven."

"Samuels, you are indeed a good man." He slipped out of his overcoat then retrieved the bottle of expensive brandy he'd tucked away in one of the deep pockets. "See that the duke receives this upon his return, will you?"

"Certainly, sir."

"And these..." Morgan patted his pockets absentmindedly. "Where did I put them? Oh, yes." He reached inside a smaller pocket and withdrew two thin boxes. "This is a little something I purchased for Isabelle and my sister. Put them in my room, if you please."

"As you wish, sir."

Morgan handed over his overcoat, and a square-shaped package wrapped in brown paper fell to the floor. "I almost forgot. Here, Samuels. I purchased this with you in mind."

The weather-worn mask of a loyal servant turned to genuine surprise. "For me, sir?"

Morgan smiled. "Yes, Jasper Samuels. For you. Did you not inform me just last week that in your youth you preferred full-bodied Jamaican smokes?"

"Yes, sir, but these...they would've cost—"

"Never mind the cost. Am I not allowed to present a gift to a valued servant and friend?"

"Forgive my ingratitude, Mister Spence." One corner of Samuels' mouth twitched upward. "I shall indeed enjoy this luxury."

By devil, I almost had him. I almost tugged a smile from the old man!

"Well then," Morgan declared in a casual tone. "I'd better hurry upstairs and wash up."

"If you like, I can serve your meal in the privacy of your suite."

"Privacy? I have no privacy, Samuels. Not since Miss Lindley arrived. I apologize for the feeble attempt at humor. No, I'll take my meal in the dining room. I suppose the others have already eaten?"

"Several hours past, sir."

"I thought so. Well then, I shall return shortly."

His stomach growling with a modest amount of urgency, Morgan bounded up the stairs, two at a time. After washing his face, running a comb through his hair, and changing out of his damp clothes, he hurried downstairs to the dining room where Samuels brought out his lunch.

"Ah, roasted quail. My favorite."

"I noticed."

"And apple tarts. I once assumed this was a rare treat, but apparently that's not the case. Have we apple trees, Samuels?"

"Oh, yes, sir. Several." The servant cut a portion of meat and placed it upon Morgan's plate. "They grow not far from the tenant cottages."

"I wasn't aware of that."

"There was, at one time, a pear orchard, but the trees suffered some sort of catastrophe." He set a small ladle in the bowl of boiled turnips. "I take it Constable Foley will not be visiting the manor later on this evening to speak with Miss Isabelle?"

"Correct. Apparently my explanation of what happened was sufficient enough. And I daresay Reverend Lindley hit the mark in regards to his distrust of certain officials."

"Foley's arrogance and questionable character vastly infuriated the vicar. So much so that he stopped speaking to the man altogether."

"I can well understand why."

Samuels poured a cup of hot tea and set it inside a china saucer. "Before I leave you to your lunch, Mister Spence, will there be anything else?"

"Yes. Where is the duke?"

"His Grace is off to inspect the tenant cottages."

"Splendid. Perhaps if I eat quickly, I can join him."

"He has likely departed by now, sir. It was my understanding that he intended to travel on to Chase Manor."

"Did my sister travel with him?"

"No, sir. Her Grace retired to one of the guest rooms for a bit of solitude."

"I see. And Miss Lindley?"

"I'm afraid solitude and Miss Isabelle never quite got along, sir. She's roaming about the manor, inspecting the new furnishings as we speak. Rather overjoyed at the prospect, I daresay. I spotted her slipping down to the wine cellar not more than ten minutes ago."

Morgan cocked a brow. "In search of a bottle of port, was she?"

"Unlikely. I fear this venture into the cellar is a clear attempt to offer her services to clean, which so far I've not allowed her to do, but I suspect she intends to ask for your permission."

"Not to worry, Samuels. I'll stand firmly by your position on the matter."

"Thank you, sir."

Morgan cut a chunk of bread then spread butter on it. "Did you ever meet Magnus Lindley?"

"Oh, yes, sir. A rather jolly soul, he was. Fond of Miss Isabelle and quite generous with his coin."

"But careful not to offend the watchful and often disapproving eye of his older brother?"

"I've no cause to speak ill of the dead, sir. Reverend Lindley was a good man. Never too proud to put his hand to a plow or his back to the wheel. But above all, he possessed a kind heart. I've seen him use money from his own coffers to help some poor family who could not afford medicine or the services of a doctor. He'd hand you the coat right off his back, should you request it. If he was strict with Miss Isabelle, it wasn't because he didn't love the girl. As we now know, he feared for her very life."

"But still...I fail to understand why he wanted nothing to do with his brother's wealth. By limiting Isabelle's funds, could he not see she'd have fewer options? Which is precisely the case now, I might add."

"I'm certain the vicar acted as he thought best."

A pity he didn't think to secure his daughter's future.

Dismissing Samuels to see to Ares, Morgan finished his lunch alone. Afterward, he headed into the kitchen. Finding the door to the wine cellar ajar, he peeked inside. A faint flicker of light broke the darkness below. As he cautiously descended the narrow stone steps, the air grew cooler while the smell of earth and decay became stronger. Reaching the bottom, he walked straight into a thick cobweb, bringing a string of foul curses to his lips which thankfully he had the decency to keep to himself.

Pausing to brush the clinging spidery web from his face allowed enough time for his eyesight to adjust. Following the trail of dim light, he found Isabelle standing behind a tall wine rack in the far corner, the lantern hung on a hook above her head.

What the devil is she doing?

No longer wearing the fancy gown, she'd changed into a more practical day dress. With her back to him and her head bowed, she appeared to be praying. He had no desire to disturb a sacred conversation between her and the Good Father but when a full minute passed, he began to wonder if she'd fallen into some sort of trance.

Deciding she was entitled to all the spiritual time she wished, Morgan glanced around. Darkness crowded in from every corner of the cellar, creeping through several of the wine racks and depositing shadows behind whatever object the soft light from the lantern touched. He turned his attention downward where several broken bottles littered the floor between them.

A hazardous return.

Especially for a woman who usually walked about in her bare feet.

Morgan's gaze trailed the length of her gown to the floor.

Dainty slippers.

He ended the silence. "I'll have to carry you."

Her head snapped up, but she kept her back rigid and did not turn.

When she failed to offer a verbal response, it suddenly dawned upon him that something was amiss. "Isabelle?"

A short pause. "Yes?"

"What the devil are you doing down here?"

Another hesitation, longer this time. "Exploring."

"Just as I thought." He moved forward. "You ventured down into this dark dungeon hoping to find another secret room with a peephole."

She sighed. "Must you constantly needle me until we are at odds with one another once again?"

"Sadly, provoking you has become my sacred duty."

"Apparently," she quipped.

Annoyed she hadn't taken a liking to his attempt at humor, as well as the fact that she still refused to face him, Morgan marched around in front of her.

She quickly turned her back.

His heart twisted. "Isabelle, have you been crying?"

"No, I...I've simply gotten a speck of dust in my eye."

"Which eye?"

"What does it matter?" she snapped, moving a short distance away.

Morgan strolled up behind her and placed his hands upon her shoulders. "What matters to me is the fact that you just lied. A sin I suspect you rarely if ever commit. And don't bother denying it." He turned her about and lifted her chin so she'd be forced to look at him. "Your lovely brown eyes betray you, Belle. What's wrong?"

Profound sadness cast a shadow upon her beauty. Then all of a sudden her expression lightened, and she almost smiled. "You called me Belle."

"When?"

"Just now."

"Did I?"

She nodded.

"Forgive me, but..." Releasing her chin, he lightly stroked her cheek before dropping his hand to his side. "An endearment spoken out of turn cannot be the cause of your tears."

"No, of course not."

"Then what the devil is? Do you not know by now that you can trust me? Have I not proven myself worthy in your sainted eyes?"

He expected a sharp rebuttal.

Instead, she handed him a loosely rolled parchment, yellowed from age.

Morgan had been so concerned with the cause of her sorrow that he hadn't even noticed it before. "What's this?"

Isabelle released a slow breath, and her bottom lip quivered. "A long overdue farewell."

Chapter Thirteen

October, 1801

My dearest Belle,
Your smile is the sun that warms my soul and the
stars that light my path by night. No matter how far away
my ship sails, your laughter never fades from my heart. If
God had given me a wee daughter of my very own, she
would not have been more dear to me than you.

Watch over your father, little one. He's been far too
preoccupied lately and refuses to take me into his
confidence. Whatever troubles his soul, I pray for its
resolution long before my return.

Until we meet again...
Your devoted uncle,
Magnus

"His ship was lost at sea six days later," Belle
explained, tears blurring her vision once again.

Morgan Spence glanced up from the note. "Where did
you find this?"

She raised an empty wine bottle. "In here."

"Just now?"

Belle nodded. "Not long before I heard your voice."

"I'm not sure I understand. Why would Magnus leave
a note for you inside a bottle?"

"Because it was our favorite game."

"Game?" One corner of his mouth lifted in a quirky
half-grin. "Rummaging about the cellar?"

"This bottle was likely discovered above stairs. I have
no idea how it got to the cellar." She took the parchment then
returned it to the bottle for safekeeping. "This was my
hidden treasure...notes like this one. You see, my uncle was

often called away on business, but he always left me a written farewell because he knew I expected one. The note would sometimes be amusing, sometimes heartfelt, but it always ended with the words 'until we meet again'. When he went away that last time it was in the middle of the night, and I thought..."

"You thought he had forgotten?"

She nodded, guilt twisting like a knife inside her stomach. "I searched and searched but..." Like a sudden gust of wind, a wave of deep-rooted rage, brought forth by all the pain she'd held inside for so long, slammed into Belle.

Morgan Spence steadied her. "Perhaps you should sit down for a moment."

His strong hands about her waist comforted her, but his touch also made her breathless and quite warm.

Belle tore herself from his embrace. "Why must I be the last of my family?" she cried, her heart heavy with an accumulation of suppressed indignation. "Why me? Why was *I* chosen?"

"I'm sorry, Isabelle." He spun her around and pulled her into his arms. "Life is rarely fair and often cruel." After a few moments, he set her at arm's length and produced a handkerchief. "We endure our time upon this wretched earth because we've little choice."

The compassion in his voice did more to undermine Belle's courage than finding her uncle's letter, and the brief surge of outrage scattered like dust in a windstorm. She accepted the handkerchief, buried her face in his chest, and sobbed until her eyes felt swollen.

Finally, she raised her head. "My father would've chided me for this gaudy display of weakness and then pointed out that my life has been blessed in so many ways. He would've been correct. I never meant to burden you, Mister Spence. It's just..." She pushed the hair from her face. "I so desperately miss my father and uncle."

"I understand. I cannot imagine the loneliness you've suffered."

No, you cannot.

Deeply ashamed by the thought, she backed away, returning a comfortable space between them.

"Why did you venture down here, Isabelle?"

Dabbing at the tears with his handkerchief, she replied, "I thought I might inspect the place. Perhaps give it a thorough cleaning."

He raised his gaze toward the darkness of the ceiling. "Good God, Samuels! You were right."

"What do you mean?"

"He observed your journey down here and warned me you were up to something. You should know by now that Samuels will not allow you to put your hand to the task of cleaning."

"But you...you can assign me chores."

"No, I cannot."

"For what reason?"

"You are a guest in my house, and I do not assign chores to guests."

"I'm no guest. In fact, did you not recently refer to me as an intruder?"

"I wasn't aware of your situation. Forgive my ignorance." He blew the dust from a pair of garden gloves then promptly lost interest. "Samuels is quite fond of you. I think he considers you a long lost princess who will one day reclaim her thrown."

"I doubt he's that gullible," Belle remarked. "Slightly blind, perhaps, but otherwise sound of mind."

"Do not be angry with a kind old man who cannot bear the thought of seeing you perform work of any sort."

"I'm not angry, but Mister Samuels coddles me without cause. I am not a princess or a fine lady. Nor am I an invalid who needs constant attention. I well know what it means to work."

"I have no doubt you do."

She exhaled a long sigh. "I'm sorry. I should not have ranted and carried on as though I'd been raised without proper manners."

"My mother is fond of ranting and carrying on. She swears that such behavior is often beneficial to the mind and soul. Except when my father does the ranting, of course."

Belle suspected her own father would disagree with such behavior, but she didn't think it polite to point this out.

"I've been meaning to ask..." His prolonged hesitation ended with a pronounced grin. "Does Samuels ever smile?"

"I'm sure he did early on...before tragedy scarred his life."

"What sort of tragedy?"

"According to Uncle Magnus, Mister Samuels was married barely two years before the fever took his beloved wife and infant daughter. He was so heartbroken and bitter that he tried to end his life twice."

"The devil, you say. How?"

"By drinking whatever spirits he could buy, beg, or steal. One winter many years ago, my father found him lying in a ditch, near death from the frigid cold. Father took him in, nursed him back to health, gave him spiritual counsel, and then offered him the position of caretaker to the church. I can tell you with complete honesty, there never came a day my father voiced a single regret for that decision."

"Poor Samuels. He's endured more than his season of troubles. I must find a solution. Give him a reason to smile again."

"That would be a kindness indeed, and in this matter I will pray for your immediate success."

"In this matter?" He raised a brow. "But not in others?"

She frowned. Had he read her private thoughts? The negative musings regarding his future bride? "You have my word, sir, I will pray for your success in everything your heart holds dear."

"Thank you, Isabelle, for any and all appeals to the Good Father on my behalf."

"You are most welcome." She stuffed the handkerchief in a pocket of her gown. "Mister Spence, may I be so bold as to ask a question?"

"You may."

"What prediction did Old Edwina make regarding your future?"

He stared, obviously surprised. "Why do you wish to know?"

She toyed with the empty wine bottle. "Curiosity, I suppose."

"I see, but you should know...I never trust in visions or grand predictions."

"I didn't inquire as to your beliefs. I merely asked—"

"I understood the question, Isabelle," he countered. "And my answer is the same. Edwina's predictions were of no value to me."

Belle frowned. "Why do you avoid the truth? Did she not correctly foretell of your sister's marriage to the Duke of Chase?"

"Nothing strange or mystical about that. Everyone who knew Margaret expected her to marry well."

"So...Edwina's description of the duke was mere coincidence?"

"No, it was simply a clever deduction. She described Margaret's future husband only *after* I brought Bartholomew to Dragon's Breath one year to celebrate Christmas."

"What does the timing matter?" Belle argued. "Her prediction still came true, did it not?"

"You're far too naïve, Isabelle. Do you realize that if Edwina had lived beyond the shores of Dragon's Breath, or with people other than the infamous Macgregor Clan, she would've most likely been considered a witch?"

"I do not believe in witches."

"And yet you believe in seers and actually hold them in high regard?"

"Have you not read the Bible? It is filled with stories of seers and prophets. What are you afraid of? Was Edwina's vision of your future so horrible you're afraid to speak of it?"

"Afraid? No."

"Then what did she say?"

"It's none of your business."

"Oh, my...can you not think up a better reason to avoid a genuine reply?"

He scowled. "Isabelle Lindley, you are a very persistent woman."

"And you, Morgan Spence, have been taking hedging lessons from Mister Samuels. Tell me. What was her prediction?"

On a sigh of irritation, he relented. "Do not think for one second you have won this battle. I'm only giving in because your questions have become most annoying." A slight pause. "Edwina told me that one day I must choose between my heart's desire and Canderlay Manor, but Canderlay *is* my heart's desire, and I already possess it. So you see...her prediction means nothing. My future came about exactly as I planned it."

"Except for the fact that you've yet to acquire a wealthy bride." Belle met his hard stare with one of her own. "A lady such as Miss Adderly."

"Margaret's been talking out of turn again, has she not?"

"You're her brother, and she loves you. It upsets her Grace that you place acquiring wealth above the affections of an adoring wife."

"Then she's upset without cause. I admit that wealth is somewhat crucial to this estate as it cannot survive without a modest amount of coin, but the selection of a devoted wife is just as important."

"I'm pleased to hear it. I adore Canderlay but if you cannot see beyond its shadow, your heart might miss the chance to find love."

"Are you now a prominent expert on the subject of matchmaking and matrimony, Miss Lindley?"

"You know very well I've lived a sheltered life," she retorted. "I doubt I have enough experience with any subject to be considered sophisticated, but I have clear vision, and I know what's before me. Seek love above all else, Mister Spence. I believe that's what Edwina was trying to tell you." She almost placed her hand upon his arm before it occurred to her that this might seem improper. "I couldn't bear it if you died as Uncle Magnus did. Alone and without ever knowing the comfort of a dearest love."

"Give thought to your own comfort, Isabelle," he chided before moving away. "Any idea where you'll travel after Dublin?"

"I haven't decided." Belle lifted the lantern from its hook and followed. "I've no cottage in Kent. No home to return to."

"Why did Magnus not purchase Canderlay?"

"He tried, but King George refused to sell. My uncle

was never sure why."

"Who knows the thoughts of a vengeful king? If it hadn't been for the Duke of Chase urging the Prince Regent to rid himself of this abandoned and desolate estate, I would've never been allowed to purchase it."

"And you and I would've never met on the third floor."

"Met?" Sporting a twisted grin, he shook his head. "The correct term for what happened that night is...*collided*."

"I suppose so, but I was pointing to the fact that Canderlay is no longer abandoned. No longer desolate. You brought it back to life. Brought me back from the edge of despair."

Unrecognizable emotion clouded his gaze.

"I meant..." All of a sudden her throat became dry. "Well, you...you've kept me safe."

His reaction was instantaneous. He became distant, as though a different person now stood in his place. "No, Isabelle. Margaret is your noble champion." He turned his back to her. "I had little to do with vanquishing your despair."

Oh, but you are very much mistaken, sir.

"Why did you purchase Canderlay?"

He shrugged. "To right a wrong. Close the book on a past injustice."

"A wrong done to you? Or to your father?"

He faced her. "Both, I suppose."

"I understand. After all, you are the eldest son of a marquis and were next in line for his title."

"Noble titles hold little interest for me and as you pointed out once before, I'm no lord."

"I was angry. I shouldn't have said that. It was rude and unforgivable."

"It was indeed rude...but not unforgivable." He closed the short distance between them. "Are you still angry?"

"I'm not sure." Belle smiled. "Perhaps you should ask me again tomorrow."

"Perhaps I will." Without warning, he scooped her up in his arms.

Face burning with immediate heat, Belle struggled to keep the lantern from tilting and thereby extinguishing their only light while her other hand held onto the bottle containing the precious note from her uncle.

"Mister Spence..." Breathless, her heart pumping with pure exhilaration, she managed to add, "What are you doing?"

"Rescuing your tender feet."

"My feet are not tender nor are they in need of rescue."

"You may not have noticed, Isabelle, but there's broken glass scattered about the floor."

"Yes, I'm aware of that particular hazard, sir, but I managed to avoid it earlier, and I can do so again. Now please...put me down."

"Give me a reason why I should grant your request."

"I'll give you two," she quipped. "One...this lantern is rather awkward and I'm deathly afraid of setting your backside afire. On the other hand, if I drop it, we could be thrown into complete darkness."

"Valid enough. And the other reason?"

"I've an empty wine bottle in my hand, and you're carrying me in an undignified and all too familiar manner."

"Point taken," he muttered. Nevertheless, he carried her across the room before setting her feet down upon the bottom step.

Heart still racing and unable to look him in the eye, Belle issued a curt thank you. Depositing the lantern on the third step then setting the bottle at her feet, she pretended to smooth the wrinkles from her gown in order to hide the fact that her entire body trembled.

"I learned something significant this afternoon," he remarked casually.

"Oh?" She glanced up. "Opened a book, did we?"

"Amusing." Morgan Spence leaned forward so that they were almost at eye level. "While in Maidstone this afternoon," he added, the soft whisper of his breath caressing her lips, "I discovered something concerning Mary B."

Her embarrassment bolted in a split second. "That's wonderful."

"I thought that bit of news might interest you."

"Tell me then," Belle pressed. "Who was she?"

"The daughter of a local tenant farmer."

"And the name of the family she worked for?"

"I'm afraid my stroke of good fortune ended at that point. No one knew." He turned away, drew a well-used and unraveling straw-bottom chair from a pile of refuge, and then sat down. "But perhaps we should postpone this conversation until later."

"For what reason?"

"To avoid repeating myself when explaining this to my sister and the duke. But mainly in the hope that your ill manners might miraculously improve."

He enjoyed teasing her. She could see it in the sparkle of his eyes.

"You are correct, sir. I sincerely apologize for my thoughtless comment. I'm sure you've opened many books."

"Are you trying to annoy me?"

"Certainly not." Belle sat on the third step, her arms draped loosely about her knees. "If you've information about Mary, you mustn't keep me in the dark a moment longer."

"Since you asked nicely...and I'm in a generous mood...very well." He leaned forward in the rickety chair, his elbows resting lightly upon his thighs. "Mary B was none other than Mary Barlow."

"Barlow?"

He nodded and imparted all he'd learned earlier that afternoon.

Belle exhaled a long sigh. "But that would mean..." A sudden chill washed over her, and she wrapped her hands about her upper arms. "Mister Spence, are you implying that Amos Barlow was Lord H's brother?"

"Half-brother, to be precise."

"Then his death really was connected to me. Mister Samuels denied it, but I knew in my heart it was true. And now..." She shivered. "Lord H will come for me."

He ran a hand through his dark hair and leaned against the back of the chair. "I'm sorry I frightened you."

"These past few months I learned to coexist with fear and to adjust my life accordingly. But this..."

"No harm will befall you, Isabelle. I swear it."

Warmth spread throughout her body. "I believe your words are sincere, Mister Spence, but I'm not sure such a promise is within your power to keep." An odd stillness descended upon the cellar, reminding Belle of the long years of neglect this house had endured. Before sadness conquered the moment, she shifted her thoughts back to the present. "What about the constable? Am I to meet with him this evening?"

"No. He accepted my explanation regarding your hesitation in reporting Barlow's crimes."

"Then...you did not mention Lord H's involvement?"

"For the reasons we'd already discussed, no, I did not. And I believe your father was right not to trust Constable Foley."

"That does not surprise me. Father was a good judge of character."

"Makes me wonder what the vicar would've thought of me."

"Perhaps he would've asked my opinion on the matter."

"Would you have berated my character?"

"Not at all. I would've sworn you are generous and most kind."

"High praise from a vicar's daughter. I'm not sure I deserve it."

Insides aquiver, Belle lowered her gaze, fidgeting with the lace on one sleeve of her gown. Distracted, she inadvertently knocked over the bottle she'd set aside earlier. It rolled between them, and they both reached out for it at the same time, bumping heads.

"Heavens," she moaned, massaging the tender spot on her forehead. "I suspected from the start that your head was as hard as stone, but now I've been given proof."

"My original thought regarding the thickness of your head was a bit stronger," he remarked, mirroring her actions. "Thankfully I possessed the good sense not to voice my opinion." Keeping his hand upon his brow, he tilted his head to the side. "Are you all right?"

"I believe so, but I fear my vision is permanently blurred."

"We'd better go before we inflict further injury upon one another."

"Agreed." Belle stood, but when Morgan Spence did not immediately rise, she added, "You wish to remain?"

"Hardly." He rocked back and forth in the chair before shifting his attention to her. "I cannot move."

"What do you mean?"

He frowned as though she were daft to ask such a question. "My backside seems to have sunk into this straw seat, and I cannot budge it."

Belle laughed.

"Stop giggling like an adolescent and help me."

"Yes, Mister Spence. Certainly, Mister Spence. Whatever you wish."

"And wipe that smirk off your lips, Isabelle."

"I'm terribly sorry for your discomfort. How can I help?"

"Give me your hand."

She did.

"All right then," he said. "You pull while I try to free my bottom from this blasted predicament. Are you ready?"

Belle braced herself. "Yes."

She had just begun to yank on his hand when suddenly the chair collapsed. As it crashed to the floor, Morgan Spence failed to release her hand, sending her tumbling on top of him in an unladylike manner. Stunned by the fall, she lay still for several seconds before raising her head.

He lay on his back, motionless beneath her and with his eyes closed, amid the splintered debris of a once serviceable straw chair.

"Are you hurt?" she asked, her voice shaky.

"Severely," he whispered.

"Oh, dear lord." She struggled to her knees, dread snatching the breath from her throat. "Where are you injured? Your neck? Your back?"

"My pride."

Realizing the ruse, Belle jabbed her finger into his chest. "You wicked scoundrel. You worried me without cause."

"Were you, Isabelle?" He rolled onto his side, leaning upon one elbow, and stared at her. "Worried for me?"

"Well, of course. Did you not recognize the horrified look upon my face? Or perhaps you'd care to see it again?"

"That's quite all right. I'm pleased to have provided your amusement."

"I was far from amused. Well...not exactly far but..." She paused then smiled. "Oh, very well. I confess. The situation was rather humorous."

"To you, I'm sure. I broke your fall." He sat up, and his expression quickly turned into an unsettling stare. As though he searched for something but wasn't sure what. "I was mistaken about you, Isabelle." The stilled silence became almost deafening. "You were never the ghost of Canderlay Manor." He leaned forward and gently curled a finger beneath her chin. "You're the lost treasure."

Belle thought he was poking fun at her again, but the serious tone of his voice along with the emotion in his eyes told her otherwise.

"A rare find," he added in a whisper.

And with those last words, he lowered his head, his lips seeking hers.

Chapter Fourteen

Belle closed her eyes, committing his tender kiss to memory. He did not pull her close or crush her against him. His gentle embrace demanded nothing. Promised nothing in return. Nevertheless, a seed of hope began inside her soul then suddenly blossomed, brought to life by the yearnings of her body.

A crack of thunder, real or imagined, split the silence, as though declaring that this moment had been destined from the very beginning of time. In the following stillness, a calm whisper from within urged her to back away, but her heart insisted she stay where she was.

In Morgan Spence's arms.

"Isabelle?" Lady Chase called from somewhere in the house above.

He broke the kiss, pushing her at arm's length.

She stared at him, heart pounding strangely in her ears and her stomach twisted in jittery knots. Alarm manifested in his apprehensive expression. What was he thinking? It wasn't long before he provided the answer.

"I'd wager everything I own that Margaret will misunderstand the reason you and I are alone in this cellar," he whispered.

Acute disappointment jolted Belle's senses, turning her joy into a stinging setback.

He regrets the kiss!

She stood, her emotions as unsteady as her knees. "Why would her Grace misunderstand? We are innocent of any wrongdoing."

"I agree, but Margaret will view our situation as improper."

"And just what, sir..." She faltered, struggling to keep

the pain of her wounded soul from entering her voice. "What is our situation?"

"You're a clever woman. Can you not see how this will look?"

"Oh, I can definitely see, Mister Spence," Belle snapped, angry she'd been duped. "Quite clearly. In fact, much more than I did a few moments ago." Pain formed a spiked club inside her chest. "You used me for a bit of sport, did you not? Now you fear you're in danger of being caught and will be forced to make amends. Well, you inconsiderate and arrogant oaf, allow me to put your fears to rest. I would never force myself into any gentleman's life but especially a man whose heart is made of ice."

"Ice?"

"And besides...you're practically already spoken for."

"Listen to reason, Isabelle. Unless you can convince Margaret that I'm Father Christmas, ours will be a most awkward explanation."

"Then you should've thought of your precious reputation *before* you followed me," she retorted and turned to head up the stairs.

He grabbed her arm. "It's not my reputation I'm concerned with, you silly goose. Can you not understand my concern?"

"I understand plenty," Belle replied, embarrassed by her anger. "Your concern is strictly for Morgan Spence."

"That's not true."

Thunder rumbled through the cellar, rattling the empty wine racks.

"Would you please..." Her voice broke, in recognition of her own weakness. Through clenched teeth she ordered him to release his hold upon her arm.

After a brief hesitation, he obeyed.

At the top of the steps the cellar door opened. "Isabelle?" A woman's silhouette appeared, blocking the light from the kitchen. "Are you down there?"

Morgan Spence backed into the shadows, away from the lantern's light.

"One moment, your Grace," Belle replied. "I'm coming up." She picked up the bottle containing her uncle's note before retrieving the lantern. "No need to worry, Mister Spence," she said beneath her breath. "Your plans for securing a wealthy bride will not be altered by me. I wish you complete success in your attempt to attain true happiness."

* * *

Like a thief concealed in the night, Morgan waited at the edge of darkness.

As Isabelle reached the top of the stone steps, Margaret commented, "I thought I heard voices. Who were you speaking with?"

"No one of importance, your Grace."

Bloody hell! That stung.

"Who, dear?"

"I was merely conversing with myself, my lady."

"I see. Well, I suspect we women are forced into such one-sided conversations due to the incredibly thick heads of our gentlemen friends."

And then...

"Good lord, Isabelle, is that a wine bottle in your hand?"

Morgan did not hear the response for the door closed immediately behind them, blanketing the cellar in blackness once again. Surrounded by a smothering silence, his mind became entangled in an emotional battle he could not possibly hope to win.

What have I done?

Why had he dared be so bold?

Taking liberties when he had no right.

To deny Isabelle's beauty had failed to catch his eye would be an absolute lie. A falsehood the Good Father might someday ask him to explain. Had he not noticed she was unique? Unlike any woman he'd ever met? And was it not clear that her heart was the purest form of innocence? Other women could not compare to Isabelle Lindley. She was gold. They were more like tarnished silver.

I didn't mean to hurt her...make her feel worthless.

Guilt cut a wide path inside his chest.

What must she think of me?

The worst, no doubt.

And in this particular instance, her assumptions would be justified.

Morgan made his way back to the steps. He could've handled things better. Instead, he'd opened his mouth and allowed thoughtlessness to rush out. Yes, he'd been overly concerned as to what Margaret would think, but his concern had not been for himself. He needed no help to defend his honor, but Isabelle...she was an unmarried woman.

Confused as to how he'd gotten on the wrong side of their disagreement, he leaned against the wall. A pity most females were cursed with stubbornness. And the vicar's lovely daughter had received more than her share. If only she had permitted the courtesy of an explanation.

But no. That simple consideration was shot in the back before he could get two words out of his mouth. Instead of seeing his point, a valid point no less, she'd allowed an unintended offense to distort her reasoning. Surely when she took time to consider their situation...

Thunder rumbled in a low moan, the sound dying almost as soon as it seeped through the ancient walls of the cellar.

A deepening chill fell upon the room, hovering over Morgan. He began a careful ascent to the top of the steps. Good manners demanded he offer Isabelle an apology. And he would.

But not on this day.

Nor tomorrow.

Perhaps he'd apologize when she stopped acting like a spoiled child. The best course of action might be to allow her pride to simmer in a bitter stew of her own making.

A punishment for stubbornness.

Was this not precisely how his father dealt with his beloved Macgregor lass? And was theirs not a strong union?

A sudden and deep longing caught Morgan off-guard. There would be no union with Isabelle. No second kiss. Her opinion of him did not matter. The more she despised him, the safer her virtue. Never again would he give in to the temptation to touch her. She didn't belong to him, and his plans did not include taking the hand of the vicar's daughter in marriage.

No matter how lovely her face or how enticing her form.

Och! What a wise mon ye've become, lad.

A strange sensation crawled along Morgan's skin. He hadn't heard that voice in almost fifteen years. The biting sarcasm was still the same, but she had never before intruded upon his private thoughts.

He waited a full minute as silence became his only companion. No footsteps or sound above. Nothing stirred in the cellar. Not even the storm intruded.

Releasing a pent-up breath, Morgan almost laughed aloud. The error in talking to one's self is you never know who's going to wander into the conversation. Like an old Scotswoman highly touted and strangely feared for her supernatural powers. Her predictions were practical, not magical. She simply paid close attention to everyone she came in contact with. Besides, she was long dead now, and there were more important matters to consider at present.

Such as...trying to interpret the meaning of an enraged woman's parting comment. What did Isabelle mean...

In your attempt to attain true happiness.

He *would* indeed attain happiness. True or otherwise.

That's it, lad. Spit inta the wind ta spite yer face.

Morgan glanced around the cellar. "You know, madam, I was once quite fond of you. More so than I let on."

Silence met the remark.

"Although I truly appreciate your selfless devotion to the Macgregor Clan, and to my mother in particular, I feel I should warn you that I have every intention of living my life exactly as I planned. I ask that you respect my wishes and stay out of my head."

He could see her in his mind's eye. Spine bent from years of administering to others, strands of white hair escaping from beneath her gray cap, skin tougher than the leather soles of his grandfather's shoes. She may not have looked the part, but she had often reminded him of a fierce dragon, breathing fire as she warned the family of her most recent visions.

Morgan chuckled. "And those of ye who dinna heed my warnin' will vanish like mist in the early morn."

An eerie scraping came from behind him, as though in anger someone had pushed aside one of the wine racks.

Morgan scrambled up the steps, stumbling midway and losing his balance. By sheer good fortune he managed to right himself and keep going.

Careful where ye place yer feet, lad. Though a misstep be fergiven, the scar it brings about will forever remain.

A shiver crawled up the back of his neck. He'd never heard that particular advice before. Had his mind simply made up the words to fit the circumstance?

Heedless of the danger, he took the rest of the steps two at a time and burst through the door. It smacked against the kitchen wall as light flooded his vision. Thankfully no one was present to witness such an undignified entrance.

Morgan closed the door and leaned against it until the beat of his heart slowed to normal. No longer was he a frightened lad of six, clinging to Grandfather Ethan's hand as he recounted tales of phantom apparitions who roamed the corridors of Dragon's Breath. No longer must he endure the odd predictions of an old Scotswoman who claimed to be a seer. Had he not long ago distanced himself from such primitive beliefs?

The beginnings of a contented smile emerged before dying a quick death.

No! Good Father, you cannot be this cruel.

Of the four brothers, she had worried about Morgan's future the most.

Promised to watch over him.

Promised it upon her deathbed.

The voice whispering inside his mind as he stood on the stone steps had sounded as familiar as rain falling upon a rooftop. He had instantly recognized the thick Scottish brogue. How could he not? He'd heard it half his life.

A slow pounding began inside his temples. Holding on to the latch of the cellar door to keep his balance, he closed his eyes.

In life, Edwina Mason had been a clever and willful

old woman. If her ghost had indeed taken up residence inside Morgan's head, he'd have a devil of a time getting rid of it.

* * *

Belle awoke early the next morning determined not to allow Morgan Spence's crude behavior to dampen her spirits. During dinner the previous evening, he had been polite yet curt. A clear indication he wished to distance himself from the incident that had transpired between them in the cellar.

Renewed pain unfurled inside her chest. Rejection stung. She would never again place heart at the mercy of an insensitive gentleman.

Belle finished the morning toiletries, dressed, then brushed and coifed her hair. Lady Chase would soon be waiting downstairs. Humming a familiar tune, she extinguished the candle. Upon leaving the secret room, she instantly noted the darkened bedroom. Behind the sheer drapes, rain beat against the window in a slow pattern, trickling down the glass.

Her enthusiasm ground to a decided halt.

Not outing today. Not in this dreary weather.

Someone walked beneath the window...a man cloaked in rain attire. She suffered a moment of agonizing fear before realizing this was one of the duke's men.

Belle unlocked the bedroom door and hurried through the antechamber. Outside in the corridor, she found Lady Chase pacing the floor. "Is something wrong, your Grace?"

The duchess placed a finger to her lips then clasped Belle's hand and drew her back inside the antechamber. Once the door closed, she turned. "I swear, Isabelle, this day has not started on a good note."

"Why? What's wrong?"

"Our plans have been spoiled, dear girl."

"Oh, you're referring to the nasty weather."

"Indeed. Morgan and my husband had planned to ride into Maidstone today to inquire about tenant farmers but with this much rain, the roads will be treacherous. Now they will be underfoot all day."

"A pity our escape from drudgery has been cancelled."

"Not cancelled. Postponed. I'm sorry, Isabelle."

"Perhaps in a day or two we'll be able to travel, but the guards...will they not betray us?"

"Since the men believe their task is guarding Canderlay Manor from curious intruders, I doubt they'll interfere."

"I cannot pretend I'm not disappointed. I was looking forward to the carriage ride this morning."

"As was I, but we simply must be patient a bit longer. Listen, my dear. I've another matter to speak with you about before it slips my mind."

"Very well."

"You've likely noticed that Morgan enjoys a fair amount of playful teasing."

Belle frowned. "You're referring to his piercing barbs aimed at me?"

"I admit my brother is a mischievous rogue, Isabelle, but he means you no harm. The point I wish to make is this...do not let your guard down. Morgan is far too clever for his own good. If you arouse his suspicions in the slightest, he'll uncover our plan in the blink of an eye."

"Then I should avoid him?"

"No. Be pleasant. More agreeable to him."

"That's asking a great deal, your Grace. I'm not sure my limited deception skills will suffice in this instance. Besides, if I suddenly turn agreeable, wouldn't your brother become suspicious and charge me with being an imposter?"

"Yes, I see your point. Well...at the very least, you might wish to ignore his attempts to provoke you."

"I will do my best," Belle promised.

In fact, she had planned to ignore Morgan Spence until the very day she left for Dublin. A mere two weeks away. The snub likely wouldn't have mattered to him, but it would've been quite satisfying to her.

And now she was to be pleasant to the man?

After the shameful way he'd treated her?

Dear God, it would be a miracle if this farce did not turn against her.

* * *

Morgan set the household accounts ledger aside and stood. It had rained the last four days, and for four days now Isabelle had successfully avoided him. By taking meals in her room...*his room*...she had handed him an obvious slight.

But perhaps his recent shameful conduct was now pressing upon his conscience, making him believe a more devious explanation.

Though they spoke only in passing, during those brief encounters she'd been pleasant enough. In fact, now that he thought about it, a bit too pleasant.

Leaving the study, he crossed the corridor and entered the library where Margaret and Bartholomew had become preoccupied in a game of chess. "I had no idea you played, Mags."

"She doesn't," Bartholomew quipped.

"One day, husband, you'll regret those words."

"Perhaps, my lovely wife, but not this day."

"Keep a close eye out for cheating, Bart."

"I do not cheat," Margaret retorted.

"Of course not, my sweet. Oh, Morgan..." The duke held up his glass in a hearty salute. "I appreciate the brandy."

"It met with your approval then?"

"Excessively."

"Splendid. Margaret, did the oriental fan please you?"

"It was lovely, Morgan. Thank you. By the way, I adore the new wallpaper in here. Palm trees and sandy beaches are infinitely more pleasing to the eye than white sheep and yellow daffodils."

"I'm glad you approve," Morgan said and decided to find an enjoyable book to read. After several minutes of searching, he finally chose a slender volume on the history of Scotland's kings and sat down on the sofa to thumb through it. But his mind was far from Scotland or kings. He glanced up. "I purchased a bronze cross for Miss Lindley."

Margaret offered no comment.

"Something to remember her time at Canderlay," he added.

"How thoughtful, dear," she responded.

"Yes, well...I haven't had the chance to give it to her yet. I noticed she took supper in her room again this evening. Is she ill?"

"If you've a genuine concern for Miss Lindley's health," Bartholomew muttered, his attention on the chess board, "you might wish to inquire in person."

"Oh, no," Margaret declared, suddenly alert. "Don't disturb her, Morgan. I'm sure Isabelle is fine."

"Then why has she taken the last three suppers in her room?"

"Dearest brother, do you know so little of women?"

He frowned.

Margaret sighed. "I suspect she's merely contemplating the approaching journey to Dublin. It's a huge step toward freedom, and I'd wager she's a bit overwhelmed."

"And more than a little concerned with the bloody scoundrel who wishes her dead," the duke remarked. "I am amazed what you learned from the constable regarding Mary B and her illegitimate offspring. Margaret, keep your attention on the game. Remember what I told you about the queen?"

"What queen?" she inquired.

"Your queen. The one sitting on the board."

"No need to get irritable, Bartholomew. I'm not addlebrained."

"Children," Morgan admonished. "Play nice or I'll send you to your room."

Bartholomew grinned at his wife. "I've no objection to such punishment."

She blushed. "Behave, rogue."

Morgan's attention returned to the book he'd selected, but his brain refused to interpret the printed words. How he envied his sister's happiness. The love she held for her husband was clear in every word she spoke.

"Bartholomew, would you please cease that infernal humming? You're trying to rush me into making a mistake."

"Apologies, love."

Morgan smiled. Well, perhaps not in every word. Even though the duke and duchess teased, disagreed, and sometimes provoked one another, the tenderness they shared could never be misinterpreted as anything but love.

Would there ever come a time when he could look into a woman's eyes and know with complete certainty that she loved him with her entire heart? He doubted Lydia Adderly truly understood the definition of selfless love. Was she even capable of loving someone other than herself?

Unlikely.

Why then had he been so infatuated?

Why had he asked Lydia's father for permission to call upon her?

At one time he knew the answer to both questions.

Now...

"Margaret..." Morgan paused, wondering how to make his next words sound logical. "Do you ever think about Old Edwina? What I mean is...does she occasional intrude upon your thoughts?"

She smiled. "Yes, quite often."

"And you believe this is normal?"

"Well of course it's normal. Edwina handed out advice like whiskey at a Scottish wedding. It would be foolish to think our minds didn't retain at least some of what she said." She smacked Bartholomew's hand. "Release my pawn."

"I'm offering you a suggestion, wife."

"No need for a handout. I understand this game perfectly."

"Then why is your queen in danger from my next move?"

Morgan closed the book. "Must I remind you two I'm trying to read?"

"You initiated this conversation, Morgan, not I," Margaret defended. "But if you intend to read, you might wish to flip the book over."

He glanced down. The book was indeed upside down. He quickly righted it and then pretended to be deeply engrossed.

"I concede defeat, Bartholomew," Margaret declared after a few moments. "At least for the present. Shall we return to the drawing room? I'll play the fortepiano if you turn the pages."

"If you insist, my love."

"Pleasant dreams, Morgan."

He smiled. "Good night, Mags. Bart."

Once again Morgan turned his attention to Scotland's kings, and once again he was again interrupted as Samuels entered the library to check and lock the windows. Halfway through the next page, he realized someone had followed the old man. And that someone now demanded his undivided attention.

His gaze lifted. "Good evening, Miss Lindley."

She offered a warm smile. "Good evening, Mister Spence. May I have a moment of your time?"

"Certainly." He set the book aside. "Won't you sit down?"

"I'd rather stand, thank you."

Reluctantly Morgan stood as well. "What's on your mind?"

"A desire to earn money."

"I beg your pardon?"

"I will be leaving for Dublin by the end of next week, and I wish to earn enough for passage on a ship as well as a room at a suitable inn. I realize this is rather short notice but if I earn my keep, I'll not be forced to borrow from Mister Samuels nor will I be obligated to accept your charity."

"Charity?"

"Well what would you call it?"

"Hospitality."

"May I remind you, sir, I am not your relative nor am I a friend. What valid reasons have I to exhaust your generosity? What right have I to intrude?"

"Isabelle—"

"Canderlay belongs to you, and I did intrude."

He could not find fault with either of those statements.

"Fire's down to coals, sir," Samuels declared. "Shall I bring in more wood?"

"No. I'll be retiring soon."

"Very well then."

But the old caretaker hovered about the library, taking his time, as though looking for an excuse to eavesdrop.

Morgan's attention returned to Isabelle. "I admire your forethought as well as your eagerness to work, but exactly what do you have in mind?"

"Cleaning and dusting. Making beds. Washing clothes. I can sew and mend socks as well. Or I can serve as maid to Lady Chase."

"Do whatever you like to assist Margaret. As for Canderlay Manor, limit chores to your private suite."

In the background, Jasper Samuels began humming a tune as he tidied up.

I've pleased the old man. Splendid. Perhaps a smile is forthcoming.

"But...how will I earn money for my travels?"

"I will provide you with more than enough."

Her eyes narrowed. "I'm to accept your charity and be grateful then?"

"You're welcome." Morgan picked up the book he'd been reading earlier and despite the fact that Isabelle remained standing, he sat down.

"You can refuse to pay," she declared, "but your stubbornness will not prevent me from making myself useful. In fact, I might try my hand at cooking, leaving Mister Samuels free to go about his numerous other duties."

Samuels cleared his throat in a lengthy manner.

Morgan chanced a quick look at the man, who promptly shook his head. Steering his attention back to Isabelle, he asked, "You've experience?"

"As a cook? Well, no. Not as a profession, but I routinely prepared small meals throughout the day for my father."

"Not a glowing recommendation, since your father is now deceased."

Her chin lifted. "Nevertheless, I *can* cook."

Another clearing of the throat from Jasper Samuels.

Isabelle turned. "You really should do something about that cough, Mister Samuels. Before it grows worse." Facing Morgan, she demanded, "Well?"

"You're right."

She smiled, her beautiful brown filled with delight.

"Samuels," Morgan added, keeping his tone flat. "Take care of that cough immediately."

"Yes, sir."

Though strained, her pleasant expression remained intact. "Have I your permission then?"

"To serve as cook? No, you do not."

"Give me one valid reason."

"Very well, but you must answer one question first."

She capitulated with a quick nod.

"Can you prepare a more appetizing meal than Samuels?"

The light in her eyes vanished in a defeated sigh. "No, I cannot."

"Then you've no point to argue, and this conversation is finished." Morgan stuck his nose in the book once again, half expecting her to grab some object and hurl it at his head.

Instead, she spun around.

Hiding a grin, he peered over the top of the book.

Back as rigid as stone, she stormed off.

"Miss Isabelle?" Samuels called as she reached the door. "I could use your help with a chore."

She halted and turned. "You could?"

"Certainly."

"Oh...well splendid."

Morgan stared at the caretaker. What the devil was he up to? Had they not entered into this conspiracy together?

As they departed the library, Morgan gave up on the book. Arising, he headed for the nearest window.

The sun tried valiantly to break through the clouds for one last appearance, but it was not to be, for dusk was quickly stealing over the manor house. The constant rain had saturated the roads, making travel unwise and thereby delaying his search for tenant farmers. Of course the cottages would need to be rebuilt before the farmers and their families moved in.

The sound of a pianoforte came to life in wave after wave of beautiful music. Margaret. He'd forgotten how brilliantly she played. Forgotten how music could force every worry from his mind.

He stared at the approaching darkness. Truth be told, when it came to the sanctimonious Miss Lindley, he rather preferred insults to polite conversation. Theirs was a duel he often looked forward to. Or perhaps the constant foul weather had soured his disposition somewhat.

The fast tempo changed to a slow rhythm. To a sad tune his grandfather used to sing about a Scotsman mourning the death of a loved one. It isn't until the end of the song that the listener realizes the singer isn't lamenting the loss of a cherished wife, but the absence of his beloved hunting dog.

Morgan groaned.

Ares!

Bartholomew's driver seemed more than capable around the other horses, but he probably found it difficult to control the Arabian. Especially during a thunderstorm. Hopefully Ares hadn't injured anyone.

Exiting the library, Morgan hurried down the corridor and out the front door, almost colliding with one of the armed guards patrolling the grounds. After a brief exchange of pleasantries, he thanked the man for not shooting him. Walking toward the west end of the manor, he heard the distinct sound of a flute. As he neared the stables, the music grew louder. Inside, he found Jasper Samuels leaning against a stall, playing a mournful tune while Isabelle stood on a wooden crate singing to Ares.

Hush, the waves are rolling in.
White with foam, white with foam.
Father toils amid the din
But baby sleeps at home.

Morgan held his breath, his heart producing a strange and uneven rhythm. Her beautiful voice belonged in an opera. Not a foul smelling stable.

Hush, the winds roar hoarse and deep.
On they come, on they come.
Brother seeks the wandering sheep
But baby sleeps at home.

Samuels played the melody while Isabelle stroked Ares' head.

Bloody hell, she's charmed my horse!

197

He glanced around the stalls. Not only Ares, but the other five horses, ears perked and listening, appeared to be enchanted as well.

Hush, the rain sweeps o'er the Knowes.
Where they roam, where they roam.
Sister goes to seek the cows
But baby sleeps at home.

With carefree laughter, Isabelle picked up her skirts, hopped down from the crate, and twirled about in rhythm with the flute. As Samuels ended the tune on a final drawn-out note, she curtsied low to him and then to the horses. One would've thought she performed in front of a group of noble dignitaries or the Prince Regent himself.

Emerging beneath the light of a low-hanging lantern, Morgan clapped his hands together in approval.

Isabelle blushed before presenting a deep curtsy.

"Ares has been quite restless these past few days, sir," Samuels explained. "Miss Isabelle often sang for her father, and I suspected her soothing voice might provide some comfort to the horses instead of the sound of a lonely flute."

Morgan eyed his horse. The beast stood so docile one would never suspect he possessed a temperamental spirit. "An excellent performance, Miss Lindley. What was the song you were singing?"

"An old Irish lullaby Uncle Magnus taught me."

"Well, you sang it beautifully. And you, Samuels, are an expert flutist. Who would've guessed you've skills in this vocation as well?"

Samuels bowed with humble acceptance of the compliment. "If you'll excuse me, sir, I'll be going about my duties. Would you see that Miss Isabelle returns to the manor safely?"

"Yes, of course."

The servant turned to leave, and the flash of a grin appeared in a corner of his mouth. But only one corner and only for a split second.

Morgan was so stunned, he instantly questioned his vision.

"Mister Spence?"

He turned. "Yes, Miss Lindley?"

Her expression revealed mild concern. "Is something amiss?"

"Yes." He shook his head. "No. Devil take it, Isabelle, I thought I saw..."

She frowned. "What?"

"Samuels," Morgan replied then laughed aloud. "I could've sworn the old man cracked a grin."

A moment of pure surprise flickered to life in her eyes. "When?"

"Just now. As he was leaving."

"Are you sure?"

"Absolutely sure."

Ares snorted, as though he didn't care a farthing for the current conversation because it didn't concern him or his well-being.

"Hush, my good lad." Isabelle picked out an apple from a nearby barrel and stepping upon the empty crate she'd used earlier, she held it out to Ares. He tried to pry the offering from between her fingers, but it ended up on the floor at her feet.

"Would you like me to teach you how to feed a horse without getting your fingers nibbled?" Morgan inquired.

She nodded.

He approached the stall. Choosing a smaller apple, he turned her hand over and placed it into her palm. "Now...don't grip it." He moved behind her, holding onto her elbow and breathing in her delicate scent of roses and honey. "Hold it out. Like this." He extended her arm. "And never ever show fear."

Ares snatched the apple from her hand and devoured it.

Isabelle shivered.

"Did he nibble?" Morgan inquired.

"No, his...his lips tickle."

He released her elbow and stood back. "Better a tickle than a bite."

"Yes, that's true." She wiped her hand on her skirt before fetching apples for each of the other horses. At length, she faced him. "I do wish you happiness, Mister Spence. It would be most unkind to wish you anything less."

"I know your heart, Belle. It beats true."

Unbidden, Morgan's thoughts returned to the kiss they'd shared in the cellar. The taste of her lips had been incredibly sweet, stirring his manhood with predictable urgings. He wanted Isabelle. Longed to hold her. Comfort her. And that need grew stronger each time he touched her. But in the end, a momentary pleasure would cause more harm than good. And he wouldn't be that selfish.

Not again.

Tears pooled in her eyes, and she turned away.

Morgan caught her arm, but she refused to look at him. "If my circumstances were not so dire...if this were another time, another life—"

An unexpected shout shattered the quiet outside the stables.

Before Morgan could move a muscle, the discharge of a rifle exploded into the night.

Chapter Fifteen

Fear slammed into Belle.

Mister Spence snatched the lantern from its hook. "Stay here."

As he exited the stables, darkness crowded in around Belle. Alone, except for an occasional snort from the horses, her anxiety tripled.

Had one of the guards fired his weapon?

Wounded someone?

Lord H?

Her heart pounded, each painful beat burdened with a terror that choked the air from her lungs. Cold crept into her body, and her hands tingled with numbness. She found it difficult to breathe, let alone move. Standing in the darkness, acute vulnerability swept over her.

Panic set in. Despite her fear and an overwhelming urge to cower inside one of the empty stalls, Belle grabbed her cloak and rushed outside, keeping to the shadows of the building.

Several men had gathered nearby, their faces illuminated by the glow of an oil lamp carried by Samuels. The duke appeared to be questioning Oxley, his driver. By the occasional shake of the servant's head, he knew nothing of importance.

Long minutes passed.

What had Morgan Spence said before the shot rang out?

If my circumstances were not so dire...

Did he imply that if his finances were more favorable, he might...what?

Ask for the privilege of calling upon her?

If my circumstances were not so dire...

He might be more agreeable and less arrogant?

If this were another time...another life...

He might leave his heart unguarded for once? Yield to the tender stirrings of love?

Her heart soared for one brief second before the voice of reason stole into her joy. This wasn't another time, another life. This was all she had. All he had. And wishing something could be different rarely made circumstances change or become more favorable.

Morgan Spence and I are oceans apart.

Especially in the matter of social standing.

Belle, me girl, certain truths are chiseled in stone before birth, but do not let them be a discouragement. Some folks embrace challenges. Others lack the courage. Which are you?

She smiled.

Mister Spence is indeed a challenge, Uncle.

The seconds ticked by with the speed of a tortoise, and Belle had to force a patience she did not possess. Finally three men headed back across the courtyard toward the duke. The leader carried a lantern, his long strides covering more ground than the others who had to quicken their pace in order to keep up.

"There you are, Morgan," Chase called as they neared. "Did you see anyone?"

"Not one bloody soul. No clue as to who Clancy shot at and apparently missed."

"He was there, sir," the guard declared. "Saw him plain as day. I'd swear to it upon my sainted mother's life."

"Whom did you see? Who was it?"

"A shadow, your Grace. Bent low and creeping around the carriage house."

"Good God, that could've been Samuels," Mister Spence roared. "Or the duke's driver. You could've shot an innocent person."

"Begging your pardon, sir, but I'd just spoken to Samuels and Oxley before they entered the rear of the manor and since I took the first watch, I knew for certain Dix had bedded down in the carriage house."

"He could've gone to relieve himself."

"Yes, sir, but then he usually makes me aware of his goings."

"What about the ladies? You could've endangered—"

"Morgan, there was never any possibility of mistaken identity," the duke insisted in a calm tone. "Procedures were put in place for that very purpose."

"And that's what I done, your Grace. I followed procedure. Mister Spence, I called for whoever it was to halt, but he didn't, sir. He purposely ran. Up to no good, he was."

"Did you notice if he carried a weapon?"

"Too dark, sir, and I wasn't about to ask. Whoever he was, he had no business sneaking about in the shadows."

"I agree. Samuels, did you see anything suspicious?"

"No, sir. I had just walked into the kitchen with Mister Oxley to prepare a meal for Mister Dix. That's when we heard the shot and ran outside."

"What about you, Oxley?"

"I'm afraid I've nothing to add to what Samuels said, Mister Spence."

"Dix, did you hear or see anything?" the duke asked.

"Nothing unusual, your Grace."

"That'll be all then. You and Clancy may return to your duties. Oxley, if you've nothing further to add, you may return to your quarters."

"Yes, your Grace."

After the men walked off, Samuels inquired of his employer, "What of Miss Isabelle, sir?"

"I'm here." Belle emerged from the shadows and hurried toward the others. "My nerves are a bit unsteady, but otherwise I'm fine."

The old caretaker raised a brow. "Since I left you in good hands, miss, I had no doubt of your wellbeing."

Morgan Spence's gaze traveled from her head to her feet then back to her face. "Your attire brings to mind a certain memory. One I'm not too fond of."

Belle knew immediately what he referred to. "I apologize if my cloak disturbs you, sir. In the future, I shall refrain from wearing it in your presence."

He nodded once in acknowledgement.

"Mister Spence, the person Mister Clancy caught sneaking about...could it have been Lord H?"

"It's possible, but there's no way to be certain."

"It could've been a thief," the duke remarked.

But more likely a devious murderer.

Dear God...the nightmare begins again.

If her knees weren't threatening to buckle, she would've raced to the manor and headed straight to the safety of the secret room.

"Isabelle, you'd better go inside with Samuels." Mister Spence urged. "Perhaps you can inform my sister what's occurred while the duke and I take another look around the carriage house and grounds."

"Very well."

"Do not concern yourself with my wife, Miss Lindley. I left her deep in slumber not more than half an hour ago. I doubt she heard the shot."

"Oh...then I'll not disturb her." Belle turned a timid smile upon Morgan Spence, and the look in his eyes betrayed a possessiveness she had not expected. Her breath hitched as though she'd just ran a hundred yards in heavy boots through shifting sand.

He cares for me.

Suddenly her thoughts turned from her own safety...to his. "Mister Spence, I wonder...would you permit me to accompany you and his Grace?"

"About the grounds? In search of a prowler?" His gaze narrowed. "No, I would not. And before my refusal prompts you to say something regretful, I'd like you to consider your welfare as justification."

"My welfare? Then teach me to fire a weapon so I can protect myself."

"Actually, Morgan, that's a sensible request."

"No, Bart, it's a disaster waiting to occur. Go inside, Isabelle. We'll discuss this later."

But they wouldn't. She could see it in his eyes.

Inside the foyer, Belle said good night to Samuels before climbing the stairs. Locking both the antechamber door as well as the bedroom door, she lit the oil lamp before opening the panel. Alone in the secret room, she slipped out of the cloak and tossed it aside. After changing into nightclothes, she climbed into the narrow cot.

The terrifying shadows began almost immediately. Lurking in every corner of her mind. Chasing her through the dark forest. Through every room of Canderlay Manor.

Sleep held a delicate balance over her consciousness. It could be a trusted friend or brutal enemy.

At present...it was the latter.

Frustrated, Belle tossed back the covers and sat up. If sleep would not come of its own accord, perhaps she could persuade it. Draping the cloak about her, she picked up the lamp then headed down the stone steps.

Nearing the secret panel, she heard voices coming from inside the library and realized they belonged to Mister Spence and the duke.

"Devil take it," announced the duke. "That's the last of the brandy."

"Good riddance. I much prefer the taste of Scottish whiskey."

And with that declaration, both gentlemen launched into a friendly debate over spirits. It wasn't long before the conversation turned to women.

Hoping to avoid a gentleman's private thoughts on the matter, Belle turned to leave.

"I noticed the look in Miss Lindley's eyes, Morgan."

She paused.

"What look?"

"Was it not obvious?"

"Bart, what the devil are you talking about?"

"Good God! I cannot believe you've remained blind to the truth."

"What truth? Must you constantly speak in riddles?"

"She worries for you, Morgan. It's the first sign of a woman's love."

Strained silence.

Belle didn't dare move for fear she'd miss his response.

"Isabelle has been sheltered her entire life," Mister Spence explained. "She's not yet experienced the love between a man and a woman. Her kindness comes from her heart. And if you haven't noticed, her concern extends to everyone. Nobles, guards, and servants alike. And it even includes my restless horse and his stable companions."

"I never doubted the girl's innocence or her kindness, Morgan. And unlike your beloved Edwina, I've never claimed to be a seer. Still, I know the future expectations you've designed for yourself and for this estate. Admirable expectations, I might add. I simply wish to caution you regarding the usual and predictable distractions."

"I'll not argue that Isabelle is a worthy distraction, Bart, but you've no cause for concern." A short-lived silence. "I've no plans to include the vicar's daughter in my future."

* * *

A week later, Morgan dismounted and leaving Ares to wander, he walked down to the old rundown barn near the ruins of the tenant cottages. One of the doors had been propped open, and inside straw littered the floor. The horse stalls were unrecognizable as most lay buried beneath a partially collapsed roof.

He glanced up. A portion of the loft remained intact but would be useless for storage. The barn would have to be torn down and rebuilt. He proceeded to the rear door. The remains of several cottages stood scattered within a few yards of one another.

Bartholomew walked up beside him. "All this should be torn down and carted off. Build two barns and a row of smaller pens to hold livestock. Six to seven cottages should serve as sufficient living quarters."

"That sounds reasonable."

"There are several families of tenant farmers living on the outskirts of Maidstone. Some highly respected and well-known for their excellent crops. We should start there."

"Your knowledge of such matters is precisely the reason I asked you to ride along with me this morning. By the way, you should probably steer clear of the King's Men Tavern."

"Not that it bothers me in the least but...why?"

"I may have led the owner to believe he was speaking with you."

"What the devil...Morgan, please tell me you did not fondle a barmaid."

"There was lovely young maiden available, however, I did not fondle her nor did I proposition her. Assuming the title of a nobleman was the only way to ensure the owner would speak honestly with me."

"That better be truth, or Margaret will place a noose about my neck."

"Better your thick neck than your tender manhood."

As they walked back to their horses, the duke's attention settled upon a distant pasture. "As to the matter of raising sheep, I'm not sure it's a good idea. They will require plenty of land."

"That venture can be postponed for now. My main concern is rebuilding these cottages. I've asked the men who repaired Canderlay to return next week to discuss the repairs here."

"Excellent. It would seem you have *this* matter well in hand."

"Yes, I believe I..." Morgan turned, staring at his friend. "What do you mean *this* matter? Is there something I've neglected?"

Bartholomew mounted his horse. "Did I imply as much?"

"No, but your tone of voice did. I've no time for games, Bart." Morgan grabbed Ares' reins and lifted himself into the saddle. "If you've something on your mind, by all means...speak up."

"Very well. It's come to my attention that you've been sleeping in a chair in the corridor outside the master suite for the past several nights."

"How do you know how I've been spending my nights?"

"Margaret."

"I should've guessed. And to set matters straight, I wasn't sleeping."

"She said your eyes were closed."

"She was mistaken. I was resting."

"With a pistol in your lap?"

"I had need of its companionship."

"I know precisely what you were doing, Morgan, and it's rather reckless, if you ask me. What if Miss Lindley or any of the others had startled you?"

"I would not have fired upon a friendly face." Several birds flushed from the nearby underbrush, and Morgan briefly glanced up as they took flight. "I stood watch in the corridor these past few nights to keep Samuels from doing it. I couldn't have that old man sitting in a chair all evening and then going about his duties during the day."

"And so you took his place? While I highly applaud your sense of chivalry, there was no need for such heroics. Clancy and Dix have been—"

"Performing their duties well. Yes, I'm fully aware of that fact but try to convince Samuels. He's quite stubborn, and he worries about Isabelle as though she were his own daughter."

"He's a decent man."

"You'll get no argument about that."

Bartholomew urged his horse toward the path leading out of the clearing. "It might be wise to warn Miss Lindley to be careful of you and your companion. That is...your pistol."

"I'd rather you didn't tell her. My discomfort, however brief, might add an unintended weight upon her shoulders, and I wouldn't want that."

"You know...she's leaving at the end of next week?"

Morgan nodded. He didn't care to think about losing Isabelle.

"You simply intend to let her go?" Bartholomew inquired.

"I've no say in the matter."

"I see."

"What do mean by that?"

"Nothing. Nothing at all." They rode in silence for several minutes until Bartholomew added, "Did she approve of your gift?"

"Who?"

"Miss Lindley. You gave her the cross, did you not?"

"No."

"Why the delay?"

Morgan sighed. "Perhaps I'm waiting for Isabelle to stop avoiding me."

"Why would she avoid you?"

"Do I know the strange workings of a woman's mind? You've more experience in these matters than I."

"No reason to get prickly." Another long silence. "Margaret believes Miss Lindley will do well with the proper teaching."

"Planning to sacrifice Isabelle to the bloody wolves, is she?"

"Why does it concern you? You've no interest in the girl."

"Good God, Bart, we're talking about decency. And as far as interest, are you not the same gentleman who warned me against distractions?"

"Yes, well...that was Margaret's idea. She hoped to measure your feelings."

"Did she now? And so she recruited you to carry out the shameful deed. Tell me, your Grace. Do you always perform at your wife's request?"

The duke grinned. "If there is sufficient motivation."

"You disappoint me, Bart."

"As do you, Morgan."

"Then what would you have me do? Allow Isabelle to leave or hold her prisoner? If she leaves, do you suppose she might eventually change her mind and return to Canderlay?"

"Margaret was correct. You care for Miss Lindley, do you not?"

"Well of course I..." Morgan's eyes narrowed. "Oh, I see. I know precisely where you're going with this conversation. Yes, I care about Isabelle. More than I should, but I can offer her nothing. If I don't acquire a wealthy bride within the year, this estate will sink faster than a ship perched atop a rotted hull."

"I realize Canderlay is vastly important to you, my friend, and understandably so, but there is far more to life than what a gentleman owns. And if Canderlay is all you possess, then what have you gained? A bleak existence?"

"Bart, you suddenly remind me of Old Edwina."

"Odd that you should mention Margaret's beloved seer. I dreamed of her recently. A most disturbing occurrence, and one I pray never to repeat."

Caught off guard by the duke's odd confession, Morgan laughed. The sound invaded the quiet forest before its echo gently faded.

"Amused, are we?"

"How could I not be?" Morgan hadn't forgotten his own disturbing experience in the cellar a week past, and at the time he had heartily questioned his mental stability. Now...he was more than pleased someone else had encountered a similar incident. "I'm curious, my friend. What on earth caused you to dream of Edwina Mason?"

"I wish to God I knew."

"Do I detect fear in your voice?"

"Not at all. I'm merely as perplexed as you."

"When did this dream occur?"

Bartholomew reined in abruptly. "Seven nights past."

Morgan halted Ares beside the other horse. "The evening Clancy shot at our mysterious trespasser?"

The duke nodded. "In my fretful sleep, I saw Edwina hovering over my bed like a wasp buzzing about."

"What did she want?"

"How would I know? She never spoke, not one word. She simply stared at me, shaking her head, as though I'd somehow displeased her."

"Odd."

"Indeed. Why would I dream of an old Scotswoman who's not walked this earth in years?"

"If you displeased Edwina, her ghost likely intends to seek retribution."

"Good God, Morgan!" Fire lit Bartholomew's black eyes. "I had hoped you'd gotten past such nonsense. Believe me, that ridiculous thought never once crossed my mind. Ghost, indeed." He slapped the reins, urging his horse up the embankment toward the road. "I simply encountered the memory of an old woman," he shouted over his shoulder. "Not a bloody ghost."

Once on the road, Morgan caught up, and they rode side by side. "I wouldn't speak lightly of the matter, Bart. Old Edwina could be listening."

"Then her bloody ears will burn. Poke fun all you like, Morgan, but I will say this again for your benefit and yours alone. I do not believe in ghostly apparitions or spirits, and no argument will persuade me otherwise."

"Until a storm descends upon you with the vengeance of an old Scotswoman."

With a daunting glare, Bartholomew spurred his horse into a quick pace.

Amused, Morgan glanced toward the heavens, offering silent thanks to the Good Father that Edwina Mason had decided to haunt someone else's thoughts.

* * *

Belle crept down the stairs, following Lady Chase's lead. "We'll never get past Mister Samuels," she whispered. "He may have only one good eye, but it's the eye of a hawk."

"Do not worry about Samuels," her Grace stated, keeping her voice low. "He's around back, hitching up the cart. I overheard him telling my brother this morning that he's traveling to Maidstone for supplies."

"How fortunate."

"Yes, the Good Father must be watching over us. Did you bring the journal?"

"It's hidden in my bodice. Where are we going?"

"Westwood Hall."

"Why?"

"I'll explain in the carriage."

Excitement surged through Belle, and she sucked in a deep breath. "I feel like a condemned prisoner who's finally getting a long-awaited taste of freedom."

"We've yet to escape, my dear," her ladyship warned as they reached the foyer. "But I have to admit, this was far easier than I expected. Wait here while I see if the carriage has been brought around."

Belle instinctively retreated into the shadow of the stairwell.

Lady Chase crossed the foyer, out of sight.

"Your Grace?" called a voice from the nearby corridor.

"Oh, it's you, Mister Samuels. Did you wish to speak with me?"

"Yes, my lady. One moment, if you please."

Curse the foul misfortune!

Belle sped around the stairwell to the other side.

"Oh, forgive me, your Grace," begged Samuels. "I had no idea you planned an outing this morning."

"That's quite all right. Is there a problem?"

"I apologize for the delay, my lady, but Mister Wilkerson just arrived, and he's awaiting approval."

"Who?"

"The gentleman who cleaned and repaired Lady Canderlay's portrait. I thought you might like to inspect it."

"Morgan found a portrait of our grandmother?"

"Yes, your Grace. Did Mister Spence not inform you?"

"No, he did not." Her voice sounded slightly perturbed. "I've always suspected my brother was a bit absentminded. Now I've been given proof. Where did you put it?"

"In the library."

"Not the most advantageous location. What not the formal drawing room?"

"The library was the portrait's previous home, and the room her ladyship personally chose."

And then their voices and footsteps faded down the corridor.

With nothing to do except wait, Belle leaned against the wall. She hadn't spoken to Morgan Spence since that night in the barn, and she didn't plan to. His conversation with the duke had made things quite clear.

I've no plans to include her in my future.

He would never care for Belle the way she cared for him. The injury caused by that knowledge still bled. Perhaps it would bleed indefinitely.

Why must I yearn for a man who values wealth over love?

And yet...she did yearn.

Hopelessly.

Foolishly.

A self-inflicted wound.

Morgan Spence wasn't to blame but then again, he wasn't blameless. He seemed to enjoy tugging her heart in one direction and then shoving it in another. His casual disinterest had wounded what little pride she possessed, but that was nothing compared to the damage he'd inflicted upon her heart.

Footsteps accompanied by voices came from the corridor.

"Thank you again, Mister Wilkerson," said the duchess. "You and your son did a remarkable job on my grandmother's portrait. And thank you kindly for setting it in its proper place above the mantel. I'm certain my brother will be extremely pleased with your work."

"You are most welcome, your Grace. If Mister Spence has any other portraits in need of repair, have Samuels contact me."

"I certainly will."

The main door opened and then closed.

"Well, Mister Samuels," her ladyship said in a cheery tone. "I suppose you're eager to be off to Maidstone."

"Indeed, your Grace. Allow me to escort you to the carriage."

"Oh...well..."

Samuels, you are ruining my escape!

The main door opened.

Belle's hopes dropped like a stone in deep water. She emerged from her hiding place only to find Dix standing at the door, hat in hand.

She quickly retreated behind the stairwell.

"Pardon me for using the front entrance, your Grace, but I feared you'd take the carriage out before I got the chance to speak with you."

"That's perfectly all right, Mister Dix. Is something amiss?"

"There's a woman waiting at the rear of the manor, my lady. Claims you hired her and her daughter to do laundry."

"Dear me. Is it Friday? With all the rain, I lost track of the days. Very well. Show these women to the laundry house and inform them I'll be right out."

Once again the main door opened then closed promptly.

This time Belle did not move.

"Do not let me keep you, Mister Samuels," the duchess said. "I'm sure you have a tedious journey ahead."

"Quite so. I'd best see if Miss Isabelle requires anything before I go."

"Oh, no. I just spoke with her, and I believe she intends to pass the morning deep in a mystery."

"Nose in a book, has she? It'll likely ease the worry from her mind. Well then, I'll be off. Good day, your Grace."

"Good day, Mister Samuels."

Within a matter of seconds, the old caretaker passed Belle's hiding place, heading for the rear of the manor.

Lady Chase peered around the stairwell. "Hurry, Isabelle. My driver is expecting you. I'll be along shortly."

Belle nodded and without a backward glance, she raced through the foyer and out the front door. It was only after she reached the safety of the carriage that it occurred to her that perhaps she should've brought along the pistol Samuels kept on the night table beside his bed.

Chapter Sixteen

Hawk adjusted the wide-brimmed hat low over his eyes. Dressed in normal attire, he would've garnered too much attention lurking about Maidstone with no apparent purpose. Disguised as a common worker, he blended in perfectly with the locals.

He stared at the buildings on the opposite side of High Street. The old caretaker had been busy this morning loading his cart with supplies before entering the butcher shop.

Waiting for Samuels to exit, Hawk leaned against the stone wall, and his thoughts inevitably drifted. He must be careful this time. Everything must go as planned. Unlike a few nights ago when he'd been surprised by the armed guard patrolling the grounds of Canderlay.

Morgan Spence had set a clever trap.

Does he know my identity?

No, or he would've confronted me.

Impatient, he crossed the cobbled street to the butcher shop and glanced through the window. Samuels stood near the fish table, speaking with the owner.

Hawk paced several feet away. He'd been careful to reveal nothing of importance to his brother. And he'd never spoken to Isabelle Lindley. Never met her. With Barlow dead, she had no valid reason to stay hidden. No reason to remain at Canderlay.

Unless she'd read her father's journal and realized she was in grave danger.

But perhaps she knows nothing of me at all.

If that were true...

A door opened behind Hawk.

"Pleasant day to you, Mister Samuels," called the shopkeeper. "My son place your purchases in the cart."

"I appreciate your kindness, sir. Good day."

"Good day. I'll expect you in a fortnight."

Keeping the upper portion of his face concealed in the shadow of his hat, Hawk nodded once as the servant passed by, but his greeting went unnoticed. Apparently the uppity Samuels was unaware he worked for a man who possessed no noble title. A fact Hawk would enjoy pointing out.

Near the end of the street, a young boy approached Samuels. After a brief conversation, the caretaker reached inside his pocket, withdrew something, and placed it in the boy's palm. Nodding with enthusiasm, the lad ran down the street in Hawk's direction, stumbling twice in his eagerness to reach the old man's cart.

Ah, the price of loyalty.

Hawk smiled. The lad's greed would serve him well.

* * *

Belle glanced out the window as the carriage traveled the long drive toward Westwood Hall. The house itself looked much like a castle, tall and imposing in the distance. Old as time but magnificent nonetheless.

The carriage soon rolled to a stop near the main entrance.

"You seem anxious, Isabelle," Lady Chase remarked.

"No, not anxious. Merely hopeful."

The carriage door opened, and the driver lowered steps to the ground.

Lady Chase alighted first then waited for Belle. "Stay calm, my girl." She linked arms as they climbed the wide stone steps to the door. "I shall do most of the talking."

"To which I am most grateful, my lady. Do you truly believe the Earl of Westwood will remember Mary Barlow?"

"If his lordship is anything like Great Uncle Charles, he's probably aware of every scandal that ever occurred in Kent. And if he does not recall Mary the servant girl, perhaps he will remember Lord H."

"One can only hope."

Lady Chase halted at the door and lifted the brass knocker, allowing it to fall in place several times. Not long after, the door opened. "Good morning," she said to the grim-faced servant. "I am the Duchess of Chase, and this is Miss Isabelle Lindley."

The man offered a dutiful nod to her ladyship, but he did not acknowledge Belle nor did he permit a glance in her direction.

"I realize it's rather early in the day to entertain visitors," the duchess added with smile, "but I've an urgent matter to discuss with Lord Westwood. Is he in residence?"

"He is, your Grace. Step inside, if you please."

Belle followed her ladyship into Westwood Hall, and they were shown to a large room that appeared to be a formal parlor.

"I am Carlton," the servant stated. "His lordship's butler. Would you care for refreshments?"

"That would be lovely," Lady Chase replied.

"I'll see that it's brought in," he said before departing.

As they waited, her Grace glanced about the room. "Most intriguing. Or perhaps that's not the correct word. I daresay I would've never had the courage to use such bold colors as red and black. Well, not concurrently. And to be honest, the haphazard pattern in the drapes is rather overwhelming. This is proof, Isabelle, why a gentleman should never be allowed to decorate his castle."

"How can you be certain Lord Westwood chose these colors?"

"The earl is a widower. He lost his wife several decades ago."

"You've met him?"

"I've not had the pleasure, but Great Uncle Charles spoke of him with genuine fondness."

The door opened, and a servant girl brought in a tray of tea and biscuits. A tall, dark-haired young woman wearing a red gown with a black sash tied at the waist trailed behind. Her gaudy attire fit the room, but it did not fit her youthful figure or tender age.

Was this the earl's daughter?

"Your Grace." After a brief hesitation, the woman held out her hand to the duchess in greeting. "I am Louise Westwood. That is...Lady Westwood."

"Oh..." Lady Chase's eyes widened. "I thought..." In a matter of seconds, her composure returned. "Forgive me, my dear countess. I had no idea his lordship had remarried."

"I'm not surprised." She dismissed the servant girl and waited until the door closed before adding, "My husband and I live in seclusion, cut off from the friends he once admired."

"Envious of the earl's good fortune, are they?"

"If that were true, their insults would be almost bearable. No, I am despised because my blood is not noble." Her eyes narrowed with suspicion. "Which brings me, your Grace, to the purpose of your unexpected visit."

Belle admired the girl's blatant honesty.

Lady Chase placed her hand upon the girl's arm. "Do not allow pompous and arrogant fools to make you feel less worthy than you truly are. Once you open that particular door, it will be difficult to close."

Suspicion faded from Lady Westwood's eyes, replaced by a modest amount of respect. "I will try to remember your advice." For a brief second, she looked lost, as though she had no idea what to do next. "Shall I pour the tea?"

"Yes, thank you," her Grace replied. She sat on the sofa and pulled Belle down beside her. "I truly must apologize for the intrusion, Lady Westwood, but Miss Lindley and I were hoping to speak with your husband in regards to an urgent matter."

The young countess hesitated, her hand upon the teapot. Finally she glanced at Belle before pouring the tea. "Forgive me, Miss Lindley. I have very little experience in social matters. I learned about proper manners under my husband's gentle tutelage but when asked to put that knowledge to use, it would seem I have failed. I am ashamed I neglected to offer you a polite greeting."

"That's quite all right, my lady. I was not offended."

"I'm relieved then." Lady Westwood's hand shook as she replaced the teapot on the table.

She's nervous.

Belle understood exactly how she felt, and compassion for this young woman warmed her heart. "I was just thinking, my lady, that for one so young, your manners are quite impressive."

Lady Westwood offered a smile of gratitude before shifting her attention. "Your Grace, you spoke of an urgent matter?"

"Yes, but I'm afraid the explanation is rather long and complicated. Perhaps if his lordship joined us..."

"I'm sorry, but that would be impossible. You see, Miles has been quite ill these past few months, and he's taken to his bed."

Bitter disappointment surrounded Belle, but she realized she mustn't be selfish and think only of herself. "I am truly sorry, Lady Westwood. I will say a prayer for you and his lordship."

"Thank you, Miss Lindley."

"We had no idea," declared Lady Chase. "Is there anything Miss Lindley or I can do?"

"No. My husband's condition is a result of his extreme age. Some days are kind. Others are not."

"Then we won't keep you from his bedside a moment longer. Good day, Lady Westwood. Come, Isabelle."

As they reached the door, the countess stopped them. "I've no wish to appear rude. Perhaps I can give my husband a message when he wakes."

Lady Chase glanced at Belle. "Let's finish our tea, shall we?"

"I'd like that, your Grace."

After a few minutes of polite conversation, Lady Chase set down her cup and got to the point of their visit, explaining everything she knew or suspected regarding all that had happened to Belle. She ended with, "Since your husband has lived in Kent for many years, we had hoped his memory would provide the answers Miss Lindley so desperately seeks."

"I understand. You wish to learn the identity of Lord H." Lady Westwood folded her hands in her lap. "Miss Lindley, I admire your courage. In your position, I doubt I would've survived a week."

"You are stronger than you realize, my lady. I can hear it in your voice."

Momentary surprise reflected in the girl's eyes. "I'm not sure that's true. However I appreciate the thought." Her attention returned to the duchess. "Forgive me, your Grace, if this suggestion is viewed as improper but if you still wish to speak to my husband, I can take you up to his room."

"We shall ignore the strict rules of impropriety for the moment, my dear. Although..." Lady Chase offered an apologetic grimace. "Perhaps it would be best if Isabelle remained here."

Another wave of disappointment crushed Belle. This type of setback had become habitual. A routine frustration. Nevertheless, when Lady Chase requested the journal, she handed it over without argument.

Alone in the parlor, Belle tried not to think about Morgan Spence. Tried not to scrutinize her feelings for the gentleman. She paced about the room. Drank tea. Nibbled on biscuits. Inspected several portraits. Drank another cup of tea, cold by now. Glanced out the window. Returned to pacing.

In the end, the truth became impossible to hide. She had fallen in love, and nothing Mister Spence said or did would likely ever change that. He desired wealth and when he looked at her, he saw only a poor vicar's daughter. A woman whose current funds stood several inches below the poverty line.

During the third round of anxious pacing, the parlor door opened.

Belle turned, her heart in her throat, but only Carlton stood there.

"Her Grace awaits," he declared, his tone indifferent.

Like a blast of cold air, excitement rushed over her. "Thank you."

In the foyer, Lady Chase stood with her arm around Lady Westwood's shoulders, and it appeared as though they were intentionally keeping their voices low. Was Lord Westwood more ill than his wife believed?

Belle approached them, a thousand questions littering her mind, but compassion for a dying old man forced itself to the forefront. "Is his lordship worse?"

"He's resting," the countess replied, and she did not appear overly worried.

"Goodbye, Lady Westwood," Lady Chase said before giving the girl a quick hug. "I shall pray diligently for your husband's health. If all goes well, I shall expect to see you at Chase Manor's Harvest Ball at the end of September."

"Forgive me, your Grace. I realize you gave that invitation because Miles expected it of you, but you are under no obligation to honor it."

"You misunderstand my motives. I agree with your husband. Whatever your upbringing, you are now a lady of quality, and you must act accordingly. Stand against adversity with both feet planted firmly on the ground. Look stupidity in the eye and take what belongs to you."

"You are very kind, Lady Chase. I shall speak to my husband again. Perhaps he will recall something of importance."

"Yes," the duchess agreed. "Perhaps he will."

Belle's hopes dashed to the floor. Nevertheless she thanked the countess, bid her farewell, and waited until she and Lady Chase were assisted into the carriage before inquiring, "What did his lordship say?"

"Nothing of interest," the duchess replied. "I repeated Mary's sad story and made it clear your life was still in danger, but the earl could offer no useful information. There was a brief moment though when I suspected he wished to say more, but I must've been mistaken."

"His lordship is quite old. He may lack the memory he once had."

"He recalled his friendship with Great Uncle Charles and how they once courted the same young lady. He even remembered my mother, and he met her only once. I cannot be sure, Isabelle, but I strongly suspect the earl is hiding something. I remember thinking that Mary's pitiful story did not surprise him, but the fact that I knew the details did."

"Then...how do we persuade his lordship to confide in us?"

Expelling a weary sigh, the duchess glanced out the carriage window. "That, my dear Isabelle, is a very good question."

* * *

Hawk lifted the old man's body from the back of the cart, threw it across his shoulder, and headed for the rundown barn several yards away. He would not have struck the servant with such force, causing the wound to his brow, if the Samuels had not reached for his pistol.

"You surprise me, Caretaker. Carrying a weapon at your age. A dangerous practice. One that could've gotten you killed. Of course..." He grunted, shifting the majority of Samuels' weight higher upon his shoulder. "Death might still come for you before this day ends."

Hawk entered the barn and chose a spot near the center. Placing his burden down upon the straw-littered floor, he pulled a short rope from his coat then bound the unconscious man's hands and feet. After rechecking the knots, he stood and admired his handy work.

Nothing but a bag of old bones. As frail as a wounded butterfly.

He'd be doing Samuels a favor by finishing him off.

What wrong has he committed?

Why waste sentiment on a useless servant?

Hawk withdrew a handkerchief and wiped the sweat from his brow. The stark white of the cloth brought an image to his cluttered mind. A long ago vision of blood on snow. His father had shot a man. A servant who angered him by sending for a physician without his master's permission.

Felicia.

She had been far too ill for a cure.

Laughter bubbled like a vile spring inside his chest until finally it escaped his throat. How he had despised that woman! Hated her more than his weak-minded prostitute of a mother. If anyone deserved a brutal end, it was Felicia Glenhawk. Five long weeks she'd writhed in her bed, her once beautiful face contorted with pain.

And Hawk had enjoyed every moment of his stepmother's agony.

The sins of the father shall fall upon the son.

"No!" A moment of weakness followed the unexpected outburst. "My son will never be touched by my sins." Hawk shook his fists toward heaven. "My demons are my bloody own."

Fool! Insanity follows your bloodline like a trained hound follows his master's every step. Your children will never be safe. Never!

Hawk recognized the voice. It had tormented him for over a decade. "It's you, is it not, reverend?" He glanced around the barn as though he expected to see the vicar's ghost. "It doesn't matter. You can no longer save your precious daughter."

Something scurried past his feet. A rat searching for a way out of the barn.

As raw emotions subsided, sanity returned, and he decided to champion his actions towards Samuels. "The old man reached for his weapon. Am I not allowed to defend myself?"

Present your argument to God. Not me.

"Must I remind you, Reverend..." His voice rose in anger. "I do not fear your God, nor will I run from His wrath!"

Samuels moaned.

Hawk nudged him with the toe of his boot. "Wake up, caretaker."

His eyes opened. "Who..." Eventually his gaze came into focus. "Who...are you?"

"Do you not recognize me?"

The old servant's eyes dimmed. "No, sir." He drew a labored breath. "I've never seen...you before."

"A fortunate response. One that will keep you alive, for the moment."

Samuels wet his lips. "Why...?"

"Why have I abducted you? Bound your hands and feet?"

A barely perceptible nod.

"Because your Miss Lindley has something I want. Can you guess what that is?"

No response.

"The bloody journal, caretaker. The one discovered in the church. And you must know by now what I intend to trade for it."

"My life...no doubt."

"Precisely."

Samuels drew another shallow breath, pain in his expression. "I am a lowly servant. No one...of importance."

"You underestimate Miss Lindley's loyalty. I've no doubt she'll come."

"And I'm just as certain...Mister Spence...will prevent her."

"Yes, I've noticed how your annoying employer enjoys interfering with my plans. Fortunately he knows nothing of this latest ploy."

"If you dare harm Miss Isabelle, there will be no place to hide." With difficulty, Samuels rose to a sitting position, and a trail of blood ran from the gash on his brow down between his eyes. "Your speech betrays a worthy upbringing, sir. Whoever you are...your noble title will not protect you."

"We'll see, old man," Hawk quipped. "We will bloody well see."

* * *

"Is this not a splendid afternoon, Isabelle?" Lady Chase asked as they climbed the stairs to the second floor together.

Splendid?

No.

Frustrating? Depressing? Exhausting?

Definitely!

Belle frowned. "I'm not sure I understand what you mean, your Grace."

"Listen. Do you not hear this blissful silence? Since we returned to Canderlay before my brother and husband, we avoided a stern lecture and the need to offer an explanation of where we've been for the last several hours. And believe me, dear girl, those two would've been quite angry."

"So...you do not intend to tell them?"

"Why on earth would I commit such a foolish blunder?"

Belle followed her down the second floor corridor. "I'm looking forward to exchanging my formal attire for a comfortable day dress." She paused outside the master suite. "Afterward, I believe I'll visit the library."

"That sounds lovely, Isabelle. My son Jonathan adores reading. Actually he's rather obsessed with it."

"I'd forgotten you have a child, your Grace. How old is he?"

"Seven. At present he and Bartholomew's mother are enjoying a visit with relatives. They'll be home in October. I must say...I do miss him."

"I'm sure he misses you as well."

Her Grace smiled. "You are such a dear young woman, Isabelle, and I have grown quite fond of you. What you said to Lady Westwood was most kind."

"I meant it, your Grace."

"You must be extremely disappointed our visit did not end the way we had hoped. Still, you mustn't give up. As always, the Good Father watches over those who place their trust in Him. My mother taught me that."

"Faith comes with ease to the lips, but the heart must learn to embrace what it cannot see," Belle quoted from memory. "Words my father often spoke."

"He was quite gifted. Run along now. The library is waiting."

"Would you care to join me?"

"No, thank you. The last book I chose put me to sleep in quick fashion."

"Oh? What book was that?"

"One dedicated to flowering plants. Morgan recently gave it to me as a gift. He found it downstairs when he first arrived."

The book I left on the old sofa in the library.

"He mistakenly assumed I'd treasure it because of my love for roses. Please do not misunderstand. I've nothing against reading, but this book was quite boring. In fact, it was mostly nonsense. My dear husband is the only reason I've not tossed it into the fire."

"He enjoyed the book?"

"Heavens, no. When we return to Chase Manor, I plan to read a chapter to his Grace each evening until he gives me permission to build my solarium."

"Well then, I shall pray for your immediate success."

"That would indeed be a blessing."

Belle laughed. "Would you like me to bring up a lunch tray?"

"That won't be necessary. This may be difficult to believe, Isabelle, but I am well able to forage for food on my own."

"Very well but if you change your mind or if you need help undressing..."

"I can manage, my dear. I'll see you at dinner," the duchess called over her shoulder as she headed down the corridor.

Belle entered the antechamber and walked straight to the bedroom. Selecting a simple white gown from the wardrobe, she quickly changed. After taking the pins from her hair, brushing and then braiding it, she returned downstairs. Half an hour later, and with several books in hand, she was about to exit the library when she thought of Samuels. He should've returned by now and was likely preparing a late lunch. Perhaps she could assist.

After carrying the books upstairs and setting them on the table beside the bed, Belle returned downstairs. Strolling through the dining room and into the kitchen, she noticed the cook stove gave off no warmth. In fact it was cold to the touch. She opened the door to the larder but found the contents to be sparse.

Obviously the caretaker had not yet returned with supplies. Nevertheless, she headed to his private quarters and knocked upon the door. "Mister Samuels?"

No response.

Belle returned to the kitchen and opened the rear door. She immediately noticed the boy wearing a faded brown cap. Although his clothing appeared a bit worn, he was no street urchin or beggar. Not with that adorable ruddy face.

"Best run along, lad," Clancy instructed, his tone imposing. "I'll not be turnin' you loose inside the manor house."

"But, sir, I've come to speak with Miss Isabelle."

"What business have you with young miss?"

The boy's chin trembled, as though he were about to burst into tears.

He's no more than nine or ten.

"Mister Clancy?" Belle stepped outside so he could see her. "Who is this?"

"Didn't ask, Miss Lindley. Says I'm to fetch you."

Belle smiled at the boy then took his hand. "I am Isabelle. And you are?"

"Andrew, miss. 'Tis urgent I speak with you."

"Very well, Andrew. Shall we go inside the kitchen and see if we can find something to eat?"

With a bright grin, he nodded.

"Splendid. Oh, Mister Clancy, have you seen Mister Samuels?"

"Not since this morning, miss."

A tight knot curled inside Belle's stomach. An uneasy sensation she could not ignore. "Then I daresay you've not eaten lunch?"

"Samuels said he might be delayed. Gave me and Dix permission to help ourselves to any food we found in the kitchen." Clancy offered a lopsided grin. "Which we did."

"Oh...very good then."

Samuels was merely delayed.

Nothing to cause concern.

Returning to the kitchen, Belle showed the boy where to wash his hands and then sat him down at a side table before searching for food. She found bread wrapped in a cloth and a hearty stew in a pot inside the stove. After placing the food on the table, she headed to the cabinet for a bowl.

"It's been many years since Canderlay entertained visitors." Taking a spoon from the drawer, she turned. "Not since my uncle..."

Young Andrew had not waited for the convenience of a bowl and spoon. He had pulled the pot to his side of the table so he could dip chunks of bread into the stew before stuffing it into his mouth. He had not, however, forgotten to remove his cap.

Belle sat down across from him. "No need to rush. You may have as much as you like."

He paid no mind to her advice. Several minutes of gorging went by before he pushed the pot to the center of the table. "Heard you speak of Samuels, miss." He wiped his mouth on a dirty sleeve. "You trust him?"

An odd question from a child.

"He's earned my trust, yes. Why do you ask?"

"Don't want no harm to come to you, miss."

"I see. Well rest assured that Mister Samuels would never harm me."

Andrew reached inside a pocket of his trousers and withdrew a slip of folded parchment. "I was told to give you this, miss."

Curious, Belle took the note and unfolded it.

Come alone to the old barn west of Canderlay and bring the journal. You will not be harmed. If you inform the others, if you allow anyone to follow you, Samuels will die. You have one hour.

Her heart plummeted to the bottom of her stomach. Questions swirled inside her head. None of them made any sense.

The boy pushed a white handkerchief across the table.

Belle stared at the cloth stained with several drops of blood and recognized the initials stitched into the bottom right corner.

JS.

"Andrew...can you describe the man who gave you this note?"

A guarded look surfaced in boy's eyes. Finally he shook his head, broke off a chunk of bread, and stuffed into his mouth.

She allowed him to swallow before pressing the issue. "Did you notice anything unusual about him?"

"Give me two pence to do his bidding." A sudden frown marred the boy's brow. "Dressed as a commoner, he was, but he spoke like a gentleman."

"Did he tell you his name?"

"No, miss. He said you'd know."

And indeed she did.

A fact that mattered very little at this point.

Lord H intended to take possession of the journal. If she refused, Samuels would surely die. On the other hand, if she did exactly as this treacherous man asked, would he keep his word?

Chapter Seventeen

Stuffing the short-blade knife into her boot, Belle hitched her skirts to climb the steep slope. Twice she slipped and nearly fell. Pausing to catch her breath, her hand slid instinctively to the journal hidden beneath her bodice.

Reaching the top, she pushed back the hood of her cloak then turned and glanced down the hill. Dix walked from the rear entrance of the manor over to the laundry house where Clancy stood peering inside. After a brief exchange of words, Clancy headed off to the carriage house while his companion walked around the manor.

The timing had been near perfect.

Belle entered a copse of trees, quickening the pace. Was Lord H somewhere in the forest, watching and waiting? The more distance she placed between herself and Canderlay, the higher her anxiety rose. She briefly considered turning around...pretending Andrew hadn't found her to deliver the message. But that would've been cowardly.

And Samuels' life depended upon her.

Further into the forest, sound came from every direction. Birds flittered from tree to tree, chirping happily as they went about their business. Nearby, a twig snapped, drowning out the other noises.

She spun around in every direction.

Was evil following her, waiting for the opportunity to pounce?

A hollow chill crept inside her chest. She swallowed the lump wedged in her throat and continued on. No point in dwelling on negative thoughts.

Picking her way through low hanging branches and dense undergrowth, she almost missed the narrow road.

Actually it wasn't much wider than a pathway. Trampled weeds along with deep grooves in the dirt confirmed that a small conveyance had recently traveled this way.

Belle emerged onto the road. It took a moment to figure out the layout of the land. If she remembered correctly, the cottages were due west. Uncle Magnus had referred to the tenants as gypsy farmers because every few years they packed up and moved on.

She turned toward the sun and headed in that direction. As she walked, a sensation of vulnerability enveloped her once again. Heaviness encompassed her legs, altering every breath. Her boots seemed to be made of iron instead of soft leather. Anxiety crushed her chest. Suffocating, as though she stood in chin deep quicksand.

She glanced left.

Then right.

No shadowy figure kept pace.

Gather your courage. Do not betray your fear.

Nevertheless she couldn't resist a final glance over her shoulder.

Eventually the pathway opened up to a large clearing. So different than when she'd last seen this place. Where a circle of tenant cottages once dotted the landscape, cluttered ruins lay scattered now. Off to the left stood a good-sized barn. One large door propped open, the other closed. A portion of the roof, wood tiles weathered and curled with age, had collapsed over one corner. Still hitched to the small cart, Samuels' horse waited obediently nearby.

The figure of a man appeared in the loft's square-shaped opening above the barn doors.

Fear lunged at Belle, striking deep within her heart. She tried to commit his appearance to memory, but she couldn't see his face. He wore a dark hat and dark overcoat. Nothing else stood out. Somehow she found her voice. "Where is Mister Samuels?"

"The old man still breathes. I give you my word."

"Does the word of a coward possess any value?"

Silence met the harsh accusation.

"What have you done to him?" she demanded.

"Come inside where we can speak privately."

"Am I a child to fall for such trickery?"

"If you've brought the journal, I'll not harm you. Why would I?"

Belle stared, unsure what to do. Concern for the caretaker forced her to stand her ground instead of fleeing into the woods behind her.

"You call me a coward, Miss Lindley. As we have never met, I'm curious as to how you've come to that dishonorable conclusion."

"What would you call someone who hires another to commit murder?"

He laughed, the odd sound echoing through the trees and back. "I believe the word would be...cautious. However, I am willing to forgive such a grievous offense as I know precisely its origination. So tell me, girl. Did your father never once disclose my identity to you?"

"No. His only reference to you was Lord H."

"How quaint of the vicar. And you've no wish to learn my name?"

"I came here merely to see to the release of my dear friend. After that, I want nothing more to do with you."

A gentle wind stirred the branches of a tall elm beside the barn. Something else moved as well. A rope strung from one sturdy bough. It disappeared just inside the bottom of the loft's opening.

"The saintly Reverend Lindley was all eyes and ears," his lordship spouted. "Fool dared to place a curse upon my head. How I despised that man."

"I doubt he cared much for you either," Belle countered. "And since you and I must forever disagree as to the sainthood of my beloved father, there is no point in speaking of him. I am, however, concerned as to the welfare of Mister Samuels. There was blood on the handkerchief you sent me."

"A mere scratch. Your servant is in good health."

Maintaining a calm voice became almost more than she could bear. "Then I demand you bring him outside at once."

A bitter laugh resonated throughout the ruins. "Come inside, Miss Lindley, and we'll discuss your *demands*."

Belle longed to run to Samuels' rescue, but she lacked the courage to move. "Forgive me, my lord, if I do not trust you. Was it not you who hired Amos Barlow to burn my cottage? Was it not you who asked him to murder me?"

"Barlow was a simpleton. A regrettable mistake."

"A mistake you felt the need to correct?"

"Why bemoan the death of a hideous snake?" he retorted. "Barlow acted without my consent or approval, Miss Lindley. I merely asked him to retrieve the vicar's journals."

"I do not believe you."

"It matters not. Did you bring the journal?"

"Do you not recall they were destroyed?"

"Except for the one Samuels discovered at the church."

How did he know?

A foreboding chill enveloped her, choking the breath from her lungs. Like a mouse hoping to outrun a cruel predator, she spun around. Instinct urged her mind to search for the nearest method of escape, and her vision found it.

The horse and cart.

If I can return to Canderlay...

"Think carefully," his lordship's voice taunted. "I've a fast horse hidden on the other side of this barn. Even if you manage to outpace him, what happens to the caretaker? Would you risk his life to save your own?"

No, she would not.

Belle faced him, her fists clenched.

"You surprise me, girl. I had no idea you were this spirited. Indeed, the vicar must've been most proud. No...no, I suppose he would've suffered quite the opposite. A thought that gives me great satisfaction." He laughed. "Come inside. Ignore the request, and you'll force me to shoot your beloved caretaker."

Emotion smothered Belle. Tears closed her throat. She loved Jasper Samuels dearly. If bartering for his life meant losing her own...

"I suppose I have little choice," she responded.

Of course there's a choice! Run!

Not without Samuels.

Belle made her way to the entrance. She feared going into the barn, but there was no other way to learn the extent of Samuels' injuries. With a silent prayer to God for protection, she stepped inside the shadowy building. The door at the opposite end had been closed, but light filtered through the cracks in the wall, allowing her to spot a figure sitting on the floor.

"Mister Samuels!" She rushed over to him, dropping to her knees.

He blinked and stared, as though he didn't recognize her. Dried blood stained his brow, between his eyes, and nose.

"Are you all right?" she asked.

Finally the confusion cleared from his good eye, and he nodded once. "You should not...have come, miss."

"What's done is done, dear friend. Can you stand?"

"No. My feet...bound."

His hands had been bound as well.

"Did I not speak the truth?" a voice shouted from above.

Belle glanced up. At one time the loft area appeared to have run the length of the barn from one end to the other but only on one side...above the stables. And that area had incurred severe damage from the collapse of the roof, leaving only a fraction of the original space.

Lord H appeared near the loft's edge, the upper portion of his face hidden behind the brim of his hat. "The caretaker will live, will he not?"

"You assault a frail old man and expect me to be grateful? Your mind is as twisted as your character."

"Enough! Toss up the journal."

"Your obsession regarding my father's writings is unfounded," Belle snapped, working to free Samuels' hands. "He never mentioned you by title or name. So you see, you've nothing to fear from me or this poor man."

"I pray that's the truth, Miss Lindley. If not..." He raised his hand, and the outline of a pistol materialized. "Toss up the journal." Lowering the long barrel, he pointed the weapon at her. "I'll not ask again."

If she did as requested, would he allow them to leave?

234

"Should your father's words prove harmless," he added, as though reading her thoughts, "you will be free to leave, and I shall never again trouble you."

That would indeed be welcome.

Removing the journal from her bodice, Belle stood then tossed it upward.

He caught the small book with one hand and pocketed it. "Stay where are, Miss Lindley. Until you can no longer hear the sound of my horse." He backed away, out of sight.

Belle nearly fainted with relief. This unstable and unpredictable man had kept his word. Standing in the middle of the barn, he could've shot her. She would've been an easy target. For some reason he'd let her live.

Her attention returned to freeing Samuels. Recalling the knife she'd stuffed inside her boot, she retrieved it and cut through the rope binding his hands and feet. Finally she stood. "We must get you home, Mister Samuels. And quickly."

"You heard him, miss. If he's outside—"

"Look at you, Jasper Samuels. You're as helpless as a day old kitten. I doubt you could walk much farther than the length of this barn, and I cannot carry you. If I do not bring the cart to you, I shall have to go for help. And I wouldn't care to leave you."

A creaking noise sounded behind Belle. Alarmed, she twisted around.

The huge barn door slammed into place beside the other, and a series of sharp taps began.

The hammering of nails into wood!

Realizing they were being boarded up inside the barn, Belle raced to the door. "I spoke the truth, my lord, did I not?" She shoved her shoulder into the door, pushing against it, but it held fast. "You've no cause to imprison us. Read the journal."

The hammering continued.

"Release us!" she shouted through the door.

Finally the noise ceased.

"Apologies, Miss Lindley. I'm afraid I cannot honor your request."

A sickening dread pitted in her stomach. "You speak of honor as though you were acquainted," she retorted. "Mister Samuels is innocent. If you possess even the smallest trace of decency, you will spare his life."

"He's seen my face."

"He's an old man, near blind. For heaven's sake, have pity on him."

"Pity is a luxury I cannot afford."

"Did you murder young Andrew as well? Rid yourself of another witness?"

"The boy knows nothing. I merely offered him coin to deliver a message, and he eagerly accepted. It's the harsh reality of poverty. A sad truth your father should've taught you."

"Your truth is a bloody lie!" Belle pounded her fists against the door, too angry to be afraid and too desperate to hold her tongue. "You cannot hide your crimes behind a noble mask. Your sins will cry out for justice long after your soul leaves this life!"

Samuels grabbed her hand, pulling her away, as the smell of burning wood entered the enclosed building.

She glanced down. A thin wisp of smoke slithered in beneath the bottom of the door, swirling about her feet before drifting up. She staggered backward, overcome by an agonizing recognition. "He intends to burn us alive."

Alarm overshadowed the caretaker's usual calm expression. "If we give in to panic, miss, we will surely perish."

Belle acknowledged this logic with a single nod. Rushing to the other side of the barn, she used as much force as she could muster to test the strength of the rear doors. They moved barely an inch.

She backed away. Confusion ran rampant inside her mind. Overwhelmed, she whirled about in a desperate search for other options.

The loft!

"Lord H must've exited through the opening in the loft and used the old elm to climb down," she said to the caretaker. "I doubt he was decent enough to leave us the rope but if I can climb up there, perhaps I can lower myself to the ground and then pry open this door."

"The tack room had a fixed ladder...at one time."

"Where?"

He pointed to the area where the roof had collapsed. Could she get through?

Removing the cloak, Belle tossed it over their shoulders before grabbing the servant's arm and guiding him across the room. Establishing a clear direction inside a dim barn and through the acrid stench of smoke was by no means simple. The pace was slow, and Samuels staggered twice before placing his hand upon her shoulder for support.

"We must hurry," she insisted.

Reaching the tack room, she directed Samuels to a sitting position and left the cloak with him before turning her attention to the loft. "There's no ladder. No way up." Behind her, the caretaker's coughs had become more frequent. She turned. "There must be another way."

The old man slumped forward.

Belle rushed to his side.

"Leave me...Miss Isabelle. Save yourself."

She would not waste precious breath arguing such a ridiculous request. Briefly overcome by a profound coughing spasm, she held the cloak to her nose and mouth, motioning for him to do the same.

In between several agonizing coughs, Samuels raised his hand, pointing to a far corner of the tack room.

She twisted around. On the inside wall, two boards had buckled beneath the roof's weight, leaving a jagged but vertical opening. Hauling Samuels to his feet, she guided him there and peered inside. This part of the barn had once been used as stalls. Now it was a treacherous path littered with jagged planks and mangled posts.

Belle lowered Samuels to a sitting position. As she entered through the slender opening, she stumbled, her feet tangled amid the clutter. She reached out but found nothing to hold on to. Colliding with the floor, she lay there, gasping for breath. All of a sudden, a surge of fresh air filled her lungs. Revitalized, she rolled onto her stomach.

Dear God, is that..?

"Light!" Excited, she pushed herself to her knees. "Mister Samuels, there's light...at the far end." A fierce round of coughing threatened to strangle her. "You must crawl toward me. Stay close to the floor. The air is more breathable."

He stared as though confused by her words.

"Do you understand?" she asked. "I may have discovered a way out."

Samuels nodded once before a violent cough snatched his attention.

Belle yanked the damaged boards from the wall then helped him through the opening. "Crawl to the far end."

He must've regained a portion of his strength for he adopted a quick pace as he scuttled along the floor.

Like dense fog over the moors, smoke continued to penetrate every space, distorting each speck of light. Soon there would be insufficient air to breathe. If not for the last few days of heavy rain, the entire barn would've been turned to ashes quicker than dry straw.

Her temples throbbed with each movement. She grew lightheaded and nauseated. Eyes watering, her vision blurred. Her nose and throat burned with the intensity of hot embers on open wounds.

Wood sizzled and popped as the fire drew new life. Soon heat from the flames would become unbearable.

Belle wiped away blinding tears but could no longer see Samuels moving ahead of her. She drew a shallow breath. Immediately the sensation of choking overwhelmed her lungs. Her chest ached with each effort to expel the damaging smoke. That she had reached the end of her life was too difficult to contemplate, so she continued forward.

Continued to focus upon one goal.

Escaping certain death.

Through the coughing and choking, the urge to survive became embedded in her mind. Stronger than before. With a sudden start, she realized she had caught up with Samuels. "Why did you...stop?"

"Impossible," he replied between spasms of coughing.

Belle stared through the haze at a massive accumulation of debris. Fragments of posts, boards, and planks stood between them and the wall, stacked in the haphazard way they had fallen. Behind that, two thick ceiling beams leaned precariously against one another. Moving them would be out of the question and if they fell, she and Samuels would likely be crushed.

Where was the fragment of light that had looked so promising?

She focused her attention on the tight space beneath the beams.

There!

An opening in the wall, but it was no bigger than a small pumpkin. A feline might squeeze through but not a grown man. Not even a petite woman. Even if they could somehow manage to get back there, there wasn't enough room to aim a swift kick. No room to do any damage or even attempt a forceful exit.

How long did they have?

Mere seconds?

She swallowed, temporarily relieving the raw dryness in her throat. A roaring sounded in her ears. Like thousands of soldiers marching together in single formation.

The last gasp of a dying heart?

Or a raging fire obsessed with consuming everything in its path?

Merciful Lord, do not allow my life to end in this manner!

Chapter Eighteen

Morgan drew Ares to a standstill at the top of a long slope above a lush valley and waited for the duke to join him. "Is this not perfect?"

Bartholomew sighed. "And again I say...raising sheep is a business not well suited for a gentleman."

"You mean a nobleman."

"Have you mud in your ears? I said you precisely what I meant."

"Your arrogance astounds me, Bart."

"And as usual, Morgan, you've twisted my words. Raise your bloody sheep, if you must. Your tenant farmers can work the land." The duke took a moment to survey their surroundings. "Your expertise this morning at the negotiating table was impressive, receiving an agreement from three families to begin planting crops next spring."

"Four," Morgan corrected.

"You cannot rely on that last family. Their reputation is not as sterling as the others."

"Forgive me, your Grace, if I chose to believe otherwise."

"You realize those ruins have to be removed and the land cleared before the new cottages can be built?"

"Yes, and my humble gratitude for pointing out the obvious." When the duke offered no instant rebuttal, Morgan followed his friend's line of vision to the valley below.

A man on horseback tarried for a second, turning his mount one way and then the other, before heading west across the valley.

"Who the devil is that?" Bartholomew inquired

"He rides like a man possessed," Morgan remarked.

"More like the devil himself chases after him."

"Which causes me to question what mischief he's been up to."

"Mischief, indeed. Look there." Bartholomew pointed east where a thin trail of smoke rose above the forest.

"Bloody fool!"

Morgan urged his horse down the slope and onto the narrow pathway. As he rode hard into the forest, he kept an eye on the smoke through the trees until he came upon the familiar clearing. Engulfed in a thick haze, a steady fire burned at the barn's front entrance.

Something moved toward him through the smoke.

A horse drawn cart.

Samuels' cart!

Apprehension churned inside Morgan's gut. Sliding from the saddle, he smacked his horse hard on the rump. Ares bolted toward the safety of the forest, nearly trampling the duke in the process.

"Bart, get that horse and cart out of here! I'll search for Samuels."

"Be reasonable, Morgan. If the old man is inside that barn—"

"He could still be alive."

"Morgan—"

"Go! See to the horses."

Morgan didn't wait to see if the duke complied. Placing his nose in the bend of his elbow, he hurried along the length of the barn, searching for the rear entrance. Smoke immediately engulfed him, stinging his eyes and confusing his sense of direction.

Racing to the far end, he shouted Samuels' name. With each breath, he choked on the smell of burning wood. It filled his nostrils. He could even taste it.

Suddenly the wind picked up, dispersing the smoke in all directions.

He sucked in a thankful breath. "Samuels!"

"Morgan!"

He spun around, his heart hammering.

It couldn't be!

"Belle?"

"Help us!" she cried.

"Where are you?"

"Trapped...behind the stalls. Running out of...air."

Her muffled voice sounded close.

Once again smoke surrounded Morgan, though not as thick as before. "Use your fists to beat against the wall. Keep pounding until I tell you to stop."

She did exactly as he instructed.

Within a matter of seconds, he located her position near the back corner of the barn. "Is Samuels with you?"

"Yes."

He could hear her choking and struggling to breathe.

If she dies...

Terror twisted its long blade deeper into his heart. "Listen to me, Belle. I'm going to have to smash through this wall. You and Samuels must move back as far as possible."

"Hurry!"

Using the heel of his boot, Morgan kicked the wall. Immediate pain from the impact jolted through his lower leg and knee, and he staggered backward.

Damnation!

He must've connected with a support joist.

Morgan moved down and tried again. With a forceful kick, two boards snapped in half, the bottom portions splintering and falling to the ground. The duke joined him and working together, they created a sizeable gap in the wall.

Samuels crawled through...coughing, dazed, and confused.

"Get him out of this smoke," Morgan instructed his friend. Wiping his eyes on the sleeve of his shirt, he turned, expecting to see Isabelle coming through the opening.

Where the devil is she?

"Belle?"

No response.

Morgan ducked through the gap in the wall and into a suffocating murkiness. He struggled with each breath. Heaviness crushed his chest with the weight of an ox. He could see very little, and the burning in his eyes and nose increased tenfold. He opened his mouth but could draw no breath to call her name. Lightheaded and disoriented, he realized he was mere seconds from passing out.

* * *

Warmth cushioned Belle in a gentle embrace. A familiar voice spoke softly in her ear, urging her to do something, but she couldn't quite understand what. Someone lifted her head and placed something cold to her lips. Liquid sloshed against her tongue and down her throat, burning all it touched.

"Isabelle, can you hear me?"

Belle forced her eyes open.

Morgan Spence's handsome face came into focus.

"Am I...dead?"

He smiled. "No, love. You are very much alive. How do you feel?"

"Not my best," she replied in a hoarse croak.

"Here." He lifted her head. "Have another sip of brandy."

Brandy?

He placed a flask to her lips.

She pushed it away

"You should drink," he insisted. "It will soothe your throat."

Belle shook her head. "Water."

"I'm sorry, but you'll have to wait until we reach Canderlay."

"The fire...Samuels...is he..?"

"Resting in the back of the cart. The duke is attending him."

Relieved, she silently thanked God. "It was Lord H. He trapped us inside the barn before setting the fire."

"Why did you and Samuels come here?"

"We had no choice." Belle explained about the caretaker's abduction, the note demanding the journal, and the bloodied handkerchief. After she finished, her throat was as raw and as painful as if she'd swallowed hot coal. "How did you know we were trapped inside the barn?"

"I didn't. We saw the smoke and hurried to investigate." He paused, his eyes studying her with deep concern. "God, Belle...I thought I'd lost you."

Tears gathered behind her eyes. How she had longed to hear such tender words. She wanted nothing more than to belong to this man for eternity.

"Do you know..." He reached out to caress her cheek but must've changed his mind. "I had to threaten Samuels with termination before he would allow Chase to tend to his wounds. Stubborn man. He was more concerned for you."

"Found my bloody horse," declared the duke just before his face appeared beside Morgan's. "Oh...hello, Miss Lindley. You gave us quite a scare."

Belle suddenly realized she was lying on her back, looking up at them. Strange she hadn't noticed sooner.

"I hope Morgan did not bore you by recounting his recent gallantry."

Confused, she focused on one man and then the other.

"He saved you," the duke added. "Found you unconscious amid the rubble, picked you up, and carried you to safety before falling to his knees with exhaustion. Thankfully he recovered or I would've had to tend to all three of you."

Belle turned her full attention on Mister Spence.

He tilted his head to the side, a slight indication of acknowledgment.

She opened her mouth to offer her gratitude.

He shook his head. "No need to speak."

She smiled, her heart content.

"An impressive rescue," Chase remarked. "I daresay, Miss Lindley, this tale of heroics will expand considerably before it reaches my wife." He glanced at Morgan. "It will grow dark soon. Is she well enough to travel?"

"Take Samuels in the cart. We'll follow shortly."

"You've a weapon?"

"Yes."

"Very well then. Your horse waits beyond those trees. I'll see you both at Canderlay."

Alone with the man she so desperately loved, Belle studied him, committing every feature to memory. Dark hair damp and clinging to his brow. Blue eyes, red and irritated now. Soot-streaked face.

Her disheveled rescuer.

Still the most handsome man she could ever imagine.

"Think you can manage to sit?" he asked.

Despite feeling a bit unsteady, she rose tentatively upon one elbow. Her blurry vision searched for the remains of the old barn. It had been reduced to charred rubble, dark smoke still hovering above the ruins. Nauseated, she drew a quick breath. Blood rushed to her head, pounding with an intense rhythm inside her ears.

"You look a bit pale," Mister Spence surmised. "Like a woman about to toss her breakfast." Once again he offered the flask.

After a brief hesitation, she accepted and drew a long swig. Liquid fire swelled in the back of her throat before sliding down into her stomach.

Burnt wine and oak.

Not the most pleasant taste. But then again...not the worse.

Again Belle lifted the flask to her lips, this time emptying it.

* * *

Morgan paced the antechamber, impatience accompanying each step. While waiting for Margaret to exit the bedroom with news of Isabelle, his thoughts returned to the previous two hours.

As they rode back to Canderlay on a strangely docile Ares, he had wrapped an arm about her waist, drawing her against his chest. Her long hair had flowed freely down her back, the smell of smoke clinging to each strand. He'd made the mistake of pushing the bulk of her tresses over her shoulder, captured immediately by the rose scent lingering on her skin.

"Comfortable?" he'd whispered against her ear.

She had barely nodded. The fact that she narrowly escaped a horrible death would make anyone speechless. Or perhaps she had been simply too exhausted to make light conversation.

I thought I'd lost you.

He should've never spoken those words. And yet...

Those very words had generated such a tender expression. Her brown eyes had softened, glimmering with emotion. A look he would never forget.

How can you lose something you do not possess?

She would leave for Dublin soon.

He didn't plan to stop her.

Morgan suspected that the very moment Isabelle Lindley stepped out of his life, his heart would never again beat the same. And he dreaded that moment.

She belongs at Canderlay.

Belongs with...

He didn't finish that last thought. Couldn't face what he feared his heart already knew.

Morgan cared for Isabelle. Wanted to protect her. Keep her safe. Did this affection translate into an undying love?

The bedroom door opened, and Margaret exited carrying a dinner tray.

"How is she?" he asked.

"Considering all she's endured, I'd say remarkably well. I managed to coax her into eating some stew, and she finally dozed off a little while ago."

"Did she insist on sleeping in the secret room?"

"Thankfully, no."

"That is indeed unexpected."

"I agree. If I'd suffered through the same harrowing ordeal, I might've shut myself inside that secret room and never come out again. Has Bartholomew sent Dix and Clancy to search for Lord H?"

"No need. He's likely far from Canderlay by now."

"How can you be sure?"

"If you believed you'd just caused two innocent people's deaths, would you not ride as far away from your crime as possible?"

"When you put it that way, yes, I suppose so. Well, I shall return this tray downstairs and then check on Mister Samuels. Be a dear, Morgan, and get the door for me."

Before he could oblige, the antechamber door opened.

Bartholomew stood in the corridor.

"You sent for the doctor?" Morgan inquired.

"No."

"Well why the devil not?"

"Samuels refused."

"I'll speak with him," Margaret said.

"And perhaps he'll listen," her husband stated. "How is Miss Lindley?"

"Asleep." Margaret slipped past Morgan then stood on tiptoe to kiss her husband's cheek. "A reward for your recent gallantry, dearest. Come downstairs. There's stew warming in the kettle, and I'll heat another pot of tea."

"I'll be down shortly, my love," Bartholomew said, keeping his attention on his wife as she departed.

"Bart?" Morgan prompted. "The doctor?"

Reluctantly he turned. "Did I forget to mention that Samuels insists he doesn't need one?"

"He's ill. I highly doubt his judgment is rational. Send one of your men to Maidstone. I'll deal with Samuels later."

"You'd better deal with him now," the duke warned.

Stubborn old man!

Determined to have his way in the matter, Morgan strode out of the antechamber and bounded down the stairs. As he passed through the kitchen, Margaret opened her mouth to speak but must've glimpsed his determined expression. At the door to the butler's private quarters, he didn't even bother to knock but burst right in.

A bleary eyed Samuels stared at him from the bed, his gray hair in mild disarray. "Miss Isabelle?"

"Resting." Morgan marched straight up to him. "What the devil are you trying to prove, Samuels? That you are self-sufficient and do not require rest? That there is no task you cannot perform, no illness you cannot overcome? If you wish me to believe you're invincible, fine. I bow to your superiority."

"By the harsh tone of your voice, sir, am I to assume I've angered you?"

"Assume? No. It's a bloody fact. You are a trustworthy servant, Jasper Samuels, and a good man, but you listen to me and listen well. I'm sending for the doctor. Not only for you, but for Isabelle, and I'll tolerate no argument."

"I would never dare argue with you, Mister Spence," the old man said, his voice barely above a strained whisper. "But you must hear me out on this matter."

Morgan hesitated. "What matter?"

"Earlier this morning, when I was in Maidstone, several of the town folk came up to me and told me how relieved they were that Miss Isabelle had not perished in the fire that destroyed her cottage." He coughed before continuing. "The news that she is now under the care of the Duchess of Chase has served as a welcome relief by all who knew and loved Reverend Lindley."

"Constable Foley. How foolish of me to hand that blubbering, incompetent idiot any information at all."

"An honest mistake, sir. We still have no idea who Lord H truly is, and we may never know. If you send for the doctor, his lordship might eventually discover that his latest attempt on Miss Isabelle's life has failed."

"Endangering her further. Yes, I understand. She saw his face."

"No, sir. He kept himself hidden from her."

"But he attacked you. Can you not identify the man?"

Samuels shook his head. "I've only one eye, and it does not serve me as well as it once did."

A slight noise came from behind Morgan, and he turned.

Margaret stood in the doorway, alarm in her expression. "Lord H took possession of the journal. Why would he still consider Isabelle a threat?"

"Evil resides in that man's soul, your Grace. I could hear it in his voice, and his actions speak clearly of his character."

She turned away.

But not before Morgan glimpsed her tears. He fixed his attention on Samuels. "You've good reason to fear this man."

"I care not for my own life, Mister Spence. Haven't cared in many a year. If I die within the hour, it will be a great relief. Indeed a comfort. I'll rest in the arms of my dearest Hennie, holding our baby daughter once again. My only concern at this moment is for Miss Isabelle."

His respect for the caretaker grew. Samuels could've spent the remainder of his years living on a modest stipend. Instead, he'd watched over the vicar's innocent daughter and worked as he always had, suffering through much discomfort. Never once had he spoken of his deceased wife and infant child. Never once shared a fraction of his grief.

Until now.

Morgan sighed. "Are you certain you do not need a doctor?"

"Quite, sir."

"Very well, but if you die in your sleep, go into that heavenly realm with the knowledge that it will be many a year before I forgive you for deserting me."

One corner of the servant's mouth twitched. "I'll keep that in mind, sir."

Morgan headed for the door.

"Mister Spence?"

He halted then turned. "Yes?"

"Miss Isabelle cannot remain at Canderlay. It's no longer safe. She should leave without delay. You must press the issue."

"And how am I to do that?"

"By whatever method you think best." Samuels picked up a black drawstring pouch sitting on the night table beside his bed. "Please, sir...take this. It's a gift for her birthday. Money to secure ship's passage."

Morgan walked back to the bed.

"When she reaches Dublin, there should be enough for several nights at a respectable inn. Convince her to leave, sir. You must."

"It's not that simple. How can I ask Belle to leave...to walk away from Canderlay as though it never existed?"

As though I never existed.

"Do you wish her to hide in the secret room for the remainder of her life?"

"No, of course not."

"But that is precisely what she will do, sir. You are an honorable gentleman, Mister Spence, like your father. If you care for Miss Isabelle, as I very much suspect you do, you must convince her to leave England. For her own safety, she must never return."

Never return.

Two words.

Effortless to speak but difficult to contemplate.

"You'd send her away on her own?" Morgan asked. "She is an innocent who has no idea the dangers a young woman can face traveling alone."

"If Lord H discovers she did not perish in that barn, he will return to Canderlay, and you can be certain he will finish the evil he started." Samuels drew a labored breath. "She will be safer in Dublin than in all of England."

"Keep the money pouch for now. I will speak with her come morning."

Samuels closed his eyes and lay back against the pillows.

Morgan exited the room, pausing outside the door. Samuels was right. Isabelle was no longer safe at Canderlay, but how could he ask her to leave when Canderlay had been the one place she'd truly felt safe?

Entering the kitchen, he was disappointed not to find Margaret. Passing by the dining room, he spotted her and the duke on the other side of the long table. Bartholomew held his wife in his arms, comforting her.

Morgan suspected his sister was upset over what Samuels had said and decided not to interrupt. He proceeded to the foyer and climbed the stairs. As he entered the second floor corridor, a soft whisper surprised him.

Whit's fer ye'll no go past ye.

"What's meant to happen will happen. Yes, I agree, Edwina." He halted at the door to the guest room he'd been using. "If that's true, it leaves you with no say in the matter of my private business."

Och...listen ta the mon blether noo.

"Off you go, love. Leave me in peace." Morgan glanced down the deserted corridor, half expecting to see a translucent figure drifting toward him. The fact that he saw nothing frightening bolstered his bravado. "Leave, or I'll find a witch to dig up your lifeless bones and place a curse upon them."

An ah'll gie ye a skelpit lug, ye arse!

"A slap on the ear? An idle threat, old woman. Empty and pointless."

Good God! I'm engaged in an argument with myself!

Why was Edwina's spirit angry with him? It's not as though this were the first time he'd told her to stay out of his affairs.

Morgan opened the door and entered the room. Sliding the bolt into place, he drew a relieved breath. The dead did not possess the power to threaten the living nor could they rise from the grave.

Not even Edwina Mason.

But if she *could* leave her place of rest, a locked door would not keep her from entering his room and speaking her mind.

Shaking his head over such irrational behavior, Morgan unbolted the door before crossing the room to the wash basin.

Ceann-laidir amadan.

A parting shot. In Gaelic.

What did the words mean?

Morgan splashed water upon his face and glancing into the mirror above the washstand, a disturbing thought trickled into his mind.

Good God! Has Old Edwina just placed a curse upon my head?

Chapter Nineteen

"You look much better this morning," Belle informed Samuels. Setting the food tray at the end of his bed, she fluffed the pillows behind his back and helped him sit up. "How do you feel?"

"Like a useless old nag who should be let out to pasture, miss."

"You are not useless. Not to me and certainly not to Canderlay." She picked up the tray and placed it across his lap. "Your voice sounds strained. Does your throat still bother you?"

"Somewhat. Your voice seems remarkably strong."

"I drank four cups of hot tea." She frowned. "Oh, dear. I forgot your tea." Rushing back to the kitchen, she returned with the teapot and a container of sugar. Pouring a cup, she handed it to Samuels before sitting in the chair opposite his bed. "Did you sleep well?"

"Like the dead, miss. And you?"

"Quite well, thank you. Strange, is it not? After what happened, we both enjoyed a peaceful slumber."

"I fear my mind was far too exhausted to overly dwell upon anything." He spooned sugar into his cup before eyeing the food tray. "What do we have here?"

"Eggs with ham, bread, and marzipan."

"You prepared all this?" He cleared his throat. "For me?"

Belle smiled. "Except for the bread and marzipan."

"On your own, miss?"

"Well Mister Dix brought in the wood for the stove, but I prepared the meal. I suspected you'd be unable to go about your usual chores this morning, but I also feared poor health wouldn't keep you from the attempt."

"I see. I'm pleased your strength has returned, Miss Isabelle, but there was no need to concern yourself for me. Mister Spence came downstairs around dawn this morn, found me in the kitchen, and ordered me back to bed. Informed me he'd see to the meal after he took Ares on a brisk run."

She laughed. "Mister Spence intends to cook, does he?"

"That was my understanding."

"Would he even recognize the stove?"

"I most certainly would," declared a stern voice.

Belle turned in the chair.

Morgan Spence stood in the doorway, his blue eyes boring into hers. "I realize your estimation of my skills is rather opinionated, Miss Lindley, but I can prepare a decent meal if and when the situation warrants."

Miss Lindley?

Had he not carried her to her room mere hours ago? Had he not held her tenderly, whispered her given name when he thought she couldn't hear?

And now...cold formality replaced the warmth of affection.

Disappointed and more than a little wounded, she muttered an apology.

"Did you enjoy the outing, sir?" Samuels asked.

"I did. Ares let me know in no uncertain terms that I've neglected him these past few weeks. I shall have to do better."

"That horse is a restless spirit, if there ever was one, sir."

Like his master.

Samuels sipped tea. "Oh..." He swallowed with difficulty. "Very nice, miss. Delightful."

She frowned. "Then why has your expression soured?"

"The tea traveled down the wrong pipe."

"Oh...I'm sorry. You know, Father enjoyed his tea brewed in this manner, but I feared it might be too strong for your tastes."

"No, no." He spooned more sugar into his cup. "It's rather stimulating."

"That's probably the sugar," Mister Spence insisted. "And I'd wager your health is not as good as you led me to believe earlier."

"If you require it, sir, I'm more than well enough to leave this bed."

"Yes, but I'd feel more comfortable if you didn't rush your recovery. That means no chores the entire day."

"Yes, sir." He spooned more sugar into his cup, but he did not drink.

"And how are you, Miss Lindley?"

"Nothing more painful than a slight headache, Mister Spence."

"I'm glad then." He hesitated. "There is a matter I'd like to speak with you about, if you'd care to step outside."

"Yes, of course. Mister Samuels, I'll return shortly for the tray."

The old man nodded in acknowledgement.

Belle exited the room. Once she reached the kitchen, she nervously faced him. "Actually, Mister Spence, if you don't mind, I've a rather pressing matter upon my heart, and I'd like to speak first."

"By all means. Should we sit?"

"If you like, but I'll remain standing as this will not take long."

"Very well but before I forget, Oxley sends his regards. He's been worried about you."

"How considerate."

"Oh...and Dix and Clancy thank you for breakfast this morning."

"It was no trouble. What did you tell them? About the fire, I mean."

He shrugged. "That you and Samuels were the victims of a cruel prank and to keep a sharp eye out for strangers. No point going into further detail."

"No, I suppose not. I hope you didn't lecture them. Neither Mister Clancy nor Mister Dix had any idea I'd left Canderlay or that Mister Samuels was in trouble."

"Actually, I had decided to lecture you, Isabelle. After you fully recovered of course. But when I realized I would've acted the same had I found myself in your position, I reconsidered."

"Thank you for understanding. And for not lecturing or scolding me."

"Yes, well you're not a child, are you?"

Belle smiled, pleased he had noticed.

"So, Miss Lindley, what did you wish to speak with me about?"

Please, Lord, do not let me weep.

She tucked a stray curl behind her ear. "I'm departing for Dublin today. In fact...within the hour."

He stared as though he could find nothing to say.

Keep the sadness from your voice.

Belle paced to the rear door then back. "I wanted to thank you, Mister Spence, for your kind generosity. You cannot begin to understand how much your friendship, along with the Duke and Duchess of Chase, has comforted me."

"I wish I...we...could've done more."

"You did more than I had any right to expect. Regrettably my dire situation endangered all of you. If you had not pulled Mister Samuels out of that barn when you did, we would now be planning arrangements for his burial."

"And quite possibly yours."

"Yes, I suppose so. I've no desire to further jeopardize you or your family, as I care deeply for each of you."

"When did you make the decision to leave?"

"Last evening. I spoke with Lady Chase, and she graciously offered the use of her carriage and driver. I asked her not to say anything to you or to Mister Samuels until I'd had a chance to inform you."

Though his unyielding expression betraying nothing of his emotions, he continued to stare. "Perhaps it is for the best, Isabelle."

His detached reaction caught her off-guard.

What did you expect?

That he would argue?

Beg you to stay?

Belle forced a brave smile. "I shall miss you."

He ignored the heartfelt remark. "Have you carefully considered your travel plans?"

"I'm not sure I understand the question."

"Merchant ships usually avoid the English Channel in times of war. It's far too treacherous."

"Oh, yes. I've been so concerned with my own problems that I completely forgot England and France were at war."

"Take the carriage to Bristol. You should arrive by evening on the third day. Once in Bristol, you can board a ship bound for the St George Channel and then on to the Irish Sea. It's a much safer route."

"Three days to Bristol?"

"And another four or five by ship. You'll be in Dublin within a week. Plenty of time before your birthday." He withdrew a black pouch from his coat pocket and tossed it onto the table. "This will help pay for the journey."

Belle eyed him with curiosity. "Where did you get this?"

"I didn't steal it, wench," he retorted, the playful teasing returning to his tone. "The monies came from Samuels. Take it and be grateful."

Disappointment pricked her heart.

"For your birthday," he added.

"Why did Mister Samuels not hand it to me himself?"

"I suspect the very thought of your eventual departure might bring a tear to his one good eye."

And to my eyes as well.

"That dear man. He's likely given me his very last coin. I have now gone from beggar to thief."

"You are too hard on yourself, Isabelle. Do not concern yourself with Samuels' sudden poverty. I will replace the contents of this pouch."

"You would do that? For Mister Samuels?"

"You've my word."

The longer you gaze into his eyes, the more difficult it will be to leave.

"I will reimburse you as soon as I acquire the funds," she insisted.

He shrugged. "There's no need."

"Oh, yes. How silly of me. You will likely acquire the promise of a wealthy bride before the end of the year."

His expression turned stormy, but he did not offer the expected rebuttal.

Belle hadn't intended to sound cynical. She had merely wished to displace some of her pain by making a casual observation.

The attempt failed miserably.

"I should go," she said, her throat clogged with unshed tears. "I must finish packing and then say my farewells to the duke and duchess. Although...I should probably prepare their breakfast first."

"You're not a servant, Isabelle. You're my guest. Besides, Mags is fully capable of lending a hand in the kitchen."

"Very well then. Oh...what did you wish to speak with me about?"

He shook his head. "It's not important."

"I see."

But she really didn't. Not when it came to Morgan Spence.

Heart heavy with sadness, Belle nudged aside her prim and proper upbringing and gave in to the desire of the moment by rushing into Morgan's arms.

* * *

Morgan held Isabelle for a mere second it seemed, no longer, before she turned and fled the kitchen. He wanted more than anything to chase after her. Tell her he wished her to remain at Canderlay. Instead, all he managed to do was stare after her.

At length, he returned to Samuels' room.

"Did all go as planned, Mister Spence?"

"No, it went to bloody hell."

The old man's brow wrinkled.

Morgan strolled to the center of the room and stopped near the foot of the bed. "Isabelle is leaving for Dublin within the hour."

"Well done, sir."

"Spare me the congratulatory speech. I played no part in the decision."

"I see. She accepted the monies?"

"Yes, and she'll no doubt wish to thank you before departing. I wager Margaret is aware of Isabelle's plans since she offered the use of her carriage."

"Her Grace is a generous lady." Samuels issued a weary sigh, and several long moments passed before he spoke again. "Inside that barn, I recall thinking I was suffering a horrible nightmare." Picking up his cup, he absentmindedly added another spoonful of sugar. "It was as though I wandered in a daze, and I could not catch my breath for more than a second or two."

"Yes, the smoke was quite suffocating."

"Indeed, sir. Miss Isabelle and I were fortunate you and the duke stumbled upon us when you did. We would not have survived much longer." He sipped before spooning more sugar into his cup. "And Lord H...is there no hope of discovering his identity and handing out the punishment he deserves?"

"Not unless his conscience forces a confession."

"Evil possesses no conscience, sir. Nor soul."

Morgan agreed. "He has the journal. Perhaps we've seen the last of him."

"But we cannot be certain, can we?"

"No, I suppose not. Well, Samuels, I'll leave you to your leisure. Enjoy your breakfast."

The old man's face turned pink then ashen.

"Samuels, are you ill? You look pale."

"Must be my stomach, sir. It's become rather nauseated."

"It's all that sugar you've ingested." Morgan snatched the container. "No more of this. It's spoiled your appetite. I'll set the food tray aside for now."

"I fear you've misunderstood my misery, sir. Miss Isabelle prepared this meal especially for me."

"And this upsets you?"

"Mister Spence, that young lady's heart is the purest I've ever encountered, but she often has trouble boiling water in the kettle."

"Surely you exaggerate?"

The servant shook his head.

Morgan examined the untouched plate of eggs and ham. "Perhaps you've judged her too harshly."

"Begging your pardon, sir, but it is not a question of visual judgment. 'Tis the mouth that has the final say."

"How horrible could it be?" Morgan studied the old man. "Isabelle's cooking, I mean."

"Inferior at best, sir."

"Jasper Samuels, you are a culinary snob. No doubt your delicate palate has become accustomed to your exceptional skill in the kitchen."

One bushy brow inched upward. "Perhaps you need convincing."

It was a challenge Morgan could not resist. He picked up a fork and sampled the eggs.

Salty. Not much butter. And scorched, as though they'd simmered in a hot pan longer than necessary. A closer inspection of the ham diminished his appetite further. It had been sliced thick and therefore undercooked. The marzipan was likely safe as it had been delivered by the farmer several days ago.

"The bread looked delicious," Morgan observed.

"I baked it yesterday morning, sir."

"I see. Well at least Isabelle poured you a decent cup of coffee."

"You mean this?" Samuels held up the cup. "This is not coffee, sir."

Morgan arched a brow. "Tea?"

The servant nodded once.

"The devil you say. No wonder you spooned almost an entire container of sugar into your cup."

"And yet I assure you it did little to overpower the bitter taste."

"I'm sorry for your pain and suffering, Samuels. I'll prepare your breakfast and put on another pot of tea. Let's keep this between us, lest we damage Isabelle's feelings."

"Agreed, sir, but then you'd best dispose of the evidence."

"A valid point." Morgan picked up the tray and headed across the room. At the door he hesitated. "Samuels, you wouldn't by chance speak Gaelic, would you?"

"Not a word, sir."

With a nod, Morgan exited the room. As he entered the kitchen, he found Margaret beside the stove. "Good morning, Mags." He set the tray on the table. "I was just about to prepare your breakfast."

She eyed the eggs and ham. "What's amiss with this one?"

"Let's call it a failed attempt, shall we?"

"Well...how fortunate I chose to come downstairs when I did."

"And I offer you my sincere gratitude, love." He kissed her cheek. "What's become of your noble husband? Surely he's not still abed?"

"Bartholomew informed me he'd be in the carriage house speaking with our driver. Perhaps you should join him."

"An excellent suggestion, but shouldn't you be upstairs with Isabelle? She's leaving for Dublin soon."

"I well know her plans, Morgan, but she wished to be alone. Besides, watching Isabelle pack would make me extremely sad. And I will not tolerate sadness on such a lovely morning." Margaret turned away. "How is Mister Samuels?"

"Recovering nicely. I insisted he spend the day at his own leisure."

"How thoughtful of you."

"On the off chance that you haven't noticed, your brother is a kind and an exceptionally thoughtful fellow."

"Which brother would that be, dear?"

Morgan frowned. "Och noo. Listen ta the lass. She's no' the full shill'n."

Margaret faced him with a sly grin. "I remember that barb," she said with a chuckle. "But it was usually aimed at the mischievous laddies. Let me think now...what was it Old Edwina would say to our cousin Derek when he bragged about how the ladies found him charming and irresistible?"

"Aye, an yer bum's oot the windae, heathen."

Her eyes lit up. "Yes, that's it. Edwina enjoyed verbal sparring. She claimed it kept her mind sharp."

"Say, Mags, you became proficient in the old language, did you not?"

"Gaelic?" She reached for a large bowl of eggs and set them on the baker's table beside the stove. "I haven't heard it spoken in years."

"Nor I. At least by anyone who still draws breath."

She stared at him. "Morgan...you dreamed of Edwina?"

"Certainly not, but I have been thinking of her lately. Occasionally hearing her raspy voice entangled with my own thoughts."

"And what words of wisdom, dear brother, did she impart?"

He hesitated. "Ceann-laidir amadan."

Amusement lightened her expression. "Do you wish an interpretation?"

Morgan shrugged. "If it pleases you to boast of this particular skill."

"Ceann-laidir means stubborn. Amadan is the word for fool."

Stubborn fool.

"Well," he muttered. "I suppose I've heard worse."

"Why is Edwina's spirit angry with you?"

"I have no idea."

"Have you asked her?"

"No, Margaret, and I don't intend to. Why engage in a one-sided conversation with the dead when I have difficulty getting my point across to the living? Ask Edwina? What a ridiculous suggestion."

Margaret approached him. "You know, Morgan, at the tender age of two, I began to follow you about. You were my oldest brother, and I worshipped you beyond reason. I was completely devoted to you."

"I remember, Mags, and you well know I adored you. Still do."

"Yes, I believe you. Therefore I pray you will forgive me and will not take this as a sign of my disaffection."

"Forgive you for what?"

With a slight grimace, Margaret raised her hands and then soundly boxed Morgan's ears.

* * *

Belle waited alone in the foyer as Clancy and Dix loaded two trunks on the platform at the rear of the carriage. Heavy with sorrow, her heart beat a slow thud in her ears. She'd bid an emotional farewell to Samuels a few minutes earlier. Had willed herself not to cry. Now, throat aching with unshed tears, how would she hold back the flood of grief that threatened to drown her?

"Isabelle?"

She turned.

Carrying a straw basket, Lady Chase approached her. "You will likely be famished before Oxley stops the carriage for the night. I've wrapped a loaf of bread and plenty of cheese." She handed over the basket. "Oh, and I tossed in a few apples."

"I'll be sure to share with Mister Oxley."

Her Grace sighed. "Safe journey, my dear." She hugged Belle. "And may the Good Father bring you back to us one day."

The duke walked up behind his wife. "It has been a pleasure meeting you, Miss Lindley, although I wish your circumstances had not been so dismal."

"As do I, your Grace." Belle curtsied. "Thank you for the generous use of your carriage and driver."

"You are quite welcome. As a precaution, I'm sending along Dix and his rifle. God speed on your journey, Miss Lindley."

"Thank you, your Grace." Belle fixed her attention upon the duchess. "You've been far too kind, my lady. If not for your generosity, I would be traveling to Dublin in rags."

"And you would still be the loveliest woman aboard ship. You will write to us, will you not?"

"I will. After the matter of my inheritance is settled."

"Are you remaining in Dublin then?" the duke inquired.

"It's possible, your Grace, though I cannot be certain."

The main door opened, and Dix appeared. "Carriage is ready whenever you are, Miss Lindley. I'll take that basket and place it inside."

Belle handed it over but hesitated to follow him.

Where was Morgan Spence?

Her gaze drifted up the stairs.

Was he so eager to be rid of her that he couldn't make a brief appearance to wish her farewell?

Pushing aside an ocean of wounded pride, she smiled at Lady Chase. "Give my gratitude to your brother, if you please."

The duchess wiped a tear before nodding.

"Where is Morgan?" the duke inquired.

"We had a slight disagreement," his wife replied. "He's likely a bit miffed."

"Disagreement? Over what?"

"Nothing serious, Bartholomew. I'll explain later."

The remark prompted mild curiosity. Nevertheless, Belle held her tongue and hugged Lady Chase one last time. Before losing her courage, she turned and marched across the foyer and through the open door. Outside, the morning sun shone as bright and as cheery as before, but it did nothing to dispel the blackness that now hovered over her. She forced herself to walk the short distance to the carriage...to Dix who stood holding the door.

"Isabelle!"

Surprised, she spun around.

Morgan Spence hurried toward her.

Her heart soared for one brief and glorious moment. "I thought that you..."

"That I didn't intend to say goodbye?" He smiled, the warmth in his gaze mesmerizing. "Do you truly think so little of me?"

"Well, no. I...I merely assumed you had become distracted."

"Actually, yes. By your gift. I'd gone upstairs to search for it."

"My gift?"

He grinned. "First you must turn around."

"Why?"

"No more questions." His expression softened. "Will you not trust me this one last time, Belle?"

One last time.

Forever.

Heart pounding in an unpredictable rhythm, she obeyed.

He slipped something about her neck.

She glanced down. A long silver chain lay nestled at her bosom. At the end of the chain hung a bronze cross that shimmered in the sunlight. "Oh, my...it's lovely."

His hands rested upon her shoulders. "And if this cross fails to protect you..." He gently spun her around. "I've something that will." He lifted a leather scabbard from the belt of his trousers. "This dragon dagger was a cherished gift given to my mother many years ago. She gave it to me the year I turned ten. And now..." He took her hand and placed it into her palm. "I'm giving it to you."

Belle shook her head. "No, I cannot accept this. One day you'll wish to present it to your son. Your heir."

"When and if that day comes..." A slow grin spread across his lips. "You can return the dagger to me in person."

Unlikely.

For Belle didn't possess the proper strength or courage to stand before him again. To face his devoted wife and not despise the woman.

"Thank you, Mister Spence."

He touched her cheek, his fingers lingering.

A delicate shiver traveled up her spine.

"Safe journey, Belle." Taking her free hand, he raised it to his lips, his breath like a loving whisper upon her skin. "I will indeed miss you."

He'd given in...said the words she longed to hear.

Fighting the tears and unable to trust her voice, she accomplished a nod.

His attention rose above her head. "Dix, you and Oxley take good care of this lady, or I'll have your heads."

"Understood, sir."

Morgan Spence helped her into the carriage and with one last affectionate glance, he closed the door.

The vehicle jerked into motion.

Alone inside the carriage, Belle could no longer hold back the tidal wave. Closing her eyes, she stuffed her face into the soft cushions as deep sobs racked her body from within. Leaving behind everything familiar and everyone she loved overwhelmed and frightened her. Her heart ached with severe loneliness. The same loneliness she'd suffered when her uncle died. And then later, her father.

Tears finally spent, she raised her head. The carriage swayed from side to side, the silent minutes ticking by one after the other. The farther she traveled from Canderlay Manor, the more distant its memory would become. She had no trouble foreseeing her future. Indeed, the remainder of her life. A pitiful life that would serve no purpose and end in spinsterhood.

And when she could no longer envision Morgan Spence's handsome face or recall his tender voice, her wounded heart would finally succumb to sadness and beat no more.

Chapter Twenty

Morgan set aside the book he'd tried in vain to read. He had purposely come to the library to be alone, but now he couldn't bear the solitude.

Five days ago Isabelle had departed Canderlay, and for five long days he'd been more miserable than he could ever remember. The truth could no longer be denied. He missed her dreadfully. More than he ever thought possible. Missed hearing her voice and seeing the fire in her brown eyes whenever he teased her.

Why did I not accompany her to Dublin?

He knew why. She confused him. He couldn't decide how he felt about her. Obviously his sentiments ran deeper than expected or his sour mood would've improved by now.

Margaret entered the library.

"How is Samuels?" Morgan inquired.

"The doctor didn't seem too concerned. He gave the poor man something for his cough, along with a vial of laudanum."

"He should sleep well this evening. I'll check on him throughout the afternoon and into the night."

"Yes, I'm sure you will, Morgan, but..."

"But what?"

"I should like to remain at Canderlay until he's completely recovered."

"That's kind of you, Mags, but there's no need. I'll take good care of him. Besides, how could I ask you to abandon your devoted husband?"

"Abandon Bartholomew? What on earth do you mean?"

"As he departed for Chase early this morning, I assume he'll be returning by carriage this afternoon in order for you to travel back to London together."

"Your assumption is incorrect," she insisted. "What would I do in London this time of year?"

"Whatever ladies normally do."

"Morgan, are you trying to get rid of me?"

"Certainly not. I was merely hoping to save your sanity. I know the grand life you are accustomed to as the Duchess of Chase, and I cannot help but suspect you've become bored at Canderlay."

"Where would you get such a foolish notion? Have I ever once complained of boredom?"

"No, but—"

"Or implied it?"

Morgan considered telling his sister the truth, that he wished to be left alone to wallow in his misery, but she would likely scold him before offering advice he had no wish to hear. "I didn't mean to offend you, Mags, but I know with certainty that emptying bedpans holds little interest for you."

"Indeed, not."

"Nor should you be responsible for preparing our meals." He placed his hands on her shoulders. "I'll leave Clancy to care for Samuels and accompany you to Chase. Hopefully we can catch Bart before he departs for London."

"No, Morgan. I'll not be returning to London. By now the gaiety and never-ending stream of invitations have ceased." She strolled to a window and pushed aside the heavy drapes. "As for joining Bartholomew...he will spend the first few hours of the day with his head inside the Morning Post, his afternoons arguing in the House of Commons, and his evenings ranting about the war with Napoleon. You spoke of boredom. I wouldn't wish that particular dreariness upon any woman. Besides..." She turned, a devilish twinkle in her eyes. "I've a Harvest Ball to plan."

"Will you be inviting Miss Lindley?"

"If she decides to return to England, yes." Her smile broadened before once again she faced the window. "I'll not deny I've plans for Isabelle."

"Plans that include procuring a wealthy husband?"

"You're one to talk, Morgan. What do you care? Are you not plotting your own scheme to land a well-endowed bride? Good heavens, it's not as though..." Something outside the window caught her eye. "Are you expecting a visitor?"

"No. Why do you ask?"

"There's a carriage coming up the drive."

Had Isabelle changed her mind?

Morgan hurried across the room and nudged Margaret away from the window. Two horses trotted to the end of the drive, pulling a black carriage behind them. After the driver drew both horses to a standstill, he set the brake then jumped down and opened the door.

Dressed in bright canary yellow, a young woman exited the vehicle, slender dark ringlets escaping a fashionable hat of the same color.

"It's Lady Westwood," Margaret exclaimed.

"Who?"

"Wife to the Earl of Westwood. Go on now. She'll be standing at the door any second."

"This woman is your friend, Mags. Not mine."

"Stop being a petulant child, Morgan, and do as I ask this once."

"Very well, but I am not dressed to entertain."

"Sadly, no."

"Nor will I be your butler."

"And an incompetent one you'd make," she teased. "Bring the countess to the drawing room. Afterward you are free to do whatever you wish."

"Your generosity astounds me, your Grace," he quipped.

As Morgan reached the foyer, the bronze knocker outside the front door clanged twice. He proceeded to the door and opened it.

Lady Westwood offered a timid smile.

The devil of it! She's younger than Belle!

"Good morning," she greeted.

"Good afternoon, my lady."

"Oh, yes. Of course it is," she said, reaching up to adjust her hat. "I hope you will forgive the intrusion. I dropped by Chase Manor earlier and was informed that the duchess was still visiting her brother. If it's no trouble, sir, I've something of the utmost importance to give her Grace."

"Certainly." Morgan opened the door wide and moved aside.

Once inside the foyer, she turned and extended her hand. "I am Louise Westwood, the Earl of Westwood's wife."

He raised her gloved hand to his lips. "Forgive my manners, Lady Westwood. I am Morgan Spence. Margaret's brother."

"Oh..." Her smile widened. "How do you do, Mister Spence."

"Margaret is in the drawing room. I'll take you to her," he said and led the way down the corridor. "I apologize, my lady, but I've yet to acquire domestic help, and my one servant has fallen ill. I'm afraid tea is all I can offer."

"Thank you, Mister Spence, but I must decline as I cannot stay long."

Margaret appeared in the corridor. "My dear Lady Westwood, I thought I heard your voice. What a delight to see you again. Have you met my brother? Well of course you have. Morgan, will you bring us a pot of tea?"

"No, madam, I will not."

She turned a harsh scowl upon him.

"I offered tea," he defended. "But my lady refused."

"He did, your Grace, and I explained I was rather pressed for time."

"I see. Well, come into the drawing room, Lady Westwood, so we may speak in private, Morgan, I believe you had a pressing matter to attend to?"

"Did I?"

"Leave, scoundrel."

"As you wish, your Grace." He bowed with exaggerated formality. "It was a pleasure meeting you, Lady Westwood,"

"And you as well, Mister Spence."

Morgan had just entered the corridor when Lady Westwood inquired if Isabelle could join them. Margaret's sharp intake of breath and ensuing silence warned him that something was definitely in the wind. He promptly turned around and waited near the door, listening to their conversation without an ounce of gentlemanly remorse.

"Another attempt was made on Isabelle's life recently," Margaret declared.

"How horrible. Is she...?"

"Unharmed, for the most part, but we felt it best she leave the country."

"I see."

"Lady Westwood, did your husband send you?"

"He did, your Grace."

A long moment of silence followed.

Morgan peered around the door and into the drawing room.

Lady Westwood drew a thin parchment from her reticule. "This was written in my husband's own hand and sealed with his crest. It contains all the information you requested."

Margaret accepted the letter.

"Your Grace, when you told Miles the story about Mary Barlow, he wanted to speak up, but he was too ashamed. After you and Miss Lindley departed, his shame turned to guilt."

Morgan stormed into the room. "Precisely what sin is your husband guilty of, my lady?"

She appeared momentarily startled. "The sin of silence, Mister Spence."

Pink dotted Margaret's cheeks. "Morgan, I am utterly appalled. Were you eavesdropping?"

"I was, madam. Apparently placing my ear to the door is less problematic than simply asking what goes on in my own house. Lady Westwood, I apologize if I offend you, but Miss Lindley's wellbeing is vastly important to me. And you, Mags...you disappoint me."

Both women stared at him.

"This is the first I've heard about a visit to Westwood Hall," he added. "Nor did Isabelle mention it."

"Well of course not. I persuaded her to keep silent."

"Why, may I ask?"

"Is it not obvious? You and Bartholomew would've objected."

"Most likely, but you could've mentioned the visit after you returned."

"Well heavens, Morgan." A charming smile curled his sister's lips. "Since we learned very little from his lordship, the visit became unimportant."

"But if you suspected the Earl of Westwood knew the identity of Lord H, you had an obligation to come straight to me or to your husband."

Margaret sighed. "You are correct."

The meek surrender left him speechless.

Literally.

And highly suspicious.

"This conversation is far from finished, Mags."

"Sadly, I've come to realize that. Am I to assume you will soon beat the subject of my disobedience to death?"

"No, madam, but I certainly intend to inform your husband."

"Yes, yes, dear tattler. Do what you will," Margaret quipped. She covered Lady Westwood's hand with her own. "I apologize for our silly bickering."

"That's quite all right, your Grace. I have a brother as well."

"Do you? Well then you understand, I dare say."

An overpowering urge to pinch Margaret's cheek came into Morgan's mind, but he decided to suggest a stronger punishment to her husband. "Lady Westwood, have you read the letter you gave my sister?"

"There was no need, Mister Spence. Miles explained everything."

"What does he know of Lord H?" Margaret asked the countess.

"Perhaps my explanation should begin with my husband's first wife, Millicent, and her younger sister, Felicia. Both were daughters of a wealthy baron. Both wed an earl at the age of sixteen. But neither woman could give her husband children. Although the news devastated Miles, he devoted his life to consoling his wife. Felicia's husband was not so gracious. Over time, he grew bitter and vowed to produce an heir by any means."

"By forcing himself upon Mary Barlow?"

"Yes. As a result, Mary got with child. My husband offered to help, but she refused. Miles never understood why. And Felicia...that spiteful woman took every opportunity to remind the boy of his shameful origins."

"To subject a child to such hatred is unconscionable," Margaret noted.

The past did not interest Morgan. What was done could never be undone. His only concern lay in the present. "Lady Westwood, are we to assume your husband is Lord H's uncle?"

"Yes, Mister Spence. Though not by blood."

"Give me his name, my lady."

"Philip," the countess replied. "Earl of Glenhawk."

* * *

Belle stared at the plump clerk sitting across the desk. "What do you mean...proof?"

His impudent sigh lasted a full three seconds. "Verification, Miss Lindley, if that be yer name."

"Well of course it's my name, Mister Curzon. Why would I say it was if it truly wasn't?"

His beady eyes narrowed over wire-rimmed spectacles. "There be the wee matter of an inheritance we've been discussin' fer the past half hour."

"An inheritance, may I remind you, that rightfully belongs to me."

"Greed lurks in all folks, lass. Young and old. At the promise of a few coins bein' rubbed together, it's sure to rear its ugly head." He leaned across the desk. "I need proof afore ye'll get a half penny."

"I appreciate your position, Mister Curzon, but how can I convince you that I am indeed Isabelle Lindley?"

He offered a disingenuous smile. "By providin' the letter sent to yer papa when Magnus Lindley perished at sea."

"But I told you. My cottage was—"

"Burned to cinders with all ye owned. Aye...the chickens flew the coop and the goats and cows ran off as well. A pitiful tale, and one I've heard afore."

Belle drew a slow breath, reminding herself once again that it would be most unladylike to punch this insufferable Irishman in his bulbous nose. "My father was a vicar, not a farmer. We owned a few chickens. No goats or cows. And I swear upon everything holy that I lost all my possessions in that fire."

"Is that so?" He leaned into his chair, appraising her attire. "Then where did ye find the fancy gown ye're wearin'? Hangin' in the barn?"

"There was no barn. Only a cottage. And if you had listened earlier, you might recall my explanation that the Duchess of Chase took pity on me and kindly provided me with this gown and several others."

A smirk appeared upon his thick lips. "Rather convenient, eh?"

Forgive me, heavenly Father, but I am mere seconds away from strangling this dimwitted oaf.

The door behind the clerk opened, and a tall, thin gentleman with gray hair walked out of the office. "Is there a problem, Curzon?"

"Aye, Mister Barrington. The lass here claims to be Magnus Lindley's niece, but if ye ask me—"

"I *am* Magnus Lindley's niece," Belle insisted.

Barrington turned his sole attention on her. "You've proof?"

Tears of frustration closed her throat. Discouraged, she shook her head.

"I'm afraid she brought with her nothin' but a sad tale of misfortune, sir," Curzon stated, his expression smug. "I was about to send her on her merry way."

Belle's shoulders slumped in despair. She would soon be shoved none too gently out the door and quickly forgotten.

Penniless. Reduced to begging.

What will happen to me?

Hot tears spilled over.

"Misfortune is never planned, Curzon. You'd do well to remember that."

Her attention quickly fixated on the elderly gentleman.

"I am Edgar Barrington," he announced. "Magnus Lindley's solicitor."

"How do you do. I'm Isabelle Lindley."

"A pleasure. Step inside my office, and we'll discuss this matter in private."

Belle accepted.

"I must apologize for Curzon," Barrington said, closing the door and motioning her to a high-backed chair. "His behavior was less than sympathetic."

"Then you understand my dire circumstances?"

"I do indeed." He sat down behind the desk, studying her. "I knew Magnus for many years. Long before ML Shipping. He persuaded me to leave my London office and come to Dublin. After his death, I decided to remain. Met my dear wife here. I imagine you must miss your uncle tremendously."

"Yes, dreadfully. My father as well."

"I only recently learned of the vicar's death. Last spring, was it?"

"Winter," she corrected.

"Oh...yes. Well, I'm terribly sorry for your loss. Magnus didn't always agree with his brother, but I know for certain he held a deep respect for him. And he was a devoted uncle to Isabelle."

Belle frowned. "Mister Barrington, you speak as if I am not Isabelle Lindley. As though a stranger sits across from you."

"A habit of my occupation, I suppose. Forgive me, Miss Lindley, but you must realize that without proof of your identity, I cannot release those funds."

She had traveled full circle.

Again.

Belle pushed aside the disappointment. "As I explained to Mister Curzon, the letter I received from this firm outlining the contents of my uncle's will was recently destroyed by fire. There is no longer any proof. I have nothing to give you except my word, and apparently my word is unacceptable."

"Unfortunately, yes. What about the old caretaker? Jacob Samuels?"

"Jasper Samuels."

"Yes, yes. Write to him. Ask him to travel to Dublin to sign a statement confirming you are who you claim."

"But that would take at least three weeks. Perhaps a month. The letter clearly stated that the monies would be held in trust until midnight on my twentieth birthday. That's tomorrow. If I fail to prove my claim, the trust will expire, and I will forfeit all rights to the entitlement."

"You're mistaken. The funds will remain in the bank until your return."

"Are you certain?"

"I dictated the letter myself, Miss Lindley. You must've misread it."

No, I did not.

But she suspected it would be pointless to pursue the argument.

Over a deep sigh, Barrington withdrew a pocket watch and flipped open the cover. After a brief glance at the dial, he snapped the cover shut before replacing the watch inside his breast coat pocket.

He wishes to be rid of me.

In the awkward silence, Belle stood, all hope floundering. "Thank you, Mister Barrington, for generously offering your valuable time. Obviously there can be no pleasant resolution to my problem. I'm sorry to have troubled you. Good day."

Gathering whatever remained of her dignity, she walked out of the office, refusing to acknowledge the annoying clerk on her way to the door.

"One moment, Miss Lindley."

She turned.

Barrington stood outside his office. "Perhaps there is a solution after all." He approached. "Would you care to take a walk?"

Belle nodded, her spirit revitalized by a spark of hope.

Outside, he tucked her hand in the crook of his arm, and they strolled down the busy cobbled street. "Did you enjoy the voyage over?"

"Not particularly."

"Oh? And why not?"

"The seas were a bit rough, pitching the ship about."

"Lost our supper, did we?"

"Thankfully only once," she replied.

Across the street, a lady in a peach-colored hat and matching taffeta gown with flounced skirt belted at the waist peered in the window of a pastry shop. Her maid waited patiently the proper steps behind.

"Your first experience aboard ship?" the solicitor inquired.

"My second actually. My first occurred many years ago when my father and I accompanied Uncle Magnus to Belfast to visit his mother. I believe I was seven at the time. Strange, but I don't recall ever being ill on that particular voyage."

"Children and pirates."

"Pardon?"

"They have less sensitive stomachs," Barrington remarked. "Magnus loved the sea. Whether it was calm or tumultuous, you'd often find him above deck."

Belle smiled, fond memories of her uncle flooding her thoughts.

"More than once I accused him of being a pirate," the solicitor added. "But I never got up the nerve to refer to him as a child. And yet he was childlike in many ways. Especially with his generosity."

A handsome and well-dressed gentleman passed by, tipping his hat to them. His casual glance toward Belle lingered longer than necessary.

Had Morgan Spence ever looked at her with such interest?

Such appreciation?

"What was your opinion?" Barrington inquired.

Drawn from her thoughts, Belle stared with complete bewilderment. "My opinion of what, sir?"

"Cleona."

"Oh...you mean my uncle's mother. I don't recall much about her except she was rather pleasant. My father often expressed a fondness for his stepmother, and I believe he admired her almost as much as his own mother."

"The vicar was older than Magnus, was he not?"

"Yes. By eleven years."

A fashionable gentleman exited a nearby dress shop, two giggling, barrel-chested ladies clinging to each arm.

Barrington nodded in passing. "No sooner than Magnus began to acquire wealth, he asked me to draw up the paperwork for several prominent charities he wished to support. They were later included in his will. Did he tell you?"

"No, but it comes as no surprise. He and Father often discussed how he could be of assistance to the poor. He gave generously to the church, but it was the orphanages that tugged urgently at his heart."

"Yes, Magnus adored children and animals. Claimed they were the truest form of pure innocence. There was this one bad-tempered feline he discovered in an alley one afternoon. Named the silly thing Buttons, I believe."

Belle laughed.

"Did I say something witty, my dear?"

"Buttons was a brown and white beagle, Mister Barrington. And he wasn't bad-tempered. He was merely lost until my uncle found him a good home."

"A dog? Are you certain?"

"I am. Uncle Magnus couldn't go near a cat without sneezing or breaking out in hives."

"Oh, yes. It must've slipped my mind. The vicar teased his brother about this feline aversion, did he not?"

"Relentlessly, but my uncle got even later by referring to my father as Reverend Bow Legs."

Barrington chuckled. "I suppose brothers cannot help but engage in such youthful antics. A pity Magnus wasn't allowed to purchase Canderlay. Without a doubt he enjoyed being near his family."

"Many a night we prayed Uncle Magnus would return to Kent, but he constantly traveled from one port to the next."

"The disadvantages of a thriving shipping business." Barrington guided her to a bench beneath a tree. "Now then, let's discuss your problem, shall we?"

"Very well, but I fail to see what can be done."

"You never know." He sat down beside her. "Three orphanages are the main recipients of your uncle's generosity. One here in Dublin, one in Belfast, and another in London. They receive annual donations. At the end of each year, my firm reevaluates their expenses to determine if the amount should be adjusted."

An open landau rolled past them, drawn by a well-groomed chestnut. A gentleman sat in the seat, pointing at something in the distance. The lady beside him leaned close, the gray feathers in her stylish hat fluttering in the breeze.

The solicitor cleared his throat, garnering her attention. "The WCMS foundation is unique. It receives a monthly allotment that can be increased or decreased, depending upon maritime disasters. At the moment there is a generous surplus sitting in this account. Should circumstances warrant, the monies can be delayed or discontinued at my sole discretion."

"WCMS?"

"Widows and Children of Merchant Seamen."

"Why would you wish to delay or discontinue such a worthy cause?"

"Normally I would do neither, Miss Lindley, but you've presented me with quite a dilemma. In order to provide for your immediate needs, I must come to a compromise. Give you time and the necessary funds to bring Mister Samuels or the Duchess of Chase to Dublin to substantiate your claim."

"I see, but what will happen to the widows and children who depend upon this monthly allotment? Will they be cared for in the meantime?"

"Sadly, they will not."

Horrified, Belle stared at the man. "Mister Barrington, I appreciate your willingness to come to my rescue, but I confess...I am outraged and appalled you would make such a suggestion." She stood. "If I took bread from the mouths of fatherless children, if I caused one dear widow a moment of distress, how could I ever face my own shame?"

He stood as well, but offered not a word in his defense.

"What possible excuse, sir, could I give our dear heavenly father? That my wellbeing was more important than others? That I deserved to eat while others starved?"

"I apologize, Miss Lindley, but I had to be certain."

"Certain? Of what?"

"That you are indeed who you claim."

The remark caught her by surprise. "I...I don't understand."

"Given no other choice, an impostor would not have hesitated to accept my offer, no matter the burden it placed on others. But a vicar's daughter...well, she would've reacted precisely as you did. With fire and indignation."

It suddenly dawned on Belle what this clever man had been up to during their leisurely stroll and casual conversation. "The questions and misinformation. The confusion over the contents of the letter from your office...you were hoping to trick me, were you not?"

He nodded. "Instead you convinced me that you are indeed the niece of Magnus Lindley. And he was right. You are exceptional."

"He spoke of me?"

"Oh, yes. Quite often."

Belle swallowed an onslaught of emotion. "Thank you for telling me, Mister Barrington." Searching inside her reticule for a handkerchief, she noticed the faded parchment. "Whenever Uncle Magnus knew he would be going away, he would hide a farewell note for me at Canderlay Manor. It was a game between us." She withdrew the parchment and handed it to the solicitor. "I only recently found this...the last note he wrote."

Barrington unfolded the paper. "Until we meet again," he whispered at length. "Oh, yes. I recognize the hand." He glanced up. "I apologize for putting you through such an insensitive ruse."

"I understand. You carry a responsibility to your position. Am I to assume I no longer need to persuade Mister Samuels to journey to Dublin?"

He acknowledged the question with a single nod.

She smiled. "Bless you, Mister Barrington. For believing me."

"That's quite all right. Well, come along now. I've several papers that need your signature." He hooked her arm with his, and they proceeded back down the street toward the establishment of Barrington and Huff. "I wonder...did Magnus tell you the sum of your inheritance?"

"I know the amount he and my father agreed upon, and your letter confirmed it. Half of one percent. But I have no idea how much that amounts to."

"Oh, well...seems there's been a slight error. I'd wager the fault lies directly with my absentminded clerk."

"Error?"

"Allow me to explain. Upon your uncle's demise, ML Shipping sold to a fellow Irishman for roughly four hundred thousand pounds. Under the terms of the original will, you would've received two thousand pounds."

Belle halted. "Are you implying that my share of the inheritance is not point five percent?"

"Precisely. That is...the will was adjusted a month before your uncle's tragic death."

"Adjusted? By whom?"

"Magnus Lindley himself."

"I see. Well, no matter. I feel certain I can live modestly on whatever funds my uncle wished to set aside for me."

"My dear Miss Lindley..." For a brief moment his expression turned comical. "I'm afraid you still do not comprehend your enviable position."

"Enviable?"

"Let me be specific. You, Isabelle Lindley, are about to be awarded fifty percent of four hundred thousand pounds."

Her heart nearly stopped. After several long seconds, his words finally sank into her befuddled brain.

Fifty percent! Not point five.

"Two hundred...thousand...pounds?" The victim of sudden dizziness, she tightened her grip on his arm. "Are you certain?"

"Quite."

Released from the oppressive burden of poverty, Belle's situation swung from having less than nothing to possessing more than enough.

"You seem an intelligent young woman, Miss Lindley, therefore I pray you will forgive my impertinence. Since your father and uncle are both deceased, I feel it is my duty to warn you."

"Warn me? About what?"

"The dangers of your newfound wealth. It will immediately thrust you center stage, whether you wish it or not. You might encounter gentlemen...some honorable, some not...whose sole purpose is to sway your heart by offering matrimony. My advice? Turn a deaf ear to all manner of flattery in order to safeguard your fortune."

"Wise counsel, Mister Barrington, but you've no cause to worry." Belle raised her gaze to heaven and silently thanked God, her spirit soaring higher than the clouds over Dublin. "My heart has already determined my fate."

Chapter Twenty One

As his carriage entered fashionable St James Street, Hawk glanced out the window at well-lit townhouses crowded next to one another.

His life had returned to normal. He'd been set free. Reborn. The secrets of his birth, along with the vicar's journal, had all died a fitting death. Reduced to ashes. Never again would dread force him to look over his shoulder. His shameful past would soon be forgotten.

No longer menacing.

No longer feared.

He would've felt completely at ease if not for the odd sensation that accompanied him the entire day. An unpleasant feeling of being watched.

Old habits, Hawk. Get hold of yourself.

The vehicle came to a standstill in front of an impressive red brick townhouse with an elegant terrace spanning across the front from one end to the other. A decorative wrought iron fence separated the building from the street.

The carriage door opened, and the driver waited dutifully.

Hawk exited. "I'll not be long, Tibbs."

"Very good, milord."

Hawk opened the gate and climbed the narrow steps. Before he had the chance to knock, the door opened.

"Welcome, Lord Glenhawk," greeted a dignified and meticulously dressed servant. "His Grace is expecting you."

Inside the well-lit foyer, Hawk removed his hat and overcoat then handed them to a waiting maid who promptly disappeared around the wide staircase.

"This way to the study, milord."

Curious, he followed the servant down a long corridor and into a private office where the Duke of Chase stood beside an expensive desk of cherry wood.

"Good evening, Hawk. I'm pleased you accepted my invitation."

"Your message implied urgency so I came at once."

"Yes, it is indeed a matter of importance." The duke nodded to his servant, and the man departed.

"Offer me a brandy, Chase, then you can speak your mind."

"I must apologize, my lord, but I neglected to ask my butler to stock the liquor cabinet."

"Taking responsibility for a servant's inadequacies is an unwise habit. I hope you dismissed the incompetent fool."

The duke did not respond.

"If you wish to resume our previous discussion regarding the war, I must warn you...I've not changed my opinion." Hawk moved into the center of the room and sat down in a chair opposite the desk. "Surely you realize that we, as a governing body, cannot continue to provide the necessary funds to chase after smugglers. Nor can we spare the ships."

"And I say again...it is in England's best interest to rid ourselves of these traitors. But I did not request your presence in order to renew our debate regarding this matter. Indeed, I well know your opinion as I've heard it often."

"Then what shall we discuss?"

"Your confession."

"My what? Good God, Chase. Now I understand what happened to the brandy. Guzzled a bit too much, have we?"

"Not nearly enough to comprehend the workings of a depraved mind. You're about to receive a suggestion, Hawk. Weigh your options carefully."

Indignation swirled in Hawk's gut, and he jumped to his feet. "And I fear you're about to make an irreversible mistake, my friend. Though I cannot imagine of what crime I'll be accused."

The duke's black eyes narrowed. "Can you not?"

"Is this some sort of ploy? To sway me into voting for whatever ridiculous cause takes your fancy?" A noise sounded behind Hawk, and he spun around.

A dark-haired gentleman stood at the door, no expression on his face.

Hawk lowered his gaze to the weapon the man carried. A pistol aimed with deadly precision. "What the bloody hell goes on here?"

"This is Morgan Spence. My wife's brother."

"I recognize him, but why has he leveled a pistol at my chest?"

"To insure you remain in our presence."

"Holding me hostage? For what reason?"

"In order to finish our discussion."

Deep roots of fear gripped his soul and spread throughout his body. A harsh chill settled inside his chest. A feeling as familiar as his own heartbeat.

He backed a short distance away in order to observe both men. "A discussion at the point of a pistol might very well be considered an interrogation, do you not agree?"

"An interrogation," Spence echoed. "What a grand idea."

"We know about your past, Hawk," the duke declared. "The vicar's journal was most helpful."

"You have me at a disadvantage, gentlemen."

"And that's precisely where we'll keep you." Spence edged closer, his weapon unwavering. "You hired Amos Barlow to retrieve Reverend Lindley's journals and then to murder Isabelle because you feared she'd read them."

Should he deny it?

"Of what interest would a vicar's writings be to me?"

"Proof of your illegitimacy," Spence replied.

Rage uncoiled inside Hawk. "Tread lightly, sir, as I am a nobleman and an esteemed member of—"

"Esteemed? Mary Barlow's bastard son? I think not. I know precisely who you are. A blackguard who recently attempted to do away with an innocent young woman and an old man to protect a dark secret."

"Attempted?"

The word came out before Hawk even thought about the consequences.

The girl and old caretaker survived?

"Miss Lindley knew nothing of your identity," Chase said. "She had no idea who you were."

So...she'd spoken the truth.

Spence eyed him warily. "If you hadn't hired Barlow to burn the vicar's cottage, hadn't trapped Isabelle and Samuels inside the old barn, no one would've ever known the shameful details of your birth."

"No one except Lord Westwood," the duke commented.

"What has my uncle to do with this?"

"He confessed all," Chase replied. "Betrayed your family secrets."

They think to trick me.

"Uncle Miles is old and forgetful. I doubt he can recall his own name."

"Precisely the reason his lordship provided a letter in his own hand and sealed with his personal crest."

Hawk clenched his fists. "Letter?"

"Not to worry. I entrusted it to a friend for safekeeping."

"And what, pray tell, do you intend to do with it?"

"Is it not obvious?" Spence retorted.

"The Prince Regent returns to London tomorrow evening," the duke remarked. "I intend to request an audience."

"You would ruin me, Chase? Shame my wife and children?"

"The shame is yours, Hawk. Consider yourself fortunate. Morgan wanted to put a ball of lead between your eyes."

"Still do."

Hawk smiled. "If it's a duel you wish, Mister Spence, I've no objection."

"There will be no duel," insisted the duke. "It would serve no purpose."

"Except to give me great pleasure," Spence quipped.

"You know how to reach me," Hawk countered. He had never before given up or given in to anyone, but he concluded the present situation warranted a temporary retreat. "Get on with it, Chase. What do you want?"

"It's simple. Resign your seat in the House."

"Resign?"

"And leave England. Take your family with you, if you so desire. You have until tomorrow evening."

"To forfeit my wealth? My title?"

"If you place your fortune and esteemed title in the hands of the Prince Regent, the outcome will be the same. His Highness will never accept your illegitimacy. Nor will your peers."

"So I'm to be thrust into calamity? Become a commoner?"

"A tragic turn of events," Morgan Spence noted sarcastically. "And one I look forward to."

"I pity your wife, Hawk, but your callous and brutal actions have caused your downfall."

"Your pity be damned. Do not preach to me from your ducal pedestal. You would've done the same, committed a higher crime, to save your noble family lineage."

"You are mistaken. And just so we understand one another...there is no higher crime than murder."

A moment of silence ensued.

"And if I do as you suggest?" Hawk prompted.

"There can be no compromise," the duke insisted. "To ensure you keep your word and never return to England, never again try to harm Miss Lindley, the letter will seal your fate."

They had him stretched over a foul-smelling barrel. And he'd foolishly left his only means of deliverance in the carriage beneath the seat.

"What you offer is not to my advantage," Hawk muttered.

"It wasn't meant to be," Spence insisted, anger smoldering in his eyes.

"Shall we settle the matter like gentlemen then?" His glare shifted to the duke. "Do not deny me this small amount of respect. You owe me."

"I owe you nothing. Particularly my respect."

"The predator becomes the prey." Spence sidestepped a chair. "Tell me, Glenhawk. Are you frightened? Did you feel an ounce of remorse when you trapped Isabelle and Samuels inside that barn?"

"It was never my intention to harm the girl."

"Wasn't it? My sympathies to your dear wife. But perhaps your evil deeds will come as no surprise to the lady."

Hawk swallowed the bitter taste of hatred. "You'd best pray, sir, that our paths never again cross. Should that occur—"

"I'll not hesitate to end your miserable existence," his adversary declared, the pistol steady in his hand. "I give you my solemn vow on that." His eyes narrowed, never straying from the target. "Are we finished, Bart?"

"We are indeed. Enjoy the remainder of your evening, Glenhawk."

"Gloat if you must, Chase, but you've not yet won the hand."

"This is not a game of chance, Hawk. You've no choice in this matter."

Hawk hesitated a moment before storming from the room. In the foyer, the servant who'd greeted him at the door handed over his hat and overcoat. Once outside, Tibbs waited expectantly beside the carriage door.

He briefly considered retrieving the pistol from beneath the carriage seat and returning to dispose of the duke and his smug companion. It would produce a moment of great satisfaction, but it would also be extremely unwise. Particularly since he had no clue as to the whereabouts of that damaging letter.

Why had his uncle betrayed him?

He descended the steps toward the wrought iron gate.

Who else knew the truth?

Uncle Miles' young trollop?

The duke's wife?

Tibbs opened the carriage door and let down the steps. "Home, milord?"

"No," Hawk replied. "Drive me to Whites."

* * *

Just before noon, Morgan strolled through St James Park, scarcely paying attention to the nobles who milled about in leisurely fashion. Would Glenhawk leave England without an argument? Thank God he was no longer a threat to Isabelle.

Isabelle.

He could gain no restful sleep because of her. She was constantly on his mind. Especially when he closed his eyes. Had she departed Dublin? Did she ever intend to write? Let anyone know how she was getting along?

Something touched his shoulder. He spun around, half expecting a pistol to be shoved into his chest.

Lydia Adderly flashed a brilliant smile. "Forgive me, Mister Spence, for startling you. I called out, but you must've been deep in thought."

"Apologies, Miss Adderly."

Long lashes fluttered over hazel eyes. "By what were you so distracted?"

"By life, I imagine. I expected you and your family would've returned to Devonshire by now. Has the London Season been extended?"

"Sadly, no. Father is off on another business venture, and Mother decided we should remain until he returned."

"I see."

Lydia turned. "Wait here," she ordered the young maid who followed close behind. "Mister Spence and I wish to speak privately."

The girl curtsied.

Lydia tucked her arm inside Morgan's, guiding him along a well-worn path. "I've thought of you often."

"What happened to the gentleman you were so eager to wed at the beginning of the Season?"

"The duke?" Her lips pouted briefly. "Penniless. A near pauper with hardly two coins to rub together."

"Neither do I. Or have you forgotten?"

She sighed. "When you asked to call upon me, Father had no idea you were the brother of the Duchess of Chase. Heavens, why would he?"

"Indeed. Margaret is wealthy. I am not. What possible connection would there be between us?"

"Morgan, your pride has done you in. If you had mentioned her Grace, Father would not have hesitated to give you his blessing to call upon me."

"Yes, well...I suppose it's a point no longer worthy of discussion."

She greeted an affluent couple with a nod as they strolled past. "Dearest Morgan, do you truly believe I desire nothing more from my future husband than his wealth?"

"No, you'll covet his noble title as well."

"You wish to trade insults? Very well. I've been told you're in the market for a wealthy bride. I imagine your motives are no different than mine."

Bloody hell, she spoke the truth!

"What do you want, Lydia?" He halted. "What could you possibly want from me?"

"I'm about to suffer a grievous humiliation, dearest." Her eyes misted. "Before next Season, I will turn ten and nine. A spinster with no visible prospects. Laughed at. Ridiculed by the *Ton*. But you can be the handsome gentleman who gallantly rushes to my rescue."

"And why would I do that?"

"Because you once claimed to care for me. Heavens, Morgan, all you need do is ask, and I will agree to become your wife."

"Until a more favorable proposition comes along?"

"You truly believe I could be so cruel?"

Morgan didn't know what to believe. The only certainty he trusted came from his heart. A heart that no longer raced with anticipation when this woman drew near. Why had he been so fascinated before?

"I'm sorry, Miss Adderly." He disentangled her arm from his. "You do not fit my high standards for a wife. In fact, now that I have standards, you fall quite short of them."

Lydia's eyes rounded with disbelieve then shock. And her mouth parted, as though her lungs had difficulty drawing air.

Offering a polite bow and a generous smile, Morgan turned and walked away. Belle was the one who had claimed his heart. He desired no other.

Why then had he allowed her to leave Canderlay?

Amadan.

Yes, Edwina. I am a fool. I should've followed her to Dublin. Kept her safe. Made sure she returned home.

She will, lad.

Will she?

Dinna ye fret. She'll be placed in safe hands.

I trust she will, love. Thank you.

Whistling an old Scottish tune, Morgan headed across St James Park. It wasn't until a fashionable carriage drew alongside that he halted.

Bartholomew's face appeared in the window. "Get in."

Morgan climbed inside the carriage opposite the duke, and the vehicle jerked forward. "Have we a particular destination?"

"No," the duke replied, his expression somber. "I merely wished to avoid any chance of this discussion being overheard."

"Oh? What secrets are we to discuss?"

"Your whereabouts at dawn this morning."

"I couldn't sleep so I took a long stroll."

"Did you by chance meet up with Hawk?"

"No. Why the devil would I?"

"I received a message a short while ago. Seems he became involved in a duel at dawn."

"A duel? Well, I must say the news is rather unexpected. I hope his injury is most painful."

The duke glanced out the window.

"Bart, you're not giving in to remorse, are you? Please tell me you've no plans to destroy Lord Westwood's letter?"

"The letter is no longer important."

"Are you insane? It is vastly important."

"Morgan..." Bartholomew sighed. "The Earl of Glenhawk is dead."

* * *

Looping the strings of her reticule tightly about her wrist, Belle waited on deck as the crew of the *Phoenix* secured the ship alongside the dock. Glasgow was a busy and fascinating port, but at the moment it was not her destination.

Catching sight of the ship's captain, she rushed to his side. "Please, Captain Richmond. I beg you to reconsider. It's of the utmost importance that I return to England. Can I not persuade you to take me as far as Bristol?"

"I wish I could accommodate you, Miss Lindley, but as I said before..." He tipped his hat to a curious female passenger as she strolled by on the arm of her gentleman companion. "This ship is not headed for English shores."

"But, captain, I've already wasted three weeks waiting for passage home. It's imperative I return and soon."

"Then you'd best hire a carriage."

"Travel by carriage across Scotland? That will take weeks if not months."

"Yes, well..." He stared off into the distance, tweaking his well-groomed mustache. "You could inquire of the two ships docked alongside us. One might offer you passage."

"How would I know whom to trust?"

"Cyrus Edmonds is the captain of the *Welsh Lady*. He's a fatherly man. A Christian soul. Speak with him."

"Beggin' yer pardon, captain," declared a weathered old seaman. "Edmonds retired from the sea two months past." He jabbed a mop into a pail, sloshing water about his feet. "The lass 'ere would do well ta inquire of the *Dragon Master*."

"What the devil are you talking about?" Richmond snapped. "And why are you standing there like a simpleton?"

"Ye asked me ta swab the deck, sir."

"Not when there are passengers strolling about." The captain's thin lips drew into a tight grimace as he turned to Belle. "I have no idea who hired that old Scotsman, but it certainly was not me."

Belle opened her mouth to defend the helpful crewman, but the captain was called away before she could issue a word.

"Pay no mind ta that blowhard, lass," the Scotsman remarked. "His cold heart lies with his coin. Go ta the *Dragon Master*. Ye'll be safe."

"Who captains her?"

"Lucian Adams. An honorable mon if e'er there be."

"Thank you, sir. Will you see that my trunks remain on board until I can make arrangements to send for them?"

"Aye, lass. Safe journey noo."

After the gangplank had been lowered, Belle departed ship and made her way to the opposite end of the dock. Standing beneath the bow of the *Dragon Master*, she glanced up, instantly intimidated by the painted figurehead of a fierce dragon. With its mouth slightly ajar and revealing two rows of sharp teeth, the carved beast eyed her with manufactured interest. She could almost imagine it breathing fire upon an enemy ship.

Drawing a deep breath, she shouted up to the crew.

A red-haired crewman leaned over the railing. "What's that, lass?"

"I wish to speak with Captain Adams."

"Who?"

Belle hesitated. Did this man not recognize his captain's name? Perhaps the old Scot had made a mistake. "Is your captain aboard?"

He shook his head. "Gone to the King James to find his missus."

"King James? Is that an inn?"

"Aye. Just up the street past the old church." He pointed east. "Ye'll see the blacksmith's shop and then a tannery. Cut through the alley between the warehouses. Takes ye straight ta the inn."

Belle thanked the crewman and hurried off, following his directions with little trouble. Near the warehouses, several men loitered about. As she passed by, some stared with unusual interest.

Entering the alley, she hitched up her skirts, heading toward the busy street at the opposite end. As she hurried along, a prickling sensation crawled up her spine, but she dared not look over her shoulder.

Keep walking. A few more steps and...

Without warning, a hand clenched the back of her neck, drawing her backward and to a sharp standstill.

"Ye're a bit dull, English," a voice taunted beside her ear. "Strollin' about the docks without an escort."

"Release me," Belle ordered, her heart thumping wildly as she struggled to free herself from his tight grip.

"Apologies, milady, but I canna be honorin' yer request."

"Let me go, and I promise my guardian will forgive this transgression."

"Am I dimwitted?" He spun her around then shoved her backward.

She slammed into the wall and fell to her knees, her entire body trembling from the jolting impact.

"I watched ye depart the *Phoenix* nary more than half an hour ago," her attacker declared. "Ye've no guardian. No one ta look out fer ye."

He was correct. No one would come to her rescue this time.

Belle stood, leaning against the wall for support. "Is it your intent to bully me? Or am I to be murdered?"

"Ye've a mind fer the morbid, lass. Robbery's my game." He approached, his eyes bright with anticipation. "That purse around yer wrist. Hand it o'er."

Morgan's cherished dagger lay inside. If she could retrieve it...

"Och, girl. Dinna be stubborn."

"I've nothing that could be of any possible value to a thief."

"I'll be the judge of that. Let's have a look, shall we?"

He snatched the purse with the strings still attached to her wrist, and a tug-of-war began between them.

"Let go, you brute."

"Ye let go, wench, or ye'll force me ta smack ye."

"Strike that young woman, and it will be the last blow you ever land," countered a stern female voice.

Belle ceased struggling, as did the thief, their gaze instantly rushing to the alley's front entrance where a woman stood.

"Careful, madam. This be no concern of yers."

"As of this moment, I'm making it my concern." She walked forward, a long barreled pistol in her right hand. "Step away, thief, or you'll leave this alley sporting a quick change of gender."

"Ye expect me ta believe ye ken how ta use that weapon?"

"I expect nothing from the likes of you except extreme stupidity, but I'd be more than pleased to provide a demonstration of my marksmanship."

He relinquished his hold on the reticule but nevertheless stood his ground.

She lowered the weapon slightly. "Leave now or forfeit your manhood."

After a brief hesitation, he fled down the alley in the opposite direction, never once looking back.

Belle released a shaky breath. "Thank you, my lady. I am most grateful you came along when you did."

"Are you all right?"

"Yes, I believe so."

As the woman drew near, Belle realized she was a bit older, but the years had been kind to her face and slender figure.

And her deep blue eyes...

An odd sense of familiarity washed over Belle. "Have we met before?"

She laughed. "Perhaps in another life. I'm Dreya."

"I am Isabelle."

"Hello, Isabelle. Shall we leave this dreadful place?"

"I would like that." Once they'd emerged from the alley, Belle studied her champion out of the corner of her eye. "I admire your bravery with a pistol."

"A necessary precaution, I'm afraid. Glasgow is far too dangerous to go traipsing about on your own. Forgive me, my dear, but have you no chaperon?"

"No, unfortunately I am traveling alone."

"I see. Well in the future you must be more careful."

"I will. I came to the King James hoping to find Captain Adams."

"Who?"

"The captain of the *Dragon Master*."

"Oh...*that* Captain Adams." The woman sat down on a nearby bench near the entrance to the inn. "I've no wish to sound mysterious, Isabelle, but it's been many years since I heard Lucian referred to by that name."

Belle joined her on the bench. "Then you know him?"

"At times and to some extent."

"I beg your pardon?"

She smiled. "He's my husband."

"Oh, then...you're Mrs. Adams?"

The woman hesitated, faint amusement entering her expression. "Yes, I suppose I am."

"May I please speak with him?"

"If you like. Lucian went to the stables to pay for a purchase I recently made. He should return shortly. I'm curious. Why do I see such desperation in your lovely brown eyes?"

Belle explained how she urgently needed to return to England and that Captain Adams was perhaps her last hope. "There is a gentleman who resides in Kent that I...well, I've become rather fond of. No, that's not exactly the truth. You see, I am hopelessly besotted with this man."

"Oh, I see. And does he return your affection?"

"I'm not sure but if I do not return soon, he'll be tempted to seek a wealthy bride. And should that occur..." Belle sighed. "I daresay I will never recover."

"A wise old healer once told me that love grows where the Good Father plants it. Trust your heart, Isabelle. If this gentleman prefers wealth over love, perhaps you should abandon him to his own fate."

"If only I could." Belle stood, and the strings tied about her wrist suddenly untangled. The reticule fell to the walkway, emptying the contents on the way down. She knelt, gathering the items.

Mrs. Adams did the same. "Here, let me help you."

Belle stuffed a handkerchief inside the small purse then added her uncle's letter. "There have been times when I felt he cared for me." She paused to touch the bronze cross beneath her chemise. "And then there were other times when there was nothing but hopeless confusion between us."

"I can well sympathize. My husband and I were at odds with one another from the moment we met."

"Truly?"

The woman nodded. "In fact, we found ourselves on opposite sides of a rather nasty war."

"How intriguing."

"I can assure you, Isabelle, at the time it was most distressing."

"When it comes to matters of the heart, I am dreadfully inexperienced."

"As are most proper young ladies your age. Have you discussed this gentleman with your mother?"

"She died when I was but a child. My father joined her a year ago."

"Oh, I'm terribly sorry." Mrs. Adams picked up the scabbard then unsheathed the dagger. In the space of a breath, all emotion vanished, leaving a startled expression. "Isabelle, may I ask how this came to be in your possession?"

"From the gentleman I spoke of. His name is Morgan Spence. Before I departed for Dublin, he insisted I take the dagger for protection. I did so simply to please him, but I intend to give it back. I believe it's a family treasure as it once belonged to his mother."

"Indeed, it did."

Belle paused, stunned by mild curiosity. "Pardon me, Mrs. Adams, but are you familiar with the Spence family of Dragon's Breath?"

"Yes, quite familiar. You see..." She sported an impish grin. "Morgan is my son."

Chapter Twenty Two

As Morgan stood behind noble lords and perfumed ladies all dressed in elaborate finery, he couldn't help but admire the stylish carriages lining both sides of Chase Manor's lamp-lit drive.

There would be numerous Harvest Balls hosted by Kent's elite, one each Saturday evening, until the end of October. As Duchess of Chase, Margaret was given the task of planning the first gala, and judging by the volume of attendance, this was a well-anticipated event.

The distant sound of music floated on the light breeze. Light illuminated every visible window of the manor, dazzling the eye.

If Margaret had not provided her carriage, he would've been forced to suffer through a dreadfully long ride with a short-tempered Ares. A journey that would've likely ended in dishevelment.

His.

While he waited for admittance, invitation in hand, his mind wandered. It had been a hectic three weeks since he'd departed London. Preoccupied with rebuilding the tenant cottages and barn, his thoughts had often returned to Isabelle. It had taken over a month, thirty five long and torturous days, but he'd finally come to a decision.

He intended to go after her.

Inside the foyer, Morgan handed his hat and overcoat to a young maid as a lively orchestra played in the background. Depositing the invitation into the hand of a waiting butler, he was promptly escorted to the rear of the manor. The music grew louder with each step, and now he could detect individual instruments. Violin. Flute. Clarinet.

At the entrance to the enormous ballroom, couples twirled about while onlookers chatted away. Hoping to catch a glimpse of his fashionable sister, Morgan skirted the dance floor and headed to the far end of the room. After several minutes of searching, he finally spotted Margaret standing with two ladies near the large center windows. The younger woman he recognized as Lady Westwood.

Margaret unexpectedly shifted her attention. As their eyes met, a brief smile curved her lips. She whispered a few words to her companions before hurrying to his side. "Morgan, dearest, you've come."

"Well of course, darling sister." He accepted an enthusiastic hug before setting her at arm's length. "Was I not invited?"

"Scoundrel," she teased. "In light of your annoying tendency for avoiding social gatherings, I was afraid you would ignore the invitation."

"Acceptance was forced upon me."

"Oh? By whom?"

"Samuels," Morgan replied. "He made me swear an oath that I would not disappoint you."

"Lovely man. I must reward him."

"I believe you already have."

The current dance ended on a quick note, and a deafening round of applause and cheers made polite conversation almost impossible.

"Margaret?" Morgan grabbed her arm. "What did you do to him?"

She shook her head. "I cannot hear you."

He drew her to a quiet corner of the room. "Samuels is not the same."

"What do you mean?"

"He smiled, Mags. Not once but twice."

"Oh, but that's wonderful news."

"Normally I would agree, but you will never guess what I discovered him doing this morning."

"I'm afraid to ask."

"Skipping about in the middle of the kitchen as though he hadn't a care in the world. Without a partner upon his arm or a flute to his lips. Strange, is it not? So I ask you again. What did you do to Jasper Samuels?"

"Perhaps his newfound joy stems from the fact that I hired a few servants to keep him company."

"A few? When I departed Canderlay at the end of August, Jasper Samuels was the only domestic servant I could claim. Upon my return, I find a housekeeper, cook, scullery maid, two upstairs maids, and three stable hands."

She smiled. "You are quite welcome, dearest."

"Wipe that smug grin off your face, Mags. The two maids resigned their position last week, the poor scullery maid jumped at every unexplainable sound and could no longer be trusted to do the simplest of chores, and none of the stable hands were qualified to handle Ares. Oh, and I dismissed the cook."

"Dismissed? Good heavens, whatever for?"

"Incompetence. Her meals were a complete disaster. Worse than..."

He'd almost said Isabelle.

"Surely you exaggerate, Morgan. Well...no matter. I'll simply have to find another cook."

"Absolutely not. Samuels is my cook."

She responded with a frown. "What about the housekeeper?"

"Her, I like. Did you know she's Dix's wife? Well of course you did. I'm hoping he'll wish to remain as well."

"Debate that subject with Bartholomew. Not me."

"Very well. Where is he?"

"In his usual setting," Margaret replied with a sigh. "The gaming room."

"I believe I'll join him then. Coax him into a round of Pharo. The winner receives Dix."

"Careful, brother. Since last you played, Bartholomew has been studying the game with a keen eye. I've no wish to see you lose a cherished possession."

"Pardon?"

"Canderlay, silly."

"Oh...yes." He hesitated. "Mags, have you received a letter from Isabelle?"

"A letter? No."

"And this does not trouble you?"

"Not particularly."

"How do you know she's not found herself in some sort of dangerous situation?"

"Because I have faith in the Good Father."

"Regrettably, my faith is not as sturdy as yours. I've made up my mind, Margaret. I'm leaving for Dublin come morning."

She touched his arm. "You love her, do you not?"

He hesitated, unwilling to expose raw emotions. "I'm not sure how I feel."

"Then you'd best sort it out, Morgan. And quickly. Isabelle is here."

"At the Harvest Ball?" He briefly glanced about. "Why the devil did you not tell me?"

"I believe I just did." Margaret indicated a group of gentleman who'd gathered around the stairs to the upper balcony. "They've had her cornered for half an hour or better. I'm sure the dear girl is longing for someone to rescue her."

Morgan occasionally glimpsed the top of an auburn head or the shimmer of a blue gown. "It appears she's enjoying the attention."

"Yes, well...appearances can be deceptive, dear boy. However I do see your point. Surrounded by such an impressive crowd of admirers, an inexperienced young woman might easily lose her heart."

"Apologies, Margaret, but I see nothing impressive about those dandies."

"No? Look again. A well-to-do marquis waiting at her right elbow. A dashing earl to her left. A young and handsome viscount standing before her, gazing into her eyes as he raises her hand to his lips."

Is this what she desires?

Admiration from the nobility?

Jealousy gnawed at Morgan's gut.

"Go to her, Morgan," Margaret whispered in his ear. "Steal Isabelle's heart. Before someone less worthy does."

"What if the lady resists?"

"Bless the Good Father. Edwina was correct. Men are such fools. Allow me to simplify matters, dearest brother. If you prevent your heart from choosing your direction, you will regret it."

Had he not been living with regret for a solid month now?

"You argue a valid point, Mags."

"Ah...commonsense makes a grand appearance," she declared with a grin. "And just as I was about to box your ears again."

* * *

Belle's stomach fluttered. Not from the attention of her ardent but uninteresting companions. Her nervousness stemmed from the fact that Morgan Spence had discovered her, and he did not appear pleased.

As he approached, annoyance in his expression, she tried to recall the advice the duke and duchess had offered the evening before, but not one precious word came to mind. In fact, her memory seemed to be a complete and awkward blank. Amidst her mental confusion, the gentlemen continued their trivial chatter, unaware she no longer listened.

Her beloved halted, his eyes glistening with fire and blue ice. He offered a polite bow before extending his hand. "Miss Lindley, I believe you promised me this waltz."

"Did I?" She became acutely aware of a certain amount of curiosity from her companions. "Oh, yes, Mister Spence. Thank you for reminding me. Will you excuse me, gentlemen?"

And then he whisked her away, his hand firm at her waist.

Belle enjoyed a moment of pure bliss until the dance ended. Afterward he guided her across the room and out the French doors.

Reaching the terrace overlooking Chase Manor's vast gardens, he released her before turning away.

The silence standing between them seemed to last an eternity.

"You wished to speak with me, Mister Spence?"

He turned, but his disagreeable expression intact.

"When did you return to England?"

"Last week."

"And you didn't bother to visit Canderlay to let me know you were well?"

"Oh, but I did."

"Samuels has been worried—" His eyes narrowed as her previous words obviously sank in. "You visited Canderlay? When?"

"Three days ago."

"Samuels failed to mention it."

"You were busy overseeing the rebuilding of the tenant cottages. Perhaps it slipped his mind."

"Yes, I suppose, but I've...that is, we...Samuels and I...we've been worried about you. Could you not have sent a note?"

"I should have. I realize that now. I'm sorry."

He ran his hand along the terrace, tapping his long fingers upon the white stone. "I neglected to tell you how lovely you look, Isabelle. And that gown is quite stunning. The color suits you."

"I'm glad it pleases you," she said, joy cascading throughout her body like a vibrant waterfall. "I've been informed my tormentor was the Earl of Glenhawk."

"Hawk to his peers. Lord H to your father."

"Though news of his death comes as quite a surprise, I cannot claim remorse. A duel, was it?"

He shrugged. "The duke suspects it was a case of death before dishonor."

"I'm not sure I understand."

"Glenhawk faced his opponent from a short distance. A fairly easy shot. While the powder in the earl's pistol flashed, it expelled no ball. His adversary, however, suffered no such misfortune."

"I see, although I find it strange a murderer would purposely forfeit his life in this manner."

"A fitting end, do you not think?"

"I suppose so," Belle replied. "I journeyed to Westwood Hall recently to properly thank his lordship for exposing Lord H. And of course to express my gratitude to Lady Westwood."

"And yet you avoided me?"

"I did not avoid you, Mister Spence."

"No? What would you call it?"

"A postponement of sorts."

"For what purpose?"

"I suppose it no longer matters."

"It does to me."

He's sulking.

Belle hid a smile. "I apologize for offending you. It was not my intent."

He nodded once.

"The duke told me you convinced him to destroy Lord Westwood's letter," she added. "For the sake of Lady Glenhawk and her children. A kind gesture and most benevolent."

"Under the circumstances it seemed the only decent thing to do." A mask of uncertainly changed his appearance, and for a brief moment he appeared older than his twenty and nine years. "Do you enjoy all this, Belle?" His attention drifted to Chase Manor's well-lit ballroom. "Do you long to attend endless balls and parties? Summers in London during the height of the Season, entertaining the nobility?"

"Truthfully, no. I'm sure it would be rather exciting for a month, perhaps two, but I've a suspicion it would quickly become tedious. For me, at least."

"I'm relieved, because I cannot give you that sort of life," he stated, his expression as solemn as his tone. "I can only give you this." Taking her hand, he placed it over his heart.

A strong pulse beat beneath his shirt. A rhythm that matched her own.

Had he learned of her newfound wealth? Lady Chase had been against telling her brother, warning Belle that she owed herself the luxury of learning a suitor's true intentions before handing over her fortune.

But perhaps the duke had suffered no such misgivings.

"Mister Spence, I am a vicar's daughter. And although your heart is a worthy sacrifice to offer any woman, are you certain it belongs with me?"

A serious twinkle appeared in his eyes. "Undeniably certain," he replied. "You once told me to look beyond the shadow of Canderlay Manor to find happiness. Well I did, Belle. And found you. I was an *amadan*, a fool, to let you go that day without telling you what my heart had already accepted. I won't make that mistake again." Clasping both her hands, he added, "Isabelle Lindley, would do you me the honor of agreeing to become my bride?"

The question was more beautiful than Belle could've ever imagined. And there was no need to consider her reply. "Yes."

He drew her into his arms. "Shall we seal the agreement with a proper kiss?" He lowered his head. "A kiss that will tease my mind and torment my soul long after this night ends."

She turned her head in order to avoid his kiss. "Perhaps I should've cautioned you that my earlier response is subject to two conditions."

Amusement curved his bottom lip. "If one of those stipulations includes the use of my private suite as well as my bathtub—"

"Oh...the bathtub. Correction. Three conditions."

"As I was saying, Miss Lindley, if you wish to bargain for the use of my bathtub, I will insist on scrubbing your back."

Heat rushed to her cheeks, stealing her breath with provocative thoughts. "I agree to your terms, Mister Spence. After we become husband and wife, of course."

"Of course. As for the present, I would prefer my fiancée refer to me by my given name. You do remember it, do you not?"

"Yes, Morgan, I do. Now then, condition number two...I would like a dog. No, two dogs to run about the house and grounds."

"I see no reason to object. On to the third condition."

"The third...yes." Belle drew a quick breath. "I wish to be wed at Dragon's Breath."

He stared for a long moment. "May I ask why?"

"I made a promise to your mother."

Mild curiosity reflected in his eyes. "My mother?"

She nodded.

"You met my mother in Dublin?"

"No, in Glasgow."

"Glasgow? What the devil were you doing in Scotland?"

"Trying to book passage home. A most distressing ordeal."

"I can well imagine. So...you approached the *Dragon Master* and inquired if the captain would take you to England?"

"Actually, no. Your mother and I met in the most unlikely place. An alley. You see, at the time I was struggling with an infuriating thief, and he—"

"Thief?" His eyes widened with concern. "Good God, Isabelle. You were robbed? What were you doing strolling down a side street?"

"Following directions to the King James Inn. And I was not robbed, although I likely would've been if not for your brave mother. She's quite handy with a pistol."

"And even more deadly with a rifle."

"I met your delightful father as well. Are you aware he was once known as Lucian Adams, the notorious French privateer?"

"In service to King George III, no less. Yes, I'm quite familiar with the tale. Did he explain how he and my mother met?"

She nodded. "Incredible, was it not? I cannot believe your dear mother was wrongfully imprisoned by the king during the war with the colonies."

"That terrifying experience is the very reason she rarely sets foot on English soil, but I'm curious, Isabelle. How did you determine the woman in that alley was my mother?"

"Well I didn't until..." How could she avoid an embarrassing explanation of how she had shamelessly confessed her love for him to a complete stranger? And then it came to her. "Until she recognized the dagger. I imagine you'd like it back. It's in my room."

"Keep it. If you promise to give me your heart and hand in exchange."

"My heart and hand? Is that all?"

"No." Momentary fire simmered in the depths of his eyes. "But it will have to suffice until after the nuptials."

A tingling sensation began in her stomach before settling lower. She drew a nervous breath. "Then you agree? We will wed at Dragon's Breath?"

"How can I refuse? Besides, it wouldn't do to disappoint my future bride or my mother. I would never hear the end of it."

Engulfed in happiness, she blurted, "I do so love you, Morgan. More than you could possibly know."

He tucked a finger beneath her chin. "And I love and adore you, Belle Lindley."

She leaned close, awaiting his tender kiss.

A sudden frown extinguished his smile. "I am a complete cad."

"For asking me to be your wife or for agreeing to my terms?"

"For failing to inquire about your trip to Dublin. Did all go well with the solicitor?"

"Yes, but not as I'd planned. As the document from Mister Barrington's office was lost in the fire, I could think of no way to prove my identity."

"I never considered that particular problem. But you did manage to prove you were Magnus Lindley's niece, did you not?"

"I believe so."

"And now you are a tad wealthier. By at least a half percent."

"Well...my inheritance wasn't what I expected."

His expression became serious. "I'm sorry, my sweet. I had no idea."

He believes I'm still a pauper.

"It doesn't matter," he added. "Whatever funds your uncle left is yours. And you and I will survive with or without Canderlay. It is no longer my heart's desire. That title belongs exclusively to my future wife. To you, my love."

"While I am pleased I rate a level above your beloved estate, I believe you misunderstood. You see, for reasons unknown, Uncle Magnus changed his will a month before he perished at sea. Instead of point five percent of the value of his shipping business, he awarded me fifty percent."

He stared as though she'd suddenly grown a second head. "Am I to assume you are now a wealthy young woman?"

"Immensely wealthy. Two hundred thousand pounds to be exact."

A strange look came into his eyes, and he released her.

"Morgan, are you not pleased?"

"For you, certainly. On the other hand, I no longer feel worthy of asking you to become my wife."

"Well, Mister Spence, that is indeed unfortunate," Belle stated as she forced her way back into the circle of his arms. "Because I have no intention of releasing you from our previous agreement."

He brushed a lock of hair from her cheek, his touch a loving caress. "You would force me to marry you?"

She smiled. "I would indeed."

"Very well, my lovely wench. I surrender to your will." He lowered his head, covering her mouth with his.

The moment their lips touched, the music ended and brief applause erupted from the grand ballroom, as if directed by the hand of an invisible maestro.

In the quiet of a beautiful autumn evening, a very old spirit smiled with contentment before vanishing like fine mist on a sultry Scottish morn.

The End

Excerpt from *The Macgregor's Daughter*

"What's your hurry, my sweet?" whispered a deep voice against her ear.

Warm breath kissed her skin, sending shivers down her spine. A whiff of brandy and cigars. By the polished tone of his voice, he wasn't one of the king's guards. Probably a guest who'd wandered away from the masquerade ball.

No, not hopeless. Merely an unfortunate delay.

"Are you aware how this entrance to Queen's House differs from all the others?" he added.

Dreya shook her head.

He spun her around but did not release her. "It was once used for secret liaisons."

She steadied her vision and scrutinized her unexpected companion. Slender build. A good five inches taller than she. Darkness hid the rest of his features. If she surrendered to the impulse to run, no doubt he would catch her before she reached the gate.

Dreya straightened her backbone. "How dare you assault me," she snapped, assuming the proper English accent. "Release me at once."

Surprisingly, he did. "I apologize, my lady. I simply wished to place myself between you and the opportunity to disappear beyond this wall."

Did he recognize her? Unlikely, or he would've alerted the guards. However inconvenient, the situation had not become dire.

Yet.

She gathered her wits and sweetened her tone. "My lord, apparently you've mistaken me for someone else. Now if you will step aside..."

His fingers brushed her chin before inching upward. "You're quite the mystery, slipping away as you did."

Dreya backed out of his reach.

He followed. "It's past midnight. Shall I remove your mask?"

"I'd rather you didn't."

The awkward silence stretched for several moments.

"Why did you leave the ball?" he inquired.

"I grew bored."

"I can offer a cure."

A different type of caution prevailed now for his seductive tone left little doubt why he'd followed her.

Dreya calmed her fears. "An intriguing proposition, my lord, but I--"

"Let me guess. You've another liaison?"

She didn't bother responding to the vulgar taunt.

He leaned close. "I'd be happy to take his place."

"And I'd be pleased if you stepped aside."

"A bit eager are we, my lady?"

"Only to be rid of your company, my lord."

He laughed low, but it sounded more like an unpleasant huff. "No gentleman escort and too inexperienced to be a man's mistress. If I were of a mind to make a wager, I'd say that more than likely..." His seductive game of cat and mouse ended abruptly. "You're a thief. "

"Thief?" Her face flushed. "How dare you insult me, you...you..."

"If I searched your bodice, would I find a collection of stolen jewels?"

"You lay one finger upon my bodice or any other part of my person, and I'll..." Instead of finishing the verbal threat, Dreya stomped on his booted foot.

The man groaned, swearing beneath his breath.

She darted toward the gate.

He quickly caught her, snagging the hood of her cape and yanking her back against his chest. "I admire your spirit, my lady, but you've just committed a foolish mistake."

"Let go of me," she hissed.

His hands slid down her arms. "Is the word 'please' missing from your vocabulary?"

She clenched her fists. "What the devil do you want?"

"An interesting question, but first..." Again he spun her around. Roughly this time. "Who are you?"

"Who are *you*? And why have you accosted me?"

"Any lady who attends a ball yet refuses to join in the festivities is worthy of attention, wouldn't you agree? As to your first question..." He tucked a finger beneath her chin.

"I'm the gentleman who intends to call the king's guards unless you tell me your name within the next five seconds."

This Englishman possessed some intellect, for clearly he'd watched her from afar. A rather disturbing thought.

She relaxed her tone. "Ana."

"Thank you. Do you possess a surname as well?"

Dreya slid one hand inside the pocket of her cape. "My lord, I understand your suspicions, but I'm no thief." Her fingers closed around the handle of the pistol. "I merely overheard a guest speaking of this secret entrance and thought to see it for myself."

"In the dark of night?"

"It never occurred to me to bring along a candle."

"Or an escort?"

"Yes, how silly of me to forget both."

"How did you obtain the key to the gate?"

"I borrowed it. Now let me pass."

"You're in no position to make demands, Lady Ana."

With the utmost satisfaction, Dreya withdrew the pistol and shoved the barrel beneath his chin. "I disagree, my lord."

CPSIA information can be obtained
at www.ICGtesting.com
Printed in the USA
LVOW13s2339250617

539357LV00007B/745/P